THE PROPOSAL
BY
BRENDA JACKSON

AND

TO TEMPT A SHEIKH
BY
OLIVIA GATES

MILLS & BOON

Dear Reader,

This is it! The twentieth book in THE WEST-MORELANDS series and the fifth book about those Denver Westmorelands. For those two reasons alone I knew this book was special from the moment I began writing it.

I always thought of Jason Westmoreland as the quiet storm. Of the three, Derringer, Zane and Jason, Jason was the one who didn't have a lot to say and wouldn't have a lot to say…until it was his time to take centre stage. Now, it is his time.

Jason is a man who thinks he knows what he wants, but when he meets Bella Bostwick he isn't so sure anymore. He thinks he would be happy to make Bella an offer, the ultimate proposal, one he thinks she can't refuse. What he doesn't count on is awakening to passion the likes of which he's never had before. And it doesn't take long for him to figure out that Bella is the one woman whose heart he needs to conquer.

I present you with another Westmoreland man who has to come up with a plan to get the woman he wants. That one woman who will make his life complete. It's going to be up to him to prove to Bella that together they can have a forever kind of love.

Happy reading!

Brenda Jackson

THE PROPOSAL

BY
BRENDA JACKSON

Published in Great Britain 2012
by Mills & Boon, an imprint of Harlequin (UK) Limited,
Eton House, 18-24 Paradise Road, Richmond, Surrey TW9 1SR

© Brenda Streater Jackson 2011

ISBN: 978 0 263 89124 9

51-0212

Harlequin (UK) policy is to use papers that are natural, renewable and
recyclable products and made from wood grown in sustainable forests. The
logging and manufacturing processes conform to the legal environmental
regulations of the country of origin.

Printed and bound in Spain
by Blackprint CPI, Barcelona

Brenda Jackson is a die "heart" romantic who married her childhood sweetheart and still proudly wears the "going steady" ring he gave her when she was fifteen. Because she's always believed in the power of love, Brenda's stories always have happy endings. In her real-life love story, Brenda and her husband of thirty-eight years live in Jacksonville, Florida, and have two sons.

A *New York Times* bestselling author of more than seventy-five romance titles, Brenda is a recent retiree who now divides her time between family, writing and traveling with Gerald.

You may write Brenda at PO Box 28267, Jacksonville, Florida 32226, USA, by e-mail at WriterBJackson@aol.com or visit her website at www.brendajackson.net.

To Gerald Jackson, Sr. My one and only.

To all my readers who enjoy reading about the Westmorelands, this book is especially for you!

To my Heavenly Father. How Great Thou Art.

He hath made everything beautiful in his time.
—Ecclesiastes 3:11 KJV

Prologue

"Hello, ma'am, I'm Jason Westmoreland and I'd like to welcome you to Denver."

Even before she turned around, the deep, male voice had Bella Bostwick's stomach clenching as the throaty *sound* vibrated across her skin. And then when she gazed up into his eyes she had to practically force oxygen into her lungs. He had to be the most gorgeous man she'd ever seen.

For a moment she couldn't speak nor was she able to control her gaze from roaming over him and appreciating everything she saw. He was tall, way over six feet, with dark brown eyes, sculpted cheekbones and a chiseled jaw. And then there was his skin, a deep, rich chocolate-brown that had her remembering her craving for that particular treat and how delicious it was. But nothing could be more appealing than his lips and the way they were shaped. Sensuous. Sumptuous. A perfect pair for the sexy smile curving them.

He said he was a Westmoreland and because this charity ball was given on behalf of the Westmoreland Foundation, she could only assume he was one of *those* Westmorelands.

She took the hand he'd extended and wished she hadn't when a heated sizzle rode up her spine the moment she touched it. She tried forcing the sensation away. "And I'm Elizabeth Bostwick, but I prefer just Bella."

The smile curving his lips widened a fraction, enough to send warm blood rushing through her veins. "Hi, Bella."

The way he'd pronounce her name was ultrasexy. She thought his smile was intoxicating and definitely contagious, which was the reason she could so easily return it. "Hi, Jason."

"First, I'd like to offer my condolences on the loss of your grandfather."

"Thank you."

"And then I'm hoping the two of us could talk about the ranch you inherited. If you decide to sell it, I'd like to put in my bid for both the ranch and Hercules."

Bella drew in a deep breath. Her grandfather Herman Bostwick had died last month and left his land and prized stallion to her. She had seen the horse when she'd come to town for the reading of the will and would admit he was beautiful. She had returned to Denver from Savannah only yesterday to handle more legal matters regarding her grandfather's estate. "I haven't decided what I plan on doing regarding the ranch or the livestock, but if I do decide to sell I will keep your interest in mind. But I need to make you aware that according to my uncle Kenneth there are others who've expressed the same interest."

"Yes, I'm sure there are."

He had barely finished his sentence when her uncle suddenly appeared at her side and spoke up. "Westmoreland."

"Mr. Bostwick."

Bella immediately picked up strong negative undercurrents radiating between the two men and the extent of it became rather obvious when her uncle said in a curt tone, "It's time to leave, Bella."

She blinked. "Leave? But we just got here, Uncle Kenneth."

Her uncle smiled down at her as he tucked her arm underneath his. "Yes, dear, but you just arrived in town yesterday and have been quite busy since you've gotten here taking care of business matters."

She arched a brow as she stared at the grand-uncle she only discovered she had a few weeks ago. He hadn't been concerned with how exhausted she was when he'd insisted she accompany him here tonight, saying it was her place to attend this gala in her grandfather's stead.

"Good night, Westmoreland. I'm taking my niece home."

She barely had time to bid Jason farewell when her uncle escorted her to the door. As they proceeded toward the exit she couldn't help glancing over her shoulder to meet Jason's gaze. It was intense and she could tell he hadn't appreciated her uncle's abruptness. And then she saw a smile touch his lips again and she couldn't help reciprocate by smiling back. Was he flirting with her? Was she with him?

"Jason Westmoreland is someone you don't want to get to know, Bella," Kenneth Bostwick said in a gruff

tone, apparently noticing the flirtatious exchange between them.

She turned to glance up at her uncle as they walked
out into the night. People were still arriving. "Why?"

"He wants Herman's land. None of the Westmorelands
are worth knowing. They think they can do whatever
the hell they please around these parts." He interrupted
her thoughts by saying, "There're a bunch of them and
they own a lot of land on the outskirts of town."

She lifted an arched brow. "Near where my grandfather lived?"

"Yes. In fact Jason Westmoreland's land is adjacent
to Herman's."

"Really?" She smiled warmly at the thought that
Jason Westmoreland lived on property that connected
to the land she'd inherited. Technically that made her
his neighbor. *No wonder he wants to buy my land,* she
thought to herself.

"It's a good thing you're selling Herman's land, but
I wouldn't sell it to him under any circumstances."

She frowned when he opened the car for her to get
in. "I haven't decided what I plan to do with the ranch,
Uncle Kenneth," she reminded him.

He chuckled. "What is there to decide? You know
nothing about ranching and a woman of your delicacy,
breeding and refinement belongs back in Savannah and
not here in Denver trying to run a hundred-acre ranch
and enduring harsh winters. Like I told you earlier, I
already know someone who wants to buy the ranch
along with all the livestock—especially that stallion
Hercules. They're offering a lot of money. Just think of
all the shoes, dresses and hats you'll be able to buy, not
to mention a real nice place near the Atlantic Ocean."

Bella didn't say anything. She figured this was

probably not the time to tell him that as far as she was concerned there was a lot to decide because none of those things he'd mentioned meant anything to her. She refused to make a decision about her inheritance too hastily.

As her uncle's car pulled out of the parking lot, she settled back against the plush leather seats and remembered the exact moment her and Jason Westmoreland's eyes had met.

It was a connection she doubted she would ever forget.

One

"**D**id you hear Herman Bostwick's granddaughter is back in Denver and rumor has it she's here to stay?"

Jason Westmoreland's ears perked up on the conversation between his sister-in-law Pam and his two cousins-in-laws Chloe and Lucia. He was at his brother Dillon's house, stretched out on the living room floor playing around with his six-month-old nephew, Denver.

Although the ladies had retired to the dining room to sit at the table and chat, it wasn't hard to hear what they were saying and he thought there was no reason for him not to listen. Especially when the woman they were discussing was a woman who'd captured his attention the moment he'd met her last month at a charity ball. She was a woman he hadn't been able to stop thinking about since.

"Her name is Elizabeth but she goes by Bella," Lucia, who'd recently married his cousin Derringer, was saying. "She came into Dad's paint store the other day and I swear she is simply beautiful. She looks so out of place here in Denver, a real Southern belle amidst a bunch of roughnecks."

"And I hear she intends to run the ranch alone. Her uncle Kenneth has made it known he won't be lifting one finger to help her," Pam said in disgust. "The nerve of the man to be so darn selfish. He was counting on her selling that land to Myers Smith who promised to pay him a bunch of money if the deal went through. It seems everyone would love to get their hands on that land and especially that stallion Hercules."

Including me, Jason thought, as he rolled the ball toward his nephew but kept his ears wide-open. He hadn't known Bella Bostwick had returned to Denver and wondered if she remembered he was interested in purchasing her land and Hercules. He definitely hoped so. His thoughts then shifted to Kenneth Bostwick. The man's attitude didn't surprise him. He'd always acted as if he was entitled, which is probably the reason Kenneth and Herman never got along. And since Herman's death, Kenneth had let it be known around town that he felt the land Bella had inherited should be his. Evidently Herman hadn't seen it that way and had left everything in his will to the granddaughter he'd never met.

"Well, I hope she's cautious as to who she hires to help out on that ranch. I can see a woman that beautiful drawing men in droves, and some will be men who she needs to be leery of," Chloe said.

Jason frowned at the thought of any man drawn to her and didn't fully understand why he reacted that way. Lucia was right in saying Bella was beautiful. He had been totally captivated the moment he'd first seen her. And it had been obvious Kenneth Bostwick hadn't wanted him anywhere near his niece.

Kenneth never liked him and had envied Jason's relationship with old man Herman Bostwick. Most people around these parts had considered Herman mean, ornery and craggy, but Jason was not one of them. He would never forget the one time he had run away from home at eleven and spent the night hidden in Bostwick's barn. The old man had found him the next morning and returned him to his parents. But not before feeding him a tasty breakfast and getting him to help gather eggs from the chickens and milk the cows. It was during that time he'd discovered Herman Bostwick wasn't as mean as everyone thought. In fact, Herman had only been a lonely old man.

Jason had gone back to visit Herman often over the years and had been there the night Hercules had been born. He'd known the moment he'd seen the colt that he would be special. And Herman had even told him that the horse would one day be his. Herman had died in his sleep a few months ago and now his ranch and every single thing on it, including Hercules, belonged to his granddaughter. Everyone assumed she would sell the ranch, but from what he was hearing she had moved to Denver from Savannah.

He hoped to hell she had thought through her decision. Colorado's winters were rough, especially in Denver. And running a spread as big as the one she'd inherited wasn't easy for an experienced rancher; he didn't want to think how it would be for someone who knew nothing about it. Granted if she kept Marvin Allen on as the foreman things might not be so bad, but still, there were a number of ranch hands and some men didn't take kindly to a woman who lacked experience being their boss.

"I think the neighborly thing for us to do is to pay her a visit and welcome her to the area. We can also let her know if there's anything she needs she can call on us," Pam said, interrupting his thoughts.

"I agree," both Lucia and Chloe chimed in.

He couldn't help but agree, as well. Paying his new neighbor a visit and welcoming her to the area was the right thing to do, and he intended to do just that. He might have lost out on a chance to get the ranch but he still wanted Hercules.

But even more than that, he wanted to get to know Bella Bostwick better.

Bella stepped out of the house and onto the porch and looked around at the vast mountains looming before her. The picturesque view almost took her breath away and reminded her of why she had defied her family and moved here from Savannah two weeks ago.

Her overprotective parents had tried talking her out of what they saw as a foolish move on her part mainly because they hadn't wanted her out of their sight. It had been bad enough while growing up when she'd been driven to private schools by a chauffeur each day and trailed everywhere she went by a bodyguard until she was twenty-one.

And the sad thing was that she hadn't known about her grandfather's existence until she was notified of the reading of his will. She hadn't been informed in time to attend the funeral services and a part of her was still upset with her parents for keeping that from her.

She didn't know what happened to put a permanent wedge between father and son, but whatever feud that existed between them should not have included her. She'd had every right to get to know Herman Bostwick and now he was gone. When she thought about the summers she could have spent here visiting him instead of being shipped away to some camp for the summer she couldn't help but feel angry. She used to hate those camps and the snooty kids that usually went to them.

Before leaving Savannah she had reminded her parents that she was twenty-five and old enough to make her own decisions about what she wanted to do with her life. And as far as she was concerned, the trust fund her maternal grandparents had established for her, as well as this ranch she'd now inherited from her paternal grandfather, made living that life a lot easier. It was the first time in her life that she had anything that was truly hers.

It would be too much to ask David and Melissa Bostwick to see things that way and they'd made it perfectly clear that they didn't. She wouldn't be surprised if they were meeting with their attorney at this very moment to come up with a way to force her to return home to Savannah. Well, she had news for them. This was now her home and she intended to stay.

If they'd had anything to say about it she would be in Savannah and getting engaged to marry Hugh Pierce. Although most women would consider Hugh, with his tall, dark and handsome looks and his old-money wealth, a prime catch. And if she really thought hard about it, then she would be one of those women who thought so. But that was the problem. She had to think real hard about it. They'd dated a number of times but there was never any connection, any spark and no real enthusiasm on her part about spending time with him. She had tried as delicately as she could to explain such a thing to her parents but that hadn't stopped them from trying to shove Hugh down her throat every chance they got. That only proved how controlling they could be.

And speaking of controlling...her uncle Kenneth had become another problem. He was her grandfather's fifty-year-old half brother, whom she'd met for the first time when she'd flown in for the reading of the will. He'd assumed the ranch would go to him and had been gravely disappointed that day to discover it hadn't. He had also expected her to sell everything and when she'd made the decision to keep the ranch, he had been furious and said his kindness to her had ended, and that he wouldn't lift a finger to help and wanted her to find out the hard way just what a mistake she had made.

She sank into the porch swing, thinking there was no way she could have made a mistake in deciding to build a life here. She had fallen in love with the land the first time she'd seen it when she'd come for the reading of the will. And it hadn't taken long to decide even though she'd been robbed of the opportunity to connect with her grandfather in life, she would connect with him in death by accepting the gift he'd given her. A part of her felt that although they'd never met, he had somehow known about the miserable childhood she had endured and was giving her the chance to have a way better adult life.

The extra men she had hired to work the ranch so far seemed eager to do so and appreciated the salary she was paying them which, from what she'd heard, was more than fair. She'd always heard if you wanted good people to work for you then you needed to pay them good money.

She was about to get up to go back into the house to pack up more of her grandfather's belongings when she noticed someone on horseback approaching in the distance. She squinted her eyes, remembering this was Denver and people living on the outskirts of town, in the rural sections, often traveled by horseback, and she was grateful for the riding lessons her parents had insisted that she take. She'd always wanted to own a horse and now she had several of them.

As the rider came closer she felt a tingling sensation in the pit if her stomach when she recognized him. Jason Westmoreland. She definitely remembered him from the night of the charity ball and one of the things she remembered the most was his warm smile. She had often wondered if he'd been as ruggedly handsome as she recalled. The closer the rider got she realized he was.

And she had to admit that in the three times she'd been to Denver, he was the closest thing to a modern-day cowboy she had seen. Even now he was riding his horse with an expertise and masculinity that had her heart pounding with every step the horse took. His gaze was steady on her and she couldn't help but stare back. Heat crawled up her spine and waves of sensuous sensations swept through her system. She could feel goose bumps form on her skin. He was definitely the first and only man she'd ever been this attracted to.

She couldn't help wondering why he was paying her a visit. He had expressed interest in her land and in Hercules when she'd met him that night at the charity ball. Was he here to convince her she'd made a mistake in moving here like her parents and uncle had done? Would he try to talk her into selling the land and horse to him? If that was the case then she had the same news for him she'd had for the others. She was staying put and Hercules would remain hers until she decided otherwise.

He brought his horse to a stop at the foot of the porch near a hitching post. "Hello, Bella."

"Jason." She gazed up into the dark brown eyes staring at her and could swear she felt heat radiating from them. The texture of his voice tingled against her skin just as it had that night. "Is there a reason for your visit?"

A smile curved his lips. "I understand you've decided to try your hand at ranching."

She lifted her chin, knowing what was coming next. "That's right. Do you have a problem with it?"

"No, I don't have a problem with it," he said smoothly. "The decision was yours to make. However, I'm sure you know things won't be easy for you."

"Yes, I'm very much aware they won't be. Is there anything else you'd like to say?"

"Yes. We're neighbors and if you ever need my help in any way just let me know."

She blinked. Had he actually offered his help? There had to be a catch and quickly figured what it was. "Is the reason you're being nice that you still want to buy Hercules? If so, you might as well know I haven't made a decision about him yet."

His smile faded and the look on his face suddenly became intense. "The reason I'm being *nice* is that I think of myself as a nice person. And as far as Hercules is concerned, yes, I still want to buy him but that has nothing to do with my offering my help to you as your neighbor."

She knew she had offended him and immediately regretted it. She normally wasn't this mistrusting of people but owning the ranch was a touchy subject with her because so many people were against it. He had wanted the land and Hercules but had accepted her decision and was even offering his help when her own uncle hadn't. Instead of taking it at face value, she'd questioned it. "Maybe I shouldn't have jumped to conclusions."

"Yes, maybe you shouldn't have."

Every cell in her body started to quiver under the intensity of his gaze. At that moment she knew his offer had been sincere. She wasn't sure how she knew; she just did. "I stand corrected. I apologize," she said.

"Apology accepted."

"Thank you." And because she wanted to get back on good footing with him she asked, "How have you been, Jason?"

His features relaxed when he said, "Can't complain." He tilted his Stetson back from his eyes before dismounting from the huge horse as if it was the easiest of things to do.

And neither can I complain, she thought, watching him come up the steps of the porch. There was nothing about seeing him in all his masculine form that any woman could or would complain about. She felt her throat tighten when moments later he was standing in front of her. Something she could recognize as hot, fluid desire closed in on her, making it hard to breathe. Especially when his gaze was holding hers with the same concentration he'd had the night of the ball.

Today in the bright sunlight she was seeing things about him that the lights in the ballroom that night hadn't revealed: the whiteness of his teeth against his dark skin, the thickness of his lashes, the smooth texture of his skin and the broadness of his shoulders beneath his shirt. Another thing she was seeing now as well as what she remembered seeing in full detail that night was the full shape of a pair of sensual lips.

"And what about you, Bella?"

She blinked, realizing he'd spoken. "What about me?" The smile curving his lips returned and in a way that lulled her into thoughts she shouldn't be thinking, like how she'd love kissing that smile on his face.

"How have you been…besides busy?" he asked.

Bella drew in a deep breath and said. "Yes, things have definitely been busy and at times even crazy."

"I bet. And I meant what I said earlier. If you ever need help with anything, let me know."

"Thanks for the offer, I appreciate it." She had seen the turnoff to his ranch. The marker referred to it as Jason's Place. And from what she'd seen through the trees it was a huge ranch and the two-story house was beautiful.

She quickly remembered her manners and said. "I was about to have a cup of tea. Would you like a cup, as well?"

He leaned against the post and his smile widened even more. "Tea?"

"Yes."

She figured he found such a thing amusing if the smile curving his lips was anything to go by. The last thing a cowboy would want after being in the saddle was a cup of tea. A cold beer was probably more to his liking but was the one thing she didn't have in her refrigerator. "I'd understand if you'd rather not," she said.

He chuckled. "A cup of tea is fine."

"You sure?"

He chuckled again. "Yes, I'm positive."

"All right then." She opened the door and he followed her inside.

Beside the fact Jason thought she looked downright beautiful, Bella Bostwick smelled good, as well. He wished there was some way he could ignore the sudden warmth that flowed through his body from her scent streaming through his nostrils.

And then there was the way she was dressed. He had to admit that although she looked downright delectable in her jeans and silk blouse she also looked out of place in them. But as she walked gracefully in front of him, Jason thought that a man could endure a lot of sleepless nights dreaming about a Southern-belle backside shaped like hers.

"If you'll have a seat, Jason, I'll bring the tea right out."

He stopped walking as he realized she must have a pot already made. "All right."

He watched her walk into the kitchen, but instead of taking the seat like she'd offered, he kept standing as he glanced around taking in the changes she'd already made to the place. There were a lot of framed art pieces on the wall, a number of vases filled with flowers, throw rugs on the wood floor and fancy curtains attached to the windows. It was evident that a woman lived here. And she was some woman.

She hadn't hesitated to get her back up when she'd assumed his visit here was less than what he'd told her. He figured Kenneth Bostwick, in addition to no telling how many others, probably hadn't liked her decision not to sell her land and was giving her pure grief about it. He wouldn't be one of those against her decision.

He continued to glance around the room, noting the changes. There were a lot of things that remained the same, like Herman's favorite recliner, but she'd added a spiffy new sofa to go with it. It was just as well. The old one had seen better days. The old man had claimed he would be getting a new one this coming Christmas, not knowing when he'd said it he wouldn't be around.

Jason drew in a deep breath remembering the last time he'd seen Herman Bostwick alive. It had been a month before he'd died. Jason had come to check on him and to ride Hercules. Jason was one of the few people who could do so mainly because he was the one Herman had let break in the horse.

He glanced down to study the patterns on the throw rug beneath his feet thinking how unique looking they were when he heard her reenter the room. He looked up and a part of him wished he hadn't. The short medium brown curls framing her face made her mahogany colored skin appear soft to the touch and perfect for her hazel eyes and high cheekbones.

There was a refinement about her, but he had a feeling she was a force to be reckoned with if she had to be. She'd proven that earlier when she'd assumed he was there to question her sanity about moving here. Maybe he should be questioning his own sanity for not convincing her to move on and return to where she came from. No matter her best intentions, she wasn't cut out to be a rancher, not with her soft hands and manicured nails.

He believed there had to be some inner conflict driving her to try to run the ranch. He decided then and there that he would do whatever he could to help her succeed. And as she set the tea tray down on the table he knew at that moment she was someone he wanted to get to know better in the process.

"It's herbal tea. Do you want me to add any type of sweetener?" she asked.

"No," he said flatly, although he wasn't sure if he did or not. He wasn't a hot tea drinker, but did enjoy a glass of cold sweet tea from time to time. However, for some reason he felt he would probably enjoy his hot tea like he did his coffee—without anything added to it.

"I prefer mine sweet," she said softly, turning and smiling over at him. His guts tightened and he tried like hell to ignore the ache deep within and the attraction for this woman. He'd never felt anything like this before.

He was still standing and when she crossed the room toward him carrying his cup of tea, he had to forcibly propel air through his lungs with every step she took. Her beauty was brutal to the eyes but soothing to the soul, and he was enjoying the view in deep male appreciation. How old was she and what was she doing out here in the middle of nowhere trying to run a ranch?

"Here you are, Jason."

He liked the sound of his name from her lips and when he took the glass from her hands they touched in the process. Immediately, he felt his stomach muscles begin to clench.

"Thanks," he said, thinking he needed to step away from her and not let Bella Bostwick crowd his space. But he also very much wanted to keep her right there. Topping the list was her scent. He wasn't sure what perfume she was wearing but it was definitely an attention grabber, although her beauty alone would do the trick.

"You're welcome. Now I suggest we sit down or I'm going to get a crook in my neck staring up at you."

He heard the smile in her voice and then saw it on her lips. It stirred to life something inside of him and for a moment he wondered if her smile was genuine or practiced and quickly came to the conclusion it was genuine. During his thirty-four years he had met women who'd been as phony as a four-dollar bill but he had a feeling Bella Bostwick wasn't one of them. In fact, she might be a little too real for her own good.

"I don't want that to happen," he said, easing down on her sofa and stretching his long legs out in front of him. He watched as she then eased down in the comfortable looking recliner he had bought Herman five years ago for his seventy-fifth birthday.

Jason figured this was probably one of the craziest things he'd ever done, sit with a woman in her living room in the middle of the day and converse with her while sipping tea. But he was doing it and at that moment, he couldn't imagine any other place he'd rather be.

Bella took a sip of her tea and studied Jason over the rim of her cup. Who was he? Why was she so attracted to him? And why was he attracted to her? And she knew the latter was true. She'd felt it that night at the ball and she could feel it now. He was able to bring out desires in her that she never felt before but for some reason she didn't feel threatened by those feelings. Instead, although she really didn't know him, she felt he was a powerhouse of strength, tenderness and protectiveness all rolled into one. She knew he would never hurt her.

"So, tell me about yourself Jason," she heard herself say, wanting so much to hear about the man who seemed to be taking up so much space in her living room as well as in her mind.

A smile touched his lips when he said, "I'm a Westmoreland."

His words raised her curiosity up a notch. Was being a Westmoreland supposed to mean something? She hadn't heard any type of arrogance or egotism in his words, just a sense of pride, self-respect and honor.

"And what does being a Westmoreland mean?" she asked as she tucked her legs beneath her to get more comfortable in the chair.

She watched him take a sip of his tea. "There's a bunch of us, fifteen in fact," Jason said.

She nodded, taking in his response. "Fifteen?"

"Yes. And that's not counting the three Westmoreland wives and a cousin-in-law from Australia. In our family tree we've now become known as the Denver Westmorelands."

"Denver Westmorelands? Does that mean there are more Westmorelands in other parts of the country?"

"Yes, there are some who sprung from the Atlanta area. We have fifteen cousins there, as well. Most of them were at the Westmoreland charity ball."

An amused smile touched her lips. She recalled seeing them and remembered thinking how much they'd resembled in looks or height. Jason had been the only one she'd gotten a real good close-up view of, and the only one she'd held a conversation with before her uncle had practically dragged her away from the party that night.

She then decided to bring up something she'd detected at the ball. "You and my uncle Kenneth don't get along."

If her statement surprised him the astonishment was not reflected in his face. "No, we've never gotten along," he said as if the thought didn't bother him, in fact he preferred it that way.

She paused and waited on him to elaborate but he didn't. He just took another sip of tea.

"And why is that?"

He shrugged massive shoulders and the gesture made her body even more responsive to his. "I can't rightly say why we've never seen eye-to-eye on a number of things."

"What about my grandfather? Did you get along with him?"

He chuckled. "Actually I did. Herman and I had a good relationship that started back when I was kid. He taught me a lot about ranching and I enjoyed our chats."

She took a sip of her tea. "Did he ever mention anything about having a granddaughter?"

"No, but then I didn't know he had a son, either. The only family I knew about was Kenneth and their relationship was rather strained."

She nodded. She'd heard the story of how her father had left for college at the age of seventeen, never to return. Her uncle Kenneth claimed he wasn't sure what the disagreement had been between the two men since he himself had been a young kid at the time. David Bostwick had made his riches on the east coast, first as a land developer and then as an investor in all sorts of moneymaking ventures. That was how he'd met her mother, a Savannah socialite, daughter of a shipping magnate and ten years her senior. The marriage had been based more on increasing their wealth instead of love. She was well aware of both of her parents' supposedly discreet affairs.

And as far as Kenneth Bostwick was concerned, she knew that Herman's widowed father at the age of seventy married a thirty-something-year-old woman and Kenneth had been their only child. Bella gathered from bits and pieces she'd overheard from Kenneth's daughter, Elyse, that Kenneth and Herman had never gotten along because Herman thought Kenneth's mother, Belinda, hadn't been anything but a gold digger who married a man old enough to be her grandfather.

"Finding out Herman had a granddaughter came as a surprise to everyone around these parts."

Bella chuckled softly. "Yes, and it came as quite a surprise to me to discover I had a grandfather."

She saw the surprise that touched his face. "You didn't know about Herman?"

"No. I thought both my father's parents were dead. My father was close to forty when he married my mother and when I was in my teens he was in his fifties already so I assumed his parents were deceased since he never mentioned them. I didn't know about Herman until I got a summons to be present at the reading of the will. My parents didn't even mention anything about the funeral. They attended the services but only said they were leaving town to take care of business. I assumed it was one of their usual business trips. It was only when they returned that they mentioned that Herman's attorney had advised them that I was needed for the reading of the will in a week."

She pulled in a deep breath. "Needless to say, I wasn't happy that my parents had kept such a thing from me all those years. I felt whatever feud was between my father and grandfather was between them and should not have included me. I feel such a sense of loss at not having known Herman Bostwick."

Jason nodded. "He could be quite a character at times, trust me."

For some reason she felt she could trust him…and in fact, that she already did. "Tell me about him. I want to get to know the grandfather I never knew."

He smiled. "There's no way I can tell you everything about him in one day."

She returned the smile. "Then come back again for tea so we can talk. That is, if you don't mind."

She held her breath thinking he probably had a lot more things to do with his time than to sip tea with her. A man like him probably had other things on his mind when he was with someone of the opposite sex.

"No, I don't mind. In fact I'd rather enjoy it."

She inwardly sighed, suddenly feeling giddy, pleased. Jason Westmoreland was the type of man who could make his way into any woman's hot and wild fantasies, and he'd just agreed to indulge her by sharing tea with her occasionally to talk about the grandfather she'd never known.

"Well, I guess I'd better get back to work."

"And what do you do for a living?" she asked, without thinking about it.

"Several of my cousins and I are partners in a horse breeding and horse training venture. The horse that came in second last year at the Preakness was one of ours."

"Congratulations!"

"Thanks."

She then watched as he eased his body off her sofa to stand. And when he handed the empty teacup back to her, she felt her body tingle with the exchange when their hands touched and knew he'd felt it, as well.

"Thanks for the tea, Bella."

"You're welcome and you have an open invitation to come back for more."

He met her gaze, held it for a moment. "And I will."

Two

On Tuesday of the following week, Bella was in her car headed to town to purchase new appliances for her kitchen. Buying a stove and refrigerator might not be a big deal to some, but for her it would be a first. She was looking forward to it. Besides, it would get her mind off the phone call she'd gotten from her attorney first thing this morning.

Not wanting to think about the phone call, she thought about her friends back home instead. They had teased her that although she would be living out in the boondocks on a ranch, downtown Denver was half an hour away and that's probably where she would spend most of her time—shopping and attending various plays and parties. But she had discovered she liked being away from city life and hadn't missed it at all. She'd grown up in Savannah right on the ocean. Her parents' estate had been minutes from downtown and was the place where lavish parties were always held.

She had talked to her parents earlier today and found the conversation totally draining. Her father insisted she put the ranch up for sale and come home immediately. When the conversation ended she had been more determined than ever to keep as much distance between her and Savannah as possible.

She had been on the ranch for only three weeks and already the taste of freedom, to do whatever she wanted whenever she wanted, was a luxurious right she refused to give up. Although she missed waking up every morning to the scent of the ocean, she was becoming used to the crisp mountain air drenched in the rich fragrance of dahlias.

Her thoughts then shifted to something else or more precisely, someone else. Jason Westmoreland. Good to his word he had stopped by a few days ago to join her for tea. They'd had a pleasant conversation, and he'd told her more about her grandfather. She could tell Jason and Herman's relationship had been close. Part of her was glad that Jason had probably helped relieve Herman's loneliness.

Although her father refused to tell her what had happened to drive him away from home, she hoped to find out on her own. Her grandfather had kept a number of journals and she intended to start reading them this week. The only thing she knew from what Kenneth Bostwick had told her was that Herman's father, William, had remarried when Herman was in his twenties and married with a son of his own. That woman had been Kenneth's mother, which was why he was a lot younger than her father. In fact her father and Kenneth had few memories of each other since David Bostwick had left home for college at the age of seventeen.

Jason had also answered questions about ranching and assured her that the man she'd kept on as foreman had worked for her grandfather for a number of years and knew what he was doing. Jason hadn't stayed long but she'd enjoyed his visit.

She found Jason to be kind and soft-spoken and whenever he talked in that reassuring tone she would feel safe, protected and confident that no matter what decisions she made regarding her life and the ranch, it would be okay. He also gave her the impression that she could and would make mistakes and that would be okay, too, as long as she learned from those mistakes and didn't repeat them.

She had gotten to meet some of his family members, namely the women, when they'd all shown up a couple of days ago with housewarming goodies to welcome her to the community. Pamela, Chloe and Lucia had married into the family, and Megan and Bailey were Westmorelands by birth. They told her about Gemma, who was Megan and Bailey's sister and how she had gotten married earlier that year, moved with her husband to Australia and was expecting their first child.

Pamela and Chloe had brought their babies and being in their presence only reinforced a desire Bella always had of being a mother. She loved children and hoped to marry and have a houseful one day. And when she did, she intended for her relationship with them to be different than the one she had with her own parents.

The women had invited her to dinner at Pamela's home Friday evening so that she could meet the rest of the family. She thought the invitation to dinner was a nice gesture and downright neighborly on their part.

They were surprised she had already met Jason because he hadn't mentioned anything to them about meeting her.

She wasn't sure why he hadn't when all the evidence led her to believe the Westmorelands were a close-knit group. But then she figured men tended to keep their activities private and not share them with anyone. He said he would be dropping by for tea again tomorrow and she looked forward to his visit.

It was obvious there was still an intense attraction between them, yet he always acted honorably in her presence. He would sit across from her with his long legs stretched out in front of him and sip tea while she talked. She tried not to dominate the conversation but found he was someone she could talk to and someone who listened to what she had to say. She could see him now sitting there absorbed in whatever she said while displaying a ruggedness she found totally sexy.

And he had shared some things about himself. She knew he was thirty-four and a graduate of the University of Denver. He also shared with her how his parents and uncle and aunt had been killed in a plane crash when he was eighteen, leaving him and his fourteen siblings and cousins without parents. With admiration laced in his voice he had talked about his older brother Dillon and his cousin Ramsey and how the two men had been determined to keep the family together and how they had.

She couldn't help but compare his large family to her smaller one. Although she loved her parents she couldn't recall a time she and her parents had ever been close. While growing up they had relinquished her care to sitters while they jet-setted all over the country. At times she thought they'd forgotten she existed. When she got older she understood her father's obsession with trying to keep up with his young wife. Eventually she saw that obsession diminish when he found other interests and her mother did, as well.

That was why at times the idea of having a baby without a husband appealed to her, although doing such a thing would send her parents into cardiac arrest. But she couldn't concern herself with how her parents would react if she chose to go that route. Moving here was her first stab at emancipation and whatever she decided to do would be her decision. But for a woman who'd never slept with a man to contemplate having a baby from one was a bit much for her to absorb right now.

She pulled into the parking lot of one of the major appliance stores. When she returned home she would meet with her foreman to see how things were going. Jason had said such meetings were necessary and she should be kept updated on what went on at her ranch.

Moments later as she got out of her car she decided another thing she needed to do was buy a truck. *A truck.* She chuckled, thinking her mother would probably gag at the thought of her driving a truck instead of being chauffeured around in a car. But her parents had to realize and accept her life was changing and the luxurious life she used to have was now gone.

As soon as she entered the store a salesperson was right on her heels and it didn't take long to make the purchases she needed because she knew just what she wanted. She'd always thought stainless steel had a way of enhancing the look of a kitchen and figured sometime next year she would give the kitchen a total makeover with granite countertops and new tile flooring, as well. But she would take things one step at a time.

"Bella?"

She didn't have to turn to know who'd said her name. As far as she was concerned, no one could pronounce it in the same rugged yet sexy tone as Jason. Although she had just seen him a few days ago when he'd joined her for tea, there was something about seeing him now that sent sensations coursing through her.

She turned around and there he stood dressed in a pair of jeans that hugged his sinewy thighs and long, muscular legs, a blue chambray shirt and a lightweight leather jacket that emphasized the broadness of his shoulders.

She smiled up at him. "Jason, what a pleasant surprise."

It was a pleasant surprise for Jason, as well. He had walked into the store and immediately, like radar, he had picked up on her presence and all it took was following her scent to find her.

"Same here. I had to come into town to pick up a new hot water heater for the bunkhouse," he said, smiling down at her. He shoved his hands into his pockets; otherwise, he would have been tempted to pull her to him and kiss her. Kissing Bella was something he wanted but hadn't gotten around to doing. He didn't want to rush things and didn't want her to think his interest in her had anything to do with wanting to buy Hercules, because that wasn't the case. His interest in her was definitely one of want and need.

"I met the ladies in your family the other day. They came to pay me a visit," she said.

"Did they?"

"Yes."

He'd known they would eventually get around to

doing so. The ladies had discussed a visit to welcome her to the community.

"They're all so nice," she said

"I think they are nice, too. Did you get whatever you needed?" He wondered if she would join him for lunch if he were to ask.

"Yes, my refrigerator and stove will be delivered by the end of the week. I'm so excited."

He couldn't help but laugh. She was genuinely excited. If she got that excited over appliances he could imagine how she would react over jewelry. "Will you be in town for a while, Bella?"

"Yes. I have a meeting with Marvin later this evening."

He raised a brow. "Is everything all right?"

She nodded, smiling. "Yes. I'm just having a weekly meeting like you suggested."

He was glad she had taken his advice. "How about joining me for lunch? There's a place not far from here that serves several nice dishes."

She smiled up at him. "I'd love that."

Jason knew he would love it just as much. He had been thinking about her a lot, especially at night when he'd found it hard to sleep. She was getting to him. No, she had gotten to him. He didn't know of any other woman that he'd been this attracted to. There was something about her. Something that was drawing him to her on a personal level that he could not control. But then a part of him didn't want to control it. Nor did he want to fight it. He wanted to see how far it would go and where it would stop

"Do you want me to follow you there, Jason?"

No, he wanted her in the same vehicle with him. "We

can ride in my truck. Your car will be fine parked here until we return."

"Okay."

As he escorted her toward the exit, she glanced up at him. "What about your hot water heater?"

"I haven't picked it out yet but that's fine since I know the brand I want."

"All right."

Together they walked out of the store toward his truck. It was a beautiful day in May but when he felt her shiver beside him, he figured a beautiful day in Savannah would be a day in the eighties. Here in Denver if they got sixty-something degree weather in June they would be ecstatic.

He took his jacket off and placed it around her shoulders. She glanced up at him. "You didn't have to do that."

He smiled. "Yes, I did. I don't want you to get cold on me." She was wearing a pair of black slacks and a light blue cardigan sweater. As always she looked ultrafeminine.

And now she was wearing his jacket. They continued walking and when they reached his truck she glanced up and her gaze connected with his and he could feel electricity sparking to life between them. She looked away quickly, as if she'd been embarrassed that their attraction to each other was so obvious.

"Do you want your jacket back now?" she asked softly.

"No, keep it on. I like seeing you in it."

She blushed again and at that moment he got the most ridiculous notion that perhaps this sort of intense attraction between two people was sort of new to Bella. He wouldn't be surprised to discover that she had several innocent bones in her body; enough to shove him in another direction rather quickly. But for some reason he was staying put.

She nibbled on her bottom lip. "Why do you like seeing me in it?"

"Because I do. And because it's mine and you're in it."

He wasn't sure if what he'd said made much sense or if she was confused even more. But what he *was* sure about was that he was determined to find out just how much Bella Bostwick knew about men. And what she didn't know he was going to make it his business to teach her.

Bella was convinced there was nothing more compelling than the feel of wearing the jacket belonging to a man whose very existence represented true masculinity. It permeated her with his warmth, his scent and his aura in every way. She was filled with an urge to get more, to know more and to feel more of Jason Westmoreland. And as she stared at him through the car's window as he pulled out his cell phone to make arrangements for their lunch, she couldn't help but feel the hot rush of blood in her veins while heat churned deep down inside of her.

And there lay the crux of her problem. As beguiling as the feelings taking over her senses, making ingrained curiosity get the best of her, she knew better than to step beyond the range of her experience. That range didn't extend beyond what the nuns at the private Catholic schools she'd attended most of her life had warned her about. It was a range good girls just didn't go beyond.

Jason was the type of man women dreamed about. He was what fantasies were made of. She watched him ease his phone back into the pocket of his jeans, walk around the front of his truck to get in. He was the type of man a woman would love to snuggle up with on a cold Colorado winter night…especially the kind her parents and uncle had said she would have to endure. Just the thought of being with him in front of a roaring fire that blazed in a fireplace would be an unadulterated fantasy come true for any woman…. And her greatest fear.

"You're comfortable?" he asked, placing a wide-brimmed Stetson on his head.

She glanced over at him and she held his gaze for a moment and then nodded. "Yes, I'm fine. Thanks."

"You're welcome."

He backed up the truck and then they headed out of the parking lot in silence but she was fully aware of his hands that gripped the steering wheel. They were large and strong hands and she could imagine those same hands gripping her. That thought made heat seep into every cell and pore of her body, percolating her bones and making her surrender to something she'd never had before.

Her virginal state had never bothered her before and it didn't really bother her now except the unknown was making the naughtiness in her come out. It was making her anticipate things she was better off not getting.

"You've gotten quiet on me, Bella," Jason said.

She glanced over at him and again met his gaze thinking, yes she had. But she figured he didn't want to hear her thoughts out loud and certain things she needed to keep to herself.

"Sorry," she said. "I was thinking about Friday," she decided to say.

"Friday?"

"Yes. Pamela invited me to dinner."

"She did?"

Bella heard the surprise in his voice. "Yes. She said it would be the perfect opportunity to meet everyone. It seems all of my neighbors are Westmorelands. You're just the one living the closest to me."

"And what makes you so preoccupied about Friday?"

"Meeting so many of your family members."

He chuckled. "You'll survive."

"Thanks for the vote of confidence." Then she said, "Tell me about them." He had already told her some but she wanted to hear more. And the ladies who came to visit had also shared some of their family history with her. But she wanted to hear his version just to hear the husky sound of his voice, to feel how it would stir across her skin and tantalize several parts of her body.

"You already met the ones who think they run things, namely the women."

She laughed. "They don't?"

"We let them think that way because we're slowly getting outnumbered. Although Gemma is in Australia she still has a lot to say and whenever we take a vote about anything, of course she sides with the women."

She grinned. "You all actually take votes on stuff?"

"Yes, we believe in democracy. The last time we voted we had to decide where Christmas dinner would be held. Usually we hold everything at Dillon's because he has the main family house, but his kitchen was being renovated so we voted to go to Ramsey's."

"All of you have homes?"

"Yes. When we each turned twenty-five we inherited one hundred acres. It was fun naming my own spread."

"Yours is Jason's Place, right?"

He smiled over at her. "That's right."

While he'd been talking her body had responded to the sound of his voice as if it was on a mission to capture each and every nuance. She inhaled deeply and they began chatting again but this time about her family. He'd been honest about his family so she decided to be honest about hers.

"My parents and I aren't all that close and I can't remember a time that we were. They didn't support my move out here," she said and wondered why she'd wanted to share that little detail.

"Is it true that Kenneth is upset you didn't sell the land to Myers Smith?" he asked.

She nodded slowly. "Yes, he told me himself that he thinks I made a mistake in deciding to move here and is looking forward to the day I fail so he can say, 'I told you so.'"

Jason shook his head, finding it hard to believe this was a family member who was hoping for her failure. "Are he and your father close?"

Bella chuckled softly. "They barely know each other. According to Dad he was already in high school when Kenneth was born, although technically Kenneth is my father's half uncle. My father's grandfather married Kenneth's mother who was twenty-five years his junior."

"Do you have any other family, like cousins?"

She shook her head. "Both my parents were the only children. Of course Uncle Kenneth has a son and daughter but they hadn't spoken to me since the reading of the will. Uncle Kenneth only spoke to me when he thought I'd be selling the ranch and livestock to his friend."

By the time he had brought the truck to a stop in front of a huge building, she had to wipe tears of laughter from her eyes when he'd told her about all the trouble the younger Westmorelands had gotten into.

"I just can't imagine your cousin Bailey—who has such an innocent look about her—being such a hell-raiser while growing up."

Jason laughed. "Hey, don't let the innocent act fool you. The cousins Aiden and Adrian are at Harvard and Bane joined the navy. We talked Bailey into hanging around here to attend college so we could keep an eye on her."

He chuckled and then added, "It turned out to be a mistake when she began keeping an eye on us instead."

When he turned off the truck's engine she glanced through the windshield at the building looming in front of them and raised a brow. "This isn't a restaurant?"

He glanced over at her. "No, it's not. It's the Blue Ridge Management, a company my father and uncle founded over forty years ago. After they were killed Dillon and Ramsey took over. Ramsey eventually left Dillon in charge to become a sheep rancher and Dillon is currently CEO."

He glanced out the windshield to look up at the forty-story building with a pensive look on his face and moments later added, "My brother Riley holds an upper management position here. My cousins Zane and Derringer, as well as myself, worked for the company after college until last year when we decided to join the Montana Westmorelands in the horse training and breeding business."

He smiled. "I guess you can say that nine-to-five gig was never our forte. Like Ramsey we prefer being outdoors."

She nodded and followed his gaze to the building. "And we're eating lunch here?"

He glanced over at her. "Yes, I have my office that I still use from time to time to conduct business. I called ahead and Dillon's secretary took care of everything for me."

A few moments later they were walking into the massive lobby of Blue Ridge Land Management and the first thing Bella noticed was the huge, beautifully decorated atrium with a waterfall amidst a replica of mountains complete with blooming flowers and other types of foliage. After stopping at the security guard station they caught an elevator up to the executive floor.

"I remember coming up here a lot with my dad," Jason said softly, reflecting on that time. "Whenever he would work on the weekends, he would gather us all together to get us out of Mom's hair for a while. Once we got up to the fortieth floor we knew he would probably find something for us to do."

He chuckled and then added, "But just in case he didn't. I would always travel with a pack of crayons in my back pocket."

Bella smiled. She could just imagine Jason and his six brothers crowded on the elevator with their father. Although he would be working they would have gotten to spend the day with him nonetheless. She couldn't ever recall a time her father had taken her to work with him. In fact she hadn't known where the Bostwick Firm had been located until she was well into her teens. Her mother never worked outside the home but was mainly the hostess for the numerous parties her parents would give.

It seemed the ride to the top floor took forever. A few

times the elevator stopped to let people either on or off. Some of them recognized Jason and he took the time to inquire about the family members he knew, especially their children or grandchildren.

The moment they stepped off the elevator onto the fortieth floor Bella could tell immediately that this was where all the executive offices were located. The furniture was plush and the carpeting thick and luxurious looking. She was quickly drawn to huge paintings of couples adorning the walls in the center of the lobby. Intrigued she moved toward them.

"These are my parents," Jason said, coming to stand by her side. "And the couple in the picture over there is my aunt and uncle. My father and Uncle Thomas were close, barely fourteen months apart in age. And my mother and Aunt Susan got along beautifully and were just as close as sisters."

"And they died together," she whispered softly. It was a statement not a question since he had already told her what had happened when they'd all died in a plane crash. Bella studied the portrait of his parents in detail. Jason favored his father a lot but he definitely had his mother's mouth.

"She was beautiful," she said. "So was your aunt Susan. I take it Ramsey and Chloe's daughter was named after her?"

Jason nodded. "Yes, and she's going to grow up to be a beauty just like her grandmother."

She glanced over at him. "And what was your mother's name?"

"Clarisse. And my father was Adam." Jason then looked down at his watch. "Come on. Our lunch should have arrived by now."

He surprised her when he took her arm and led her

toward a bank of offices and stopped at one in particular
with his name on it. She felt her heart racing. Although
he hadn't called it as such, she considered this lunch a
date.

That thought was reinforced when he opened the door
to his office and she saw the table set for lunch. The
room was spacious and had a downtown view of Denver.
The table, completely set with everything, including a
bottle of wine, had been placed by the window so they
could enjoy the view while they ate.

"Jason, the table and the view are beautiful. Thanks
for inviting me to lunch."

"You're welcome," he said, pulling a chair out for her.
"There's a huge restaurant downstairs for the employees
but I thought we'd eat in here for privacy."

"That's considerate of you."

And done for purely selfish reasons, Jason thought
as he took the chair across from her. He liked having
her all to himself. Although he wasn't a tea drinker, he
had become one and looked forward to visiting her each
week to sit down and converse while drinking tea. He
enjoyed her company. He glanced over at her and their
gazes connected. Their response to each other always
amazed him because it seemed so natural and out of
control. He couldn't stop the heat flowing all through
his body at that precise moment even if he wanted to.

He doubted she knew she had a dazed look in the
depths of her dark eyes or that today everything about
her looked soft, feminine but not overly so. Just to the
right degree to make a man appreciate being a man.

She slowly broke eye contact with him to lift the lid
off the platter and when she glanced back up she was
smiling brightly. "Spaghetti."

He couldn't help but return her smile. "Yes. I recall

you saying the other day how much you enjoyed Italian food." In fact they had talked about a number of things in the hour he had been there.

"I do love Italian food," she said excitedly, taking a hold of her fork.

He poured wine into their glasses and glanced over and caught her slurping up a single strand of spaghetti through a pair of luscious lips. His gut clenched and when she licked her lips he couldn't help but envy the noodle.

When she caught him staring she blushed, embarrassed at being caught doing something so inelegant. "Sorry. I know that showed bad manners but I couldn't resist." She smiled. "It was the one thing I always wanted to do around my parents whenever we ate spaghetti that I couldn't do."

He chuckled. "No harm done. In fact you can slurp the rest of it if you'd like. It's just you and me."

She grinned. "Thanks, but I better not." He then watched as she took her fork in her hand, preparing to eat the rest of her spaghetti in the classical and cultured way.

"I take it your parents were strong disciplinarians," he said, taking a sip of his wine.

Her smile slowly faded. "They still are or at least they try to be. Even now they will stop at nothing to get me back to Savannah so they can keep an eye on me. I got a call from my attorney this morning warning me they've possibly found a loophole in the trust fund my grandparents established for me before they died."

He lifted a brow. "What kind of a loophole?"

"One that says I'm supposed to be married after the first year. If that's true I have less than three months," she said in disgust. "I'm sure they're counting on me returning to Savannah to marry Hugh."

He sipped his wine. "Hugh?"

She met his gaze and he could see the troubled look in hers. "Yes, Hugh Pierce. His family comes from Savannah's old money and my parents have made up their minds that Hugh and I are a perfect match."

He watched her shoulders rise and fall after releasing several sighs. Evidently the thought of becoming Mrs. Hugh Pierce bothered her. Hell, the thought bothered him, as well.

In a way he should be overjoyed, elated, that there was a possibility she was moving back to Savannah. That meant her ranch and Hercules would probably be up for sale. And when they were, he would be ready to make her an offer he hoped she wouldn't refuse. He knew he wasn't the only one wanting the land and no telling how many others wanted Hercules, but he was determined that the prized stallion wouldn't fall into anyone's hands but his.

And yet, he wasn't overjoyed or elated at the thought that she would return to Savannah.

He got the impression her parents were controlling people or at least they tried to be. He began eating, wondering why her parents wanted to shove this Hugh Pierce down her throat when she evidently wasn't feeling the guy. Would they coerce her to marry someone just because the man came from "old money"?

He forced the thought to the back of his mind, thinking who she ended up marrying was no concern of his. But making sure his name headed the list as a potential buyer for her ranch and livestock was. He glanced over at her. "When will you know what you'll have to do?"

She looked up after taking a sip of her wine. "I'm not sure. I have a good attorney but I have to admit my parents' attorney is more experienced in such matters. In other words, he's crafty as sin. I'm sure when my grandparents drew up my trust they thought they were looking out for my future because in their social circles, ideally, a young woman married by her twenty-sixth birthday. For her to attend college was just a formality since she was expected to marry a man who had the means to take care of her."

"And your parents have no qualms in forcing you to marry?"

"No, not one iota," she said without pause. "They don't truly care about my happiness. All they care about is that they would be proving once again they control my life and always will."

He heard the trembling in her voice and when she looked down as to study her silverware, he knew her composure was being threatened. At that moment, something inside of him wanted to get up, pull her into his arms and tell her things would be all right. But he couldn't rightly say that. He had no way of knowing they would be for her, given the situation she was in. Actually it was her problem not his. Still another part of him couldn't help regretting that her misfortune could end up being his golden opportunity.

"I thought I'd finally gotten free of my parents' watchful eyes at college, only to discover they had certain people in place, school officials and professors, keeping tabs on me and reporting to them on my behavior," she said, interrupting his thoughts.

"And I thought, I truly believed, the money I'm getting from my trust fund and inheriting the ranch were my way of living my life the way I want and an end to being under my parents' control. I was going to exert my freedom for the first time in my life."

She paused briefly. "Jason. I really love it here. I've been able to live the way I want, do the things I want. It's a freedom I've never had and I don't want to give it up."

They sat staring at each other for what seemed like several mind-numbing moments and then Jason spoke. "Then don't give it up. Fight them for what you want."

Her shoulders slumped again. "Although I plan to try, it's easier said than done. My father is a well-known and powerful man in Savannah and a lot of the judges are his personal friends. For anyone to even try something as archaic as forcing someone to marry is ludicrous. But my parents will do it with their friends' help if it brings me to heel."

Once again Bella fell silent for a moment. "When I received word about Herman and confronted my father as to why he never told me about his life here in Denver, he wouldn't tell me, but I've been reading my grandfather's journals. He claims my father hated living here while growing up. His mother had visited this area from Savannah, met Herman and fell in love and never went back east. Her family disowned her for it. But after college my father moved to Savannah and sought out his maternal grandparents and they were willing to accept him in their good graces but only if he never reminded them of what they saw as their daughter's betrayal, so he didn't."

She then straightened her shoulders and forced a smile to her lips. "Let's change the subject," she suggested. "Thinking about my woes is rather depressing and you've made lunch too nice for me to be depressed about anything."

They enjoyed the rest of their meal conversing about other things. He told her about his horse breeding business and about how he and the Atlanta Westmorelands had discovered they were related through his great-grandfather Raphel Westmoreland.

"Was your grandfather really married to all those women?" she asked after he told her the tale of how Raphel had become a black sheep in the family after running off in the early nineteen hundreds with the preacher's wife and all the other wives he supposedly collected along the way.

He took another sip of wine. "That's what everyone is trying to find out. We need to know if there are any more Westmorelands out there. Megan is hiring a private detective to help solve the puzzle about Raphel's wives. We've eliminated two and now we have two more to check out."

When they finished the main course Jason used his cell phone to call downstairs to say they were ready for dessert. Moments later banana pudding was delivered to them. Bella thought the dessert was simply delicious. She usually didn't eat a lot of sweets but once she'd taken a bite she couldn't help but finish the whole thing.

A short while later, after they'd devoured the dessert with coffee, Jason checked his watch. "We're right on schedule. I'll take you back in time to get your car so you can make your meeting with Marvin."

Jason stood, rounded the table and reached for her hand. The instant they touched it seemed a rush of heated sensations tore through the both of them at the same time. It was absorbed in their bones, tangled their flesh and he all but shuddered under the impact. The alluring scent of her filled his nostrils and his breath was freed on a ragged sigh.

Some part of his brain told him to take a step back and put distance between them. But then another part told him he was facing the inevitable. There had been this blazing attraction, this tantalizing degree of lust between them from the beginning. For him it had been since the moment he had seen her when she'd entered the ballroom with Kenneth Bostwick. He had known then he wanted her.

They stared at each other and for a second he thought she would avert her gaze from his but she didn't. She couldn't resist him any more than he could resist her and they both knew it, which was probably why, when he took a step closer and began lowering his head, she went on tiptoes and lifted her mouth to meet his.

The moment their lips connected, a low, guttural sound rumbled from deep in his throat and he deepened the kiss the moment she wrapped her arms around his neck. His tongue slid easily into her mouth, exploring one side and then another, as well as all the areas in between before tangling with her own, mating deeply, and when she reciprocated the move sent a jolt of desire all through his bones.

And then it was on.

Holy crap. Hunger the likes he'd never felt before infiltrated his mind. He felt a sexual connection with her that he'd never felt with any woman before. As his tongue continued to slide against hers, parts of him felt primed and ready to explode at any moment. Never had he encountered such overwhelming passion, such blatant desire and raw primal need.

His mouth was doing a good job tasting her, but the rest of him wanted to feel her, draw her closer into his arms. On instinct he felt her lean into him, plastering their bodies from breast to knee and as Jason deepened the kiss even more, he groaned, wondering if he would never get enough of her.

Bella was feeling the same way about Jason. No man had ever held her this close, taken her mouth this passionately and made sensations she'd never felt before rush through her quicker than the speed of light.

And she felt him, his erection, rigid and throbbing, against her middle, pressing hard at the juncture of her thighs, making her feel sensations there—right there—she hadn't felt before. It was doing more than just tingling. She was left aching in that very spot. She felt like a mass of kerosene and he was a torch set to ignite her, making her explode into flames. He was all solid muscle pressing against her and she wanted it all. She wanted him. She wasn't sure what wanting him entailed but she knew he was the only man who made her feel this way. He was the only man she wanted to make her feel this way.

When at last he drew his mouth away from her, his face remained close. Acting by instinct, she took her tongue and licked around his lips from corner to corner, not ready to relinquish the taste of him. When a guttural sound emitted from his throat, need rammed through her and when she tilted her lips toward his, he took her mouth once again. He eased his tongue into her mouth like it had every right to be there and at the moment she was of the conclusion that it did.

He slowly broke off the kiss and stared into her face for a long moment before caressing his thumb across her lips then running his fingers through the curls on her head.

"I guess we better leave now so you won't miss your meeting," he said in a deep, husky tone.

Unable to utter a single word she merely nodded.

And when he took her hand and entwined her fingers in his, the sensations she'd felt earlier were still strong, nearly overpowering, but she was determined to fight it this time. And every time after that. She could not become involved with anyone, especially someone like Jason. And especially not now.

She had enough on her plate in dealing with the ranch and her parents. She had to keep her head on straight and not get caught up in the desires of the flesh. She didn't need a lover; she needed a game plan.

And as Jason led her out of his office, she tried sorting out all the emotions she was feeling. She'd just been kissed senseless and now she was trying to convince herself that no matter what, it couldn't happen again.

Only problem with that was her mind was declaring one thing and her body was claiming another.

Three

He was in serious trouble.

Jason rubbed his hand across his face as he watched Bella rush off toward her car. He made sure she had gotten inside and driven off before pulling out of the parking lot behind her. The Westmoreland men were known to have high testosterone levels but his had never given him pause until today and only with Bella Bostwick.

He wouldn't waste his time wondering why he had kissed her since he knew the reason. She was walking femininity at its finest, temptation not too many men could resist and a lustful shot in any man's arms. He had gotten a sampling of all three. And it hadn't been a little taste but a whole whopping one. Now that he knew her flavor he wanted to savor it again and again and again.

When he brought his truck to a stop at a traffic light

he checked his watch. Bella wasn't the only one who had a meeting this afternoon. He, Zane and Derringer had a conference call with their partners in Montana in less than an hour. He hadn't forgotten about the meeting but spending time with Bella had been something he hadn't been willing to shorten. Now with the taste of her still lingering in his mouth, he was glad he hadn't.

He shook his head, still finding it hard to believe just how well they had connected with that kiss, which made him wonder how they would connect in other ways and places...like in the bedroom.

The thought of her naked, thighs opened while he entered her was something he couldn't get out of his mind. He was burning for her and although he'd like to think it was only a physical attraction he wasn't sure that was the case. But then if it wasn't the case, what was it?

He didn't get a chance to think any further because at that moment his cell phone rang. He pulled it off his belt and saw it was his cousin Derringer. The newlywed of just a little over a month had been the last person he'd thought would fall in love with any woman. But he had and Jason could see why. Lucia was as precious as they came and everyone thought she was a great addition to the Westmoreland family.

"Yes, Derringer?"

"Hey, man, where are you? Did you forget about today's meeting?"

Jason couldn't help but smile as he remembered how he'd called to ask Derringer the same question since he'd gotten married. It seemed these days it was hard for his cousin to tear himself away from his wife at times.

"No, I didn't forget and I'm less than thirty minutes away."

"Okay. And I hear your lady is joining the family for dinner on Friday night."

He considered that for a moment. Had anyone else made that comment he probably would have gotten irritated by it, but Derringer was Derringer and the two people who knew more than anyone that he didn't have a "lady" were his cousins Derringer and Zane. Knowing that was the case he figured Derringer was fishing for information.

"I don't have a *lady* and you very well know it, Derringer."

"Do I? If that's the case when did you become a tea sipper?"

He laughed as his gaze held steady to the road. "Ah, I see our precious Bailey has been talking."

"Who else? Bella might have mentioned it to the ladies when they went visiting, but of course it's Bailey who's decided you have the hots for the Southern belle. And those were Bailey's words not mine."

"Thanks for clarifying that for me." The hots weren't all he had for Bella Bostwick. Blood was pumping fast and furious in his veins at the thought of the kiss they had shared.

"No problem. So level with me, Jason. What's going on with you and the Southern Bella?"

Jason smiled. The Southern Bella fit her. But then so did the Sensuous Bella. The Sexy Bella. The Sumptuous Bella. "And what makes you think something is going on?"

"I know you."

True. Derringer and Zane knew him better than any of the other Westmorelands because they'd always been close, thick as thieves while growing up. "I admit I'm attracted to her but what man wouldn't be? Otherwise, it's not that serious."

"You sure?"

Jason's hand tightened on his steering wheel—that was the crux of his problem. When it came to Bella the only thing he was sure about was that he wanted her in a way he'd never wanted any other woman. When they'd kissed she kissed him back in a way that had his body heating up just thinking how her tongue had mated with his. He had loved the way her silken curls had felt flowing through his fingers and how perfect their bodies fit together.

He was probably treading on dangerous ground but for reasons he didn't quite understand, he couldn't admit to being sure right now. So instead of outright lying he decided to plead the fifth by saying, "I'll get back to you on that."

Irritation spread all through his gut at the thought that he hadn't given Derringer an answer mainly because he couldn't. And for a man who'd always been decisive when it came to a woman's place in his heart, he could just imagine what Derringer was thinking.

He was trying not to think the same thing himself. Hell, he'd only set out to be a good neighbor and then realized how much he enjoyed her company. And then there had been the attraction he hadn't been able to overlook.

"I'll see you when you get here, Jason. Have a safe drive in," Derringer said without further comment about Bella.

"Will do."

Bella stood staring out her bedroom window at the mountains. Her meeting with Marvin had been informative as well as a little overwhelming. But she had been able to follow everything the man had said. Heading the list was Hercules. The horse was restless, agitated and it seemed when Hercules wasn't in a good mood everybody knew it.

According to Marvin, Hercules hadn't been ridden in a while mainly because very few men would go near him. The only man capable to handling Hercules was Jason. The same Jason she had decided to avoid from now on. She recognized danger when she saw it and in this case it was danger she could feel. Physically.

Even now she could remember Jason mesmerizing her with his smile, seducing her with his kiss and making her groan over and over again. And there was the way his gaze had scanned over her body while in the elevator as they left his office after lunch, or the hot, lusty look he gave her when she got out of the truck at the appliance store. That look had her rushing off as if a pack of pit bulls were nipping at her heels.

And last but not least were Jason's hands on her. Those big, strong hands had touched her in places that had made her pause for breath, had made sensations overtake her and had made her put her guard up in a way she didn't feel safe in letting down.

Of course she'd known they were attracted to each other from the first, but she hadn't expected that attraction to become so volatile and explosive. And she'd experienced all that from just one kiss. Heaven help them if they went beyond kissing.

If he continued to come around, if he continued to spend time with her in any way, they would be tempted to go beyond that. Today proved she was virtually putty in his hands and she didn't want to think about what that could mean if it continued. She liked it but then she was threatened by it. She was just getting to feel free and the last thing she wanted to be was held in bondage by anything, especially by emotions she couldn't quite understand. She wasn't ready to become the other part of anyone. Jeez, she was just finding herself, enjoying her newfound independence. She didn't want to give it up before experiencing it fully.

At that moment her cell phone went off and she rolled her eyes when she saw the caller was her mother. She pulled in a deep breath before saying, "Yes, Mother?"

"I'm sure you've heard from your attorney about that little stipulation we found out about in your trust fund. My mother was definitely smart to think of it."

Bella frowned. "Yes, I heard all about it." Of course Melissa Bostwick would take the time to call and gloat. And of course she wanted to make it seem that they had discovered the stipulation by accident when the truth was that they'd probably hired a team of attorneys to look for anything in the trust fund they could use against her to keep her in line. If they had their way she would be dependent on them for life.

"Good. Your father and I expect you to stop this nonsense immediately and come home."

"Sorry, Mom, but I am home."

"No, you're not and if you continue with this foolishness you will be sorry. With no money coming in, what on earth will you do?"

"Get a job I guess."

"Don't be ridiculous."

"I'm being serious. Sorry you can't tell the difference."

There was a pause and then her mother asked, "Why do you always want to have your way?"

"Because it's my way to have. I'm twenty-five for

heaven's sake. You and Dad need to let me live my own life."

"We will but not there, and Hugh's been asking about you."

"That's nice. Is there anything else you wanted, Mom?"

"For you to stop being difficult."

"If wanting to live my life the way I want is being difficult then get prepared for more difficult days ahead. Goodbye, Mom."

Out of respect Bella didn't hang up the phone until she heard her mother's click. And when she did she clicked off and shook her head. Her parents were so sure they had her where they wanted her.

And that possibility bothered her more than anything.

Jason glanced around the room. All of his male cousins had Bella to the side conversing away with her. No doubt they were as fascinated by her intellect as well as her beauty. And things had been that way since she'd arrived. More than once he'd sent Zane dirty looks that basically told his cousin to back off. Why he'd done such a thing he wasn't sure. He and Bella weren't an item or anything of the sort.

In fact, to his way of thinking, she was acting rather coolly toward him. Although she was polite enough, no one would have thought he had devoured her mouth the way he had three days ago in his office. And maybe that was the reason she was acting this way. No one was supposed to know. It was their secret. Right?

Wrong.

He knew his family well, a lot better than she did. Their acting like cordial acquaintances only made them suspect. His brother Riley had already voiced his suspicions. "Trouble in paradise with the Southern Bella?"

He'd frown and had been tempted to tell Riley there was no trouble in paradise because he and Bella didn't have that kind of relationship. They had kissed only once for heaven's sake. Twice, if you were to take into consideration that he'd kissed her a second time that day before leaving his office.

So, okay, they had kissed twice. No big deal. He drew in a deep breath wondering if it wasn't a big deal, why was he making it one? Why had he come early and anticipated her arrival like a kid waiting for Christmas to get here?

Everyone who knew him, especially his family, was well aware that he dated when it suited him and his reputation with women was nothing like Derringer's had been or Zane's was. It didn't come close. The thought of meeting someone and getting married and having a family was something at the bottom of his list, but at least he didn't mind claiming it was on his list. That was something some of his other single brothers and cousins refused to do.

"You're rather quiet tonight, Jason."

He glanced over and saw his cousin Bailey had come to stand beside him and knew why she was there. She wanted to not just pick his brain but to dissect his mind. "I'm no quieter than usual, Bail."

She tilted her head and looked up at him. "Hmm, I think you are. Does Bella have anything to do with it?"

He took a sip of his wine. "And what makes you think that?"

She shrugged. "Because you keep glancing over there at her when you think no one is looking."

"That's not true."

She smiled. "Yes, it is. You probably don't realize you're doing it."

He frowned. Was that true? Had he been that obvious whenever he'd glanced over at Bella? Of course someone like Bailey—who made it her business to keep up with everything and everyone or tried to—would notice such a thing.

"I thought we were just having dinner," he decided to say. "I didn't know it was an all-out dinner party."

Bailey grinned. "I remember the first time Ramsey brought Chloe to introduce her to the family. He'd thought the same thing."

Nodding, he remembered that time. "Only difference in that is that Ramsey *brought* Chloe. I didn't bring Bella nor did I invite her."

"Are you saying you wished she wasn't here?"

He hated when Bailey tried putting words into his mouth. And speaking of mouth...he glanced across the room to Bella and watched hers move and couldn't help remembering all he'd done to that mouth when he'd kissed her.

"Jason?"

He then recalled what Bailey had asked him and figured until he gave her an answer she wasn't going anywhere. "No, that's not what I'm saying and you darn well know it. I don't have a problem with Bella being here. I think it's important for her to get to know her neighbors."

But did his brothers and cousins have to stay in her face, hang on to her every word and check her out so thoroughly? He knew everyone who hadn't officially

met her had been taken with her the moment Dillon
had opened the door for her. She had walked in with
a gracefulness and pristine elegance that made every
male in the house appreciate not only her beauty but
her poise, refinement and charming personality.

Her outfit, an electric-blue wrap dress with a flattering
scoop neckline and a hem line that hit just above her
knees greatly emphasized her small waist, firm breasts
and shapely legs, and looked stylishly perfect on her.
He would admit that his heart had slammed hard in his
chest the moment she'd entered the room.

"Well, dinner is about to be served. You better hope
you get a seat close to her. It won't take much for the
others to boot you out the way." She then walked off.

He glanced back over to where Bella was standing
and thought that no one would boot him out the way
when it came to Bella. They better not even try.

Bella smiled at something Zane had said while trying
not to glance across the room at Jason. He had spoken
to her when she'd first arrived but since then had pretty
much kept his distance, preferring to let his brothers
and cousins keep her company.

You would never know they had been two people
who'd almost demolished the mouths right off their
faces a few days ago. But then maybe that was the
point. Maybe he didn't want anyone to know. Come to
think of it, she'd never asked if he even had a girlfriend.
For all she knew he might have one. Just because he'd
dropped by for tea didn't mean anything other than he
was neighborly. And she had to remember that he had
never gotten out of the way with her.

Until that day in his office.

What had made him want to kiss her? There had

been this intense chemistry between them from the first, but neither of them had acted on it until that day. Had stepping over those boundaries taken their relationship to a place where it couldn't recover? She truly hoped not. He was a nice person, a charmer if ever there was one. And although she'd decided that distance between them was probably for the best right now, she did want him to remain her friend.

"Pam's getting everyone's attention for dinner," Dillon said as he approached the group. "Let me escort you to the dining room," he offered and tucked Bella's arm beneath his.

She smiled at him. The one thing she noticed was that all the Westmoreland men resembled in some way. "Thank you."

She glanced over at Jason. Their gazes met and she felt it, the same sensations she felt whenever he was near her. That deep stirring in the pit of her stomach had her trying to catch her breath.

"You okay?" Dillon asked her.

She glanced up and saw concern in his deep dark eyes. He'd followed her gaze and noted it had lit on his brother. "Yes, I'm fine."

She just hoped what she'd said was true.

Jason wasn't surprised to discover he had been placed beside Bella at the dinner table. The women in the family tended to be matchmakers when they set their minds to it, which he could overlook considering three of them were all happily married themselves. The other two, Megan and Bailey, were in it for the ride.

He dipped his head, lower than he'd planned, to ask Bella if she was enjoying herself, and when she turned her head to look at him their lips nearly touched. He came close to ignoring everyone sitting at the table and giving in to the temptation to kiss her.

She must have read his mind and a light blush spread into her cheeks. He swallowed, pulled his lips back. "Are you having a good time?"

"Yes. And I appreciate your family for inviting me."

"And I'm sure they enjoy having you here," he said. Had she expected him to invite her? He shrugged off the thought as wrong. There had been no reason for him to invite her to meet his family. Come to think of it, he had never invited a woman home for dinner. Not even Emma Phillips and they'd dated close to a year before she tried giving him an ultimatum.

The meal went off without a hitch with various conversations swirling around the table. Megan informed everyone that the private investigator she had hired to dig deeper into their great-grandfather Raphel's past was Rico Claiborne, who just happened to be the brother of Jessica and Savannah who were married to their cousins Chase and Durango. Rico, whom Megan hadn't yet met, was flying into Denver at some point in time to go over the information he'd collected on what was supposed to be Raphel's third wife.

By the time dinner was over and conversations wound down it was close to ten o'clock. Someone suggested given the lateness of the hour that Bella be escorted back home. Several of his cousins spoke up to do the honor and Jason figured he needed to end the nonsense once and for all and said in a voice that brooked no argument, "I'll make sure Bella gets home."

He noticed that all conversation automatically ceased and no one questioned his announcement. "Ready to go?" he asked Bella softly.

"Yes."

She thanked everyone and openly gave his cousins and brothers hugs. It wasn't hard to tell that they all liked her and had enjoyed her visit. After telling everyone good-night he followed her out the door.

Bella glanced out her rearview mirror and saw Jason was following her at a safe distance. She laughed, thinking when it came to Jason there wasn't a safe zone. Just knowing he was anywhere within her area was enough to rattle her. Even sitting beside him at dinner had been a challenge for her, but thanks to the rest of his family who kept lively conversation going on, she was able to endure his presence and the sexual tension she'd felt. Each time he talked to her and she looked into his face and focused on his mouth, she would remember that same mouth mating with hers.

A sigh of relief escaped her lips when they pulled into her yard. Figuring it would be dark when she returned she had left lights burning outside and her yard was practically glowing. She parked her car and was opening the door to get out when she saw Jason already standing there beside it. Her breathing quickened and panic set in. "You don't need to walk me to the door, Jason," she said quickly.

"I want to," he said simply.

Annoyance flashed in her eyes when she recalled how he'd gone out of his way most of the evening to avoid her. "Why would you?"

He gave her a look. "Why wouldn't I?" Instead of waiting for her to respond he took her hand in his and headed toward her front door.

Fine! she thought, fuming inside and dismissing the temptation to pull her hand away from his. Because her foreman lived on the ranch, she knew the last thing she needed to do was make a scene with Jason outside under the bright lights. He stood back while she unlocked the door and she had a feeling he intended to make sure she was safely inside before leaving. She was right when he followed her inside.

When he closed the door behind them she placed her hands on her hips and opened her mouth to say what was on her mind, but he beat her to the punch. "Was I out of line when I kissed you that day, Bella?"

The softly spoken question gave her pause and she dropped her hands to her side. No, he hadn't been out of line mainly because she'd wanted the kiss. She had wanted to feel his mouth on hers, his tongue tangling with her own. And if she was downright truthful about it, she would admit to wanting his hands on her, all over her, touching her in ways no man had touched her before.

He was waiting for her response.

"No, you weren't out of line."

"Then why the coldness today?"

She tilted her chin. "I can be asking you the same thing, Jason. You weren't Mr. Congeniality yourself tonight."

He didn't say anything for a moment but she could tell her comment had hit a mark with him. "No, I wasn't," he admitted.

Although she had made the accusation she was stunned by the admission. It had caught her off guard. "Why?" She knew the reason for her distance but was curious to know the reason for his.

"Ladies first."

"Fine," she said, placing her purse on the table. "We

might as well get this little talk over with. Would you like something to drink?"

"Yes," he said, rubbing his hand down his face in frustration. "A cup of tea would be nice."

She glanced up at him, surprised by his choice. There was no need to mention since that first day when he'd shown up she had picked up a couple bottles of beer and wine at the store to give him more of a choice. Since tea was also her choice she said, "All right, I'll be back in a moment." She then swept from the room.

Jason watched her leave and felt more frustrated than ever. She was right, they needed to talk. He shook his head. When had things between them gotten so complicated? Had it all started with that kiss? A kiss that was destined to happen sooner or later given the intense attraction between them?

He sighed deeply, wondering how he would explain his coldness to her tonight. How could he tell her his behavior had been put in place as a safety mechanism stemming from the fact that he wanted her more than he'd ever wanted any other woman? And how could he explain that the thought of any woman getting under his skin to the extent she had scared the hell out of him?

Chances were if he hadn't run into her at the appliance store he would have sought out her company anyway. More than likely he would have dropped by later for tea, although he had tried limiting his visits for fear of wearing out his welcome.

Her phone rang and he wondered who would be calling her at this late hour but knew it was none of his business when she picked it up on the second rang. He'd never gotten around to asking if she had a boyfriend or not and assumed she didn't.

Moments later Jason glanced toward the kitchen door when he heard a loud noise, the sound of something crashing on her floor. He quickly moved toward the kitchen to see what had happened and to make sure she was all right.

He frowned when he entered the kitchen and saw Bella stooping to pick up the tray she'd dropped along with two broken cups.

He quickly moved forward. "Are you okay, Bella?" he asked.

She didn't look at him as she continued to pick up broken pieces of the teacups. "I'm fine. I accidentally dropped it."

He bent down toward her. "That's fine. At least you didn't have tea in the cups. You could have burned yourself. I can help you get that up."

She turned to look up at him. "I can do this, Jason. I don't need your help."

He met her gaze and would have taken her stinging words to heart if he hadn't seen the redness of her eyes. "What's wrong?"

Instead of answering she shook her head and averted her gaze, refusing to look at him any longer. Quickly recovering his composure at seeing her so upset, he was pushed into action and wrapped his arms around her waist and assisted her up off the floor.

He stood facing her and drew in a deep, calming breath before saying, "I want to know what's wrong, Bella."

She drew in her own deep breath. "That was my father. He called to gloat."

Jason frowned. "About what?"

He watched her when she swallowed deeply. "He and his attorney were able to get an injunction against my trust fund and wanted me to know my monthly funds are on hold."

He heard the tremor in her voice. "But I thought you had three months before your twenty-sixth birthday."

"I do, but some judge—probably a close friend of Dad's—felt my parents had grounds to place a hold on my money. They don't believe I'll marry before the trust fund's deadline date."

She frowned. "I need my money, Jason. I was counting on the income to pay my men as well as to pay for all the work I've ordered to be done around here. There were a number of things my grandfather hadn't taken care of around here that need to be done, like repairing the roof on the barn. My parents are deliberately placing me in a bind and they know it."

Jason nodded. He had started noticing a number of things Herman had begun overlooking that had needed to be done. He then shook his head. He'd heard of controlling parents but felt hers were ridiculous.

"Certainly there is something your attorney can do."

She drew in a deep breath. "He sent me a text moments ago and said there's nothing he can do now that a judge has gotten involved. And even if there were, it would take time and my parents know it. It is time they figure I don't have, which will work in their favor. True, I got this ranch free and clear but it takes money to keep it operational."

He shook his head. "And all because you won't get married?"

"Yes. They believe I was raised and groomed to be the wife of someone like Hugh who already has standing in Savannah's upper-class society."

Jason didn't say anything for a few moments. "Does your trust fund specifically state who you're to marry?"

"No, it just says I have to be a married woman. I guess my grandparents figured in their way of thinking that I would automatically marry someone they would consider my equal and not just anyone."

An idea suddenly slammed into Jason's head. It was a crazy one…but it would serve a purpose in the long run. In the end, she would get what she wanted and he would get what he wanted.

He reached out and took her hand in his, entwined their fingers and tried ignoring the sensations touching her caused. "Let's sit down for a moment. I might have an idea."

Bella allowed him to lead her over to the kitchen table and she sat down with her hands on top of the table and glanced up at him expectantly.

"Promise you'll keep an open mind when you hear my proposal."

"All right, I promise."

He paused a moment and then said, "I think you should do what your parents want and get married."

"What!"

"Think about it, Bella. You can marry anyone to keep your trust fund intact."

He could tell she was even more confused. "I don't understand, Jason. I'm not seriously involved with anyone, so who am I supposed to marry?"

"Me."

Four

Bella's jaw dropped open. "You?"

"Yes."

She stared at Jason for a long moment and then she adamantly shook her head.

"Why would you agree to marry me?" she asked, confused.

"Think about it, Bella. It will be a win-win situation for the both of us. Marriage to me will guarantee you'll keep your trust fund rolling in without your parents' interfering. And it will give me what I want, as well, which is your land and Hercules."

Her eyes widened. "A marriage of convenience between us?"

"Yes." He could see the light shining bright in her wide-eyed innocent gaze. But then caution eased into the hazel depths.

"And you want me to give you my land as well as Hercules?"

"Co-ownership of the land and total ownership of Hercules."

Bella nibbled on her bottom lip, giving his proposal consideration while trying not to feel the disappointment trying to crowd her in. She had come here to Denver to be independent and not dependent. But what he was proposing was not how she had planned things to go. She was just learning to live on her own without her parents looking over her shoulder. She wanted her own life and now Jason was proposing that he share it. Even if it was on a temporary basis, she was going to feel her independence snatched away. "And how long do we have to remain married?"

"For as long as we want but at least a year. Anytime after that either of us are free to file for a divorce to end things. But think about it, once we send your father's attorney proof we're officially married he'll have no choice but to release the hold on your trust fund."

Bella knew that her parents would always be her parents and although she loved them, she could not put up with their controlling ways any longer. She thought Jason's proposal might work but she still had a few reservations and concerns.

"Will we live in separate households?" she decided to ask.

"No, we will either live here or at my place. I have no problem moving in here but we can't live apart. We don't want to give your parents or anyone a reason to think our marriage isn't the real thing."

She nodded thinking what he said made sense but she needed to ask another question. This one was of a delicate nature but was one she definitely needed to know the answer to. She cleared her throat. "If we lived in the same house would you expect for us to sleep in the same bed?"

He held her gaze intently. "I think by now it's apparent we're attracted to each other, which is the reason I wasn't Mr. Congeniality tonight as you've indicated. That kiss we shared only made me want more and I think you know where wanting more would have led."

Yes, she knew. And because he was being honest with her she might as well be honest with him. "And the reason I acted 'cold' as you put it was that I felt sensations kissing you that I'd never felt before and with everything going on in my life, the last thing I needed to take on was a lover. And now you want me to take on a husband, Jason?"

"Yes, and only because you won't have all those issues you had before. And I would want us to share a bed, but I'll leave the decision of what we do up to you. I won't rush you into doing anything you're not comfortable with doing. But I think you can rightly say with us living under the same roof such a thing is bound to happen eventually."

She swallowed. Yes, she could rightly say that. Marrying him would definitely be a solution to her problem and like he'd said, he would be getting what he wanted out of the deal as well—co-ownership of her land and Hercules. It would be a win-win situation.

But still.

"I need to think about it, Jason. Your proposal sounds good but I need to make sure it's the right answer."

He nodded. "I have an attorney who can draw up the papers so you won't have to worry about everything I'm proposing being legit and binding. Your attorney can look at them as well if you'd like. He will be bound by attorney-client privilege not to disclose the details of our marriage to anyone."

"I still need time to think things through, Jason."

"And I'll give you that time but my proposal won't be out there forever."

"I understand."

And whether or not he believed her, she *did* understand, which was why she needed time to think about it. From his standpoint things probably looked simple and easy. But to her there were several "what ifs" she had to consider.

What if during that year she fell in love with him but he wanted out of the marriage? What if he was satisfied with a loveless marriage and like her parents wanted to be discreet in taking lovers? What if—

"How much time do you think you'll need to think about it?"

"No more than a week at the most. I should have my answer to you by then." And she hoped more than anything it would be the right one.

"All right, that will work for me."

"And you're not involved with anyone?" she asked, needing to know for certain.

He smiled. "No, I'm not. Trust me. I couldn't be involved with anyone and kiss you the way I did the other day."

Bringing up their kiss made her remember how it had been that day, and how easily her lips had molded to his. It had been so easy to feel his passion, and some of the things his tongue had done inside her mouth nearly short-circuited her brain. Even now her body was inwardly shuddering with the force of those memories. And she expected them to live under the same roof and not share a bed? That was definitely an unrealistic expectation on her part. It seemed since their kiss, being under the same roof for any period of time was a passionate time bomb waiting to happen for them and they both knew it.

She glanced across the table at him and her stomach clenched. He was looking at her the same way he'd done that day right before he'd kissed her. And she'd kissed him back. Mated with his mouth and loved every minute doing so.

Even now she recognized the look in his eyes. It was a dark, hungry look that did more than suggest he wanted her and if given the chance he would take her right here, on her kitchen table. And it would entail more than just kissing. He would probably want to sample her the same way she'd done the seafood bisque Pam had served at dinner. And heaven help her but she would just love to be sampled.

She knew what he wanted but was curious to know what he was thinking at this moment. He was staring at her with such intensity, such longing and such greed. Then she thought, maybe it was best that she didn't know. It would be safer to just imagine.

Swallowing hard, she broke eye contact with him and thought changing the subject was a good idea. The discussion of a possible marriage between them was not the way to go right now.

"At least I've paid for the appliances they are delivering next week," she said, glancing over at her stove that had seen better days. "I think that stove and refrigerator were here when my Dad lived here," she added.

"Probably."

"So it was time for new ones, don't you think?"

"Yes. And I think we need to get those broken pieces of the teacups off the floor," he said.

"I'll do it later. It will give me something to do after you leave. I'm going to need to stay busy for a while. I'm not sleepy."

"You sure you won't need my help cleaning it up?"

"Yes, I'm sure" was her response.

"All right."

"I have beer in the refrigerator if you'd like one," she offered.

"No, I'm straight."

For the next ten minutes they continued to engage in idle chatter. Anything else was liable to set off sparks that could ignite into who knows what.

"Bella?"

"Yes."

"It's not working."

She knew just what he meant. They had moved the conversation from her appliances, to the broken teacups, to him not wanting a beer, to the furniture in her living room, to the movie that had made number one at the box office last weekend like either of them really gave a royal flip. "It's not?"

"No. It's okay to feel what we're feeling right now, no matter what decision you make a week from now. And on that note," he said, standing, "if you're sure you don't want me to help clean up the broken teacups, I think I'd better go before…"

"Before what?" she asked when he hesitated in completing the statement.

"Before I try eating you alive."

She sucked in a quick breath while a vision of him doing that very thing filtered through her mind. And then instead of leaving well enough alone, she asked something really stupid. "Why would you want to do something like that?"

He smiled. And the way he smiled had her pulse beating rapidly in several areas of her body. It wasn't a predatory smile but one of those "if you really want to know" smiles. Never before had she been aware of the many smiles a person's lips could convey.

In truth, with the little experience she had when it came to men, she was surprised she could read him at all. But for some strange reason she could read Jason and she could do so on a level that could set off passion fizzing to life inside of her.

Like it was doing now.

"The reason I'd try eating you alive is that the other day I only got a sample of your taste. But it was enough to give me plenty of sleepless nights since then. Now I find that I crave knowing how you taste all over. So if you're not ready for that to happen, come on and walk me to the door."

Honestly, at that moment she wasn't quite sure what she was ready for and figured that degree of uncertainty was reason to walk him to the door. She had a lot to think about and work out in her mind and only a week to do it.

She stood and moved around the table. When he extended his hand to her, she knew if they were to touch it would set off a chain of emotions and events she wasn't sure she was ready for. Her gaze moved away from his hand up to his face and she had a feeling that he knew it, as well. Was this supposed to be a challenge? Or was it merely a way to get her to face the facts of how living under the same roof with him would be?

She could ignore his outstretched hand but doing so would be rude and she wasn't a rude person. He was watching her. Waiting for her next move. So she made it and placed her hand in his. And the instant their hands touched she felt it. The heat of his warmth spread through her and instead of withstanding it she was drawn deeper and deeper into it.

Before she realized his intentions he let go of her hand to slide his fingertips up and down her arm in a caress so light and so mind-bogglingly sensual that she had to clamp down her mouth to keep from moaning.

The look in the dark eyes staring at her was intense and she knew at that moment his touch wasn't the only thing making her come apart. His manly scent was flowing through her nostrils and drawing him to her in a way that was actually making her panties wet.

My goodness.

"Maybe my thinking is wrong, Bella," he said in a deep, husky voice as his fingers continued to caress her arms, making her stomach clench with every heated stroke against her skin.

"Maybe you are ready for me to taste you all over, let my tongue glide across your skin, sample you in my mouth and feast on you with the deep hunger I need assuaged. And while your delicious taste sinks into my mouth, I will use my tongue to push you over the edge time and time again and drown you in a need that I intend to fulfill."

His words were pushing her over the edge just as much as his touch was doing. They were making her feel things. Want things. And increasing her desire to explore. To experience. To exert her freedom this way.

"Tell me you're ready," he urged softly in a heated voice. "Just looking at you makes me hot and hard," he said in a tone that heated her skin. "So please tell me you're ready for me."

Bella thought Jason's words had been spoken in the huskiest whisper she'd ever heard, and they did something to her both physically and mentally. They prodded her to want whatever it was he was offering. Whatever she was supposed to be ready for.

Like other women, sex was no great mystery to her. At least not since she had seen her parents' housekeeper Carlie have sex with the gardener when she was twelve. She hadn't understood at the time what all the moans and groans were about and why they had to be naked while making them. As she got older she'd been shielded from any encounters with the opposite sex and never had time to dwell on such matters.

But there had been a time when she'd become curious so she had begun reading a lot. Her parents would probably die of shame if they knew about all the romance novels Carlie would sneak in to her. It was there between the pages of those novels that she began to dream, fantasize and hope that one day she would fall in love and live happily ever after like the women she read about. Her most ardent desire was to one day find the one man who would make her sexually liberated. She wouldn't press her luck and hold out for love.

She swallowed deeply as she gazed up at Jason, knowing he was waiting for her response, and she knew at that moment what it would be. "Yes, Jason, I'm ready."

He didn't say anything for the longest time; he just stood there and stared at her. For a moment she wondered if he'd heard her. But his darkened eyes, the sound of his breathing alerted her that he had. And his eyes then traveled down the length of her throat and she knew he saw how erratically her pulse was throbbing there at the center.

And then before she could blink, he lowered his head to kiss her. His tongue drove between her lips at the same time his hand reached under her wrap dress. While his tongue relentlessly probed her mouth, his fingers began sliding up her thighs and the feel of his hands on that part of her, a part no other man had touched, made something inside of her uncoil and she released a breathless sigh. She knew at that moment the heat was on. Before she realized he'd done so, he had inched her backward and the cheeks of her behind aligned with the table.

He withdrew his mouth from hers long enough to whisper, "I can't wait to get my tongue inside of you."

His words sent all kinds of sensations swirling around in her stomach and a deep ache began throbbing between her legs. The heat was not just on, it was almost edging out of control. She felt it emitting even more when his fingers moved from her thighs to her panties.

And when he reclaimed her mouth again she moaned at how thoroughly he was kissing her and thinking her brain would overload from all the sensations ramming through her. She tried keeping up as his tongue did a methodical sweep of her mouth. And when she finally thought her senses were partially back under control, he proved her wrong when his fingers wiggled their way beneath the waistband of her panties to begin stroking her in a way that all but obliterated her senses.

"Jason…"

She felt her body being eased back onto the table at the same time her dress was pushed up to her waist. She was too full of emotions, wrapped up in way too many sensations, to take stock in what he was doing, but she got a pretty good idea when he eased her panties down her legs, leaving her open and bare to his sight. And when he eased her back farther on the table and placed her legs over his shoulders to nearly wrap around his neck she knew.

Her breath quickened at the smile that then touched his lips, a smile like before that was not predatory and this time wasn't even one of those "if you really want to know" smiles. This one was a "you're going to enjoy this" smile that curved the corners of his mouth and made a hidden dimple appear in his right cheek.

And before she could release her next breath he lifted her hips to bury his face between her legs. She bit her tongue to keep from screaming when his hot tongue slid between her womanly folds.

She squirmed frantically beneath his mouth as he drove her crazy with passion, using his tongue to coax her into the kind of climax she'd only read about. It was the kind that had preclimactic sensations rushing through her. He shoved his tongue deeper inside her, doing more than tasting her dewy wetness; he was using the hot tip of his tongue to greedily lick her from core to core.

She threw her head back and closed her eyes, as his tongue began making all kinds of circles inside her, teasing her flesh, branding it. But he wouldn't let up and she saw he had no intentions of doing so. She felt the buildup right there at the center of her thighs where his mouth was. Pleasure and heat were taking their toll.

Then suddenly her body convulsed around his mouth and she released a moan from deep within her throat as sharp jolts of sexual pleasure set ripples off in her body. And she moaned while the aftershocks made her body shudder uncontrollably. What she was enduring was unbearably erotic, pleasure so great she thought she would pass out from it.

But she couldn't pass out, not when his tongue continued to thrust inside her, forcing her to give even more. And then she was shoved over the edge. Unable to take anymore, she tightened her legs around his neck and cried out in ecstasy as waves after turbulent waves overtook her.

It was only when the last spasm had eased from her body did he tear his mouth away from her, lower her legs, lean down and kiss her, letting her taste the essence of herself from his lips.

She sucked hard on his tongue, needing it like a lifeline and knowing at that moment he had to be the most sensual and passionate man to walk on the planet. He had made her feel things she'd never felt before, far greater than what she had imagined in any of those romance novels. And she knew this was just the beginning, an introduction to what was out there... and she had a feeling of what was to come.

She knew at that moment, while their tongues continued to mate furiously, that after tonight there was no way they could live under the same roof and not want to discover what was beyond this. How far into pleasure could he take her?

She was definitely going to have to give the proposal he'd placed out there some serious thought.

Jason eased Bella's dress back down her thighs before lifting her from the table to stand on her feet. He studied her features and was pleased with what he saw. Her eyes glowed, her lips were swollen and she looked well rested when she hadn't slept.

But more than anything he thought she was the most beautiful woman he'd ever seen. He hoped he'd given her something to think about, something to anticipate, because more than anything he wanted to marry her.

He intended to marry her.

"Come on, walk me to the door," he whispered thickly. "And this time I promise to leave."

He took her hand in his and ignored the sensations he felt whenever he touched her. "Have breakfast with me tomorrow."

She glanced up at him. "You don't intend to make my decision easy, do you?"

A soft chuckle escaped his lips. "Nothing's wrong with me giving you something to think about. To remember. And to anticipate. It will only help you to make the right decision about my proposal."

When they reached her door he leaned down and kissed her again. She parted her lips easily for him and he deepened the kiss, finding her tongue and then enjoying a game of hide-and-seek with it before finally releasing her mouth on a deep, guttural moan. "What about breakfast in the morning at my place?" he asked huskily.

"That's all it's going to be, right? Breakfast and nothing more?" she asked, her voice lower than a whisper.

He smiled at her with a mischievous grin on his face. "We'll see."

"In that case I'll pass. I can't take too much of you, Jason Westmoreland."

He laughed as he pulled her closer into his arms. "Sweetheart, if I have my way, one of these days you're going to take *all* of me." He figured she knew just what he meant with his throbbing erection all but poking at her center. Maybe she was right and for them to share breakfast tomorrow wasn't a good idea. He would be pouncing on her before she got inside his house.

"A rain check, then?" he prompted.

"Um, maybe."

He lifted a brow. "You're not trying to play hard to get, are you?"

She smiled. "You can ask me that after what happened a short while ago in my kitchen? But I will warn you that I intend to build up some type of immunity to your charms by the time I see you again. You can be overwhelming, Jason."

He chuckled again, thinking she hadn't seen anything yet. Leaning over he brushed a kiss across her lips. "Think about me tonight, Bella."

He opened the door and walked out, thinking the next seven days were bound to be the longest he'd ever endured.

Later that night Bella couldn't get to sleep. Her body was tingling all over from the touch of a man. But it hadn't been any man, it had been Jason. When she tried closing her eyes all she could see was how it had been in her kitchen, the way Jason had draped her across the table and proceeded to enjoy her in such a scandalous way. The nuns at her school would have heart failure to know what had happened to her…and to know how much she had enjoyed it.

All her life she'd been taught—it had virtually been drilled into her head—all about the sins of the flesh. It was wrong for a woman to engage in any type of sexual encounter with a man before marriage. But how could something be so wrong if it felt so right?

Color tinted her cheeks. She needed to get to Confessions the first chance she got. She'd given in to temptation tonight and as much as she had enjoyed it, it would be something she couldn't repeat. Those kinds of activities belonged to people who were married and doing otherwise was improper.

She was just going to have to make sure she and Jason weren't under the same roof alone for a long period of time. Things could get out of hand. She was a weakling when it came to him. He would tempt her to do things she knew she shouldn't.

And now she was paying the price for her little indulgence by not being able to get to sleep. There was no doubt in her mind that Jason's mouth should be outlawed. She inwardly sighed. It was going to take a rather long time to clear those thoughts from her mind.

Five

"I like Bella, Jason."

He glanced over at his cousin Zane. It was early Monday morning and they were standing in the round pen with one of the mares while waiting for Derringer to bring the designated stallion from his stall for the scheduled breeding session. "I like her, too."

Zane chuckled. "Could have fooled me. Because you weren't giving her your attention at dinner Friday night. We all felt that it was up to us to make her feel welcome, because you were ignoring the poor girl."

Jason rolled his eyes. "And I bet it pained all of you to do so."

"Not really. Your Southern Bella is a real classy lady. If you weren't interested in her I'd make a play for her."

"But I *am* interested in her."

"I know," Zane said, smiling. "It was pretty obvious. I

intercepted your dirty looks loud and clear. In any case, I hope things get straightened out between you two."

"I hope so, too. I'll find out in five more days."

Zane lifted a curious brow. "Five days? What's supposed to happen in five days?"

"Long story and one which I prefer not to share right now." He had intentionally not contacted Bella over the past two days to give her breathing space from him to think his proposal through. He'd thought it through and it made perfect sense to him. He was beginning to anticipate her answer. It would be yes; it just had to be.

But what if yes wasn't her answer? What if even after the other night and the sample lovemaking they'd shared that she thought his proposal wasn't worth taking the chance? He would be the first to admit that his proposal was a bit daring. But he felt the terms were fair. Hell, he was giving her a chance to be the first to file for a divorce after the first year. And he—

Zane snapped a finger in front of his face. "Hellooo. Are you with us? Derringer is here with Fireball. Are you up to this or are you thinking about mating of another kind?" Zane was grinning.

Jason frowned when he glanced over at Derringer and saw a smirk on his face, as well. "Yes, I'm up to this and it's none of your business what I'm thinking about."

"Fine, just keep Prancer straight while Fireball mounts her. It's been a while since he's had a mare and he might be overly eager," Zane said with a meaningful smile.

Just like me, Jason thought, remembering every vivid detail of Bella spread out on her kitchen table for him to enjoy. "All right, let's get this going. I have something to do later."

Both Zane and Derringer gave him speculative looks but said nothing.

* * *

Bella stepped out of the shower and began toweling herself dry. It was the middle of the day but after going for a walk around the ranch she had gotten hot and sticky. Now she intended to slip into something comfortable and have a cup of tea and relax…and think about Jason's proposal.

The walk had done her good and walking her land had made her even more determined to hold on to what was hers. But was Jason's proposal the answer? Or would she be jumping out of the pot and into the fire?

After Friday night and what had gone down in her kitchen, there was no doubt in her mind that Jason was the kind of lover women dreamed of having. And he had to be the most unselfish person she knew. He had given her pleasure without seeking his own. She had read enough articles on the subject to know most men weren't usually that generous. But he had been and her body hadn't been the same since. Every time she thought about him and that night in the kitchen, she had to pause and catch her breath.

She hadn't heard from him since that night but figured he was giving her time to think things through before she gave him her answer. She had talked to her attorney again and he hadn't said anything to make her think she had a chance of getting the hold on her trust fund lifted.

She had run into her uncle yesterday when she'd gone into town and he hadn't been at all pleasant. And neither had his son, daughter and two teenage grandsons. All of them practically cut her with their sharp looks. She just didn't get it. Jason had wanted her land as well but he hadn't been anything but supportive of her decision to keep it and had offered his help from the first.

She understood that she and her Denver relatives didn't have the same bond as the Westmorelands but she would think they wouldn't be dismissing her the way they were doing over some land.

She had dressed and was heading downstairs when something like a missile sailed through her living room window, breaking the glass in the process. "What on earth!" She nearly missed her step when she raced back up the stairs to her bedroom, closing the door and locking it behind her.

Catching her breath she grabbed her cell phone off the nightstand and called the police.

"Where is she, Marvin?" Jason asked, walking into Bella's house with Zane and Derringer on his heels.

"She's in the kitchen," the man answered, moving quickly out of Jason's way.

Jason had gotten a call from Pam to tell him what had happened. He had jumped in his truck and left Zane's ranch immediately with Derringer and Zane following close behind in their vehicles.

From what Pam had said, someone had thrown a large rock through Bella's window with a note tied to it saying, "Go back to where you came from." The thought of anyone doing that angered him. Who on earth would do such a thing?

He walked into the kitchen and glanced around, dismissing memories of the last time he'd been there and his focus immediately went to Bella. She was sitting at the kitchen table talking to Pete Higgins, one of the sheriff's deputies and a good friend of Derringer's.

Everyone glanced up when he entered and the look on Bella's face was like a kick in his gut. He could tell she was shaken and there was a hurt expression in her eyes he'd never seen before. His anger flared at the thought that someone could hurt her in any way. The rock may not have hit her but she'd taken a hit just the same. Whoever had thrown that rock through the window had hit her spirit and left her shaken.

"Jason, Zane and Derringer," Pete said, acknowledging their arrival. "Why am I not surprised to see the three of you here?"

Jason didn't respond as he moved straight toward Bella and, disregarding the onlookers, he reached out to caress the soft skin beneath her ear. "Are you all right?" he whispered in a husky tone.

She held his gaze and nodded slowly. "Yes, I'm fine. I was on my way downstairs when that rock came flying through the window. It scared me more than anything."

He glanced at the rock that someone had placed on the table. It was a huge rock, big enough to hurt her had she been in her living room anywhere near the window. The thought of anyone harming one single hair on her head infuriated him.

He glanced over at Pete. "Do you have any idea who did it?"

Peter shook his head. "No, but both the rock and note have been dusted for fingerprints. Hopefully we'll know something soon."

Soon? He wanted to know something now. He glanced down at the note and read it.

"I was just asking Ms. Bostwick if she knew of anyone who wanted her off this property. The only people she could think of are her parents and possibly Kenneth Bostwick."

"I can't see my parents behind anything like this," Bella said in a soft voice. "And I don't want to think

Uncle Kenneth is capable of doing anything like this, either. However, he does want me off the land because he knows of someone who wants to buy it."

Pete nodded. "What about Jason here? I think we all know he wants your land and Hercules, as well," the deputy said as if Jason wasn't standing right there listening to his every word. "Do you think he'd want you gone, too?"

Bella seemed surprised by the question and moved her gaze from Pete to Jason. Jason figured she saw remnants of passion behind the anger in his eyes.

"No, he'd want me to stay," she said with a soft sigh.

Pete closed his notepad, evidently deciding not to ask why she was so certain of that. "Well, hopefully we'll have something within a week if those fingerprints are identified," he said.

"And what is she supposed to do in the meantime, Pete?" Jason asked in a frustrated tone.

"Report anything suspicious," Pete responded dryly. He turned to face Bella. "I'll request that the sheriff beef up security around here starting today."

"Thank you, Deputy Higgins," Bella said softly. "I'd appreciate that tremendously. Marvin is getting the window replaced and I'll be keeping the lights on in the yard all night now."

"Doesn't matter," Jason said. "You're staying at my place tonight."

Bella tilted her head to the side and met Jason's intense gaze. "I can't do that. You and I can't stay under the same roof."

Jason crossed his arms over his chest. "And why not?"

A flush stole into her cheeks when she noted Jason

wasn't the only one waiting on her response. "You know why," she finally said.

Jason's forehead bunched up. Then when he remembered what could possibly happen if they stayed overnight under the same roof, he smiled. "Oh, yeah."

"Oh, yeah, what?" Zane wanted to know.

Jason frowned at his cousin. "None of your business."

Pete cleared his throat. "I'm out of here but like I said, Miss Bostwick, the department will have more police checking around the area." He slipped both the rock and note into a plastic evidence bag.

Zane and Derringer followed Pete out the door, which Jason appreciated since it gave him time alone with Bella. The first thing he did was lean down and kiss her. He needed the taste of her to know she was really okay.

She responded to his kiss and automatically he deepened it, drawing her up out of the chair to stand on her feet in the process. He needed the feel of all of her to know she was safe. He would protect her with his life if he had to. He'd aged a good twenty years when he'd gotten that call from Pam telling him what had happened. And speaking of Pam's phone call...

He broke off the kiss and with an irritated frown on his features he looked down at Bella. "Why didn't you call me? Why did I have to hear what happened from someone else?"

She gazed right back at him with an irritated frown of her own. "You've never given me your phone number."

Jason blinked in surprise and realized what she'd said was true. He hadn't given her his phone number.

"I apologize for that oversight," he said. "You will

definitely have it from here on out. And we need to talk about you moving in with me for a while."

She shook her head. "I can't move in with you, Jason, and as I said earlier, we both know why."

"Do you honestly think if you gave me an order not to touch you that I wouldn't keep my hands off you?" he asked.

She shrugged delicate shoulders. "Yes, I believe you'd do as I ask, but I'm not sure given that same scenario, in light of what happened in this very kitchen Friday night, that I'd be able to keep my hands off you."

He blinked. Stared down at her and blinked again. This time with a smile on his lips. "You don't say?"

"I do say and I know it's an awful thing to admit, but right now I can't make you any promises," she said, rubbing her hands together as if distressed by the very notion.

He wasn't distressed, not even a little bit. In fact, he was elated. For a minute he couldn't say a word and then said, "And you think I have a problem with you not being able to keep your hands off me?"

She nodded. "If you don't have a problem with it then you should. We aren't married. We aren't even engaged."

"I asked you to marry me Friday night."

She used her hand to wave off his reminder. "Yes, but it would be a marriage of convenience, which I haven't agreed to yet since the issue of the sleeping arrangements is still up in the air. Until I do decide I think it's best if you stay under your roof and I stay under mine. Yes, that's the proper thing to do."

He lifted a brow. "The proper thing to do?"

"Yes, proper, appropriate, suitable, fitting, which of those words do you prefer using?"

"What about none of them?"

"It doesn't matter, Jason. It's bad enough that we got carried away the other night in this kitchen. But we can't repeat something like that."

He didn't see why they couldn't and was about to say as much when he heard footsteps approaching and glanced over as Derringer and Zane entered the kitchen.

"Pete thinks he's found a footprint outside near the bushes and is checking it out now," Derringer informed them.

Jason nodded. He then turned back to Bella and his expression was one that would accept no argument on the matter. "Pack an overnight bag, Bella. You're staying at my place tonight even if I have to sleep in the barn."

Six

Bella glared at Jason. It was a ladylike glare but a glare nonetheless. She opened her mouth to say something then remembered they had an audience and immediately closed it. She cast a warm smile over at Zane and Derringer. "I'd like a few minutes alone with Jason to discuss a private matter, please."

They returned her smile, nodded and gave Jason "you've done it now" smiles before walking out of the kitchen.

It was then that she turned her attention back to Jason. "Now then, Jason, let's not be ridiculous. You are not sleeping in your barn just so I can sleep under your roof. I'm staying right here."

She could tell he did not appreciate his order not being obeyed when she saw his irritation with her increase. "Have you forgotten someone threw a rock through your window with a note demanding you leave town?"

She nibbled a minute on her bottom lip. "No, I didn't forget the rock or the note attached to it, but I can't let them think they've won by running away. I admit to being a little frightened at first but I'm fine now. Marvin is having the window replaced and I'll keep lights shining around here all night. And don't forget Marvin sleeps in the bunkhouse each night so technically, I won't be here by myself. I'll be fine but I appreciate your concern."

Jason stared at her for a moment and didn't say anything. He hadn't lied about aging twenty years when he'd gotten that call from Pam. He had walked into her house not knowing what to expect. The thought that someone wanted her gone bothered him, because he knew she wasn't going anywhere and that meant he needed to protect her.

"Fine, you stay inside here and I'll sleep in your barn," he finally said.

She shook her head after crossing her arms over her chest. "You won't be sleeping in anyone's barn. You're going to sleep in your own bed tonight and I intend to sleep in mine."

"Fine," he snapped like he was giving in to her suggestion when he wouldn't do anything of the sort. But if she wanted to think it he would let her. "I need to take you to Pam's to show her and the others you're okay and in one piece."

A smile touched her lips. "They were worried about me?"

She seemed surprised by that. "Yes, everyone was worried."

"In that case let me grab my purse."

"I'll be waiting outside," he said to her fleeing back.

He shook his head and slowly left the kitchen and walked through the dining room to the living room where Marvin and a couple of the men were replacing the window. They had cleaned up all the broken glass but a scratch mark on the wooden floor clearly showed where the rock had landed once it entered the house.

He drew in a sharp breath at the thought of Bella getting hit by that rock. If anything would have happened to her he would have...

At that moment he wasn't sure just what he would do. The thought of anything happening to her sent sharp fear through him in a way he'd never known before. Why? Why were his feelings for her so intense? Why was he so possessive when it came to her?

He shrugged off the responses that flowed through his mind, not ready to deal with any of them. He walked out the front door to where Zane and Derringer were waiting.

"You aren't really going to let her stay here unprotected?" Derringer asked, studying his features.

Jason shook his head. "No."

"And why can't the two of you stay under the same roof?" Zane asked curiously.

"None of your business."

Zane chuckled. "If you don't give me an answer I'm going to think things."

That didn't move Jason. "Think whatever you want." He then checked his watch. "I hate to do this but I'm checking out for the rest of the day. I intend to keep an eye on Bella until Pete finds out who threw that rock through her window."

"You think Kenneth Bostwick had something to do with it?" Derringer asked.

"Not sure, but I hope for his sake he didn't," Jason said in a voice laced with tightly controlled anger.

He stopped talking when Bella walked onto the porch. Not only had she grabbed her purse but she'd also changed her dress. At his curious look, she said, "The dress I was wearing wasn't suitable for visiting."

He nodded and decided not to tell her she looked good now and had looked good then. Whatever she put on her body she wore with both grace and style. He met her in the middle of the porch and slipped her hand in his. "You look nice. And I thought we could grab dinner someplace before I bring you back here."

Her eyes glowed in a way that tightened his stomach and sent sensations rushing through his gut. "I'd like that, Jason."

It was close to ten at night when Bella returned home. Jason entered her house and checked around, turning on lights as he went from room to room. It made her feel extra safe when she saw a police patrol car parked near the turnoff to her property.

"Everything looks okay," Jason said, breaking into her thoughts.

"Thanks. I'll walk you to the door," she said quickly, heading back downstairs.

"Trying to rush me out of here, Bella?"

At the moment she didn't care what he thought. She just needed him gone so she could get her mind straightened out. Being with him for the past eight hours had taken its toll on her mind and body.

She hadn't known he was so touchy and each time he'd touched her, even by doing something simple as placing a hand in the center of her back when they'd been walking into the movies, it had done something to her in a way that had her hot and bothered for the rest of the evening.

But she had enjoyed the movies they'd gone to after dinner. She had enjoyed sitting beside him while he held her hand when he wasn't feeding her popcorn.

"No, I'm not trying to rush you, Jason, but it is late," she said. "If your goal this evening was to tire me out then you've done a good job of it. I plan to take a shower and then go to bed."

They were standing facing each other and he wrapped his arms around her and took a step closer, almost plastering his body to hers. She could feel all of him from chest to knee; but especially the erect body part in between.

"I'd love to take a shower with you, sweetheart," he whispered.

She didn't know what he was trying to do, but he'd been whispering such naughty come-ons to her all evening. And each and every one of them had only added to her torment. "Taking a shower together wouldn't be right, Jason, and you know it."

He chuckled. "Trying to send me home to an empty bed isn't right, either. Why don't you just accept my proposal? We can get married the same day. No waiting. And then," he said, leaning closer to begin nibbling around her mouth, "we can sleep under the same roof that night. Just think about that."

Bella moaned against the onslaught of his mouth on hers. She was thinking about it and could just imagine it. Oh, what a night that would be. But then she also had to think about what would happen if he got tired of her like her father had eventually gotten tired of her mother. The way her mother had gotten tired of her father. What if he approached her about wanting an open marriage?

What if he told her after the first year that he wanted a divorce and she'd gotten attached to him? She could just imagine the heartbreak she would feel.

"Bella?"

She glanced up at him. "Yes?"

Jason Westmoreland was such a handsome man that it made her heart ache. And at the same time he made parts of her sizzle in desire so thick you could cut it with a knife. She thought his features were flawless and he had to have the most irresistible pair of lips born to any man. Staring at his mouth pushed her to recall the way their tongues would entangle in his mouth while they mated them like crazy. It didn't take much to wonder how things would be between them in the bedroom. But she knew as tempting as it was, there was more to a marriage than just great sex. But could she really ask for more from a marriage of convenience?

"Are you sure you don't want me to stay tonight? I could sleep on the sofa."

She shook her head. Even that would be too close for comfort for her. "No, Jason, I'll be fine. Go home."

"Not before I do this," he said, leaning down and capturing her mouth with his. She didn't have a problem offering him what he wanted and he proved he didn't have a problem taking it. He kissed her deeply, thoroughly and with no reservations about making her feel wanted, needed and desired. She could definitely feel heat radiating from his body to hers and wasn't put off by it. Instead it ignited passion within her so acute she had to fight to keep a level head or risk the kiss taking them places she wasn't ready to go.

Moments later she was the one who broke off the kiss. Desperately needing to breathe, she inhaled a deep breath. Jason just simply stood there staring and waiting, as if he was ready to go another round.

Bella knew she disappointed him when she took a step back. "Good night, Jason."

His lips curved into a too-sexy smile. "Tell me one thing that will be good about it once I walk out that door."

She really wasn't sure what she could say to that and in those cases she'd always been told it was better not to say anything at all. Instead she repeated herself while turning the knob on the door to open it. "Good night, Jason.

He leaned in, brushed a kiss across her lips and whispered, "Good night, Bella."

Bella wasn't sure what brought her awake during the middle of the night. Glancing over at the clock on her nightstand she saw it was two in the morning. She was restless. She was hot. And she was definitely still bothered. She hadn't known just spending time with a man could put a woman in such an erotic state.

Sliding out of bed she slipped into her robe and house shoes. A full moon was in the sky and its light spread into the room. She was surprised by how easily sleep had come to her at first. But that had been a few hours ago and now she was wide-awake.

She moved over to the windows to look out. Under the moon-crested sky she could see the shape of the mountains in their majestic splendor. At night they were just as overpowering as they were in the daylight.

She was about to move away from the window when she happened to glance down below and saw a truck parked in her yard. She frowned and pressed her face closer to the window to make out just whose vehicle was parked in her yard and frowned when she recognized the vehicle was Jason's.

What was his truck doing in her yard at two in the morning? Was he in it?

She rushed downstairs. He couldn't be in a truck in front of her house at two in the morning. What would Marvin think? What would the police officers cruising the area think? His family?

When she made it to the living room she slowly opened the door and slipped out. She then released a disgusted sigh when she saw he was sitting in the truck. He had put his seat in a reclining position, but that had to be uncomfortable for him.

As if he'd been sleeping with one eye open and another one closed, he came awake when she rounded the truck and tapped on his window. He slowly tilted his Stetson back from covering his eyes. "Yes, Bella?"

She opened her mouth to speak and then closed it. If she thought he was a handsome man before then he was even more now with the shadow covering his jaw. There was just something ultrasexy about a man who hadn't shaved.

She fought her attention away from his jaw back to his gaze. "What are you doing here? Why did you come back?"

"I never left."

She blinked. "You never left? You mean to tell me you've been out here in the car since I walked you to the door?"

He smiled that sexy smile. "Yes, I've been here since you walked me to the door."

"But why?"

"To protect you."

That simple statement suddenly took the wind out of

her sail for just a moment. Merely a moment. That was all the time she needed to be reminded that no one had tried truly protecting her before. She'd always considered her parents' antics more in the line of controlling than protecting.

She then recovered and remembered why he couldn't sit out here protecting her. "But you can't sit out here, Jason. It's not proper. What will your family think if any of them see your car parked in front of my house at this hour? What would those policemen think? What would—"

"Honestly, Bella, I really don't give a royal damn what anyone thinks. I refuse to let you stay here without being close by to make sure you're okay. You didn't want me to sleep in the barn so this is where I am and where I will stay."

She frowned. "You're being difficult."

"No, I'm being a man looking out for the woman I want. Now go back inside and lock the door behind you. You interrupted my sleep."

She stared at him for a long moment and then said, "Fine, you win. Come on inside."

He stared back at her. "That wasn't what this was about, Bella. I recognize the fact just as much as you do that we don't need to be under the same roof alone. I'm fine with being out here tonight."

"Well, I'm not fine with it."

"Sorry about that but there's nothing I can do about it."

She glared at him and seeing he was determined to be stubborn, she threw up her hands before going back into the house, closing the door behind her.

Jason heard the lock click in place and swore he could also hear her fuming all the way up the stairs. She could fume all she wanted but he wasn't leaving. He had been sitting out there for the past four hours thinking, and the more he thought the more he realized something vital to him. And it was something he could not deny or ignore. He had fallen in love with Bella. And accepting how he felt gave his proposal much more meaning than what he'd presented to her. Now he fully understood why Derringer had acted so strangely while courting Lucia.

He had dated women in the past but had never loved any of them. He'd known better than to do so after that fiasco with Mona Cardington in high school. He'd admitted he loved her and when a new guy moved to town weeks later she had dumped him like a hot potato. That had been years ago but the pain he'd felt that day had been real and at seventeen it had been what had kept him from loving another woman.

And now he had fallen head over heels in love with a Southern belle and for the time being would keep how he felt to himself.

An hour later Bella lay in bed staring up at the ceiling, still inwardly fuming. How dare Jason put her in such a compromising position? No one would think he was sleeping in the truck. People were going to assume they were lovers and he was sleeping in her bed, lying with her between silken sheets with their limbs entwined and mouths fused while making hot, passionate and steamy love.

Her thighs began to quiver and the juncture between her legs began to ache just thinking of how it would probably be if they were to share a bed. He would stroke her senseless with his fingers in her most intimate spot first, taking his time to get her primed and ready for the next stage of what he would do to her.

She shifted to her side and held her legs tightly together, hoping the ache would go away. She'd never craved a man before and now she was craving Jason something fierce, more so than ever since he'd tasted her there. All she had to do was close her eyes and remember being stretched out on her kitchen table with his head between her legs and how he had lapped her into sweet oblivion. The memories sent jolts of electricity throughout her body, making the tips of her breasts feel sensitive against her nightgown.

And the man causing her so much torment and pleasure was downstairs sleeping in his truck just to keep her safe. She couldn't help but be touched that he would do such a thing. He had given up a nice comfortable bed and was sleeping in a position that couldn't be relaxing with his hat over his eyes to shield the brightness of the lights around her yard. Why? Was protecting her that important to him?

If it was, then why?

Deep down she knew the reason and it stemmed from him wanting her land and Hercules. He had been up-front about it from the beginning. She had respected him for it and for accepting the decision was hers to make. So, in other words, he wasn't really protecting her per se but merely protecting his interest, or what he hoped to be his interest. She figured such a thing made sense but…

Would accepting the proposal Jason placed on the table be in her best interest? Did she have a choice if she wanted the hold lifted on her trust fund? Was being legally bound to Jason as his wife for a minimum of a year something she wanted? What about sleeping under the same roof with him and sharing his bed—she'd accepted they would be synonymous—be in her best interest? Was it what she wanted to do, knowing in a year's time he could walk away without looking back? Knowing after that time he would be free to marry someone else? Free to make love to someone else the same way he'd make love to her?

And then there was the question of who was responsible for throwing the rock inside her house. Why was someone trying to scare her off? Although she doubted it, could it be her parents' doing to get her to run back home?

She yawned when she felt sleep coming down on her. Although she regretted Jason was sleeping in his truck, she knew she could sleep a lot more peacefully knowing he was the one protecting her.

Bella woke to the sound of someone knocking on her door and discovered it was morning. She quickly eased out of bed and slid into her bathrobe and bedroom shoes to head downstairs.

"I'm coming!" she called out, rushing to the door. She glanced out the peephole and saw it was Jason. Her heart began beating fast and furiously in her chest at the sight of him, handsome and unshaven with his Stetson low on his brow. Mercy!

Taking a deep breath she opened the door. "Good morning, Jason."

"Good morning, Bella. I wanted to let you know I'm leaving to go home and freshen up, but Riley is here."

"Your brother Riley?" she asked, looking over his shoulder to see the truck parked next to his and the man sitting inside. Riley threw up his hand in a wave which she returned. She recalled meeting him that night at dinner. Jason was older than Riley by two and a half years.

"Yes, my brother Riley."

She was confused. "Why is he here?"

"Because I'm going home to freshen up." He tilted his head and smiled at her. "Are you awake yet?"

"Yes, I'm awake and I know you said you're going home to change but why does Riley have to be here? It's not like I need a bodyguard or something. A rock got thrown through my window, Jason. Not a scud missile."

He merely kept smiling at her while leaning in her doorway. And then he said, "Has anyone ever told you how beautiful you look in the morning?"

She stood there and stared at him. Not ready for him to change the subject and definitely not prepared for him to say something so nice about how she looked. She could definitely return the favor and ask, had anyone ever told him how handsome he looked in the morning. However, she was certain a number of women already had.

So she answered him honestly. "No one has ever told me that."

"Then let me go on record as being your first."

She drew in a deep breath. He didn't say "the" first but had said "your" first. He had made it personal and exclusive. She wondered what he would think to know she had drifted off to sleep last night with images of him flittering through her mind. Memories of his mouth on her probably elicited pleasurable sighs from her even while she slept.

"Doesn't Riley have to go to work today?" she asked, remembering when he'd mentioned that Riley worked for Blue Ridge Management. She'd even seen his name on one of the doors when they'd exited from the elevator on the fortieth floor.

"Yes, but he'll leave whenever I get back."

She crossed her arms over her chest. "And what about you? Don't you have horses to breed or train?"

"Your safety is more important to me."

"Yeah, right."

He lifted a brow. "You don't believe me? Even after I spent the entire night in my truck?"

"You were protecting your interest."

"And that's definitely you, sweetheart."

Don't even go there. Bella figured it was definitely time to end this conversation. If she engaged in chatter with him too much longer he would be convincing her that everything he was saying was true.

"You will have an answer for me in four days, right, Bella?"

"That's my plan."

"Good. I'll be back by the time you're dressed and we can do breakfast with Dillon and Pam, and then I want to show you what I do for a living."

Before she could respond he leaned in and kissed her on the lips. "See you in an hour. And wear your riding attire."

She sucked in a deep breath and watched as he walked off the porch to his truck to drive away. The man was definitely something else. She cast a quick glance to where Riley sat in his own truck sipping a cup of coffee. There was no doubt in her mind Riley had seen his brother kiss her, and she could only imagine what he was thinking.

Deciding the least she could do was invite him in, she called out to him. "You're welcome to come inside, Riley," she said, smiling broadly at him.

The smile he returned was just as expansive as he leaned his head slightly out the truck's window and said, "Thanks, but Jason warned me not to. I'm fine."

Jason warned him not to? Of course he was just joking, although he looked dead serious.

Instead of questioning him about it, she nodded, closed the door and headed back upstairs. As she entered her bedroom she couldn't ignore the excitement she felt about riding with Jason and checking out his horse training business.

Jason had grabbed his Stetson off the rack and was about to head out the door when his cell phone rang. He pulled it off his belt and saw it was Dillon.

"Yes, Dil?"

"Pam wanted me to call and verify that you and Bella are coming for breakfast."

Jason smiled. "Yes, we'll be there. In fact I'm about to saddle up one of the mares. I thought we'd ride over on horseback. We can enjoy the sights along the way."

"That's a good idea. Everything's okay at her place?"

"Yes, so far so good. The sheriff has increased the patrols around Bella's house and I appreciate it. Thank him the next time the two of you shoot pool together."

Dillon chuckled. "I will. And just so you know, I like Bella. She has a lot of class."

Jason smiled. That meant a lot coming from his older brother. While growing up he'd always thought Dillon was smart with a good head on his shoulders. Jason's admiration increased when Dillon had worked hard to keep the family together.

"And thanks, Dillon."

"For what?"

"For being you. For being there when all of us needed

you to be. For doing what you knew Mom and Dad, as well as Uncle Thomas and Aunt Susan would have wanted you to do."

"You don't have to thank me, Jason."

"Yes, I do."

Dillon didn't say anything for a moment. "Then you're welcome. Now don't keep us waiting with Bella. We won't start breakfast until the two of you get here. At least all of us except Denver. He wakes up hungry. Pam has fed him already," Dillon said.

Jason couldn't help but smile, and not for the first time, as he thought of one day having a son of his own. Being around Denver had the tendency to put such thoughts into his head. He enjoyed his nephew immensely.

"We'll get there in good time, I promise," he said before clicking off the phone.

Bella glanced down at her riding attire and smiled. She wanted to be ready when Jason returned.

Grabbing her hat off the rack she placed it on her head and opened the door to step outside on the porch. Riley had gotten out of the truck and was leaning against it. He glanced over at her and smiled.

"Ready to go riding I see," he said.

"Yes, Jason told me to be ready. We're having breakfast with Dillon and Pam."

"Yes, I had planned to have breakfast with them as well but I have a meeting at the office."

Bella nodded. "You enjoy working inside?"

Riley chuckled. "Yes, I'll leave the horses, dirt and grime to Jason. He's always liked being outdoors. When he worked at Blue Ridge I knew it was just a matter of time before wanderlust got ahold of him. He's good

with horses, so are Zane and Derringer. Joining in with
the Montana Westmorelands in that horse business was
great for them."

Bella nodded again. "So exactly what do you do at
Blue Ridge?"

"Mmm, a little bit of everything. I like to think of
myself as Dillon's right-hand man. But my main job
is PR. I have to make sure Blue Ridge keeps a stellar
image."

Bella continued to engage in conversation with Riley
while thinking he was another kind Westmoreland man.
It seemed that all of them were. But she'd heard Bailey
remark more than once that Riley was also a ladies'
man, and she could definitely believe that. Like Jason,
he was handsome to a fault.

"So, Riley, when will you settle down and get
married?" she asked him, just to see what his response
would be.

"Married? Me? Never. I like things just the way they
are. I am definitely not the marrying kind."

Bella smiled, wondering if Jason wasn't the marrying
kind, as well, although he'd given a marriage proposal
to her. Did he want joint ownership of her land and
Hercules that much? Evidently so.

Jason smiled as he headed back to Bella's ranch with
a horse he knew she would love riding. Fancy Free was
an even tempered mare. In the distance, he could see
Bella was standing on the porch waiting for him. He
would discount the fact that she seemed to be having
an enjoyable conversation with Riley, who seemed to
be flirting with her.

He ignored the signs of jealousy seeping into his
bones. Riley was his brother and if you couldn't trust

your own brother who could you trust? A lightbulb suddenly went off in his head. Hell. Had Abel assumed the same thing about Cain?

He tightened his hands on his horse and increased his pace to a gallop. What was Riley saying to Bella to make her laugh so much anyway? Riley was becoming a regular ladies' man around town. It seemed he was trying to keep up with Zane in that aspect. Jason had always thought Riley's playboy ways were amusing. Until now.

Moments later he brought his horse to a stop by the edge of Bella's porch. He tilted his Stetson back on his head so it wouldn't shield his eyes. "Excuse me if I'm interrupting anything."

Riley had the nerve to grin up at him. "No problem but you're twenty minutes late. You better be glad I enjoy Bella's company."

Jason frowned at his brother. "I can tell."

His gaze then shifted to Bella. She looked beautiful standing there in a pair of riding breeches that fitted her body to perfection, a white shirt and a pair of riding boots. She didn't just look beautiful, she looked hot as sin and a side glance at Riley told him that his brother was enjoying the view as much as he was.

"Don't you need to be on your way to work, Riley?"

His brother gave him another grin. "I guess so. Call if you need me as Bella's bodyguard again." He then got into his truck and pulled off.

Jason watched him leave before turning his full attention back to Bella. "Ready to go riding, sweetheart?"

As Bella rode with Jason she tried concentrating on the sheer beauty of the rustic countryside instead of the sexiness of the man in the saddle beside her. He was riding Hercules and she could tell he was an expert horseman. And she could tell why he wanted to own the stallion. It was as if he and the horse had a personal relationship. It was evident Hercules had been glad to see him. Whereas the stallion had been like putty in Jason's hands the horse had given the others grief in trying to handle him. Even now the two seemed in sync.

This was beautiful countryside and the first time she'd seen it. She was stunned by its beauty. The mare he'd chosen for her had come from his stable and was the one he'd rode over to her place. She liked how easily she and the horse were able to take the slopes that stretched out into valleys. The landscape looked majestic with the mountains in the distance.

First they rode over to Dillon and Pam's for breakfast. She had fallen in love with the Westmoreland Estate the first time she had seen it. The huge Victorian style home with a wide circular driveway sat on three hundred acres of land. Jason had told her on the ride over that as the oldest cousin, Dillon had inherited the family home. It was where most of the family seemed to congregate the majority of the time.

She had met Pam's three younger sisters the other night at dinner and enjoyed their company again around the breakfast table. Everyone asked questions about the rock throwing incident and Dillon, who knew the sheriff personally, felt the person or persons responsible would eventually get caught.

After breakfast they were in the saddle again. Jason and Bella rode to Zane's place. She was given a front row seat and watched as Zane, Derringer and Jason exercised several of the horses. Jason had explained some of the horses needed both aerobic and anaerobic training, and that so many hours each day were spent on that task. She could tell that it took a lot of skill as well as experience for any trainer to be successful and achieve the goals they wanted for the horses they trained.

At noon Lucia arrived with box lunches for everyone and Bella couldn't help noticing how much the newlyweds were still into each other. She knew if she decided to marry Jason they would not share the type of marriage Derringer and Lucia did since their union would be more of a business arrangement than anything else. But it was so obvious to anyone around Derringer and Lucia they were madly in love with each other.

Later that day they had dinner with Ramsey and Chloe and enjoyed the time they spent with the couple immensely. Over dinner Ramsey provided tidbits about sheep ranching and how he'd made the decision to move from being a businessman to operating a sheep ranch.

The sun was going down when she and Jason mounted their horses to return to her ranch. It had been a full day of activities and she had learned a lot about both the horse training business and sheep ranching.

She glanced over at Jason. He hadn't said a whole lot since they'd left his brother's ranch and she couldn't help wondering what he was thinking. She also couldn't help wondering if he intended to sleep in his truck again tonight.

"I feel like a freeloader today," she said to break the silence between them.

He glanced over at her. "Why?"

"Your family fed me breakfast, lunch and dinner today."

He smiled. "They like you."

"And I like them."

She truly did. One of the benefits of accepting Jason's proposal would be his family. But what would happen after the year was up and she'd gotten attached to them? Considered herself part of the family?

They had cleared his land and were riding on her property when up ahead in the distance they saw what appeared to be a huge fiery red ball filled with smoke. They both realized at the same time what it was.

Fire.

And it was coming from the direction of her ranch.

Seven

Bella stood in what used to be the middle of her living room, glanced around and fought the tears stinging her eyes. More than half of her home was gone, destroyed by the fire. And according to the fire marshal it had been deliberately set. If it hadn't been for the quick thinking of her men who begun using water hoses to douse the flames, the entire ranch house would have gone up in smoke.

Her heart felt heavy. Oppressed. Broken. All she'd wanted when she had left Savannah was to start a new life here. But it seemed that was not going to happen. Someone wanted her gone. Who wanted her land that much?

She felt a touch to her arm and without looking up she knew it was Jason. Her body would recognize his touch anywhere. He had been by her side the entire time and watched as portions of her house went up in flames. And he had held her when she couldn't watch any longer and buried her face in his chest and clung to him. At that moment he had become the one thing that was unshakable in a world that was falling down all around her; intentionally being destroyed by someone who was determined to steal her happiness and joy. And he had held her and whispered over and over that everything was going to be all right. And she had tried to believe him and had managed to draw strength from him.

His family had arrived and had given their support as well and had let the authorities know they wanted answers and wanted the person or persons responsible brought to justice. Already they were talking about helping her rebuild and like Jason had done, assured her that everything would be all right.

Sheriff Harper had questioned her, making inquiries similar to the ones Pete had yesterday when the rock had been thrown through her living room window. Did she know of anyone who wanted her out of Denver? Whoever was responsible was determined to get their message through to her loud and clear.

"Bella?"

She glanced up and met Jason's gaze. "Yes?"

"Come on, let's go. There's nothing more we can do here tonight."

She shuddered miserably and the lungs holding back her sob constricted. "Go? Go where, Jason? Look around you. I no longer have a home."

She couldn't stop the single tear that fell from her eyes. Instead of responding to what she'd said Jason brushed the tear away with the pad of his thumb before entwining his fingers in hers. He then led her away toward the barn for a moment of privacy. It was then that he turned her to face him, sweeping the curls back from her face. He fixed her with a gaze that stirred everything inside of her.

"As long as I have a home, Bella, you do, too."

He then drew in a deep breath. "Don't let whoever did this win. This is land that your grandfather gave you and you have every right to be here if that's what you want. Don't let anyone run you off your land," Jason said in a husky whisper.

She heard his words, she felt his plea, but like she'd told him, she no longer had a home now. She didn't want to depend on others, become their charity case. "But what can I do, Jason? It takes money to rebuild and thanks to my parents, my trust fund is on hold." She paused and then with sagging shoulders added, "I don't have anything now. The ranch was insured, but it will take time to rebuild."

"You have me, Bella. My proposal still stands and now more than ever you should consider taking it. A marriage between us means that we'll both get what we want and will show the person who did this that you aren't going anywhere. It will show them they didn't win after all and sooner or later they will get caught. And even if it happens to be a member of your family, I'm going to make sure they pay for doing this."

Jason lowered his gaze to the ground for a moment and then returned it to her. "I am worse than mad right now, Bella, I'm so full of rage I could actually hurt someone for doing this to you. Whoever is behind this probably thought you were inside the house. What if you had been? What if you hadn't spent the day with me?"

Bella took a deep breath. Those were more "what ifs" she didn't want to think about or consider. The only thing she wanted to think about right now was the proposal; the one Jason had offered and still wanted her to take. And she decided at that very moment that she would.

She would take her chances on what might or might not happen within that year. She would be the best wife possible and hopefully in a year's time even if he wanted a divorce they could still be friends.

"So what about it, Bella? Will you show whoever did this today that you are a fighter and not a quitter and that you will keep what's yours? Will you marry me so we can do that together?"

She held his gaze, exhaled deeply. "Yes, I'll marry you, Jason."

She thought the smile that touched his lips was priceless and she had to inwardly remind herself he wasn't happy because he was marrying her but because marrying her meant he would co-own her land and get full possession of Hercules. And in marrying him she would get her trust fund back and send a message to whomever was behind the threats to her that they were wasting their time and she wasn't going anywhere.

He leaned down, brushed a kiss across her lips and tightened his hold on her hand. "Come on. Let's go tell the family our good news."

If Jason's brothers and cousins were surprised by their announcement they didn't let on. Probably because they were too busy congratulating them and then making wedding plans.

She and Jason had decided the true nature of their marriage was between them. They planned to keep it that way. The Westmorelands didn't so much as bat an eye when Jason further announced they would be getting married as soon as possible. Tomorrow in fact. He assured everyone they could plan a huge reception for later.

Bella decided to contact her parents *after* the wedding tomorrow. A judge who was a friend of the Westmorelands was given a call and he immediately agreed to perform the civil ceremony in his chambers around three in the afternoon. Dillon and Ramsey suggested the family celebrate the nuptials by joining them for dinner after the ceremony at a restaurant downtown.

The honeymoon would come later. For now they would spend the night at a hotel downtown. With so many things to do to prepare for tomorrow, Bella was able to put the fire behind her and she actually looked forward to her wedding day. She was also able to put out of her mind the reason they were marrying in the first place. Dillon and Pam invited her to spend the night in their home, and she accepted their invitation.

"Come walk me out to my truck," Jason whispered, taking her hand in his.

"All right."

When they got to where his truck was parked, he placed her against it and leaned over and kissed her in a deep, drugging kiss. When he released her lips he whispered, "You can come home with me tonight, you know."

Yes, she knew but then she also knew if she did so, they would consummate a wedding that was yet to take place. She wanted to do things in the right order. The way she'd always dreamed of doing them when she read all those romance novels.

"Yes, I know but I'll be fine staying with Dillon and Pam tonight. Tomorrow will be here before you know it." She then paused and looked up at him, searched his gaze. "And you think we're doing the right thing, Jason?"

He smiled, nodding. "Yes, I'm positive. After the ceremony we'll contact your parents and provide their attorney with whatever documentation needed to kick your trust fund back in gear. And I'm sure word will get around soon enough for whoever has been making those threats to hear Bella Bostwick Westmoreland is here to stay."

Bella Bostwick Westmoreland. She liked the sound of it already but deep down she knew she couldn't get attached to it. She stared into his eyes and hoped he wouldn't wake up one morning and think he'd made a mistake and the proposal hadn't been worth it.

"Everything will work out for the best, Bella. You'll see." He then pulled her into his arms and kissed her again.

"I now pronounce you man and wife. Jason, you may kiss your bride."

Jason didn't waste any time pulling Bella into his arms and devouring her mouth the way he'd gotten accustomed to doing.

He had expected a small audience but every Westmoreland living in Denver was there, except Micah, his brother who was a year older and an epidemiologist with the federal government, as well as his brothers Canyon and Stern who were away attending law school. And of course he missed his cousin Gemma who was living with her husband in Australia, and his younger brother Bane who was in the navy. Jason also missed the twins, Aiden and Adrian. They were away at college.

When he finally released Bella's mouth, cheers went

up and he glanced at Bella and knew at that moment just how much he loved her. He would prove the depth of his love over the rest of their lives. He knew she assumed after the first year either of them could file for divorce, but he didn't intend for that to happen. Ever. There would be no divorce.

He glanced down at the ring he'd placed on her finger. He had picked her up at eight that morning, taken her into town for breakfast and from there a whirlwind of activities had begun with a visit to the jeweler. Then to the courthouse to file the necessary papers so they could marry on time. Luckily there was no waiting period in Colorado and he was grateful for that.

"Hey, Jason and Bella. Are the two of you ready for dinner?" Dillon asked, smiling.

Jason smiled back. "Yes, we are." He took Bella's hand in his, felt the sensations touching her elicited and knew that, personally, he was ready for something else, as well.

Bella cast a quick glance over at Jason as they stepped on the elevator that would take them up to their hotel room in the tower—the honeymoon suite—compliments of the entire Westmoreland family. She realized she hadn't just married the man but had also inherited his entire family. For someone who'd never had an extended family before, she could only be elated.

Dinner with everyone had been wonderful and Jason's brothers and cousins had stood to offer toasts to what everyone saw as a long marriage. There hadn't been anything in Jason's expression indicating they were way off base in that assumption or that it was wishful thinking on their parts.

All of the Westmoreland ladies had given her hugs

and welcomed her to the family. The men had hugged her, as well, and she could tell they were genuinely happy for her and Jason.

And now they were on the elevator that would carry them to the floor where their room was located. They would be spending the night, sleeping under the same roof and sharing the same bed. They hadn't discussed such a thing happening, but she knew it was an unspoken understanding between them.

Jason had become quiet and she wondered if he'd already regretted making the proposal. The thought that he had sent her into a panic mode, made her heart begin to break a piece at a time. Then without warning, she felt his hand touch her arm and when she glanced over at him he smiled and reached for her and pulled her closer to his side, as if refusing to let her stand anywhere by herself…without him. It was as if he was letting her know she would never ever be alone again.

She knew a part of her was probably rationalizing things the way she wished they were, the way she wanted them to be but not necessarily how they really were. But if she had to fantasize then she would do that. If she had to pretend they had a real marriage for the next year then she would do that, too. However, a part of her would never lose sight of the real reason she was here. A part of her would always be prepared for the inevitable.

"You were a beautiful bride, Bella."

"Thank you." Warmth spread through her in knowing that he'd thought so because she had tried so hard to be. She had been determined to make some part of today resemble a real wedding—even if it was a civil one in the judge's chambers. The ladies in the family had insisted that she be turned over to them after securing a license at the Denver County Court House and had promised Jason she would be on time for her wedding.

It had taken less than an hour to obtain the marriage license and Lucia had been there to pick her up afterward. Bella had been whisked away for a day of beauty and to visit a very exclusive bridal shop to pick up the perfect dress for her wedding. Since time was of the essence, everything had been arranged beforehand. When they had delivered her back to Jason five hours later, the moment she'd joined him in the judge's chambers his smile had let her know he thought her time away from him had been well worth it. She would forever be grateful to her new in-laws and a part of her knew that Pam, Chloe, Megan, Lucia and Bailey would also be friends she could count on for life.

"You look good yourself," she said softly.

She thought that was an understatement. She had seen him in a suit the night at the charity ball. He had taken her breath away then and was taking it away now. Tall, dark and handsome, he was the epitome of every woman's fantasy and dream. And for at least one full year, he would be hers.

The elevator stopped on their floor and tightening his hand on hers, they stepped out. Her breath caught when the elevator doors whooshed closed behind them and they began walking toward room 4501. She knew once they reached those doors and she stepped inside there would be no turning back.

They silently strolled side by side holding hands. Everything about the Four Seasons Hotel spoke of its elegance and the decorative colors all around were vibrant and vivid.

Jason released her hand when they reached their room to pull the passkey from the pocket of his suit jacket.

Once he opened the door he extended his hand to her and she took it, felt the sensations flowing between them. She gasped when she was suddenly swept off her feet and into his arms and carried over the threshold into the honeymoon suite.

Jason kicked the door closed with his foot before placing Bella on her feet. And then he just stood there and looked at her, allowing his gaze to roam all over her. What he'd told her earlier was true. She was a beautiful bride.

And she was his.

Absolutely and positively his.

Her tea-length dress was ivory in color and made of silk chiffon and fitted at her small waist with a rose in the center. It was a perfect match for the ivory satin rose-heeled shoes on her feet. White roses were her favorite flower and she'd used them as the theme in their wedding. Even her wedding bouquet had consisted of white roses.

His chest expanded with so much love for her, love she didn't know about yet. He had a year to win her over and intended to spend the next twelve months doing just that. But now, he needed for her to know just how much she was desired.

He lowered his head and kissed her, letting his tongue tangle with hers, reacquainting himself with the taste of her, a taste he had not forgotten and had so desperately craved since the last time. He kissed her deeply, not allowing any part of her mouth to go untouched. And she returned the kiss with a hunger that matched his own and he was mesmerized by how she was making him feel.

He tightened his hold on her, molding his body to

hers, and was certain she could feel the hot ridge of his erection pressing against her. It was throbbing something awful with a need for her that was monumental. He had wanted her for a long time…ever since he'd seen her that night at the ball, and his desire for her hadn't diminished any since. If anything, it had only increased to a level that even now he could feel his gut tighten in desire. Taking her hands he deliberately began slowly lifting her dress up toward her waist.

"Wrap your legs around me, Bella," he whispered and assisted by lifting her hips when she wrapped her legs around him to walk her toward the bedroom. It was a huge suite and he was determined that later, after they took care of business in the bedroom, they would check out all the amenities the suite had to offer; especially the large Jacuzzi bathtub. Already he saw the beauty of downtown Denver from their hotel room window. But downtown Denver was the last thing on his mind right now. Making love to his wife was.

His wife.

He began kissing her again, deeper and longer, loving the way her tongue mated with his over and over again. He placed her on the bed while reaching behind her to unfasten her dress and slide it from her body. It was then that he took a step back and thought he was dreaming. No fantasy could top what he was seeing now.

She was wearing a white lace bra and matching panties. On any other woman such a color would come across as ultrainnocence, but on Bella it became the epitome of sexual desire.

He needed to completely undress her and did so while thinking of everything he wanted to do to her. When she was on her knees in the middle of the bed naked, he could tell from her expression that this was the first time a man had seen her body and the thought sent shivers through him as his gaze roamed over her in male appreciation. A shudder of primal pride flowed through him and he could only stand there and take her all in.

An erection that was already hard got even harder when he looked at her chest, an area he had yet to taste. Her twin globes were firm. His tongue tingled at the thought of being wrapped around those nipples.

No longer able to resist temptation, he moved toward the bed and placed a knee on it and immediately leaned in to capture a nipple in his mouth. His tongue latched on the hard nub and began playing all kinds of games with it. Games she seemed to enjoy if the way she was pushing her breasts deeper into his mouth was anything to go by.

He heard her moan as he continued to torture her nipples, with quick nips followed by sucking motions and when he reached down to let his hands test her to see how ready she was, he found she was definitely ready for him. Pulling back he eased from the bed to remove his clothes as she watched.

"I'm not on the Pill, Jason."

He glanced over at her. "You're not?"

"No."

And evidently thinking she needed to explain further she said, "I haven't been sexually active with anyone."

"Since?"

"Never."

A part of him wasn't surprised. In fact he had suspected as much. He'd known no other man had performed oral sex on her but hadn't been sure of the depth of any other sexual experience. "Any reason you hadn't?"

She met his gaze and held it. "I've been waiting for you."

He drew in a sharp breath and wondered if she knew what she'd just insinuated and figured she hadn't. Maybe she hadn't insinuated anything and it was just wishful thinking on his part. He loved her and would give just about anything for her to love him in return. And until she said the words, he wouldn't assume anything.

"Then your wait is over, sweetheart," he said, sliding on a condom over the thickness of his erection while she looked on. And from the fascinated expression on her face he could tell what she was seeing was another first for her.

When he completed that task he moved to the bed and toward her. "You are so beautifully built, Jason," she said softly, and as if she needed to test her ability to arouse him, she leaned up and flicked out her tongue, licking one of the hardened nubs on his breast like he'd done earlier to her.

He drew in a sharp intake of breath. "You're a quick learner," he said huskily.

"Is that good or bad?"

He smiled at her. "For us it will always be good."

Since this would be her first time he wanted her more than ready and knew of one way to do it. He eased her down on the bed and decided to lick her into an orgasm. Starting at her mouth, he slowly moved downward to her chin, trekked down her neck to her breasts. By the time he'd made it past her midriff to her flat tummy she was writhing under his mouth but he didn't mind. That was a telltale sign of how she was feeling.

"Open your legs, baby," he whispered. The moment she did so he dipped his head to ease his tongue between the folds of her femininity. He recalled doing this to her the last time and knew just what spots would make her moan deep in her throat. Tonight he wanted to do better than that. He wanted to make her scream.

Over and over again he licked her to the edge of an orgasm then withdrew his tongue and began torturing her all over again. She sobbed his name, moaned and groaned. And then, when she was on the verge of an explosion he shifted upward and placed his body over hers.

When he guided his erection in place, he held her gaze and lowered his body to join with hers, uniting them as one. She was tight and he kept a level of control as he eased inside her, feeling how firm a hold her clenched muscles had on him. He didn't want to hurt her and moved inch by slow inch inside her. When he had finally reached the hilt, he closed his eyes but didn't move. He needed to be still for a moment and grasp the significance of what was taking place. He was making love to his wife and she was a wife he loved more than life.

He slowly opened his eyes and met hers and saw she had been watching…waiting and needing him to finish what he'd started. So he did. He began moving slowly, with an extremely low amount of pressure as he began moving in and out of her. When she arched her back, he increased the pressure and the rhythm.

The sounds she began making sent him spiraling and let him know she was loving it. The more she moaned, the more she got. Several times he'd gone so deep inside her he knew he had touched her womb and the thought that he had done so made him crave her that much more.

She released a number of shuddering breaths as he continued to thrust, claiming her as his while she claimed him as hers. And then she threw her head back and screamed out his name.

That's when he came, filling her while groaning thickly as an orgasm overtook them both. The spasms that rammed through his body were so powerful he had to force himself to breathe. He bucked against her several times as he continued to ride her through the force of his release.

He inhaled the scent of their lovemaking before leaning down to capture her mouth, and knew at that moment the night for them was just beginning.

Sometime during the night Jason woke up from the feel of Bella's mouth on him. Immediately his erection began to swell.

"Oh." She pulled her mouth away and looked up at him with a blush on her face. "I thought you were asleep."

His lips curved into a smile. "I was but there are some things a man can't sleep through. What are you doing down there?"

She raised her head to meet his gaze. "Tasting you the way you tasted me," she said softly.

"You didn't have to wait until I was asleep, you know," he said, feeling himself get even harder. Although he was no longer inside her mouth, it was still close. Right there. And the heat of her breath was way too close.

"I know, but you were asleep and I thought I would practice first. I didn't want to embarrass myself while you were awake and get it wrong," she said, blushing even more.

He chuckled, thinking her blush was priceless. "Baby, this is one of those things a woman can never get wrong."

"Do you want me to stop?"

"What do you think?"

She smiled up at him shyly. Wickedly. Wantonly. "I think you don't. Just remember this is a practice session."

She then leaned closer and slid him back into her mouth. He groaned deep in his throat when she began making love to him this way. Earlier that night he had licked her into an orgasm and now she was licking him to insanity. He made a low sound in the back of his throat when she began pulling everything out of him with her mouth. If this was a practice session she would kill him when it came to the real thing.

"Bella!"

He quickly reached down and pulled her up to him and flipped her onto her back. He moved on top of her and pushed inside of her, realizing too late when he felt himself explode that he wasn't wearing a condom. The thought that he could be making her pregnant jutted an even bigger release from his body into hers.

His entire body quivered from the magnitude of the powerful thrusts that kept coming, thrusts he wasn't able to stop. The more she gave, the more he wanted and when her hips arched off the bed, he drove in deeper and came again.

"Jason!"

She was following him to sweet oblivion and his heart began hammering at the realization that this was lovemaking as naked as it could get, and he clung to it, clung to her. A low, shivering moan escaped his lips and when her thighs began to tremor, he felt the vibration to the core.

Moments later he collapsed on top of her, moaned her name as his manhood buried inside of her continued to throb, cling to her flesh as her inner muscles wouldn't release their hold.

What they'd just shared as well as all the other times they'd made love tonight was so unbearably pleasurable he couldn't think straight. The thought of what she'd been doing when he had awakened sent sensuous chills down his body.

He opened his mouth to speak but immediately closed it when he saw she had drifted off to sleep. She made such an erotic picture lying there with her eyes closed, soft dark curls framing her face and the sexiest lips he'd ever had the pleasure of kissing slightly parted.

He continued to look at her, thinking he would let her get some rest now. Later he intended to wake her up the same way she'd woken him.

Eight

The following morning after they'd enjoyed breakfast in bed, Bella figured now was just as good a time as any to let her parents know she was a married woman.

She picked up her cell phone and then glanced over at Jason and smiled. That smile gave her the inner strength for the confrontation she knew was coming. The thought of her outwitting them by marrying—and someone from Denver—would definitely throw her parents into a tizzy. She could just imagine what they would try to do. But just as Jason had said, they could try but wouldn't succeed. She and Jason were as married as married could get and there was nothing her parents could do about it.

Taking a deep breath she punched in their number and when the housekeeper answered she was put on hold, waiting for her father to pick up the line.

"Elizabeth. I hope you're calling to say you've come

to your senses and have purchased a one-way plane ticket back home."

She frowned. He didn't even take the time to ask how she was doing. Although she figured her parents had nothing to do with those two incidents this week, she decided to ask anyway. "Tell me something, Dad. Did you and Mom think using scare tactics to get me to return to Savannah would work?"

"What are you talking about?"

"Three days ago someone threw a rock through my living room window with a threatening note for me to leave town, and two days ago someone torched my house. Luckily I wasn't there at the time."

"Someone set Dad's house on fire?"

She'd heard the shock in his voice and she heard something else, too. Empathy. This was the first time she'd heard him refer to Herman as "Dad."

"Yes."

"I didn't have anything to do with that, Elizabeth. Your mother and I would never put you in danger like that. What kind of parents do you think we are?"

"Controlling. But I didn't call to exchange words, Dad. I'm just calling for you and Mother to share my good news. I got married yesterday."

"What!"

"That's right. I got married to a wonderful man by the name of Jason Westmoreland."

"Westmoreland?"

"Yes."

"I went to schools with some Westmorelands. Their land was connected to ours."

"Probably his parents. They're deceased now."

"Sorry to hear that, but I hope you know why he married you. He wants that land. But don't worry about it, dear. It can easily be remedied once you file for an annulment."

She shook her head. Her parents just didn't get it. "Jason didn't force me to marry him, Dad. I married him of my own free will."

"Listen, Elizabeth, you haven't been living out there even a full month. You don't know this guy. I will not allow you to marry him."

"Dad, I am already married to him and I plan to send your attorney a copy of our marriage license so the hold on my trust fund will be lifted."

"You think you're smart, Elizabeth. I know what you're doing and I won't allow it. You don't love him and he can't love you."

"Sounds pretty much like the same setup you and Mom have got going. The same kind of marriage you wanted me to enter with Hugh. So what's the problem? I don't see where there is one and I refuse to discuss the matter with you any longer. Goodbye, Dad. Give Mom my best." She then clicked off the phone.

"I take it the news of our marriage didn't go over well with your father."

She glanced over at Jason who was lying beside her and smiled faintly. "Did you really expect that it would?"

"No and it really doesn't matter. They'll just have to get over it."

She snuggled closer to him. That was one of the things she liked about Jason. He was his own man. "What time do we have to check out of here?"

"By noon. And then we'll be on our way to Jason's Place."

She had to restrain the happiness she felt upon knowing they would be going to his home where she would live for at least the next twelve months. "Are there any do's and don'ts that I need to know about?"

He lifted a brow. "Do's and don'ts?"

"Yes. My time at your home is limited. I don't want to jeopardize my welcome." She could have sworn she'd seen something flash in his eyes but couldn't be certain.

"You'd never jeopardize your welcome and no, there are no do's and don'ts that will apply to you, unless…"

Now it was her turn to raise a brow. "Unless what?"

"You take a notion to paint my bedroom pink or something."

She couldn't help bursting out in laughter. She calmed down enough to ask, "What about yellow? Will that do?"

"Not one of my favorite colors but I guess it will work."

She smiled as she snuggled even closer to him. She was looking forward to living under the same roof with Jason.

"Bella?"

She glanced up. "Yes?"

"The last time we made love, I didn't use a condom."

She'd been aware of it but hadn't expected him to talk about it. "Yes, I know."

"It wasn't intentional."

"I know that, too," she said softly. There was no reason he would want to get her pregnant. That would only throw a monkey wrench in their agreement.

They didn't say anything for a long moment and then he asked, "Do you like children?"

She wondered why he was asking such a thing. Surely

he had seen her interactions with Susan and Denver enough to know that she did. "Yes, I like children."

"Do you think you'd want any of your own one day?"

Was he asking because he was worried that she would use that as a trap to stay with him beyond the one year? But he'd asked and she needed to be honest. "Yes, I'd love children, although I haven't had the best of childhoods. Don't get me wrong, my parents weren't monsters or anything like that but they just weren't affectionate…at least not like your family."

She paused for a moment. "I love my parents, Jason, although I doubt my relationship with them will ever be what I've always wished for. They aren't that kind of people. Displaying affection isn't one of their strong points. If I become a mother I want to do just the opposite. There will never be a day my child will not know he or she is loved." She hadn't meant to say all of that and now she couldn't help wondering if doing so would ruin things between them.

"I think you would make a wonderful mother."

His words touched her. "Thank you for saying that."

"You're welcome, and I meant it."

She drew in a deep breath, wondering how he could be certain of such a thing. She continued to stare at him for a long moment. He would be a gift to any woman and he had sacrificed himself to marry her—just because he'd wanted her land and Hercules. When she thought about it she found it pitiful that it had taken that to make him want to join his life to hers.

He lifted her hand and looked at the ring he'd placed there. She looked at it, too. It was beautiful. More than she'd expected and everyone had oohed and aahed over it.

"You're wearing my ring," he said softly.

The sound of his deep, husky voice made her tummy tingle and a heated sensation spread all through her. "Yes, I'm wearing your ring. It's beautiful. Thank you."

Then she lifted his hand. Saw the gold band brilliantly shining in the sunlight. "And you're wearing mine."

And then she found herself being kissed by him and she knew that no matter how their marriage might end up, right now it was off to a great beginning.

For the second time in two days Jason carried the woman he loved over the threshold. This time he walked into his house. "Welcome to Jason's Place, sweetheart," he said, placing her on her feet.

Bella glanced around. This was the first time she'd been inside Jason's home. She'd seen it a few times from a distance and thought the two-story dwelling flanked by a number of flowering trees was simply beautiful. On the drive from town he'd given her a little history of his home. It had taken an entire year to build and he had built it himself, with help from all the other Westmorelands. And with all the pride she'd heard when he spoke of it, she knew he loved his home. She could see why. The design was magnificent. The decorating—which had been done by his cousin Gemma—was breathtaking and perfect for the single man he'd been.

Jason's eyes never left Bella's as he studied her reaction to being in his home. As far as he was concerned, she would be a permanent fixture. His heart would beat when hers did. His breath was released the same time hers was. He had shared something with her he had never done with any woman—the essence of himself. For the first time in his life he had made love to a woman without wearing a condom. It had felt wonderful being skin to skin, flesh to flesh with her—but only with her. The wife he adored and intended to keep forever.

He knew he had a job to do where she was concerned and it would be one that would give him the greatest of pleasure and satisfaction. Her pain was his pain, her happiness was his. Their lives were now entwined and all because of the proposal he'd offered and she'd taken.

Without thought he turned her in his arms and lowered his head to kiss her, needing the feel of his mouth on hers, her body pressed against his. The kiss was long, deep and the most satisfying experience he could imagine. But then, he'd had nothing but satisfying experiences with her. And he planned on having plenty more.

"Aren't you going to work today?" Bella asked Jason the following day over breakfast. She was learning her way around his spacious kitchen and loved doing it. They had stayed inside yesterday after he'd brought her here. He had kept her mostly in the bedroom, saying their honeymoon was still ongoing. And she had been not one to argue considering the glow she figured had to be on her face. Jason was the most ardent and generous of lovers.

Her mother had called last night trying to convince her she'd made a mistake and that she and her father would be flying into Denver in a few days to talk some sense into her. Bella had told her mother she didn't think coming to Denver was a good idea, but of course Melissa Bostwick wouldn't listen.

When Bella had told Jason about the latest developments—namely her parents' planned trip to Denver—he'd merely shrugged and told her not to worry about it. That was easy for him to say. He'd never met her parents.

"No, I'm not going to work today. I'm still on my honeymoon," Jason said, breaking into her thoughts. "You tell me what you want to do today and we'll do it."

She turned away from the stove where she'd prepared something simple like French toast. "You want to spend more time with me?"

He chuckled. "Of course I do. You sound surprised."

She was. She figured as much time as they'd spent in the bedroom he would have tired of her by now. She was about to open her mouth when his house phone rang. He smiled over at her. "Excuse me for a minute while I get that."

Bella figured the caller was one of his relatives. She turned back to the stove to turn it off. She couldn't help but smile at the thought that he wanted to spend more time with her.

A few moments later Jason hung up the phone. "That was Sheriff Harper."

She turned back around to him. "Has he found out anything?"

"Yes, they've made some arrests."

A lump formed in her throat. She crossed the floor to sit down at the table, thinking she didn't want to be standing for this. "Who did it?"

He came to sit across from her. "Your uncle Kenneth's twin grandsons."

Bella's hand flew to her chest. "But they're only fourteen years old."

"Yes, but the footprints outside your window and the fingerprints on the rock matched theirs. Not to mention that the kerosene can they used to start the fire at your ranch belonged to their parents."

Bella didn't say anything. She just continued to stare at him.

"Evidently they heard their grandfather's grumblings about you and figured they were doing him a favor by scaring you away," Jason said.

"What will happen to them?" she asked quietly.

"Right now they're in police custody. A judge will decide tomorrow if they will be released into the custody of their parents until a court date is set. If they are found guilty, and chances are they will be since the evidence against them is so strong, they will serve time in a detention center for youth for about one or two years, maybe longer depending on any prior arrests."

Jason's face hardened. "Personally, it wouldn't bother me in the least if they locked them up and threw away the key. I'm sure Kenneth is fit to be tied, though. He thinks the world of those two."

Bella shook her head sadly. "I feel so badly about this."

A deep scowl covered Jason's face. "Why do you feel badly? You're the victim and they broke the law."

She could tell by the sound of his voice that he was still upset. "But they're just kids. I need to call Uncle Kenneth."

"Why? As far as I'm concerned this is all his fault for spouting off at the mouth around them about you."

A part of Bella knew what Jason said was true and could even accept he had a right to be angry, but still, the thought that she was responsible for the disruption of so many lives was getting to her. Had she made a mistake in moving to Denver after all?

"Don't even think it, Bella."

She glanced across the table at Jason. "What?"

"I know what's going through your mind, sweetheart. I can see it all over your face and you want to blame yourself for what happened but it's not your fault."

"Isn't it?"

"No. You can't hold yourself responsible for the actions of others. What if you had been standing near the window the day that rock came flying through, or worse yet, what if you'd been home the day they set fire to the house? If I sound mad it's because I still am. And I'm going to stay mad until justice is served."

He paused a moment and then said, "I don't want to talk about Kenneth or his grandsons any longer. Come on, let's get dressed and go riding."

When they returned from riding and Bella checked her cell phone, she had received a call from her parents saying that they had changed their minds and would not be coming to Denver after all. She couldn't help wondering why, but she figured the best thing to do was count her blessings and be happy about their change in plans.

Jason was outside putting the horses away and she decided to take a shower and change into something relaxing. So far, other than the sheriff, no one else had called. She figured Jason's family was treating them as honeymooners and giving them their privacy.

When her cell phone rang, she didn't recognize the caller but figured it might be one of her parents calling from another number. "Yes?"

"This is all your fault, Bella."

She froze upon hearing her uncle's voice. He was angry. "My grandsons might be going to some youth detention center for a couple of years because of you."

Bella drew in a deep breath and remembered the conversation she and Jason had had earlier that day. "You should not have talked badly about me in front of them."

"Are you saying it's my fault?"

"Yes, Uncle Kenneth, that's exactly what I'm saying. You have no one else to blame but yourself."

"Why you… How dare you speak to me that way. You think you're something now that you're married to a Westmoreland. Well, you'll see what a mistake you made. All Jason Westmoreland wanted was your land and that horse. He doesn't care anything about you. I told you I knew someone who wanted to buy your land."

"And I've always told you my land isn't for sale."

"If you don't think Westmoreland plans to weasel it from you then you're crazy. Just mark my word. You mean nothing to him. All he wants is that land. He is nothing but a controller and a manipulator."

Her uncle then hung up the phone on her.

Bella tried not to let her uncle's words get to her. No one knew the details of their marriage so her uncle had no idea that she was well aware that Jason wanted her land and horse. For what other reason would he have presented her with that proposal? She wasn't the crazy person her uncle evidently assumed she was. She was operating with more than a full deck and was also well aware Jason didn't love her.

She glanced up when Jason walked through the back door. He smiled when he saw her. "I thought you were going to take a shower."

"I was, but I got a phone call."

"Oh, from who?"

She knew now was not the time to tell him about her uncle's call—especially after all he'd said earlier. So she decided to take that time to tell him about her parents' decision.

"Dad and Mom called. They aren't coming after all."

"What changed their minds?" he asked, taking a seat on the sofa.

"Not sure. They didn't say."

He caught her wrist and pulled her down on the sofa beside him. "Well, I have a lot to say, none of it nice. But the main thing is they've decided not to come and I think it's a good move on their part because I don't want anyone to upset you."

"No one will," she said softly. "I'm fine."

"And I want to make sure you stay that way," he said and pulled her closer into his arms.

She was quiet as her head lay rested against his chest and could actually hear his heart pounding. She wondered if he could hear the pounding of her heart. She still found it strange how attracted they were to each other. Getting married hadn't lessened that any.

She lifted her head to look up at him and saw the intense look that was there in his eyes. It was a look that was so intimate it sent a rush of heat sprinting all through her.

And when he began easing his mouth toward hers, all thoughts left her mind except for one, and that was how much he could make her feel loved even when he was pretending. The moment their lips touched she refused to believe her uncle Kenneth's claim that he was controlling.

Instead she concentrated on how he was making her feel with the way his mouth was mating with hers. And she knew this kiss was just the beginning.

Nine

During the next few weeks Bella settled into what she considered a comfortable routine. She'd never thought being married would be such a wonderful experience and could only thank Jason for making the transition easy for her.

They shared a bed and made passionate love each night. Then in the morning they would get up early and while he sat at the table drinking coffee she would enjoy a cup of tea while he told her about what horses he would be training that day.

While he was away she usually kept busy by reading her grandfather's journals, which had been upstairs in her bedroom and so were spared by the fire. Because she'd been heavily involved with a lot of charity work while living in Savannah, she'd already volunteered a lot of her time at the children's hospital and the West-moreland Foundation.

Hercules was now in Jason's stalls and Jason was working with the insurance company on the repairs of her ranch. He had arranged for all the men who'd worked with her before the fire to be hired on with his horse training business.

Although she appreciated him stepping in and taking charge of her affairs the way he'd done, she hadn't been able to put her uncle Kenneth's warning out of her mind. She knew it was ludicrous to worry about Jason's motivation because he had been honest with her from the beginning and she knew why he'd made the proposal for their marriage. She was well aware that he didn't love her and that he was only married to her for the land and Hercules. But now that he had both was it just a matter of time for him before he tried to get rid of her?

She would be the first to admit he never acted as if he was getting tired of her and still treated her as if he enjoyed having her around. In the afternoons when he returned home for work, the first thing he did after placing his Stetson on the hat rack was to seek her out. Usually he didn't have far to look because she would be right there, close by. Anticipating his return home always put her near the door when he entered the house.

Bella couldn't help noticing that over the last couple of days she had begun getting a little antsy where Jason was concerned because she was uncertain as to her future with him. And to make matters even worse she was late, which was a good sign she might be pregnant. She hadn't told him of her suspicions because she wasn't sure how he would take the news.

If she were pregnant, the baby would be born within the first year of their marriage. Would he still want a divorce even if she was the mother of his child or would he want to keep her around for that same reason; because he felt obligated to do so? But an even more important question was, did he even want to become a father? He had questioned her feelings on motherhood but she'd never questioned his. She could tell from his interactions with Susan and Denver that he liked kids, but that didn't necessarily mean he wanted any of his own.

Bella knew she should tell him about the possibility she could be pregnant and discuss her concerns with him now, but each time she was presented with the opportunity to do so, she would get cold feet.

She walked into an empty room he'd converted into an office and sat down at the desk to glance out the window. She would finally admit that another reason she was antsy was that she knew without a shadow of doubt that she had fallen in love with Jason and could certainly understand how such a thing had happened. She could understand it, but would he? He'd never asked for her love, just her land and horse.

She heard the sound of a vehicle door closing and stood from the desk, went to the window and looked down. It was Jason. He glanced up and saw her and a smile touched the corners of his mouth. Instantly she felt the buds of her nipples harden against her blouse. A flush of desire rushed through her and she knew at that moment her panties had gotten wet. The man could turn her on with a single look. He was home earlier than usual. Three hours earlier.

Now that he was here a lot of ideas flowed in her mind on how they could use those extra hours. What she wanted to do first was to take him into her mouth, something she discovered she enjoyed doing. And then he could return the favor by putting that tongue of his to work between her legs. She shuddered at the thought and figured her hormones were on the attack; otherwise, she wouldn't be thinking such scandalous things. They were definitely not things a Miss Prim and Proper lady would think.

He broke eye contact with her to walk up the steps to come into the house and she rushed out of the office to stand at the top of the stairs. She glanced down the moment he opened the door. Jason's dark gaze latched on her and immediately her breath was snatched from her lungs. As she watched, he locked the door behind him and slowly began removing the clothes from his body, first tossing his hat on the rack and then unbuttoning his shirt.

She felt hot as she watched him and he didn't stop. He had completely removed his shirt and she couldn't help admiring the broad shoulders and sinewy muscular thighs in jeans. The masculine sight had blood rushing fast and furious through her veins.

"I'm coming up," he said in a deep, husky voice.

She slowly began backing up when he started moving up the stairs with a look in his eyes that was as predatory as anything she'd ever seen. And there was a deep, intense hunger in his gaze that had her heart hammering like crazy in her chest.

When he cleared the top stair and stepped onto the landing, she breathed in deeply, taking in his scent, while thinking that no man had a right to smell so good, look so utterly male and be so damn hot in a way that would overwhelm any woman's senses.

At least no man but Jason Westmoreland.

"Take off your clothes, Bella," he said in a deep, throaty voice.

She then asked what some would probably think was a dumb question. "Why?"

He moved slowly toward her and it was as if her feet were glued to the spot and she couldn't move. And when he came to a stop in front of her, she tilted back her head to look up at him, saw the hunger in his dark brown gaze. The intensity of that look sent a shudder through her.

He reached out and cupped her face in the palms of his hands and lowered his head slightly to whisper, "I came home early because I need to make love to you. And I need to do it now."

And then he captured her mouth with his, kissing her with the same intensity and hunger she'd seen in his eyes. She returned his kiss, not understanding why he needed to make love to her and why now. But she knew she would give him whatever he wanted and whatever way he wanted it.

He was ravishing her mouth, making her moan deep in her throat. His kiss seemed to be making a statement and staking a claim all at the same time. She couldn't do anything but take whatever he was giving, and she did so gladly and without shame. He had no idea she loved him. How much sharing these past few weeks had meant to her.

And then he jerked his mouth away and quickly removed his boots. Afterward, he carried her into the office and stood her by the desk as he began taking off her clothes with a frenzy that had her head spinning. One part of her wanted to tell him to slow down and to assure him she wasn't going anywhere. But another part was just as eager and excited as he was to get naked, and kept insisting that he hurry up.

Within minutes, more like seconds, spooned between

his body and the desk, she was totally naked. The cool air from the air conditioner that swept across her heated skin made her want to cover herself with her hands, but he wouldn't let her. He gently grabbed her wrists in his and held them up over her head, which made her breasts tilt up in perfect alignment to his lips when he leaned down.

On a breathless sigh he eased a nipple into his mouth, sucking it in between his lips and then licking the throbbing tip. She arched her back, felt him gently ease her onto the desk and realized he was practically on the desk with her. The metal surface felt cool to her back, but the warmth of his body felt hot to her front.

He lowered his hand to her sex and the stroke of his fingers on the folds of her labia made her groan out sounds she'd never made before. She'd thought from the first that he had skillful fingers and they were thrumming through her, stirring all kinds of sensations within her. Their lovemaking would often range from gentle to hard and she knew today would be one of those hard times. For whatever reason, he was driven to take her now, without any gentleness of any kind. He was stroking a need within her that wanted it just as fast and hard as he could deliver.

He took a step back and quickly removed his jeans and boxers. When she saw him—in his engorged splendor—a sound of dire need erupted from deep within her throat. He was bringing her to this, this intense state of want and need that was fueled by passion and desire.

"I want to know your taste, baby."

It was on the tip of her tongue to say that as many times as he'd made a meal out of her that he should know it pretty well by now. Instead when he crouched down in front of her body, which was all but spread out on the desk, and proceeded to wrap her legs over his shoulders, she automatically arched her back.

And when she felt his hot mouth close in on her sex, slide his tongue through her womanly folds, she lifted her hips off the table with the intimate contact. And when he began suckling hard, using his tongue to both torture and pleasure, she let out an intense moan as an orgasm tore through her body; sensations started at the soles of her feet and traveled like wildfire all the way to the crown of her head. And then she screamed at the top of her lungs.

Shudders continued to rip through her, made her muscles both ache and rejuvenate. And she couldn't help but lie there while Jason continued to get the taste he wanted.

When her shudders finally subsided, he gave her body one complete and thorough lick before lifting his head and looking up at her with a satisfied smile on his face, and the way he began licking his lips made her feel hot all over again.

He reached out and spread her legs wide and began stroking her again and she began moaning at the contact. "My fingers are all wet, which means you're ready," he said. "Now for me to get ready."

And she knew without looking that he was tearing into a condom packet and soon would be sliding the latex over his erection. After that first time in the hotel he'd never made love to her unprotected again, which gave her even more reason to think he wasn't ready for children. At least not with her, anyway.

From the feel of his erection pressing against her thigh she would definitely agree that at least he was ready for this, probably more ready than any man had a right to be, but she had no complaints.

She came to full attention when she felt his swollen, engorged member easing between her legs, and when he centered it to begin sliding between the folds of her labia and then suddenly thrust forward without any preamble, she began shuddering all over again.

"Look at me, baby. I want to be looking in your eyes when you come. I need to see it happen, Bella."

She looked up and met his gaze. He was buried deep inside of her and then holding tight to her gaze, he began moving, holding tight to the hips whose legs were wrapped firmly around him. They began moving together seemingly in perfect rhythm, faultless harmony and seamless precision. With each deep and thorough stroke, she felt all of him…every glorious inch.

"You tasted good and now you feel good," he said in a guttural voice while holding steadfast to her gaze. "Do you have any idea how wonderful you are making me feel?"

She had an idea. If it was anything close to how he was making her feel then the feelings were definitely mutual. And to show him just how mutual, her inner muscles began clamping down on him, milking him. She could tell from the look in his eyes the exact moment he realized what she was doing and the effect it was having on him. The more she milked him the bigger he seemed to get inside of her, as if he intended for her to have it all.

Today she felt greedy and was glad he intended to supply her needs. She dug her nails into his shoulders, at the moment not caring if she was branding him for life. And then he picked up the tempo and pleasure, the likes of nothing she'd experienced before dimming her vision. But through it all, she kept her gaze locked on his and saw how every sound, every move she made, got to him and triggered him to keep it coming.

And then when she felt her body break into fragments, she screamed out his name and he began pumping into her as if his very life depended on it. The orgasm that ripped through her snatched the breath from her lungs as his intense, relentless strokes almost drove her over the edge. And when she heard the hoarse cry from his own lips, saw the flash of something dark and turbulent in the depths of his eyes, she lost it and screamed again at the top of her lungs as another orgasm shook the core of everything inside her body.

And he followed her, pushed over the edge, while he continued to thrust even deeper. He buried his fingers into her hair and leaned down and captured her mouth to kiss the trembles right off her lips. At that moment she wished she could say all the words that had formed in her heart, words of love she wanted him to know. But she couldn't. This was all there was between them. She had accepted that long ago. And for the moment she was satisfied and content.

And when the day came that he wanted her gone, memories like these would sustain her, get her through each day without him.

And she prayed to God the memories would be enough.

"So when can we plan your wedding reception?" Megan asked when the Westmorelands had assembled around the dinner table at Dillon's place a few weeks later.

When Bella didn't say anything but looked over at Jason, he shrugged and said, "Throw some dates out to see if they will work for us."

Megan began rambling off dates, saying the first weekend in August would be perfect since all the Westmorelands away at college would be home and Micah, who was presently in Beijing, had sent word he would be back in the States during that time, as well. Gemma, who was expecting, had gotten the doctor's okay to travel from Australia then.

"And," Megan continued, "I spoke with Casey yesterday and she's checked with the other Westmorelands and that will give them plenty of time to make plans to be here, as well. I'm so excited."

Jason glanced over at Bella again thinking he was glad someone was. There was something going on with his wife that he just couldn't put a finger on and whatever it was had put him at a disadvantage. He knew she was upset with the outcome of the Bostwick twins. With all the evidence mounted against the twins, their attorney had convinced their parents to enter a guilty plea in hopes they would get a lesser sentence.

However, given prior mischievous pranks that had gotten the pair into trouble with the law before, the judge was not all that lenient and gave them two years. Bella had insisted on going to the sentencing hearing and he'd warned her against it but she'd been adamant. Things hadn't gone well when Kenneth, who still refused to accept blame for his part in any of it, made a scene, accusing Bella as the one responsible for what had happened to his grandsons. Since that day Jason had noted a change in her and she'd begun withdrawing from him. He'd tried getting her to talk, but she refused to do so.

"So what do the two of you think?" Megan asked, drawing his attention again.

He glanced at Bella. "What do you think, sweetheart?"

She placed a smile on her lips that he knew was forced. "That time is fine with me, but I doubt Mom and Dad will come either way."

"Then they will miss a good party," Jason replied. He then turned to Megan. "The first weekend in August is fine."

Later, on the ride back to their place, Jason finally found out what was troubling Bella. "I rode over to my ranch today, Jason. Why didn't you tell me work hadn't begun on the house yet?"

"There was no reason to tell you. You knew I was taking care of things, didn't you?"

"Yes. But I assumed work had gotten started already."

"I saw no reason to begin work on the place yet, given we're having a lot of rainy days around here now. It's not a good time to start any type of construction. Besides, it's not like you're going to move into the house or anything."

"You don't know that."

He had pulled into the yard and brought the truck to a stop and turned the ignition off. He glanced over at her. "I don't? I thought I did."

He tilted his hat back from his eyes and stared over at her. "Why would you need to move back into the house?"

Instead of holding his gaze she glanced out the window and looked ahead at his house, which he now considered as their house. "Our marriage is only supposed to last a year and I'm going to need somewhere to live when it ends."

Her words were like a kick in the gut. She was already

planning for the time when she would be leaving him? Why? He thought things were going great between them. "What's going on, Bella?"

"Nothing is going on. I just need to be realistic and remember that although we enjoy being bed partners, the reason we married stemmed from your proposal, which I accepted knowing full well the terms. And they are terms we must not forget."

Jason simply looked at her as he swore under his breath. She thought the only thing between them was the fact they were bed partners? "Thanks for reminding me, Bella." He then got out of the truck.

That was the first night they slept in the same bed but didn't make love and Bella lay there hurting inside and wasn't sure what she could do about it. She was trying to protect her heart, especially after the results of the pregnancy test she'd taken a few days ago.

Jason was an honorable man. Just the kind of man who'd keep her around just because she was the mother of his child. She wasn't particularly thinking of herself per se but of her child. She had grown up in a loveless household and simply refused to subject her child to one. Jason would never understand how that could be because he'd grown up with parents who'd loved each other and had set a good example for their children to follow. That was evident in the way his cousins and brother treated the wives they loved. It was easy to see their relationships were loving ones, the kinds that last until death. She didn't expect that kind of long-term commitment from Jason. That was not in the plan and had not been in his proposal.

She knew he was awake by the sound of his breathing but his back was to her as hers was to him. When he had come up to bed he hadn't said anything. In fact he had barely cast a glance her way before sliding under the covers.

His family was excited about hosting a wedding reception for them but she had been tempted to tell them not to bother. Their year would be up before she knew it anyway. However, she had sat there and listened while plans were being made and fighting the urge to get pulled into the excitement.

The bed shifted and she held her breath hoping that, although she'd given him that reminder, he would still want her. He dashed that hope when instead of sliding toward her he got out of the bed and left the room. Was he coming back to bed or did he plan on sleeping somewhere else tonight? On the sofa? In his truck?

She couldn't help the tears that begin falling from her eyes. She only had herself to blame. No one told her to fall in love. She should have known better. She should not have put her heart out there. But she had and now she was paying the price for doing so.

"Okay, what the hell is wrong with you, Jason? It's not like you to make such a stupid mistake and the one you just made was a doozy," Zane stormed. "That's the sheikh's prized horse and what you did could have cost him a leg."

Anger flared up inside of Jason. "Dammit, Zane, I know what I did. You don't have to remind me."

He then glanced over at Derringer and waited to see what he had to say and when he didn't say anything, Jason was grateful.

"Look, guys, I'm sorry about the mistake. I've got a lot on my mind. I think I'll call it a day before I cause another major screwup." He then walked off toward Zane's barn.

He was in the middle of saddling his horse to leave when Derringer walked up. "Hey, man, you want to talk about it?"

Jason drew in a deep breath. "No."

"Come on, Jas, there's evidently trouble in paradise at Jason's Place. I don't profess to be an expert when it comes to such matters, but even you will admit that me and Lucia had a number of clashes before we married."

Jason glanced over at him. "What about *after* you married?"

Derringer threw his head back and laughed. "Want a list? The main thing to remember is the two of you are people with different personalities and that in itself is bound to cause problems. The most effective solution is good, open communication. We talk it out and then we make love. Works every time. Oh, and you need to remind her every so often how much you love her."

Jason chuckled dryly. "The first two things you said I should do are things I can handle but not the latter."

Derringer raised a brow. "What? You can't tell your wife you love her?"

Jason sighed. "No, I can't tell her."

Derringer looked confused. "Why? You do love her, don't you?"

"Yes, more than life."

"Then what's the problem?"

Jason stopped what he was doing and met Derringer's gaze. "She doesn't love me back."

Derringer blinked and then drew back slightly and said, "Of course she loves you."

Jason shook his head. "No, she doesn't." He paused

for a moment and then said, "Our marriage was based on a business proposition, Derringer. She needed a husband to retain her trust fund and I wanted her land—at least co-ownership of her land—and Hercules."

Derringer stared at him for a long moment and then said, "I think you'd better start from the beginning."

It took Jason less than ten minutes to tell Derringer everything, basically because his cousin stood there and listened without asking any questions. But once he'd finished the questions had begun...as well as the observations.

Derringer was certain Bella loved him because he claimed she looked at Jason the way Lucia looked at him, the way Chloe looked at Ramsey and the way Pam looked at Dillon—when they thought no one was supposed to be watching.

Then Derringer claimed that given the fact Jason and Bella were still sharing the same bed—although no hanky-panky had been going on for almost a week now—had significant meaning.

Jason shook his head. "If Bella loves me the way you think she does then why hasn't she told me?"

Derringer crossed his arms over his chest. "And why haven't you told her?" When Jason couldn't answer Derringer smiled and said, "I think the two of you have a big communication problem. It happens and is something that can easily be corrected."

Jason couldn't help but smile. "Sounds like you've gotten to be a real expert on the subject of marriage."

Derringer chuckled. "I have to be. I plan on being a married man for life so I need to know what it takes to keep my woman happy and to understand that when wifey isn't happy, hubby's life can be a living hell."

Derringer then tapped his foot on the barn's wooden floor as if he was trying to make up his mind about something. "I really shouldn't be telling you this because it's something I overheard Chloe and Lucia discussing yesterday and if Lucia found out I was eavesdropping she—"

"What?"

"Maybe you already know but just hadn't mentioned anything."

"Dammit, Derringer, what the hell are you talking about?"

A sly smile eased across Derringer's lips. "The ladies in the family suspect Bella might be pregnant."

Bella walked out of the children's hospital with a smile on her face. She loved kids and being around them always made her forget her troubles, which was why she would come here a couple of days a week to spend time with them. She glanced at her watch. It was still early yet and she wasn't ready to go home.

Home.

She couldn't help but think of Jason's Place as her home. Although she'd made a stink with Jason about construction on her ranch, she didn't relish the thought of going back there to live. She had gotten accustomed to her home with Jason.

She was more confused than ever and the phone call from her mother hadn't helped. Now her parents were trying to work out a bargain with her—another proposal of a sort. They would have their attorney draw up a legal document that stated if she returned home they would give her the space she needed. Of course they wanted her to move back onto their estate, although she would be given the entire east wing as her own. They claimed they no longer wanted to control her life, but just wanted to make sure she was living the kind of life she was entitled to live.

Their proposal sounded good but she had gotten into enough trouble accepting proposals already. Besides, even if things didn't work out between her and Jason, he deserved to be around his child. When they divorced, at least his son or daughter would be a stone's throw away.

She was crossing the parking lot to her car when she heard someone call her name. She turned and cringed when she saw it was her uncle Kenneth's daughter, who was the mother of the twins. Although Uncle Kenneth had had an outburst at the trial, Elyse Bostwick Thomas had not. She'd been too busy crying.

Drawing in a deep breath Bella waited for the woman to catch up with her. "Elyse."

"Bella. I just wanted to say how sorry I was for what Mark and Michael did. I know Dad is still bitter and I've tried talking to him about it but he refuses to discuss it. He's always spoiled the boys and there was nothing I could do about it, mainly because my husband and I are divorced. My ex moved away, but I wanted a father figure in their lives."

Elyse didn't say anything for a moment. "I hope Dad will eventually realize his part in all this, and although I miss my sons, they were getting too out of hand. I've been assured the place they are going will teach them discipline. I just wanted you to know I was wrong for listening to everything Dad said about you and when I found out you even offered to help pay for my sons' attorney I thought that was generous of you."

Bella nodded. "Uncle Kenneth turned down my offer."

"Yes, but just the thought touched me deeply considering everything. You and I are family and I hope that one day we can be friends."

A smile touched Bella's lips. "I'd like that, Elyse. I really would."

"Bella, are you sure you're okay? You might want to go see the doctor about that stomach virus."

Bella glanced over at Chloe. On her way home she had dropped by to visit with her cousin-in-law and little Susan. Bella had grown fond of the baby who was a replica of both of her parents. The little girl had Ramsey's eyes and skin tone and Chloe's mouth and nose. "Yes, Chloe, I'm fine."

She decided not to say anything about her pregnancy just yet until after she figured out how and when she would tell Jason. Evidently Chloe had gotten suspicious because Bella had thrown up the other day when Chloe had come to deliver a package to Jason from Ramsey.

Bella knew from the bits and pieces of the stories she'd heard from the ladies that Chloe was pregnant when she and Ramsey had married. However, Bella doubted that was the reason Ramsey had married her. Anyone around the pair for any period of time could tell how in love they were.

Bella never had a best friend, no other woman to share her innermost feminine secrets with. That was one of the reasons she appreciated the bond she felt toward all the Westmoreland women. They were all friendly, understanding and supportive. But she was hoping that because Chloe had been pregnant when she'd married Ramsey, her in-law could help her understand a few things. She had decisions to make that would impact her baby's future.

"Chloe, can I ask you something?"

Chloe smiled over at her. "Sure."

"When you found out you were pregnant were you afraid to tell Ramsey for fear of how he would react?"

Chloe placed her teacup down on the table and her smile brightened as if she was recalling that time. "I didn't discover I was pregnant until Ramsey and I broke up. But the one thing I knew was that I was going to tell him because he had every right to know. The one thing that I wasn't sure about was when I was going to tell him. One time I thought of taking the coward's way out and waiting until I returned to Florida and calling him from there."

Chloe paused for a moment and then said, "Ramsey made things easy for me when he came to me. We patched up things between us, found it had been nothing more than a huge misunderstanding and got back together. It was then that I told him about my pregnancy and he was happy about it."

Bella took a sip of her tea and then asked, "When the two of you broke up did you stay apart for long?"

"For over three weeks and they were the unhappiest three weeks of my life." Chloe smiled again when she added, "A Westmoreland man has a tendency to grow on you, Bella. They become habit-forming. And when it comes to babies, they love them."

There was no doubt in Bella's mind that Jason loved children; that wasn't what worried her. The big question was if he'd want to father any with her considering the nature of their marriage. Would he see that as a noose around his neck? For all she knew he might be counting the days until their year would be up so he could go his way and she go hers. A baby would definitely change things.

She glanced back over at Chloe. "Ramsey is a wonderful father."

Chloe smiled. "Yes, and Jason would be a wonderful father, as well. When their parents died all the Westmorelands had to pitch in and raise the younger ones. It was a team effort and it wasn't easy. Jason is wonderful with children and would make any child a fantastic father."

Chloe chuckled. "I can see him with a son while teaching him to ride his first pony, or a daughter who will wrap him around her finger the way Susan does Ramsey. I can see you and Jason having a houseful of kids."

Bella nodded. Chloe could only see that because she thought she and Jason had a normal marriage.

"Don't ever underestimate a Westmoreland man, Bella."

Chloe's words interrupted her thoughts. "What do you mean?"

"I mean that from what I've discovered in talking with all the other wives, even those spread out in Montana, Texas, Atlanta and Charlotte, a Westmoreland man is loyal and dedicated to a fault to the woman he's chosen as a mate. The woman he loves. And although they can be overly protective at times, you can't find a man more loving and supportive. But the one thing they don't care too much for is when we hold secrets from them. Secrets that need to be shared with them. Jason is special, and I believe the longer you and he are married, the more you will see just how special he is."

Chloe reached out and gently touched Bella's hand. "I hope what I've said has helped in some way."

Bella returned her smile. "It has." Bella knew that

she needed to tell Jason about the baby. And whatever decision he made regarding their future, she would have to live with it.

Ten

Jason didn't bother riding his horse back home after his discussion with Derringer. Instead he borrowed Zane's truck and drove home like a madman only to discover Bella wasn't there. She hadn't mentioned anything at breakfast about going out, so where was she? But then they hadn't been real chatty lately, so he wasn't really surprised she hadn't told him anything.

He glanced around his home—their home—and took in the changes she'd made. Subtle changes but changes he liked. If she were to leave his house—their house—it wouldn't be the same. He wouldn't be the same.

He drew in a deep breath. What if the ladies' suspicions were true and she was pregnant? What if Derringer's suspicions were true and she loved him? Hell, if both suspicions were true then they had one hell of a major communication problem between them, and it was one he intended to remedy today as soon as she returned.

He walked into the kitchen and began making of all things, a cup of tea. Jeez, Bella had definitely rubbed off on him but he wouldn't have it any other way. And what if she was really pregnant? The thought of her stomach growing big while she carried his child almost left him breathless. And he could recall when it happened.

It had to have been their wedding night spent in the honeymoon suite of the Four Seasons. He had awakened to find her mouth on him and she had driven him to more passion than he'd ever felt in his entire life. He'd ended up flipping her on her back and taking her without wearing a condom. He had exploded the moment he'd gotten inside her body. Evidently she had been good and fertile that night.

He certainly hoped so. The thought of her having his baby was his most fervent desire. And no matter what she thought, he would provide both her and his child with a loving home.

He heard the sound of the front door opening and paused a moment not to rush out and greet her. They needed to talk and he needed to create a comfortable environment for them to do so. He was determined that before they went to bed tonight there would be a greater degree of understanding between them. With that resolution, he placed the teacup on the counter to go greet his wife.

Bella's grooming and social training skills had prepared her to handle just about anything, but now that she was back at Jason's Place she was no longer sure of her capabilities. So much for all the money her parents had poured into those private schools.

She placed her purse on the table thinking at least she'd had one bright spot in her day other than the time spent with the kids. And that was her discussion with Elyse. They had made plans to get together for tea later in the week. She could just imagine how her uncle would handle it when he found out she and Elyse had decided to be friends.

And then there had been her conversation with Chloe. It had definitely been an eye-opener and made her realize she couldn't keep her secret from Jason any longer. He deserved to know about the baby and she would tell him tonight.

"Bella. You're home."

She was pulled from her reverie by the pure masculine tone of Jason's voice when he walked out of the kitchen. Her pulse hammered in the center of her throat and she wondered if he would always have this kind of effect on her. She took a second or two to compose herself, before she responded to him. "Yes, I'm home. I see you have company."

He lifted a brow. "Company?"

"Yes. Zane's truck is parked outside," she replied, allowing her gaze to roam over her husband, unable to stop herself from doing so. He was such a hunk and no matter what he wore it only enhanced his masculinity. Even the jeans and chambray shirt he was wearing now made him look sexy as hell.

"I borrowed it. He's not here."

"Oh." That meant they were alone. Under the same roof. And hadn't made love in almost a week. So it stood to reason that the deep vibrations of his voice would stir across her skin and that turn-you-on mouth of his would make her panties start to feel damp.

She met his gaze and something akin to potent sexual awareness passed between them, charging the air, electrifying the moment. She felt it and was sure he felt it, as well. She studied his features and knew she wanted a son or daughter who looked just like him.

She knew she needed to break into the sensual vibe surrounding them and go up the stairs, or else she would be tempted to do something crazy like cross the room and throw herself in his arms and beg him to want her, to love her, to want the child they had conceived together.

"Well, I guess I'll go upstairs a moment and—"

"Do you have a moment so we can talk, Bella?"

She swallowed deeply. "Talk?"

"Yes."

That meant she was going to have to sit across from him and watch that sensual mouth of his move, see his tongue work and remember what it felt like dueling nonstop with hers and—

"Bella, could we talk?"

She swallowed again. "Now?"

"Yes."

"Sure," she murmured and then she followed him toward the kitchen. Studying his backside she could only think that the man she had married was such a hottie.

Jason wasn't sure where they needed to begin but he did know they needed to begin somewhere.

"I was about to have a cup of tea. Would you like a cup, as well?"

He wondered if she recalled those were the exact words she had spoken to him that first time she had invited him inside her house. They were words he still remembered to this day. And from the trace of amusement that touched her lips, he knew that she had recalled them.

"Yes, I'd love a cup. Thank you," she said, sitting down at the table, unintentionally flashing a bit of thigh.

He stepped back and quickly moved to the counter, trying to fight for control and to not remember this is the woman whom he'd given her first orgasm, the woman who'd awakened him one morning with her mouth on him, the first woman he'd had unprotected sex with, the only woman he'd wanted to shoot his release inside of, but more than anything, this was the woman he loved so very much.

Moments later when he turned back to her with cups of tea in his hands, he could tell she was nervous, was probably wondering what he wanted to talk about and was hoping he would hurry and get it over with.

"So, how was your day today?" he asked, sitting across from her at the table.

She shrugged those delicate shoulders he liked running his tongue over. She looked so sinfully sexy in the sundress she was wearing. "It was nice. I spent a lot of it at the children's hospital. Today was 'read-a-story' day and I entertained a bunch of them. I had so much fun."

"I'm glad."

"I also ran into Uncle Kenneth's daughter, Elyse."

"The mother of the twins, right?"

"Yes."

"And how did that go?" Jason asked.

"Better than I expected. Unlike Uncle Kenneth, she's not holding me responsible for what happened to her sons. She says they were getting out of hand anyway and is hoping the two years will teach them discipline," Bella said.

"We can all hope for that" was Jason's response.

"Yes, but in a way I feel sorry for her. I can only imagine how things were for her having Kenneth for a father. My dad wouldn't get a 'Father of the Year' trophy, either, but at least I had friends I met at all those schools they shipped me off to. It never bothered me when I didn't go home for the holidays. It helped when I went home with friends and saw how parents were supposed to act. Not as business partners but as human beings."

Bella realized after she'd said it that in a way Jason was her business partner, but she'd never thought of him that way. From the time he'd slipped a ring on her finger she had thought of him as her husband—for better or worse.

The kitchen got silent as they sipped tea.

"So what do you want to talk about, Jason?"

Good question, Jason thought. "I want to talk about us."

He saw her swallow. "Us?"

"Yes, us. Lately, I haven't been feeling an 'us' and I want to ask you a question."

She glanced over at him. "What?"

"Do you not want to be married to me anymore?"

She broke eye contact with him to study the pattern design on her teacup. "What gave you that idea?"

"Want a list?"

She shot her gaze back to him. "I didn't think you'd notice."

"Is that what this is about, Bella, me not noticing you, giving you attention?"

She quickly shook her head. Heaven help her or him if he were to notice her any more or give her more attention than she was already getting. To say Jason Westmoreland was all into her was an understatement.

Unfortunately he was all into her, literally. And all for the wrong reasons. Sex was great but it couldn't hold a marriage together. It couldn't replace love no matter how many orgasms you had a night.

"Bella?"

"No, that's not it," she said, nervously biting her bottom lip.

"Then what is it, sweetheart? What do you need that I'm not giving you? What can I do to make you happy? I need to know because your leaving me is not an option. I love you too much to let you go."

The teacup froze midway to her lips. She stared over at him in shock. "What did you just say?"

"A number of things. Do I need to repeat it all?"

She shook her head, putting her cup down. "No, just the last part."

"About me loving you?"

"Yes."

"I said I loved you too much to let you go. Lately you've been reminding me about the year I mentioned in my proposal, but there isn't a year time frame, Bella. I threw that in as an adjustment period to not scare you off. I never intended to end things between us."

He saw the single tear flow from her eyes. "You didn't?"

"No. I love you too much to let you go. There, I've said it again and I will keep saying it until you finally hear it. Believe it. Accept it."

"I didn't know you loved me, Jason. I love you, too. I think I fell in love with you the first time I saw you at your family's charity ball."

"And that's when I believe I fell in love with you, as well," he said, pushing the chair back to get up from the table. "I knew there was a reason every time we touched a part of my soul would stir, my heart would melt and my desire for you would increase."

"I thought it was all about sex."

"No. I believe the reason the sex between us was so good, so damn hot, was that it was fueled by love of the most intense kind. More than once I wanted to tell you I loved you but I wasn't sure you were ready to hear it. I didn't want to run you off."

"And knowing you loved me is what I needed to hear," she said, standing. "I've never thought I could be loved and I wanted so much for you to love me."

"Sweetheart, I do. I love every single thing about you."

"Oh, Jason."

She went to him and was immediately swept up into his arms, held tight. And when he lowered his head to kiss her, her mouth was ready, willing and hungry. That was evident in the way her tongue mated with his with such intensity.

Moments later he pulled back and swept her off her feet and into his arms then walked out of the kitchen.

Somehow they made it upstairs to the bedroom. And there in the middle of the room, he kissed Bella again with a hunger that she greedily returned. He finally released her mouth to draw in a deep breath, but before she could draw in one of her own, he flipped her dress up to her waist and was pulling a pair of wet panties down her thighs. She barely had time to react before he moved to her hips to bury his head between her legs.

"Jason!"

She came the moment his tongue whipped inside of her and began stroking her labia, but she quickly saw that wouldn't be enough for him. He sharpened the tip of his tongue and literally stabbed deep inside of her and proceeded to lick circles around her clitoris before drawing it in between his lips.

Her eyes fluttered closed as he then began suckling her senseless as desire, more potent than any she'd ever felt, started consuming her, racing through every part of her body and pushing her toward a orgasm.

"Jason!"

And he still didn't let up. She reached for him but couldn't get a firm hold as his tongue began thrusting inside her again. His tongue, she thought, should be patented with a warning sign. Whenever he parted this life it should be donated to the Smithsonian.

And when she came yet again, he spread her thighs wide to lap her up. She moaned deep in her throat as his tongue and lips made a plaything of her clitoris, driving her demented, crazy with lust, when sensations after earth-shattering sensations rammed through her.

And then suddenly he pulled back and through glazed eyes she watched as he stood and quickly undressed himself and then proceeded to undress her, as well. Her gaze went to his erection.

Without further ado, he carried her over to the bed, placed her on her back, slid over her and settled between her legs and aimed his shaft straight toward the damp folds of her labia.

"Yes!" she almost screamed out, and then she felt him, pushing inside her, desperate to be joined with her.

He stopped moving. Dropped his head down near hers and said in a sensual growl, "No condom tonight."

Bella gazed up at him. "No condom tonight or any other night for a while," she whispered. "I'll tell you why later. It's something I planned to tell you tonight anyway." And before she could dwell too much on just what she had to tell him, he began thrusting inside of her.

And when he pushed all the way to the hilt she gasped for breath at the fullness of having him buried so deep inside her. Her muscles clung to him, she was holding him tight and she began massaging him, milking his shaft for everything she had and thought she could get, while thinking a week had been too long.

He widened her legs farther with his hands and lifted her hips to drive deeper still and she almost cried when he began a steady thrusting inside of her, with relentless precision. This was the kind of ecstasy she'd missed. She hadn't known such degrees of pleasure existed until him and when he lifted her legs onto his shoulders while thrusting back and forth inside her, their gazes met through dazed lashes.

"Come for me, baby," he whispered. "Come for me now."

Her body complied and began to shudder in a climax so gigantic she felt the house shaking. She screamed. There was no way she could not, and when he began coming inside her, his hot release thickened by the intensity of their lovemaking, she could only cry out as she was swept away yet again.

And then he leaned up and kissed her, but not before whispering that he loved her and that he planned to spend the rest of his life making her happy, making her feel loved. And she believed him.

With all the strength she could muster, she leaned up to meet him.

"And I love you so very much, too."

And she meant it.

"Why don't I have to wear a condom for a while?" Jason asked moments later with her entwined in his arms, their limbs tangled as they enjoyed the aftermath of their lovemaking together. He knew the reason, but he wanted her to confirm it.

She lifted her head slightly, met his gaze and whispered, "I'm having your baby."

Her announcement did something to him. Being given confirmation that a life they had created together was growing inside her made him shudder. He knew she was waiting for him to say something.

He planned to show her he had taken it well. She needed to know just how happy her announcement had made him. "Knowing that you are pregnant with my child, Bella, is the greatest gift I could ever hope to receive."

"Oh, Jason."

And then she was there, closer into his arms with her arms wrapped around his neck. "I was afraid you wouldn't be happy."

"You were afraid for nothing. I am ecstatic, overjoyed at the prospect of being a father. Thank you for everything you've done, all the happiness you've brought me."

She shook her head. "No, it's I who needs to thank you for sharing your family with me, for giving me your support when my own family tried to break me down. And for loving me."

And then she leaned toward his lips and he gave her what she wanted, what he wanted. He knew at that moment the proposal had worked. It had brought them together in a way they thought wasn't possible. And he would always appreciate and be forever thankful that Bella had come into his life.

Two days later the Westmorelands met at Dillon's for breakfast to celebrate. It seemed everyone had announcements to make and Dillon felt it was best that they were all made at the same time so they could all rejoice and celebrate.

First Dillon announced he'd received word from Bane that he would be graduating from the naval academy in a few months with honors. Dillon almost choked up when he'd said it, which let everyone know the magnitude of Bane's accomplishments in the eyes of his family. They knew Bane's first year in the navy had been hard since he hadn't known the meaning of discipline. But he'd finally straightened up and had dreams of becoming a SEAL. He'd worked hard and found favor with one of the high-ranking chief petty officers who'd recognized his potential and recommended him for the academy.

Zane then announced that Hercules had done his duty and had impregnated Silver Fly and everyone could only anticipate the beauty of the foal she would one day deliver.

Ramsey followed and said he'd received word from Storm Westmoreland that his wife, Jayla, was expecting and so were Durango and his wife, Savannah. Reggie and Libby's twins were now crawling all over the place. And then with a huge smile on his face Ramsey announced that he and Chloe were having another baby. That sent out loud cheers and it seemed the loudest had come from Chloe's father, Senator Jamison Burton of Florida, who along with Chloe's stepmother, had arrived the day before to visit with his daughter, son-in-law and granddaughter.

Everyone got quiet when Jason stood to announce that he and Bella would be having a baby in the spring, as well. Bella's eyes were glued to Jason as he spoke and she could feel the love radiating from his every word.

"Bella and I are converting her grandfather's ranch into a guest house and combining our lands for our future children to enjoy one day," he ended by saying.

"Does that mean the two of you want more than one child?" Zane asked with a sly chuckle.

Jason glanced over at Bella. "Yes, I want as many children as my wife wants to give me. We can handle it, can't we, sweetheart?"

Bella smiled. "Yes, we can handle it." And they would because what had started out as a proposal had ended up being a whole lot more and she was filled with overflowing joy at how Jason and his family had enriched her life.

He reached out his hand to her and she took it. Hers felt comforting in his and she could only be thankful for her Westmoreland man.

Epilogue

"When I first heard you'd gotten married I wondered about the quickness of it, Jason, but after meeting Bella I understand why," Micah said to his brother. "She's beautiful."

"Thanks." Jason smiled as he glanced around the huge guest house on his and Bella's property. The weather had cooperated and the construction workers had been able to transform what had once been a ranch house into a huge fifteen room guest house for family, friends and business associates of the Westmorelands. Combining the old with the new, the builder and his crew had done a fantastic job and Jason and Bella couldn't be more pleased.

He glanced across the way and saw Dillon was talking to Bane who'd surprised everyone by showing up. It was the first time he'd returned home since he had left nearly three years ago. Jason had gotten the chance to have a long conversation with his youngest brother. He was not the bad-assed kid of yesteryears but standing beside Dillon in his naval officer's uniform, the family couldn't be more proud of the man he had become. But there still was that pain behind the sharpness of Bane's eyes. Although he hadn't mentioned Crystal's name, everyone in the family knew the young woman who'd been Bane's first love, his fixation probably since puberty, was still in his thoughts and probably had a permanent place in his heart. He could only imagine the conversation Dillon was having with Bane since they both had intense expressions on their faces.

"So you've not given up on Crystal?" Dillon asked his youngest brother.

Bane shook his head. "No. A man can never give up on the woman he loves. She's in my blood and I believe that no matter where she is, I'm in hers." Bane paused a moment. "But that's the crux of my problem. I have no idea where she is."

Bane then studied Dillon's features. "And you're sure that you don't?"

Dillon inhaled deeply. "Yes, I'm being honest with you, Bane. When the Newsomes moved away they didn't leave anyone a forwarding address. I just think they wanted to put as much distance between you and them as possible. But I'll still go on record and say that I think the time apart for you and Crystal was a good thing. She was young and so were you. The two of you were headed for trouble and both of you needed to grow up. I am proud of the man you've become."

"Thanks, but one day when I have a lot of time I'm going to find her, Dillon, and nobody, her parents or anyone, will keep me from claiming what's mine."

Dillon saw the intense look in Bane's face and only

hoped that wherever Crystal Newsome was that she loved Bane just as much as Bane still loved her.

Jason glanced over at Bella who was talking to her parents. The Bostwicks had surprised everyone by flying in for the reception. So far they'd been on their good behavior, probably because they were still in awe by the fact that Jason was related to Thorn Westmoreland—racing legend; Stone Westmoreland—aka Rock Mason, *New York Times* bestselling author; Jared Westmoreland, whose reputation as a divorce attorney was renowned; Senator Reggie Westmoreland, and that Dillon was the CEO of Blue Ridge. Hell, they were even speechless when they learned there was even a sheikh in the family.

He saw that Bella was pretending to hang on to her parents' every word. He had discovered she knew how to handle them and refused to let them treat her like a child. He hadn't had to step in once to put them in their place. Bella had managed to do that rather nicely on her own. They had opted to stay at a hotel in town, which had been fine with both him and Bella. There was only so much of her parents that either of them could take.

He inwardly smiled as he studied Bella's features and could tell she was ready to be rescued. "Excuse me a minute, Micah, I need to go claim my wife for a second." Jason moved across the yard to her and as if she felt his impending presence, she glanced his way and smiled. She then excused herself from her parents and headed to meet him.

The dress she was wearing was beautiful and the style hid the little pooch of her stomach. The doctor had warned them that because of the way her stomach was growing they shouldn't be surprised if she was having twins. It would be a couple of months before they knew for sure.

"Do you want to go somewhere for tea…and me," Jason leaned over to whisper close to her ear.

Bella smiled up at him. "Think we'll be missed?"

Jason chuckled. "With all these Westmorelands around, I doubt it. I don't even think your parents will miss us. Now they're standing over there hanging on to Sheikh Jamal Yasir's every word."

"I noticed."

Jason then took his wife's hand in his. "Come on. Let's take a stroll around our land."

And their land was beautiful, with the valley, the mountains, the blooming flowers and the lakes. Already he could envision a younger slew of Westmorelands that he and Bella would produce who would help take care of their land. They would love it as much as their parents did. Not for the first time he felt as if he was a blessed man, his riches abundant not in money or jewelry but in the woman walking by his side. His Southern Bella, his southern beauty, the woman that was everything to him and then some.

"I was thinking," he said.

She glanced over at him. "About what?"

He stopped walking and reached out and placed a hand on her stomach. "You, me and our baby."

She chuckled. "Our babies. Don't forget there is that possibility."

He smiled at the thought of that. "Yes, our babies. But mainly about the proposal."

She nodded. "What about it?"

"I suggest we do another."

She threw her head back and laughed. "I don't have any more land or another horse to bargain with."

"A moot point, Mrs. Westmoreland. This time the stakes will be higher."

"Mmm, what do you want?"

"Another baby pretty soon after this one."

She chuckled again. "Don't you know you never mention having more babies to a pregnant woman? But I'm glad to hear that you want a house filled with children because I do, too. You'll make a wonderful father."

"And you a beautiful mother."

And then he kissed her with all the love in his heart, sealing yet another proposal and knowing the woman he held in his arms would be the love of his life for always.

* * * * *

"Not fair…" she moaned into his lips. "I don't know your name… Let alone what it means…"

"Harres…Harres Aal Shalaan…"

She suddenly gasped, then pushed away.

He stared down at her, all his being rioting, needing her back against him, her lips crushed beneath his, her heat enveloping his suddenly chilled body.

She gaped up at him.

Then she finally rasped, "You're an Aal Shalaan?"

Harres nodded, already acutely sorry that he'd told her.

Now it would end, the spontaneity of the attraction that had exploded into life between them. Now that he'd told her who he was, nothing could ever be the same.

Dear Reader,

I can't tell you how I much I loved writing Harres and Talia's story. But wait, I can! And I'm here to do so.

This story was one I'd longed to write. A true desert romance. Not one taking place in Zohayd's palaces among luxury and man-made grandeur, with the only threats being the insidious royal conspiracies and political intrigue, but one out there in the desert, where nature is the ultimate enchantment and enemy, and where constant danger to the hero's and heroine's lives and hearts is omnipresent.

It was an adrenaline rush to write every word, from the moment Harres burst in to save Talia, to every moment of their journey back to safety as peril and passion rose to unmanageable levels. That journey ended only for another to begin—one of tumultuous surrender to their desires—in the sanctuary of an oasis whose beauty and magic deepened every meaning and sharpened each sensation. Then came the return to the metaphorical royal jungle, where no one was an ally of their bond and their enemies were ready with brutal tests to force it to the breaking point. Even I was wondering how their love would survive!

So now I've told you how much I adored writing this story! I can only hope you enjoy it as much.

Thank you so much for reading, and I'm always eager to hear from readers. Please contact me at oliviagates@gmail.com and visit me at www.oliviagates.com. I'd love it if you friend me on Facebook or follow me on Twitter.

Happy reading!

Olivia

TO TEMPT A SHEIKH

BY
OLIVIA GATES

Published in Great Britain 2012
by Mills & Boon, an imprint of Harlequin (UK) Limited,
Eton House, 18-24 Paradise Road, Richmond, Surrey TW9 1SR

© Olivia Gates 2011

ISBN: 978 0 263 89124 9

51-0212

Harlequin (UK) policy is to use papers that are natural, renewable and
recyclable products and made from wood grown in sustainable forests. The
logging and manufacturing processes conform to the legal environmental
regulations of the country of origin.

Printed and bound in Spain
by Blackprint CPI, Barcelona

Olivia Gates has always pursued creative passions like singing and handicrafts. She still does, but only one of her passions grew gratifying enough, consuming enough, to become an ongoing career—writing.

She is most fulfilled when she is creating worlds and conflicts for her characters, then exploring and untangling them bit by bit, sharing her protagonists' every heart-wrenching heartache and hope, their every heart-pounding doubt and trial, until she leads them to an indisputably earned and gloriously satisfying happy ending.

When she's not writing, she is a doctor, a wife to her own alpha male and a mother to one brilliant girl and one demanding Angora cat. Visit Olivia at www.oliviagates. com.

To my mother.
No words can describe how relieved I am
that the worst is over.
Here's to many, many more books with us together.

One

Harres Aal Shalaan tightened his shroud, narrowing the opening across his eyes to a slit. He didn't need more than that to monitor his target.

The midnight wind buffeted him, pelted him with sand as he stilled once more, flattened himself at the uppermost edge of the dune. His cloth-smothered breathing still rivaled the wind's hubbub across the endlessness of the desert in his ears.

He absently reached for his sand car much as he would have his prized horse. The vehicle wasn't there. He'd left it behind over two miles away. Any closer and the engine noise would have transmitted across this sound-hurling landscape. Ideally, he would have dragged it to this vantage point, but that would have slowed him down at least twenty minutes. Twenty minutes he couldn't afford.

He wouldn't let the stationary status of the scene he'd been watching for the past five minutes fool him. Everything could change at any moment. Then it would be too late for him to intervene.

For now, all remained the same. The two sentries guarding the only entrance were huddled around a makeshift container where a fire struggled for survival against the merciless desert wind. Three more guard duos surrounded the weather-eaten, sand-brick cabin. From inside the shabby construction, gaslight flickered through the seams of shoddy wooden shutters.

He had to give it to the Aal Ossaibis. The Aal Shalaan's rival clan had constructed a watertight plan, and at the spur of the moment, too. This cabin was in the middle of nowhere. Literally. The nearest inhabited areas were over five hundred miles away in any direction. It was an ideal place to hold a hostage.

The hostage Harres was here to free.

He only found this place because he'd deduced the identity of one of those who hired the people inside the cabin. Since he'd uncovered the plot early enough, he'd managed to tag all the players in transit. He'd followed their phone signals before coverage vanished two hundred miles away. He'd since employed all the technology at his fingertips, and found this place only through some advanced satellite triangulation.

Anyone with less specific knowledge and less-than-limitless access and power at his disposal would have been stymied. Even with all of his resources, he never would have found it if not for his timely deductions.

And time was running out. From what he'd learned of the enemy's plans he had less than twenty minutes to complete the extraction. It was then that the masterminds of this kidnapping would arrive to interrogate the hostage and they'd be bringing their army of guards along.

Under any other circumstances, he wouldn't have considered this the ticking bomb he did now. He would have been here with his own major strike force. The very appearance of his finest Black Ops men would have forced anyone with any survival instincts to throw down his arms in surrender.

But as Zohayd's Minister of Interior and head of Central Intelligence and Homeland Security, he no longer knew whom to trust. His team tonight consisted of three men from his highest-ranking teams whom he would trust with his life. They didn't just work under him—they were family, prince soldiers who, like him, would give their lives for their kingdom. Though in other circumstances he trusted many of his men the same way, he couldn't afford the luxury of belief right now. There was too much at stake, and mixed loyalties could tip the whole region into chaos. He had to treat everyone else as suspect.

How could he not when the royal palace itself had already been breached? He wouldn't put infiltrating his ministry and operations, the forces responsible for keeping Zohayd secure, beyond the royal house's enemies.

He closed his eyes. He could still hardly believe it.

A conspiracy to overthrow his father as king and the Aal Shalaans as the ruling house of Zohayd had been brewing right under their noses for months now. The priceless Pride of Zohayd jewels, believed universally throughout the tribes to give the royal house the right to rule, had been stolen and replaced with fakes just in time for Exhibition Day, when they were to be paraded in public for all to see. No doubt the thief planned to publicly expose the jewels as fakes and begin the chaos that would see the Aal Shalaans removed from power.

For the past weeks, Harres had been casting his net throughout the region using information his brother Shaheen and his new wife, Johara, had secured. Early that morning,

Harres had gotten a lead that might take him straight to the conspiracy's mastermind.

A man claiming to be an American reporter was said to be in possession of all the vital details of the conspiracy.

Within twenty minutes, Harres had arrived at the man's rented condo. But their enemies had already made their move. The man had been gone. Abducted.

Harres hadn't missed a beat since, had followed the trail of the abductors to this desolate place. He had no doubt what the orders of the ruthless patriarch of the Aal Ossaibis were. Extract the info from the man, then let the desert claim him and his secrets.

That alone was reason enough for Harres to be out here. No one would be unjustly hurt on Zohaydan soil on his watch. Not even if it was someone whose agenda was to bring the Aal Shalaans down. Not even if it was this T. J. Burke.

T. J. Burke. The man was an enigma. In his databases Harres possessed up-to-the-moment information on every reporter in the world. He kept tight tabs on each since they wielded the most dangerous weapon of all, the media and its inexorable effect on global movements and the manufacturing of worldwide public opinion.

But T. J. Burke had slipped under his radar. Since Harres had learned of the reporter's existence, the unprecedented had happened. He'd failed to learn anything about the man. It was as if T. J. Burke had come into existence the moment he'd arrived in the region one week ago.

He'd found one reference to the only T. J. Burke who'd ever been in the region, an American IT specialist who'd worked for a multinational corporation in Azmahar. But that man had gone back to the States just over a year ago. A few months later, he'd been tried for the crimes of fraud and embezzlement, perpetrated while he'd been in

Harres's region. He was now serving a five-year sentence in a maximum-security penitentiary and was still securely in his cell as of a couple hours ago.

The current T. J. Burke had probably latched on to the name, or else he'd come up with a random persona for his fictional character and it coincided with an actual person's identity.

Which drove Harres to one conclusion. The man must be a spy. An uncanny one at that, hiding his origins from Harres's networks, and his movements and affiliations, too.

But he would save T. J. Burke even if he were the devil. Once he had him safe, he would extract the info he had. If it was what he hoped, what he feared, he would see what impossible price this man had intended to demand for the invaluable info and double it. Then he'd do everything in his considerable power to ensure he'd never resell it.

The sentries were nodding off in front of the fire now. He signaled to Munsoor, his second-in-command. Munsoor relayed his order counterclockwise to Yazeed at the cabin's south side, who then relayed it to Mohab at its west.

Twice they simultaneously fired their tranq darts, each felling their designated sentries.

Harres erupted to his feet. In seconds he was jumping over the guards' crumpled bodies and landing soundlessly on the stone steps leading to the cabin's door. The others were converging on him.

He exchanged a terse nod with his men, seeing only their intense gazes in the eerie combination of steady-as-time starlight and erratic firelight. They'd deal with any surprises. He'd go straight for their target.

He pushed on the door. It swung open with a creak that gutted the silence.

His gaze swept around the dim interior. Burke wasn't there. There was another room. He had to be there.

He bounded to its skewed door, slowly pushed it open.

A slim, trim-bearded man in a sand-colored quilted jacket rounded on him.

A heartbeat stretched as their eyes clashed.

Even in the faint light, Harres did a double take at the impact of the man's gaze, which seemed to be spewing electric azure. Then there was the rest of him. He seemed to glow in the gloom, both with an incandescent tan and a shock of gleaming gold hair spiking around his face.

Next heartbeat, Harres tore his gaze away, assessed the situation. This was a bathroom. Burke hadn't been using it. He'd been attempting an escape. He'd already pried the six-foot-high window open even with his hands tied in front of him. Harres had no doubt his captors wouldn't have made the mistake of tying them like that. Which meant the man had enough flexibility to get his hands where he could use them. A minute more and he *would* have escaped.

It was clear he didn't know there was nowhere to escape to. He must have been either knocked out cold or blindfolded on the way. But from what he'd seen in Burke's eyes, Harres bet he would have tried to escape regardless. This man was one who'd rather be shot in the back escaping than in the face while he pleaded for his life. He was beyond canny. He was resourceful, fearless.

And he'd be dead if Harres didn't get him out of here.

Harres had no doubt his captors would rather kill the man and lose the info his mind contained than let it fall into Aal Shalaan hands.

Observations segued into action. He lunged, grabbed the man's arm. Next second, he could swear a rocket launched through his teeth and exploded behind his eye sockets. It took him seconds to realize what had happened.

The man had hit him.

Still half-blind, Harres ducked, employing his other senses to dodge the barrage of blows the man rained on him. Harres charged him again, detained him in a crushing bear hug. He had no time for a more intimate introduction to those fists that packed such an unexpected wallop.

The man writhed in his hold with the ferocity of a tornado, almost breaking it.

"Quit struggling, you fool," Harres hissed. "I'm here to save you."

Seemed the man couldn't decipher Harres's words through the shroud covering his mouth. Or he didn't believe him. The man simultaneously delivered a bone-cracking kick to his left shin and kneed him. Harres barely avoided that last crippling impact, marveling at Burke's agility and speed even as he squeezed the man harder. The much smaller, wiry man would give him a run for his money if he had the use of both hands and more space.

Harres wrenched the cloth from his mouth, plastered the man against the uneven stone wall, a forearm against his throat applying enough pressure to make him stop fighting, pushing his face up to his so they again made eye contact.

A buzz zapped through him again as those glowing eyes slammed into his, as the body he imprisoned seethed against his with a mixture of defiance and panic.

Harres shook away the disorientation, firmed his pressure. "Don't make me knock you out and carry you like a sack of dirty laundry. I don't have time for your paranoia. Now, do as I tell you, if you want to get out of here alive."

He didn't wait for the man's consent. But in the second before he wrenched away, he thought he saw the fearful hostility in Burke's eyes soften. He filed away the observation for later dissection as he began dragging Burke back where he'd come from.

A fire exchange ripped the night, aborted his momentum.

Reinforcements must have arrived. His heart stampeded with the need to charge to his men's aid. But he couldn't. They'd all signed on knowing that only securing their target mattered. Anything—and anyone else—was expendable.

Feeling his blood boiling and curdling at once, he turned to the man. They'd have to use the escape route he'd already secured.

The man was ahead of him, already turning there. Harres snatched a dagger from the weapon belt around his thigh, slashed Burke's tethers, put it away, then bent to give him a boost so he could climb out of the window. And the man did another uncanny thing. He leaped up from a standstill, like a cat, clutched the six-foot-high ledge for the moment it took him to gain leverage and impetus to catapult himself through the opening. He cleared it in one fluid move. In a second, Harres heard the distinctive sound of someone hitting the ground on the other side of the wall in a rolling landing.

Was this guy an acrobat? Or was he a Black Ops agent, too?

Whatever he was, he was far more than even Harres had bargained for. He just hoped the tenacious sod didn't take off, forcing him to pursue Burke once he got out of here. It would take him more than the three seconds flat the man had taken to clear that tiny hatch with his size.

In about ten seconds, Harres flipped himself backward through the opening, the only way he'd been able to get enough leverage to squeeze himself through. As he let his mass drag him down, meeting the ground with extended arms, he had an upside-down view of the man's waiting silhouette. So

Burke was intelligent enough to know where his best chances lay.

He landed on flat palms, tucked and flipped over to his feet, standing up and starting to run toward the man in one continuous motion. "Follow me."

Without a word, the man did.

They ran across the sand dunes guided only by Harres's phosphorescent compass and a canopy of cold starlight. He couldn't use a flashlight to find his trail back to his sand car. There was no telling if any of their adversaries had slipped his men's net. A flashlight in this darkness would be like a beacon for the enemy to follow and all this would have been for nothing.

He ran with his charge in his wake, telling himself the others were safe. He wouldn't know for certain until they reached their own helicopter several miles away and entered coverage zones where he could communicate with them.

For now, he could think only of getting T. J. Burke to safety.

Ten minutes later, he felt secure enough to turn his senses back to the man. Burke was keeping up with him. The rhythm of his feet said he was running faster than Harres to make up for the difference in the length of their legs. So not only an agile and ready fighter, but in great shape, too. Good news. He hadn't been looking forward to hauling the guy to the sand car if he collapsed. But it was clear there was no danger of that. Burke was pacing himself superbly. No gasping, just even, deep inhalations and long, full exhalations.

And again something…inexplicable slithered down Harres's body as those sounds seemed to permeate the night, even with his own ears being boxed by the wind. The sensation originated from somewhere behind his breastbone and traveled downward, settling low, then lower.

He gritted his teeth against the disturbance as they reached his sand car. He jumped inside the open-framed, dune-buggy-style four-wheel vehicle. "Get in behind me."

Without missing a beat, Burke slid behind him on the seat, spread his legs on either side of Harres's hips, plastered his front to his back and curled himself around him as if they'd been doing this every day.

A shudder spread through Harres as he revved the motor. In seconds, he was hurtling the sand car over the dunes, driving with even more violence than the urgency of the situation dictated.

He drove in charged silence, catapulting the car over dune edges, crashing it in depressions, spraying sand in their wake and pushing the engine to its limit. With every violent jolt, the man's arms tightened around his midriff, his legs grabbing him more securely, his cheek pressing deeper into his back until Harres felt they'd been fused together.

His breath shortened by the moment as the heat of the man's body seeped through every point of contact, pooled in his loins.

Adrenaline. That was what it was. Discomfort. At having someone pressed so close, even in these circumstances.

Yes. What else could it possibly be?

In minutes, the crouching silhouette of his Mi-17 transport helicopter came into view. It was the best sight Harres had ever seen. He'd not only managed to reach their way out, but now he could get the man off of him.

He screeched the sand car into a huge arc, almost toppling it before bringing it to a quaking stop by the pilot's door.

He wrenched Burke's hands from his waist and leveraged himself out of the car in one motion. The man jumped out behind him, again with the stealth and economy of a cat, then waited for directions.

He took in details now that his vision was at its darkness-adapted best. With his windswept golden hair and those iridescent eyes, Burke looked like some moon elf, ethereal, his beauty untouched by the ordeal—

His *beauty?*

"Jump into the passenger seat and buckle yourself up." He heard his bark, knew all his aggression was directed at his insane thoughts and reactions. "I'll stuff the car in the cargo bay—"

The crack of thunder registered first.

Second, comprehension. A gun's discharge.

The shock in the man's eyes followed.

Last, the sting.

He'd been hit.

Somewhere on his left side, level with his heart. He had to assume not in it. He didn't feel any weakening. Yet.

Someone had slipped his men's net, had managed to sneak up on them. This could be the last mistake he ever made.

He exploded into action, charged the man to stop him from taking cover. They had no time for that.

He shouldn't have worried. Burke was no cowering fool. He was bolting to the helicopter even as more and more gunshots rang around them. He now knew the shot that had connected had been random. That was no sniper out there. That still didn't mean whoever it was couldn't hit a huge target like the chopper.

In seconds they were in their seats and Harres had the monster of a machine roaring off the ground, levitating into the sky.

He pressed the helicopter for all the altitude and velocity it was capable of. In less than a minute he knew they were too far for anyone pursuing them on foot or ATV to even spot anymore.

Only then did he let himself investigate his body for the

damage it had sustained. It had no idea yet. All it reported back was a burning path traversing his left side back to front just below his armpit. Flesh wound, he preferred to assume. Maybe with some bone damage. Nothing major. If no artery had been hit.

But the idea of losing blood too fast and spiraling into shock gave way to more pressing bad news. The chopper was losing fuel. The pursuer had hit the tank.

He eyed the gauge. With the rate of loss, the fuel wouldn't take them back to the capital. Nor anywhere near the inhabited areas where he could make contact with his people.

He had to make a detour. Head for the nearest oasis. At fifty miles away it was still four hundred and fifty miles closer than any other inhabited area. The inhabitants hadn't joined the modern world in any way, but once he and Burke were safely there, he would send envoys on horseback to his people. The trek would probably be delayed by a sandstorm that was expected to cut off the area from the world soon, a week or two during which his brothers and cousins—the only ones who knew of his mission—would probably think him dead. When weighed against his actual survival, and that of his charge, that was a tiny price to pay.

His new plan *would* be effective. Land in the oasis, take care of any injuries and contact his people. Mission accomplished.

Next minute, he almost kicked himself.

Of all times to count his missions….

The leaking fuel wasn't their only problem. In fact it was their slighter one. The damage to the navigation system had taken this long to reveal itself. The chopper was losing altitude fast. And there was nothing he could do to right its course.

He had to land now. Here. Or crash.

He turned to Burke urgently. "Are you buckled in?"

The man nodded frantically, his eyes widening with realization. Harres had no time to reassure him.

For the next few minutes he tried every trick he'd learned from his stint as a test pilot to land the helicopter and not have it be the last thing he did in his life.

As it was, they ended up crash-landing.

After the violent chain reaction of bone-powdering, steel-tearing impacts came to an end, he let out a shuddering breath acknowledging that they had survived being pulverized.

He leaned back in his seat, watching the interior of the cockpit fade in and out of focus. Had he lost too much blood or were the cockpit's lights fluctuating? He had no doubt the chopper itself was a goner.

He'd deal with his own concerns later. After he saw to his passenger.

He unbuckled his belt, flicked the cockpit lights on to maximum, turned to Burke. The man had his head turned against his seat, his eyes wide with an amalgam of panic and relief. Their gazes meshed.

And there was no mistaking what happened then.

Harres hardened. Fully.

He shuddered. What *was* this? What was going on? Was his body going haywire from the stress?

Enough of this idiocy. Check him for injuries.

He reached for him. The man flinched at his touch, as if Harres had electrified him. He knew how he felt. The same charge had forked through him. This had crossed from idiotic to insane.

He forced in an inhalation, determined to erase those anomalous reactions, drew Burke by the shoulders into the overhead light. The man struggled.

"Stop squirming. I need to check you for injuries."

"I'm fine."

The husky voice skewered through him even though he could barely hear it with the din of the still-moving rotors.

And a conviction slammed into him.

He would have thought he was beginning to hallucinate from blood loss. But he'd been feeling these inexplicable things long before he'd been hit. So he was through listening to his mind, and what it thought it knew, and heeding his body. It had been yelling at him from the first moment, just as his every instinct had been. He always listened to them.

Right now they were telling him that, even in these nightmarish conditions, they *wanted* T. J. Burke.

And knowing himself, that could only mean one thing.

He stabbed his fingers into the unruly gold silk on top of T. J. Burke's head, his body hardening more at the escaping gasp that flayed his cheek.

He traced the dewy lips with his thumb, as if to catch the sound and the chagrined shock at what he sensed was an equally uncontrollable response.

He smiled his satisfaction. "So, tell me, why are you pretending to be T. J. Burke, bearded investigative reporter, when a modern-day bejeweled Mata Hari would suit you far better?"

Two

T. J. Burke wrenched away from the cloaked, force-of-nature-in-man-form's hold, panted, voice gruff and low, a tremor of panic traversing it. "Did you hit your head in the crash?"

The man bore down again without seeming to move, making the spacious cockpit of the high-end military helicopter shrink. The smile in those golden eyes that seemed to snare the dimmest rays and emit them magnified, took on a dangerous edge. The danger was more spine-shivering for being unthreatening, more…distressing, with the response it elicited.

Then the colossus drawled in that deeper-than-the-desert-night baritone. "The only hit to the head I got tonight was courtesy of those neatly trimmed, capable hands of yours."

"Since I hit you with the intention of taking your head

off, I probably dislocated something in there. Your good sense, seemingly. Maybe your whole brain."

The man pressed closer, the freshness of his breath and the potency of his virility flooding every one of T.J.'s senses. "Oh, both my sense and my brain are welded in place. It would take maybe…" his eyes traveled up and down T.J.'s body like slow, scorching hands "…ten of you to loosen even my consciousness."

"It took only one of me to do so earlier," T.J. scoffed, not sure the supply of air in the cockpit would last much longer. "I almost took you down. With both hands literally tied, too."

"You can sure take me down, just not by hitting me. Your effect on me has nothing to do with your physical strength and is certainly not proportionate to your size."

"Is that all you got? Cheap shots at my size?"

"I'd never take any kind of shot at you." Again the man's eyes seemed to emit a force field that gathered T.J. into its embrace. "And then, I think your size is perfection itself."

Drenched in goose bumps and feeling the heart that had barely slowed down start to hammer again, T.J. smirked. "Sure you're not concussed? Or is this the way you usually talk to other men?"

The insult seemed to burn to ash in the rising temperature of the man's smile. "It's not even the way I talk to women. But it's the only way I'll talk to *you*. Among other things. Every other possible thing."

T.J. pressed against the passenger door. "So you somehow got it into your head that I'm a woman? And now you're all over me? Just minutes after barely surviving a devastating crash and landing God knows where in this forsaken, sand-infested land? And you can't hear how ridiculous you sound?"

"What's ridiculous is that you thought a fuzzy beard and

an atrocious haircut would disguise the femininity blasting off you. It got me by the…throat, from the first moment. So why don't you drop the act and tell me who you really are?"

"I *am* T. J. Burke!"

Painstakingly chiseled lips spread to reveal teeth so white they were almost phosphorescent in the dimness. "My bearded beauty, only one of us has testosterone coursing in his bloodstream right now. Don't make me offer you… tangible proof."

T.J. glowered at him, tried not to show any weakness, to meet him on the same level of audacity. "Is it the…tangible proof proving that you're attracted to small blond men?"

A chuckle rumbled deep in that huge predator's gut, zigzagged all through T.J.'s system like deadly voltage. "First thing you have to learn about me so we can move on is that I am insult-proof. I wouldn't even sock you if you *were* a man. But my body knew you weren't from the moment I laid eyes on you in that filthy hole, against all evidence and intel. So will you admit it on your own, or will you make me…establish proof myself?"

T.J. shrank back farther against the door as the man's right hand rose. "Lay a hand on me, buster, and have it chomped off."

"With the way I'm reacting to you, there's nothing I want more than your teeth on every part of me. But if anything proves your femininity, it's that so-called threat. A man would have told me he'd break my hand or tear it off, or something suitably macho."

"So you have men regularly threatening to do that? And women chomping away at any part of you they can reach?"

The man narrowed his eyes, concentrating the intensity of his amusement. "You're an expert at diversion, aren't you? Give it up, already. I'm on to you. So on to you that not even a bullet is dulling my response."

"A *bullet?*" T.J felt both eyes almost pop out with shock. "You're hit?"

The man nodded. "So will you take pity on an injured man and bestow your name on me? Make it your real one this time. And let me see how you look without that rug on your face."

"Oh, shut *up*. Are you really injured or are you playing me?"

The man suddenly sat up from his seemingly indolent pose, tugged T.J.'s right hand. T.J. ended up pressed against him, chest to chest, face in his neck, arm around his massive torso. The sensation of touching a live wire came first. Then that of sickening viscosity scorched everything away.

Before T.J. could jerk back in alarm, the man meshed his right hand in T.J.'s hair, pulling gently until their gazes once again melded. "See? I'm bleeding. For you. I might die. Can you be so cruel as to let me die without knowing who you are?"

T.J. wrenched away from him, one hand drenched in the thick heat and slickness of his blood. "Oh, just shut *up*."

Those lethal lips twitched. "I will if you start talking."

"You don't need me to talk, you need me to take care of this wound."

"*I'll* take care of it. You talk."

"Don't be stupid. Your intercostal arteries might be severed, and those bleed like gushing faucets. You might think you're stable, but there's no telling how bad your injury is, what kind of blood loss you've suffered. Your blood pressure could plunge without warning. And if it does, there's no bringing it back up!"

"Spoken like an expert. Been shot before?"

"I've treated people who were. People who weren't too stupid to jump at my offer to help them."

"Is that any way to talk to the man who took a bullet for you? And will you peel that thing off your face, already?"

"I can't believe this! You might slip into shock at any moment and you're still trying to prove this lame theory of yours?"

He just smiled, imperturbable, immovable.

"Okay," T.J. gritted. "I'll talk. After I take care of you."

"I'll let you take care of me. After you talk."

"Come *on*. Where is this chopper's emergency kit?"

"I'll tell you after you tell me what I want to hear."

"Not the truth, huh? 'Cause I already told you that."

The man backed away when T.J. lunged at him, hands reaching out to expose his wound. "Uh-uh-uh. No touching until you admit you're a woman. I only let women touch me."

T.J. glared into eyes that had a dozen devils dancing in them. "You're really out of touch with the reality—the *gravity*—of your situation, aren't you? But what do you care if I admit it or not? You *know* it, after all. And then, I'm not going to merely *touch* you, I'm going to bathe in your blood."

The appreciation in the man's eyes expanded, enveloped T.J. whole. "I knew you were a bloodthirsty wench when you almost sliced me in half with the power of your glare alone. Then you tried to powder my teeth *and* transform me from a baritone to an alto."

T.J. felt a smile advancing, dispelling the frown that by now felt etched on, and had to admit…

That man was lethal. In every sense of the word.

But though he was teasing, his irreversible deterioration

might actually come to pass. There was no telling how
serious his injury was without a thorough exam. "And to
think you seemed intelligent. Guess appearances can be
deceiving."

The man's lips twisted. "You can talk."

"Oh, but I thought my appearance didn't deceive you for
a moment, that my 'femininity' kicked you like a mule."

The man sighed, nodding in mock helplessness. "*Aih*.
But if I do succumb, remember, it's your doing, in every
way."

"Give me a break." T.J. exhaled forcibly then scratched
at the beard.

Then she snatched it away.

She yelped as a blowtorch seemed to blast her nerve
endings, forcing her to leave the beard dangling over
her lips. She rubbed at the burning sensation, gave her
tormentor a baleful glance. "Happy now, you pigheaded,
mulish ox?"

"A one-man farm, eh? No one has ever flattered me as
you do." She glared at him as he oh-so-carefully removed
the rest of the beard, making the adhesive separate from her
skin with a kneading sensation instead of a stinging one.

Then he pulled back, massaged her jaw and cheeks in
an insistent to and fro, soothing her skin with the backs of
those long, roughened, steel-hard fingers. She moaned as
a far more devastating brand of fire swept her flesh from
every point of contact.

He groaned himself. "*Ya Ullah, ma ajmalek*. How
absolutely beautiful you are. I thought I'd seen all kinds
of beauty, but I've never laid eyes on anything like you.
It's like you're made of light and gold and energy and
gemstones."

Heat rose through her at his every word. When she'd
first seen him, she'd been freezing with dread and the

desert's chill. But when she'd turned to him in that filthy bathroom, his very presence had sent animation surging into her every cell. The crash had drained her, but the heat of his solicitude, his awareness and appreciation, the stoking of his challenge, had been melting away the ice that seemed to have become a constituent of her bones.

She still couldn't believe he'd seen through her disguise. No one had during the week she'd been in Zohayd. Her captors hadn't, and she'd spent a whole day in their grasp. But he'd sensed her femininity in moments, with his senses almost blinded by the night's dimness, the urgency and her disguise. He'd also had no tactile evidence, with the buffer of clothes—especially her jacket and the corset flattening her…assets.

Yet he'd known. And just as he'd felt her vibes, she'd been immersed in his. She'd felt every hot granite inch of his formidable body, smelled him over the overpowering stench of her prison, over the dispersion of the desert and the deluge of post-accident mayhem. She'd heard each inflection of his voice through the din of her inner cacophony and the madness of their escape and crash.

And instead of reacting to his maleness as she had to her captors'—with dread, revulsion, aggression and desperation—she was finding it bolstering, soothing and, if she could believe her body's reactions in these insane circumstances, arousing.

She hadn't found a male this arousing in…ever.

And to find this man so might mean it was *she* who'd hit her head. Or something. There must be something wrong, if all she wanted right now was to snuggle into him and hold on tight.

As if responding to her need, mirroring it, he leaned in, pressed his face lightly into her neck, breathed her in and groaned again with intense enjoyment. "Even with male cologne and all the traces of your ordeal, you smell heavenly. And you still haven't told me your name, *ya jameelati*."

She pulled back from his hypnosis, from the idiocy of her untimely weakness. She had to patch up this obdurate hulk. "And you still think if you ask me enough times I'll give you a different answer."

His eyes stilled on her. Then he nodded, as if coming to a decision. "So your name is T.J. What do the *T* and *J* stand for?"

She blinked. "You believe me?"

"Yes. My instincts about you have been right-on so far. They're saying you're telling the truth now. They even insist you probably haven't developed the ability to lie."

"You make me sound like an incontinent blabbermouth. I gave my kidnappers nothing."

"Withholding the truth is not lying. It can span the spectrum of motives, from fear to nobility. Doing it under threat of harm or worse is courageous. But in almost all situations, telling an untruth is cowardly. And I had no doubt of your courage from the first moment. So, with that established…your name?"

T.J. drew in a shaky inhalation then blurted it out. "Talia Jasmine. Satisfied? Now where is that damned emergency kit?"

She heard his intake of breath, felt it sweeping inside her own chest like an internal caress. But it was the wonder that flared in those preternatural eyes that started her shivering again. With everything but cold.

Without a word, he reached overheard, opened a compartment and produced a huge emergency bag.

She pounced on it. Relief swamped her as she made a lightning-fast inventory of the contents. Everything she could possibly need.

She took out a saline bag, hooked it in an overhead protrusion, dragged his right arm over her lap and pushed the needle into his vein, then secured it with adhesive tape and turned the drip to maximum for quickest fluid replacement.

He tugged at her chin, pressed something to her lips. A bottle of water. She suddenly realized she was beyond parched. She downed the bottle in one go. He watched her as if he wanted to gulp her down himself, to decipher and assimilate her.

She licked her lips, cleared her throat. "Okay, I need you to expose the wound and hold this flashlight over it for me. Better do it in the back of this monster so you can lie down."

He smiled in that seriousness-melting way of his. "I can give you two out of three of your demands. I can with pleasure take off my clothes. And I can shed light on the mess I made when all of my senses were so focused on you that I missed the pursuer who could have killed me with one haphazard shot. I shudder to think where that would have left you."

"As if I'm in such a great situation now," she mumbled under her breath as she snapped on gloves.

"We're both in one piece, with me only slightly punctured, which in a hostage-extraction op is about the best possible situation. But I have to inform you I had to sacrifice the back end of the chopper to preserve the cockpit while crash-landing. I doubt there's any space back there for even one of *your* species to stretch out."

She looked up from preparing her surgical tray. "My species? Women you mean? Last I heard we were a gender."

"Felines." His smile widened as he reached for the swathe over his head to start the process of exposing himself...his *wound* for her. "I know of nothing else capable of exiting a six-foot-high window with as much economy of movement and grace."

"They're called gymnasts. I was one till I hit eighteen. Seems my abilities reactivated under duress."

He finished unfurling the yards of material from his head in movements she could only describe as…erotic. This was a man used to barricading himself in mere cloth before plunging into the desert, pitting his wiles and will against its cruelty and capriciousness.

Suddenly all thoughts evaporated. The last coil fell off, and a mane of gleaming mahogany cascaded in layers of satin luxury to his shoulders.

She swallowed. "You should talk."

"Oh?" One formidable wing of an eyebrow quirked as he shrugged off the outer layer of his night-colored desert raider/ninja/Black Ops hybrid outfit. He seemed to grow bigger in only a skintight, high-collared, long-sleeved top.

She gave him an encompassing gesture. "You should be on stage playing the Lion King yourself. With minimal or no makeup."

And he gifted her with another of those amused rumbles that proved his great feline origins.

Then he tried to yank off his top and groaned, his face twisting in obvious pain. "Seems raising my left arm won't be one of my favorite activities for a while."

"Do you have a change of clothes on board?"

"Yes. And other supplies that I'll access once we're done with this."

"Okay, then." She swept scissors off the tray and proceeded to cut off his top.

He hissed as the coolness of the blade slid against his hot skin, groaned as she reached the parts that had stuck to his wound, then growled as her gloved hands glided over his flesh, separating the adhesions and palpating the edges of his wound.

There should only be pain. But to ears that were hyperaware of his merest inflection, the pleasure was unmistakable, too.

Tremors invaded her hands, traveling all the way from her core. And this from gloved and accidental contact while exploring his wound. What would touching him with no barriers do to her if she were exploring his power and beauty for pleasure instead?

Work, idiot. Stop fantasizing about this hunk of impossible virility and just patch him up. You're probably in ten different types of shock and hallucinating most of this anyway. Moron.

Continuing her raucous inner abuse, she worked in silence.

Suddenly a realization dawned on her. All the time she'd been filling hypodermic needles with local anesthetic, analgesic/anti-inflammatory and broad-spectrum antibiotic, he'd been handing her vials, receiving filled syringes and placing them in the correct sequence on the tray like the best of her long-term assistants. He continued to help her with total efficiency and obvious knowledge of what went where and would be used when as she prepared forceps, scalpels, sutures, cautery, bandages, wipes and antiseptics.

He hadn't been bragging when he'd said he'd take care of his wound. This was a man versed in more than hostage-retrieval ops. He was no stranger to field emergency procedures.

Just who and what was he?

She opened her mouth to ask and one of those fingers she'd bet could bend steel feathered down her cheek again. The gentleness of his touch almost pulverized her precarious control. Tears churned at the back of her eyes. She swallowed them along with any questions.

He asked them of her. "You weren't exaggerating when you said you'd treated bullet wounds before. Just who are you, my heaven's dew?"

Her hands stilled from checking her supplies before she started the procedure.

No one had ever realized the meaning of her name.

"Your parents are to be applauded for choosing such a name to befit your wonder and delicacy."

She shot him an affronted look. "I'm not delicate!"

His smile filled with teasing indulgence. "Oh, but you are, incredibly so."

She narrowed her eyes at him. "How's your jaw?"

Something hot and delighted rumbled deep in his chest, revved in her bones like a bass line made of urges instead of sound. "My jaw will always remember its meeting with your fist. But sheathe your claws. Delicacy doesn't equate with fragility when describing you, but with refinement mixed with delectability wrapped around a core of resourcefulness. That's what you are. An exterior of pure gold, a filling of sheer delight and a center of polished steel."

Her lips twitched. "You sure you didn't hit your head? Or are you always so ready and free with spontaneous poetry?"

"I'm the very opposite. Women call me a miser with words. I never say what I don't mean. What I don't feel. It's no wonder I was chosen for law enforcement and not diplomacy."

"So among the hordes of women who've stampeded through your life, I'm the only one who, in the aftermath of a rescue mission out of a *Mission Impossible* movie, has moved you so much you've found your inner poet."

"You've summed it up perfectly."

He suddenly turned around and lay back, placing his head and shoulders on her lap.

He grinned up at her as she froze, stared down at him. "This is the only place I'm lying down around here."

She gulped, looked into his upside-down eyes and repressed the urge to smooth her hands over his face, to thread her fingers through that incredible mane fanned over her lap, and most insane of all, to bend down and kiss his forehead before she started poking him with needles and slicing him with scalpels.

Before she succumbed to any of those ridiculous urges, he transferred the tray she'd prepared to the floor, then turned to his side to present her with an optimum view of his injury.

She almost choked when he looked up from his sideways position and purred, "And that's the best way to hand you instruments as you work."

She gave a jerky nod and a throat-clearing cough, hoping to expel any mind-fogging stupidity.

Then proceeded to examine his wound.

Harres looked up at this enigma in a woman's form whom he'd saved. And who was in turn saving him.

He held the flashlight at an optimal angle for her. And while she injected his side with local anesthetic, he examined her.

She was beyond beautiful. Unique. Magical. He hadn't told her the half of it when she'd charged him with being poetic.

She finally made that throat-clearing noise he'd come to realize meant she was fighting for composure. And he bet it had nothing to do with the medical part of their situation.

"Okay. The bullet made a clear track through your muscles. It hit the tip of your scapula, grazing three ribs.

No tendons or nerves are severed. There is muscle damage at the bullet's entry point, then as it came out the front it tore a four-inch wound in your skin. But the bleeding is the worst of it, since a few arteries have recoiled out of reach. I'll have to widen the wound and deepen it, to fish them out and cauterize them, and for future drainage. I'll place deep sutures to repair the most traumatized tissues, but will leave the wound open to drain for later closure, once the swelling goes down, so no infection is trapped within."

As she spoke, she continued to implement her plan with flawless execution. He continued to assist her.

Every minute brought more unprecedented sensations. It wasn't just physical reactions to feeling her firm, warm thighs beneath his head, or breathing her hot, intoxicating scent with every breath. He'd never experienced this synergy, not even when working with his brothers or his men. He'd never let another person take charge of anything while he was around, let alone his own physical well-being. He'd never lusted after a woman anywhere near this intensely, let alone while simultaneously respecting the hell out of her capabilities, relying on her efficiency and wanting to pamper her with all he had and protect her with his life.

Was this real, or was everything being amplified by the circumstances combined with a dose of blood loss, survival elation and gratitude?

But when he added in his mounting physical response and mental appreciation, he was back to square one.

This *was* as real as anything got. And from the way she kept stroking him with her eyes after she finished each step and with her hands after each cut as if to apologize for the necessity of hurting him to heal him, from the way her hands and lips trembled at his merest indication of discomfort, he knew.

It was just as real for her.

It didn't matter who they were, or how and when they'd met. What they'd done since, the seeming lifetime of life-changing events and feelings they'd experienced together, meant they could leap over most stages of development and acknowledgment of attraction.

She finished the procedure and he sat up, helped her wrap his torso in bandages. As she began to draw back, he couldn't bear it. His right hand wove into her hair, kept her close, brought her closer. And she lurched away.

He stilled, his heart jolting with the same force.

After a long moment, he removed his hand, whispered, "Are you afraid of me?"

"No." Relief deflated him at her vehement denial. Then she grinned sheepishly at him, boosting her beauty to dizzying heights. "Which might be the stupidest thing I've ever thought or felt, considering I'm in the middle of nowhere with a hulk of a man in a hostile land where I know no one. But there you go. I'm not afraid of you. Not for a second. I'm…the very opposite."

Warmth flooded him at her admission. He'd been right. She felt the same way.

Another unknown urge took him over, the desire to tease her, even as he wanted to devour her. "Now that's a little white lie. You were so afraid of me for at least a few seconds that you almost gave me a permanent disability."

"That was before I saw your face, heard your voice. Before that, you were this…huge chunk of night that had come to claim me."

"You were right about the coming to claim you part." He reached out to her again, slid a hand around her waist, drew her to him. "So are you going to tell me where you learned to perform field surgery like that?"

"In medical school, where else?"

"You mean you *are* a doctor?"

"Last I heard that's what came off said school's production line."

"So everything I thought you were was false, from your gender to your profession. Is there no end to your surprises?"

A grin trembled on her dimpled but now colorless lips. "Now why would there be?"

The urge to capture her lips, nibble color and warmth back into them surged inside him, almost brimmed over into action.

"No reason at all, *ya shafeyati.*"

"What does this mean?"

"My healer."

"So how do you say 'my rescuer' in Arabic?"

"Monqethi."

She repeated the word after him, that voice that even when she'd tried to deepen and roughen it had coursed through him like an intravenous aphrodisiac now becoming a vocal caress that soothed his insides, infused his every cell.

Then she heightened her exquisite torture. "And 'my hero'?"

His vocal cords locked against the tide of temptation. He whispered, *"Buttuli,"* listened to her hypnotic melody begin to repeat it, before his control snapped.

He swooped down and took the rest of her tremulous homage inside him, along with that breath that had been tormenting him with its arousing fragrance. She gave him more, in one gasp after another, opened for him.

He wanted to drown in her, drown her in him, give her a glimpse of the need and ferocity she ignited in him. His lips claimed hers as if he'd brand her, his tongue thrusting deep, breaching her, draining her of moans and sweetness.

She took it all, seeming unable to meet his passion yet overwhelming him with her surrender.

"Talia…*nadda jannati*…my heaven's dew…"

"Not fair," she moaned into his lips. "I don't know your name…let alone what it means."

He drew in her plump lower lip, suckled it until she cried out and took his tongue deeper.

"Harres…Harres Aal Shalaan." He started to translate, had said only "Guardian—" when she gasped then pushed him away.

He stared down at her, all his being rioting, needing her back against him, her lips crushed beneath his, her heat enveloping his suddenly chilled body.

She gaped up at him.

Then she finally rasped, "You're an Aal Shalaan?"

Harres nodded, already acutely sorry that he'd told her.

Now it would end, the spontaneity of the attraction that had exploded to life between them. Now that he'd told her who he was, nothing could ever be the same. There hadn't been a woman of the thousands he'd met in his life, the hundreds who'd pursued him, no matter how attracted to him they were, who'd seen him as anything but an amalgam of status, power and money. He was never just a man to them. He'd cease to be just a man to her now.

He exhaled, his gaze leaving her kiss-swollen lips in regret as he waited for artificiality to settle into her guileless eyes, for calculation to take hold of her open-book reactions. He'd often chafed at the trappings of his status and position and wealth. He now positively cursed them.

Then she again did the last thing he could have expected.

Her gaping became a glare of such revulsion and hostility,

he might as well have turned into a slimy creature before her eyes.

Then she spat, "You're one of that pack of highborn, lowlife criminals?"

Three

Harres stared at this woman who'd just called him and his family a pack of criminals. And he did the only thing he could.

He threw his head back and belted out a guffaw.

Now that the local anesthetic was wearing off, his wound protested the uninhibited movement, stabbed him with a burning lance of pain. It wasn't any hotter than the glare of abhorrence Talia still scorched him with. Seemed his mirth only poured fuel on her sudden antipathy.

But he couldn't help it. There was no way he could control his relief, his thrill, that instead of fawning over him, she looked ready to sock him again.

Then she did. On his good arm, hard enough to sober him a bit, save him from tearing loose her meticulous suturing efforts with laughter.

"Don't you laugh at me, you aggravating jackass!"

As if in response to her anger, the wind exploded with sudden fury around the helicopter, rocking the wreckage.

She didn't seem to notice as she braced herself, her incandescent eyes riddling him with azure-hot holes.

And he just loved it.

He raised a placating hand, tried to pretend a measure of sobriety. It was far harder than anything he'd done tonight. Right along with not reaching out and dragging her back against him. The woman sabotaged his propriety sense and either caressed, aroused or tickled all others.

"I wouldn't dare. And then, this is delight, not ridicule." His left hand rubbed the sting of her blow, as if to trap the feel of her flesh against his, even in anger. His lips were still burning with the memory of capturing hers, his tongue from tangling with hers, tasting her intoxication and swallowing her whimpers of pleasure. All of him still tingled from having her, ton of clothes and all, pressed against him. He wanted to get this confrontation out of the way so he could have her there again. "And it's your doing again, you and your endless surprises."

She balled her fists, her bee-stung lips pressing into an ominous line. "How about I give those a fitting end? By fracturing your nose."

Her aggression made the pleasure bubbling inside him spill again into a chuckle as he gave his aching jaw a reminiscent rub. "To go with my jaw?" He turned his face, presented her with a three-quarters view of said nose. "Or do you think it could do with a new one?" He shook his head at her chagrined hiss. "Whoa, that alone could have done the job. It's a good thing I didn't tell you my name when you had your scalpels deep in my flesh."

Her eyes became slits of enraged challenge. "But now I know it, and I'll have those scalpels there again while debriding the wound before closing it. Over many stages.

Or it will fester. And don't tell me you can take care of it yourself, 'cause we both know you can't. Most of the wound track is where you can't reach it. And next time, maybe my nerve block won't be as…effective."

He gasped in mock shock. "You not only flaunt your power over me, you'd abuse that power, disregard your oath to do no harm? You would torment me while I'm under your scalpel? You'd gloat at my helplessness and need, and take pleasure in my pain?" He let excitement at her implied threat spread his lips. "I can't wait."

Her eyes swept him with now blue-cold disdain. "So you have an extreme form of masochism among your perversions, huh? Figures."

"Not to me, it doesn't. At least, it didn't. But I *am* discovering I'd welcome anything from you."

She snorted. He shook his head as he huffed another chuckle. He couldn't believe it himself, how fully he meant that.

Sighing, admitting that for the first time in his life, he was experiencing something beyond his control, he reached for what had survived of his bloody clothes. And though she aimed more detestation at him, he felt her unwilling coveting spread over every inch of his cold flesh, heating it from the inside out. He shuddered at the caress of her eyes over every bulge and stretch of his muscles as he carefully pulled his clothes back on.

His satisfaction rose. Her reactions to him had not only alternated between delightful and brutal honesty, they were as overpowering as his. Her mind might be telling her to slash him open, but everything else was clamoring for his nearness, delighting in his every detail. And of course that was making her madder. At him.

He'd finished dressing before it occurred to him to try the heater. It was still working.

He turned his gaze back to her with a smile, and she slammed him with a disapproving scowl.

"*Now* you turn on the heater. Were you trying to see how long you can last before you succumb to hypothermia? Or were you hoping I'd offer you the best remedy for it?"

"Flesh-on-flesh warming." He almost shivered with imagining the mind-melting sensuality of such an act with her. "And now you've cornered me. I must admit either that I was such a remiss male that I didn't think of it, or such an inefficient field officer that I didn't remember the onboard heater. Will I get leniency points if I cite my reason for failing to think of it to be preoccupation with your golden self?"

"Nah. I have another explanation. You didn't think of it because you're cold-blooded like all *your* species. Snakes."

A laugh overpowered him and sent another bolt of pain through him. "Ah, I've never been so inventively insulted before. I can't get enough of whatever spills from your mouth."

Her smile was one of condescension and disgust. "I'm such a refreshing acid bath after all the slimy, simpering sweetness you usually marinate in, huh, you jaded jerk?"

He put a protective hand to his side as he laughed again and groaned in pain simultaneously. "What you are is literally sidesplitting. It is positively intoxicating what an irreverent, fearless wildcat you are, *ya nadda jannati*."

"Don't you dare call me that again!" she growled.

"Talia…"

She slammed her fist on her thigh in chagrin. "And don't call me that, either. I'm T.J.—no, *Dr.* Burke to you. No—I'm nothing to you. So don't call me anything at all!" He began to say her name again but she bulldozed over his insistence. "And now I take back everything *I* called you.

You're not *monqethi* or *buttuli*. You're just one of those self-serving, criminal dictators. Or wait—since you were sent to retrieve me, you're probably one of their lower ranks, maybe even disposable. Not that it makes you any better than the higher-ups."

Everything inside him stilled.

Then he slowly asked, "You don't know who I am?"

"You're an Aal Shalaan," she spat the name. "That's all I need to know."

Would knowing exactly who he was change her attitude? For the better? By now, he was hoping it would. Her antagonism, now that it seemed there to stay, was fast losing its exciting edge.

Then he inhaled. "I'm not just an Aal Shalaan. I'm Harres."

"Yeah, I heard you the first time. But just Harres, huh? Like you're Elvis or something!"

"Around here? I'd say I'm more Captain Kirk. And you really have no idea, eh?"

Her eyes narrowed on him. "So you're some big shot?"

He huffed, the last traces of elation snuffed. "The third-biggest shot around, yes."

He saw that lightning-fast mind of hers reach the conclusion. She still stared at him, as if expecting him to say something else to negate his declaration and her deduction.

He quirked a prodding eyebrow at her. He wanted to reach the new status quo his identity always triggered and be done with it.

She shook her golden head dazedly, her lips opening and closing on many aborted outbursts, before she finally managed to voice one.

"You're *that* Harres Aal Shalaan?"

"You mean there are others? And here I thought I was the one and only."

"And here I thought the dumb-blonde stereotype had been long erased. Clearly not in Zohayd, if you think I'll believe *that*."

"Actually I think you're superiorly intelligent and extensively informed. In general. In this specific case, I think you're suffering from severe and very damaging misinformation."

"Fine. One of the hallmarks of superior intelligence is an open mind. So here's my mind, wide as the desert and ready for amending info. What is the king's second son and Zohayd's worshipped minister of interior doing on a hostage-retrieval mission?"

"You see? Brilliant. You cut to the core of logic in any situation like an arrow. And as the question is the only one to be asked, the answer is as singular. I couldn't entrust anyone else with retrieving you. I had to be here myself. And I thank the circumstances that necessitated my presence."

She cracked a bitter laugh. "Sure, because it turned out to be me, and I'm unique, magical, and our meeting under these circumstances is an unprecedented and unrepeatable act of munificent fate, and all that over-the-top drivel."

His hands itched with the need to capture that proud, obstinate head, subdue her resentment, resurrect her hunger.

But he knew that would backfire. He was finally realizing the gravity of the situation. The depth of her prejudice. He had no idea what had formed such an iceberg within her, but if he wasn't careful, all his efforts to win her trust would be wrecked against it.

He let the last trace of the smile go. This needed to be serious, heartfelt. That would be easy. He didn't have to act either sentiment. "A few minutes ago, before learning my identity turned you from an ally into an enemy, you would have agreed with all that you now consider devious nonsense."

Her eyes lashed him with more vexation. He realized that her belief that she'd been taken in was exaggerating her anger. "Sure I would have. I was being worked by a master manipulator. But then, after I escaped being interrogated to death by a gang of desert hooligans, anyone would have seemed a knight in camouflage to my fried mind and senses. But you're not being very clever. Telling me who you are was the worst mistake you could have made. You would have served your goal far better if you'd let me believe you were small fry, one of the hundreds of 'princes' with the odd drop of Aal Shalaan blood. Exposing yourself as the premium pure brew only makes you more accountable for the crimes your family perpetrated. It makes you the enemy I'm here to bring down."

Talia watched her words sink into Harres Aal Shalaan.

She'd managed to wipe away that indulgent smile that had seemed permanent on his face a couple of minutes ago. Now she'd gone a dozen steps further, causing his expression to be engulfed in a tide of grimness.

She almost bit her tongue, but she might get poisoned by the venom flowing from it.

But she couldn't stop. Disappointment urged her to pour it out before it ate through her. Her hero, her savior, the man who'd risked his life to rescue her, was an Aal Shalaan. And not just any Aal Shalaan. One of the four big guns. And the one who had as much jurisdiction and even more law-enforcement power than the king himself. Which meant only one thing.

He had more to lose than any other member of his family.

He had *everything* to lose.

And she was using her considerable provocation powers to declare herself in a position to affect those incalculable losses. While she was stranded in the desert with him, with no way of rejoining humanity except through him.

Any bets she ever would now?

She held her breath for his reaction. So rage and indignation and—damn him—*him* were loosening every last one of her discretion screws. But not to the point where she'd lost track of the possible, and expected, consequences.

He lowered his gaze, relinquishing hers for the first time. She watched the long sweep of his downcast lashes as they stilled, her heart ramming her ribcage. Next time he raised those eyes he'd take off the mask of geniality and tolerance. They'd be cold and ruthless. And he'd no longer be her persuader but her interrogator, not her rescuer but her warden.

Then he raised his eyes and almost had her keeling over in his lap.

Those golden orbs were emitting a steady energy, a calming power that seeped through hers, into her brain, flooding her whole body.

The son of a...king was trying to hypnotize her!

And he was almost succeeding. Even now.

So. She'd gravely underestimated him. She'd thought, with the novelty of her resistance depleted, his facade of endless patience and indulgence would crack, exposing his true face. That of an all-powerful prince used to having people cower before him. But it seemed he was also an infallible character-reader, realized that intimidation would get him nowhere with her. So he wasn't playing that card just yet. Not before he gave all the others in his formidable arsenal a full demo.

So Prince Harres Aal Shalaan wasn't who he was just

because he'd been delivered into the royal family, hadn't qualified for his position in the family business because he'd grown up playing desert raiders. He evidently had staying power, was in command of himself at all times. He had long-term insight and layered intelligence, remained on top of any situation. And he had uncanny people skills and truckloads of charisma, made willing followers of everyone he crossed paths with.

He had of her, too. But no more.

The bucket of drool stopped here.

Then he spoke in that polyphonic voice of his, which made her feel as if it was coming from all around her, from inside her, and she almost revised her certainty. Almost.

"I don't know what you've been hearing about the Aal Shalaans, or from whom, but you've been misled. We're neither despots nor criminals."

"Sure. And I'm supposed to take your word for it."

"Yes, until I'm in a position to prove it. I would at least demand you grant us the benefit of the doubt."

"Oh, if I had any, I'd grant it. But I don't, so I won't."

"Won't you at least make your accusations and give me a chance to come up with a defense?"

"I'm sure you can come up with anything you wish. You'd fabricate enough evidence to confuse issues with reasonable doubt. But this isn't a court of law, and I'm not a judge. I'm just someone who knows the truth. And I'm here collecting evidence to prove it."

"To prove what?"

"That you're not all above reproach as you paint yourselves to be."

He gave a shrug with his right shoulder. It was eloquent with concession and dismissal. The man spoke, expressed, with every last inch of his body. "Who in any place of power doesn't have someone with a beef against them?

Ruling a country isn't all plain sailing. Laws and rulings are contested, whether economic, military or judicial, by others with opposing views or interests. In my own peacekeeping and business capacities, I'm sure my decisions and actions always leave someone disgruntled. That doesn't mean I'm evil. I've certainly done nothing criminal in my life."

"Oh, you're too clever to do something overt. But you, Mr. Peacekeeping Entrepreneur, manipulate the law, and people. Like you did me. Like you're still trying to. But I'm on to you. I'm on to your whole family. That you call yourselves a royal family doesn't make you any less criminal. Many so-called rulers were deposed then brought to justice for crimes against their people. As you one day, and soon I hope, will be."

Okay. She'd done it. She'd ensured her place at the top of his blacklist.

And again, the tenacious man refused to get it over with and validate her fear, release his mask.

His face remained the very sight of sincerity, his voice the very sound of earnestness. "You can believe what you wish, Talia. But I will also say what I wish, my version of the truth. I would have come to save you, no matter who you were. And whomever I saved would have been safe with me. Whatever your agenda is, you are safer with me than with your own family. You scoff now, but when you weren't applying your prejudice to me, you, too, believed it was an act of fate for us to share this, to feel this powerfully about each other, to see the other for what we truly are without the help or hindrance of identities and history. I now urge you to look beyond what you think you know, to what you *do* know. Of me. You're a doctor, and you're used to seeing people stripped to their basic nature during emergencies. You've seen me as I really am through the best tests of all—the litmus of mortal danger, and your own valiant efforts at exercising your potent provocation."

She gaped at him for a long moment.

Then she shook her head on a bewildered, belligerent chuckle. "You *should* have been a diplomat. You'd hog-tie anyone in a net of platitudes and persuasions so thick, they wouldn't see the way out and would soon stop wanting one. But it's too late with me, so save it."

His gaze lengthened in turn. She could swear he was struggling not to smile again. At last he exhaled, like a man bound on tolerating a nuisance for life, leveled that supernatural gaze on her. "You believe you have reason to hate us. Tell me."

"I'm telling you nothing. As far as I'm concerned, you're no better than my kidnappers. You're actually far worse. My enmity with them was incidental. I was just the source of damaging info to their hereditary enemies. But with your family, my enmity is very specific. And don't play the 'I took a bullet saving you' card. I now realize why you did. You want what they wanted. And my answer to you is the same one I gave them. You can go take a flying leap from one of your capital's world-record-high skyscrapers."

"Is that how you always reach your verdicts, Talia? You judge by symptoms that have many differential diagnoses and insist on the first one that occurs to you and explains them?"

She gritted her teeth against the urge to punch him again. The man made perfect sense every time he opened his mouth. Was there no provoking him into making his first mistake? "Oh, don't start with the professional similes. You know nothing about me."

"I may not know the facts about you, but I know a lot about the truth. I'm certain of everything I know, through the proof of your actions in the worst possible conditions.

You're brave and daring and capable and intense. You're passionate in everything you do and about everything you believe in, most of all your sense of justice. Be fair with me now. Give me a chance to defend my family. Myself. Please, Talia, tell me."

His every word expanded in her heart like a compulsion trying to spread out and take hold of her. She resisted his influence, slammed him with her frustration. "I told you not to call me that. But since you're breath-depleting and you can talk me under the sand, just call me T.J. if you must call me at all. Everyone does."

This time he let that smile spread on his lips again. "Then something's wrong with everyone you know, if they can look on your beauty and think something as sexless and characterless as T.J., let alone articulate it. I'm calling you nothing but Talia. Or *nadda jannati*. It's impossible for me not to. Deal with it."

She gave a smothered screech. "For Pete's sake, turn off your female-enthrallment software. It won't work anymore. It's making me so sick that I'd rather you use your fists like my captors did."

It was as if she'd hit a button, fast-forwarding his face from teasing to ominous. He rasped, "They hit you?"

She instinctively rubbed the lingering ache in her gut, which had been swamped by far more pressing urgencies. "Oh, a couple did, just for laughs. It wasn't part of the interrogation, since those jerks weren't cleared to engage in that, and I bet their orders were not to damage me. But they couldn't resist bullying the smaller man they thought I was. One made it sound as if it's some duty a true Zohaydan owes any foreigner messing in the kingdom's business."

His teeth made a bone-scraping sound. "I wish I had used something other than tranq darts to knock them out. Something that would have caused permanent damage"

She gave an impressive snort. "Stop pretending to care."

"I can't stop something I'm not pretending. And I would have cared had you been a man, even the spy with the multiple agenda I thought you to be. Nothing is more despicable or worthy of punishment than abusing the helpless. Under any pretext. Those men aren't patriots as they pretended, they're vicious, cowardly lowlifes who can't pass up a chance to take their deficiencies out on those who can't retaliate."

"Right. Like you're the defender of the weak and the champion of the oppressed."

He gave a solemn nod. Then, as if he was renewing a blood oath, he said, "I am."

And she couldn't hold back, blurted it all out. "Like you defended my brother? Like you championed him against the bullies in your family who abused their power and threw him in jail?"

Four

Harres had thought he'd been ready for anything.

He had made peace with the fact that he would never know what to expect next from Talia Jasmine Burke.

But this was beyond unexpected. And he wasn't ready for it.

He stared into her eyes. They were flaying him with rage. But now anxiety muddied their luminous depths. It fit what he knew of her, that his first sighting of the debilitating emotion there wouldn't be on her own account, but on a loved one's.

Her brother.

So that was it. Why she was here.

He knew she'd been determined not to tell him, hated that she had, was madder than ever, at herself. But it was out.

At least, the first clue was. He realized she was talking

about the same T. J. Burke he'd investigated. There couldn't be another one who happened to be in jail, too.

That still didn't tell him why she'd implicated his family in her brother's imprisonment. And it was clear he had another fight on his hands until she gave him anything more.

After a long moment of refusing to give an inch, her whole body started shaking from escalating tension, her eyes growing brighter as pain welled in them. His insides itched with the need to defuse her agitation. But he was the enemy to her now. She wouldn't let him console her while she considered him—however indirectly—the cause of her brother's suffering.

Struggling not to override her resistance and to hell with the consequences, maybe even letting her vent her surplus of anguish by lashing out at him, he let out a ragged exhalation. "You've come this far. Tell me the rest."

She glared defiance at him then echoed his exhalation. "Why? So you can tell me I got it all wrong again? You've said that a few times already. I'll cut and paste on my own."

"*Oqssem b'Ellahi,* I swear to God, Talia, if you don't start talking, I'll kiss you again."

Outrage flared in her eyes. And, he was certain, unwilling remembrance and involuntary temptation, too. That only seemed to pour fuel on her indignation. He would have been thrilled that her attraction was so fierce it defied even her hostility. *If* the grimness of the situation wasn't mounting by the second. Then she thrilled him anyway.

She hissed, "My earlier 'feminine' threat of chomping a part of you off stands. It'll just be your lips instead of your hand."

He inclined his head at her, suppressing the smile spreading inside him. He couldn't exhibit any levity. She'd only put the worst possible interpretation to it. "Why bother when you'd only end up fixing it? Talk, Talia. If I'm to be punished for it, at least face me with the details of my charge."

Her scowl darkened. "I again remind you I'm not the police. I don't owe you a reading of the charges against you. I'm the family of the victim, and you're the family of the criminals."

"So what did my family of criminals do?" he prodded. "Don't leave me in suspense any longer."

She huffed some curses about his being a persistent pain in the posterior under her breath, then finally said, "My brother—my *twin*—" she paused to skewer him with a glare of pure loathing "—was working in Azmahar two years ago. He's an IT whiz, and international companies have been stealing him from each other since he turned eighteen. He met a woman and they fell in love. He asked her to marry him and she agreed. But her family didn't."

So a woman was involved. Figured. Not that he'd expected it.

"The woman's name is Ghada Aal Maleki." She watched him as she pronounced the foreign-to-her name in perfect precision, her eyes probing, shrewd. Then she smirked. "Do turn down the volume of the bells ringing in your head. Very jarring now that the desert seems to have turned in for the night."

He contemplated the implications of the new information even as his lips twitched at her latest bit of lambasting. "Excuse the racket. Bells did go off quite loudly. The woman in question belongs to the royal family of Azmahar. I know she's long been betrothed. But what caused the jangling is to whom. Mohab Aal Shalaan, my second cousin and one of the three men on my retrieval team tonight."

Her mouth dropped open. Then she threw her hands

in the air, looked around as if seeking support from an invisible audience as she protested the unfairness of this last revelation. "Oh, great. Just super dandy. So now I'm supposed to owe *him* my life, too?"

He shook his head, adamant. "You don't owe anyone anything. We were doing our duty. As for Mohab and Ghada's betrothal, it was family-arranged, but I have a feeling both have been working together to sabotage their families' intentions. She first insisted on obtaining her bachelor's degree, then she wanted to finish her postgraduate studies and he gladly agreed, granting her year after year of postponement. I think both want to escape marriage altogether and are using each other as an alibi for as long as they can put off their families. As of hours ago, there's been no sign of a wedding date being set."

She digested this then raised her chin, trying to seem uninterested. "Well, maybe your second cousin doesn't want to marry Ghada, but your family wants him to, at any cost. Must have some huge vested interest in the marriage so they'll do anything to see it comes to pass. When Ghada told them she was breaking it off with your cousin and marrying my brother, they drove him away from Azmahar. But when Ghada said she'd join him in the States, they decided to get rid of him altogether.

"They fabricated a detailed hacking-and-embezzlement history implicating him in major cyber raids. They somehow got the States to arraign him and put him on trial. He was found guilty in less than two months and sentenced to five years. After the first couple of weeks there, they even arranged for him to be attacked. When he defended himself, he became ineligible for good behavior. So now he'll serve the full sentence without possibility of parole. In a maximum-security prison."

Silence detonated after the last tear-clogged syllable

tumbled from her lips. Only the harsh unevenness of her breathing broke the expanding stillness as her eyes brimmed then overflowed with resurrected anguish, outrage and futility.

And she was waiting for him to make a comment. He had none.

She on the other hand, had plenty more. "T.J.—yeah, that's his name, too, Todd Jonas—looks like me, Prince Harres. I'm tall for a woman, but imagine a five-foot-eight man who doesn't have much on me in breadth and who's got my coloring and the eternally boyish version of my features. Do you have any idea what prison is like for him? I die each day thinking what his life is like on the inside. He's got four years and seven months more to serve. All thanks to your family."

He could only stare at her. He knew in gruesome detail what she was talking about. A prison full of the lowlifes he'd just described, preying on the weakest of the herd. With her brother as an easy, eye-catching target.

She went on, a fusion of terrible emotions vibrating in her voice. "But no thanks to all of you, he's safe. For now. I...buy his safety. I probably won't be able to afford it for long, as the premium keeps going up. In the past three months it has already tripled."

This time when she fell silent, he knew she'd said all she was going to say.

It was endless minutes before he could bring himself to talk. "Nothing I say could express my regret at your brother's situation. If it's true any member of my family was responsible—"

"*If?*" Her sharp interjection cut him off. "Oh, it is true, Prince Harres. And I've been given the chance to prove it. And to do something about it."

He couldn't help coming closer with the urgency her fiery

conviction sparked in him. "What exactly? And given? By whom?"

She looked at him as if he'd told her to jump out of a plane without a parachute and he'd catch her. "As if I'd tell you."

"It's vital that you tell me, Talia," he persisted. "If I know all the details, I can help. I will."

"Sure you will. You'll help prove your own family guilty of fraud, send those involved to jail instead of my brother."

"I can't say what will happen, since I don't know the specifics, but if there's anything I can do to help your brother, I will do it."

She smirked at him. "*That's* more like it. Be inconclusive, make insubstantial promises. Until the silly goose gives you what you bothered to come after her for."

He leveled his gaze on her, tried to convey all the sincerity he harbored in this specific situation and the rules he lived by. "I again say I don't know the specifics. But I will. And when I do, I will act. And I can and do promise you this. I deal with my family members the same way I do strangers when it comes to guilt. If they're guilty, they will pay the price."

"Oh, give me a break."

"You think I can keep the peace in a kingdom like Zohayd by playing favorites? I am where I am, as effective as I am, because everyone knows my code and believes beyond a shadow of doubt that I would never compromise it. And I never do."

Her eyes flickered before they hardened again. "Good for you. But I'm not telling you anything more. What will you do? Force it out of me like those thugs intended to?"

He ached with the need to erase that doubt, that fear, once and forever. He couldn't bear that she could be uncertain of her fate with him. "I again swear that you are safe with me, in every way, no matter what."

His gaze bored into hers, as if he'd drive the conviction inside her mind with the force of his, until she gave an uncomfortable shrug.

He knew that was all the concession he'd get now.

He exhaled. "With that settled, let's get to other vital points. Now that I know you're not the reporter you were…reported to be, and not the spy I suspected you to be, I am wondering if all this isn't a case of catastrophic misinformation on all sides, if you weren't kidnapped for the wrong reasons."

She gave him an exasperated look. "Is that your round-about way to get to the reason I was taken, the same reason you came to extract me? Okay, let's get this out of the way. I came here following a lead that can prove my brother's innocence. And I stumbled on information terminally damaging to the Aal Shalaans. I have no idea how your rival tribe, or you for that matter, got wind of that, and so quickly. Maybe when I emailed my brother's attorney with the developments. So yes, I know why I was kidnapped. Your rival tribe wants the information I have to destroy you. You want it to avoid being destroyed."

And though she was looking at him as if she'd like nothing more than to see him and his family "destroyed," another wave of admiration surged inside him for this golden lioness who was here risking everything for her twin.

He at last sighed. "At least one thing turned out as I believed. But you said you were 'given' the chance to prove your brother's innocence and refused to tell me who gave it to you. Don't you realize that someone is orchestrating all this?"

A considering look came into her eyes. "Sure. Your point?"

"My point is, that someone cares nothing about you or your brother, you're just one of the instruments they're using to their end of causing the most chaos and destruction."

She gave a slow nod. "I never thought they were doing this out of the kindness of their hearts."

"Did they give you anything that might exonerate your brother yet?" She glared at him, then gave a grudging headshake. "Don't you find it suspicious they only gave you information that will hurt the Aal Shalaans?"

Her eyes spat blue fire. "According to them, it will end your reign."

He gritted his teeth at the very real danger of that coming to pass. "Didn't you ask yourself how they intend you to use that information? How using it will help your brother?"

She shrugged again, her eyes losing their hard gleam, the first flicker of uncertainty creeping there. "I didn't have time to think. I just got the info this morning, and within a couple of hours I was snatched. But I came to one decision. I wouldn't give my kidnappers anything. For every reason there is. I knew I wasn't walking out of that hole. So not only wasn't I about to be party to your tribal feud, I sure wasn't helping my abusers become the rulers of Zohayd and the abusers of millions."

He stared at her. There really was no end to her surprises. Almost anyone in her place would have said and given anything for a chance to walk away from the situation. But he'd pegged her right in those first moments. She *would* rather die in defiance, for a cause, than beg for her life from someone she despised and have her survival mean untold misery to others.

He fought the need to pull her into his arms, chide her for being such an obstinate hero. The one thing that stopped him, besides the settling weariness of the whole thing, was that he knew she'd resist. Spontaneous expression of emotion was something he'd have to work on re-earning.

He at last said, "You seem to realize the gravity of the information you have and what having it fall into the hands of the wrong people can mean. Have you decided what you'll do with it?"

Her shoulders drooped. "If I get out of this in one piece, you mean? I'll solidify my facts first. Then I'll think long and hard how best to use it." She shot him a sullen glance. "I may announce it to the world, maybe paving the way for Zohayd to become a democracy at last."

He raised both eyebrows, answering her surliness with sarcasm. "Like one of the so-called democracies in the region? *That* is the epitome of peace and prosperity, in your opinion? You want to save Zohayd from its current wealth and stability, from the hands of a royal family who have ruled it wisely and fairly for five hundred years and place it into the hands of hungry upstarts and militia warlords? And that's only Zohayd. Do you have the first inkling what the sprouting of such a 'democracy' among the neighboring monarchies would do? The unending repercussions it would send throughout the whole region?" He waited until he again found evidence of his points sinking home, in the darkness of grim realization in her eyes, the tremor of ominous possibilities in her lips. Then he went on, "Even if we're deposed tomorrow, and that doesn't plunge the region into chaos, it still doesn't help your brother. Or would you settle for avenging him, seeing his abusers punished, and leave him in prison for the rest of his sentence?"

"I don't know, okay?" she cried out, her eyes flaring her confusion and antipathy. "I told you, I had no time to think. And it's pointless to start right now. I'm in the middle of nowhere where I'm neither help nor threat to anyone. Ask me again, if I get out of this mess in any condition to be either."

Before he could assert that he would do anything to see her to safety, she winced, almost doubled over.

His heart folded in on itself, mimicking her contortion.

Before he could move, she keened, lurched back, and a ball of panic burst in his gut.

He'd taken her word that she was fine. What if he'd left an injury she'd sustained unseen to that long?

He pounced on her, disregarding the pain the careless move shot through his side. He raised her face to his, feverishly examining its locked-in-pain features.

It was only when she tried to escape his solicitous hands that he could rasp, "Talia, stop being stubborn, not about this. Are you injured?"

"No." He firmed his hold on her shoulder, on her head, detaining her with support and solicitude, demanding a confession. She groaned, relented. "It's those punches. Guess I was too distracted to focus on anything my body was feeling till now. But suddenly it…cramps with every breath. You know, like being cripplingly sore the morning after too many sit-ups." Something feral rolled out of his gut. Her eyes shot wider. Then she gave a huff that segued into a moan as her eyes slid down his body to his abdomen then back to his eyes. "What am I saying? It's sit-ups that are probably sore after a stint with your six-pack."

She was distracting him. Even thinking she owed him nothing but hostility, even if she wasn't acknowledging the sincerity of his outrage on her behalf, she was still trying to defuse it.

Before he kissed her, compelled her to carry out her earlier threat, he said, "Talia, I'm going to take off those layers of clothes…"

"Oh, no, you're not!" she squeaked.

"Then you do it. But I will have them off. Then you're going to lie down against me. You're going to stretch those muscles, or they're only going to get worse. I'll massage them with anti-inflammatory ointment."

She remained stiff in his hands for a moment longer before she capitulated, nodded and unzipped her coat.

He followed those capable hands as they undid the layers of clothes beneath it. And when he realized she wore a corset under her man's undershirt, he felt blood desert his head, his heart seeming to pump it only to his loins. He'd been in enough trouble when he'd believed her figure was as uneventful as a boy's. She'd been subduing a very... eventful one.

When she'd moved things around to expose only her midriff, she looked at him awkwardly. She tensed again when he began to turn her, and he whispered in her ear, "Let me take care of you. Don't resist me."

A breath shuddered out of her as she let him manipulate her body onto his lap. "Resistance is futile, huh?"

He smiled down at her as he opened the ointment tube. "Oh, yes. You're in no shape for it right now. Resist me all you like when you're no longer in pain."

She murmured something, a cross between grudging consent and whimpering pain/pleasure as he carefully began to examine her, then spread the ointment he'd warmed first between him palms over her aching flesh. His own flesh ached, too, all over.

Then, as she relaxed into his touch, arched up into his soothing hands, he saw the outline where the impact had bruised her paleness.

All blood was back, shooting into his head.

He heard the viciousness in his voice as he growled,

"Just thinking they had their hands on you at all, let alone in violence, makes me contemplate murder."

She fidgeted at his intensity, her eyes scanning him from her upside-down position. "You mean you don't do that on auto?"

He gave her a chiding glance. "Murder isn't even in the same solar system as manipulation or framing innocents for fraud. Don't you think you're taking your enmity too far?"

She sighed as she relaxed again under his cosseting hands. "I don't know. Maybe you think killing someone a suitable punishment for abusing their power, as an ultimate example for others. As for taking my enmity too far, let me throw one of your brothers in jail for five years, ruin his future and destroy his psyche, and then we'll discuss the exaggeration of my beliefs and reactions."

He stopped his massaging movements when she started to quiver. She could be getting cold or tender...or aroused. He was all of that. And though all he wanted was to rip off his clothes and hers and remedy all the causes of their distress, he knew that must remain a fantasy for now.

With what stood between them, maybe forever.

He kept his hands pressed lightly into her flesh for a few more defusing moments, his gaze tangling with her turbulent one.

Then he removed his hands, helped her up. She declined his help straightening her clothes. Then, with her eyes still wrestling with his, she nestled into the farthest part of the cockpit from him, against her door.

He'd thought he could postpone this until she was less raw, until he'd decided how to go on from here. But her withdrawal snapped something inside him. He had to settle this score. Now.

He pressed closer, showing her he wouldn't take her

categorizing him as the villain and shunning him. "Let's get one thing clear, Talia. *I* was not a party to what happened to your brother. So I have no more to say on this matter. And nothing to apologize for." Satisfaction surged as he saw that sense of fairness of hers flickering in her gaze, admitting his point. "So, until I'm in a position to learn more, and do something about it, I won't let you bring it up again. The subject of your brother is closed for now."

He held her eyes until she gave him a resentful if conceding huff.

He gave her an approving nod, as if sealing their treaty.

Then he said, "Now, to the only subject we should concern ourselves with for the duration. Our survival."

Five

"What do you mean *our* survival?"

Harres frowned at Talia's glower. His was of confusion. Hers seemed to be equal measures that and a revival of anger.

"What kind of a question is that? We're in the middle of nowhere, as you pointed out. The most hostile nowhere on the planet."

"Yeah, sure. So?"

He shook his head, as if it would shake her words into making sense. "You were worried about getting out of this alive. I thought you understood the danger we're in."

"I thought *I* was in danger. The only danger I thought I was in was human-induced."

His exasperation rose to match hers. "You mean *me-*induced."

She shrugged, unfazed by his displeasure. "Yeah, you-induced. I was thinking you'd use my being out here with you as the only way of rejoining humanity, as…persuasion to get me to spill. And that once you were certain I wouldn't give you anything, you wouldn't be too gung ho about my well-being, maybe even my survival."

Blood bounded in his arteries until he felt each hammer against the confines of his body.

He forcibly exhaled frustration before he burst with it. "I thought we got this ridiculous—and let me add, most dishonoring, injuring and aggravating—misconception out of the way."

Her eyes seemed to be giving him a total mind-and-psyche scan before she gave a slow nod. "I guess so. But since that only happened in the past few minutes, I had no time to form an alternate viewpoint. I sure didn't consider for a second that you were in any danger. After the escape, the gunshot and the crash, that is. After you survived all that in one glorious piece, I thought you were home free."

"How is it even possible you think so?"

"Oh, I don't know." Her voice drenched him in sarcasm. "Maybe my first clue was how glib about the whole situation you were. You know, being so cheerful and carefree that you spent most of the past hour laughing and lobbing witticisms in between pestering me for my gender, interrogating me for my agenda and trying to deluge me with testosterone."

And he had to. He laughed again. "It's your effect on me. You make me cheerful and carefree, against all odds."

Her lips crooked up in a goading smile. "Next you'll say I made you kiss me."

"In a fashion. You made me unable to draw one more breath if I didn't. You made me thankful. That I found you, that I saved you, that you saved me, that you exist and that you're with me. And you did make me do it in the most important way, the way all of the above still couldn't have made me. Because you wanted me to."

She gave her lips, which had fallen open, an involuntary lick, her eyes glittering as if she felt his there, tasted him. Then she gave a smothered, chagrined sound before her eyes sharpened again and she thrust both hands at him in a fed-up gesture. "See? Is it any wonder I couldn't even conceive that you had anything to worry about? Who talks like that if he's in any kind of danger, let alone a potentially life-threatening situation?"

He sighed, conceding her point. "Apparently, I do. With you around. But when you talked about my needing your scalpels again, I thought that proved you were aware that I shared your danger."

She waved a hand. "Oh, I was just pointing out that if you held me here at your mercy, you'd be at mine, too."

He huffed a stunned chuckle. "We're sitting inside a crashed helicopter, *our* as well as *my* only way out of here. How can you consider that I'm not right with you at the mercy of the desert?"

Her shrug was defensive this time. "Why should I have considered that? So the helicopter crashed. But you're the one, the only, Prince Harres Aal Shalaan. You must have all sorts of gadgets on hand and can contact your people to come pick you up whenever you want."

He gave a regretful nod. "I do have gadgets, every one known to humankind. And all useless, since we are in a signal blackout zone. The nearest area with possibility of transmitting or receiving anything is over two hundred miles away."

Her eyes widened with each word until they'd expanded to a cartoonish exaggeration. "You mean your people have no way of knowing where you are?

"None."

After a moment of wrestling with descending dread, she seemed to come to a conclusion that steadied her. "Well, that alone will have your armies combing the desert to find you."

"Sure it will." He sighed in resignation. "And they'll find me. In maybe a week. We have water on board for a couple of days."

"They can't possibly take a week to find you!" Her protest came out a squeak. "With all the high-end tech stuff at their disposal, and the whole country out looking for its precious prince, I bet they find you within a couple of hours from the moment they realize you're missing!"

He wanted to press her into his flesh and absorb her worry. But he owed her the truth. He would see her to safety, but he had to prepare her for the grueling experience that he couldn't spare her before he did.

Bleakness clamped his heart, erasing any lightness as he forced himself to decimate her hope. "They have no way of knowing where to start looking. Once my men go back home and realize I didn't precede them, they'll go back to where we originally landed as a starting point to search. But they'll have no way of knowing which way I headed, or how far in which direction I crashed."

"So they'd take longer, maybe a day or two," she still argued. "Surely they'll crisscross the area with enough aircrafts, one of them is bound to spot us within that time frame."

He shook his head, needing to erase any false expectations. Those were more damaging than painful reality. "Relying on visual search over an area of a hundred thousand square miles? With some of the dunes around here over one thousand feet high? Apart from a stroke of luck, I was being optimistic when I said a week."

Silenced howled after his last word.

She stared at him with horror gathering in her eyes.

Then it burst from her lips. "Oh, *God*. You're stranded here with me."

He couldn't hold back any longer. He reached out and cupped her velvet cheek in soothing cherishing. "And I couldn't have dreamed of better company to be in mortal danger with."

Her mouth opened, closed, then again. She couldn't have looked more flabbergasted if he'd said he was actually a plant.

Then she slapped his hand away with a furious sound. "How can you joke about this now? About anything?"

"I'm not joking in the least." He reached out to her again and she snapped her teeth at him like the infuriated feline she was. He withdrew his hand with a sigh. "You can chomp any part of me you like, but it won't change the fact that what I said is the truth. Apart from not wishing you to be in any discomfort or danger, there's no one else I'd rather have with me now."

Tears suddenly eddied in a swirl of silver in her eyes, had his blood churning in his heart before two arrowed down her cheeks.

Then she choked out, "Oh, shut *up!*"

He hooted with laughter. "And you take me to task about being cheerful? I'd be mute if you had your way, wouldn't I?"

She shot him a baleful glance, even as her lips twitched, too. "You've said enough, don't you think?"

"Actually, I was getting to the interesting part."

"What interesting part? How after a few millennia they'll dig our bones from this desert and put them in an exhibit and have scientists hypothesizing that we were actually Adam and Eve?"

He dug his fingers into his seat so he wouldn't yank her to him and claim those lips under his. "How...anthropologically imaginative of you. But I have no intention of becoming a fossil just yet. To this end, we'll have to get out of this hunk of twisted metal and have us a desert trek."

She said nothing. Then she shifted, came closer and patted her lap. "You should lie down again. It's clear you did hit your head and everything you've said and done so far has originated from a swollen brain."

His eyes laughed into her in-doctor-mode ones. "You mean you don't think I have one by default?"

"Sure, as is no doubt expected of your princeliness. But when you start suggesting we take a two-hundred-mile stroll in 'the most hostile nowhere on the planet,' it's time for medical intervention."

"Actually, it's only a fifty-mile stroll. That's the distance to the oasis I was taking us to when we had this little diversion."

He winced inwardly at the hope that swept her ultra-expressive features, rearranging them into the image of relief, then reprimand. "Why didn't you say so? That's not too far."

"That's two marathons' worth. In the desert. With temperatures reaching 120 degrees Fahrenheit at midday and 20 at night. And that's if we're talking a linear path to our destination, which we're not. Not with the seas of dry quicksand in the way."

She raised her chin defiantly at him. "If you're trying to scare me, save it. I didn't come to Zohayd from an air-conditioned exam room in a five-star hospital, but from an understaffed and hectic emergency room in a teaching hospital and a couple of aid stints in Africa. I've been steeped in discomfort all my working years and I've rubbed shoulders with danger and despair quite a few times, by choice."

He had to pause to admire her for a moment before he

said, "I'm only trying to prepare you. I'll see that we get through this, in the most efficient way possible, but I need you to be aware of the facts. So far, we've gone through the easy part. Now we face the desert."

He could see her defiance and determination wavering, uncertainty and fear skirting their protective shell, scraping against it for chinks, for a way in.

But the good thing about challenge was that it kept one focused. Maybe he should escalate it, keep all her faculties locked on it, and on him.

He crooked his lips, knowing by now that would stoke her ready flames. "Anyway, great to know I won't have a swooning damsel on my hands."

"As long as I don't have a swooning dude on mine!"

There she was. Ricocheting right back at him. And he laughed again, shook his head at his helpless reaction.

They were in a demolished multimillion-dollar helicopter in what might as well be another planet for all the area's desolation. He was going to brave the desert's mercilessness in his weakened condition to ensure her safety. She seemed to wish him and his whole family erased from the face of the earth.

And yet, he had never enjoyed anything as much, never looked forward to anything more.

But though he did, and had said they'd focus on their current predicament, he couldn't forget the beef she had with his family. An unjustly imprisoned sibling was the stuff of undying grudges.

This *was* worse than anything he'd imagined. He'd thought he'd be bargaining with a news bounty hunter or an intel black marketer. But he couldn't have imagined this. Imagined her. What she was, how she affected him, what she had against his family.

Even the response he wrenched from her was one more strike against him.

Not that he'd let this, or anything, stand in his way.

He wanted her to give him everything. The info. And herself.

He always got what he wanted.

And he'd never known he *could* want like this.

Everything she knew, felt, was, had to be his. *Would* be his.

He cocked his head and her gaze slid unwilling admiration and sensuality over the hair that fell to his shoulder.

Pleasure revved inside his chest. "Now we're squared on that, how about shelving your enmity until we survive this?"

"*You're* only playing nice because you need *me*. Primary closure of a wound of that caliber is in four to ten days."

He knew that. He also knew she needed to provoke him to keep her spirits up. He let her. "And *you* need *me*. You won't find any passersby here to hitch a ride with to the nearest oasis. So how about *you* be nice to *me*?"

Her eyes stormed through vexation, futility and resignation before she harrumphed. "Okay, okay. I concede the need is mutual."

"It is. In every way. Even if you're too mad right now to concede that."

She blasted him with a glare of frustration. He only grinned and dueted her exasperated, "Oh, shut *up*."

Six

No one could know how absolutely majestic and humbling night could be until they'd been in the desert at night.

Problem was, it was also downright petrifying and alien.

Talia had known they were in the middle of nowhere. But before she got out of the helicopter, that had only been a concept, a figure of speech. Now it was reality. One that impacted her every sense and inundated her every perception. As she at last had the chance to appreciate.

And what a vantage she had to appreciate it from.

Harres had crash-landed them about five dozen feet from the top of one of those thousand-foot dunes he'd spoken of. From this spot she had an almost unlimited view of the tempestuous oceans of sand that seemed to simmer with their own arcane energy, emit their own indefinable color and eerie illumination. At the edge of her vision, they pushed in a scalpel-sharp demarcation against a dome of deepest eternity scattered with stars, the unblinking shrapnel of the big boom. Under their omnidirectional light, each steep undulation created occult shadows that seemed to metamorphose into shapes, entities. Some seemed to look back at her, some seemed to beckon, some to crawl closer. It made her realize how Middle Eastern fables had come to such vivid and sometimes macabre life. She certainly felt as if a genie or worse would materialize at any time.

Then again, she'd already met her genie.

Right now, he was taking apart the mangled rear of the helicopter to get to the gear and supplies they'd need before they set off on their oasis-bound trek.

She shuddered again, this time complete with chattering teeth, as much from expanding awe and descending dread as from marrow-chilling cold aided by a formidable windchill factor.

Though he was making a racket cutting the twisted metal with shears he'd retrieved from the cockpit, and the wind had risen again, eddying laments around them, it seemed he'd heard her.

He straightened with a groan that reminded her of his injury, made her wonder again how he ignored it, functioned—and so efficiently—with only the help of a painkiller shot.

He reached out to her face, cupped her cheek in the coolness of his huge, calloused hand and frowned. "You're freezing. Go back to the cockpit."

She shook her head. "I'm cold, yes, freezing, no. You're the one who's half-dressed."

Her last word got mangled by another teeth-rattling shiver.

His scowl deepened. "We need to set some ground rules. When I say something, you obey. I'm your commanding officer here."

She stuck her fists at her waist. "We're not in your army and I'm not one of your soldiers."

He fixed her with an adamant glare of his own. "I'm the native around here. And I'm the leader of this expedition."

"I thought we agreed we have equal billing."

"We do. In our respective areas of expertise."

"And you're the desert knight, right?"

He gave her a mock-affronted look, palm over his chest. "What? I don't look the part?"

"You sure do." *With a capital T in "the,"* she added inwardly. "But we established that looks can be deceiving."

"I thought *I* established they can't be."

"So you're the real thing. But you could be the prototype and this would remain *my* area. I'm the one qualified to judge which one of us is in danger of hypothermia. And until you get bundled up in thermal clothing like I am, that's you. So now you've done your Incredible Hulk bit and torn away debris and cleared a path to our supplies, you go back to the cockpit. I'll get the stuff we need."

He took a challenging step, crowding her against the mangled hull. "You'd spend hours trying to figure out what is where. I'm the one who knows where the stuff we'll need is, and can get it in minutes. If you can stop arguing that long."

"So I'm the uninjured, suitably dressed one, and your doctor, but you're the expert on this lost-cause aircraft and on survival in the desert. See? We end up with equal billing. So we both stay, work together and cut the effort and time in half."

His eyes had been following her mouth, explicit with thoughts of stopping it with his lips. And teeth.

Then he raised them to hers and captured her in that

bedeviling appreciation she was getting dangerously used to. "You're a control freak, aren't you?"

She let her shoulders rise and drop nonchalantly. "Takes one to know one, eh?"

His lips widened in a heart-palpitating grin. "You bet."

And even though she'd been and still was in mortal danger, and the emergency light at his feet cast sinister shadows over his hewn face, as if exposing some supernatural entity lurking inside him, she couldn't remember a time when she'd felt more...energized.

Strange how the company made all the difference when the situation remained the same.

I couldn't have dreamed of better company to be in mortal danger with.

Yeah, what he'd said.

Not that she'd agreed to it then. Or could credit it now. But there it was. She was actually looking forward to the grueling and possibly life-threatening time ahead. She'd always thrived on challenge and hardship to start with, but she'd never been anywhere near that level of danger. With Harres by her side, anything felt possible. And doable. And anything was...enjoyable?

She shook her head, as if she could dislodge the ridiculous thought. How could anything be enjoyable in their situation?

She had no idea how. But having no rationalization didn't change the fact that being with him was turning this nightmare into the most stimulating experience of her life.

She watched as he bent the last strip of protruding metal, widening the makeshift hatch, then stepped back, gestured to her.

"Report to packing duty, my obdurate dew droplet."

Her heart punched her ribs. No one, not even her parents,

had ever come up with such endearments for her. Nothing anywhere as ready and inventive and…sweet. A woman could get used to this.

And this woman shouldn't. For every reason there was.

She bit down on the bubble of delight rising inside her, popped it.

"That's your retaliation for pigheaded, mulish ox and my assortment of other insults?" she tossed over her shoulder as she preceded him into the cramped space, kneeled on the uneven floor of what remained of the cargo bay and awaited his directions.

He came down facing her, started reaching for articles as if he knew exactly where they were. And he clearly did. Prince Harres seemed to be hands-on in his operations' every level and detail.

After he hoisted on a thermal jacket, he answered her previous barb. "I am sabotaging myself by telling you this, since you might now stop them, but those aren't insults. From you, they have the effect of the most…intimate caress."

His eyes left her in no doubt of what that meant. She almost choked her lungs out imagining his body stirring, hardening, aching in response to her words, to her…

She pretended to cough, waved a hand at him. "Try another one. You're just insult-proof, as you said early on."

"You remember?" He looked disproportionately pleased that she did. "*Aih*, I've never had a hair-trigger ego. And then, most insults are falsehoods or exaggerations, attempts to get a rise. My best payback to insults is to let them slide off me, inside and out."

She gasped in mock stupefaction. "You mean people actually dare to attempt to insult you?"

"I have an older brother. A very...aggravating one. And three younger ones. I'm no stranger to insults. But you will insult me only if you fear me or distrust me."

Her heart hiccuped at the sudden seriousness in his eyes. The cross between warning and entreaty there had the mocking comeback sticking in her throat. She instinctively knew he was telling the truth. That this was the one thing he wouldn't laugh at. The one thing that would hurt him.

And even if she told herself Todd's ordeal balanced out everything Harres had done for her, that he'd only done it for the person who held the vital info he wanted to extract and to keep hushed, her fairness again intervened. He'd been right when he'd said he had nothing to do with Todd's imprisonment. And she didn't believe in guilt by association, even if she made it sound as if she did. And if she went a step further into truthfulness, she had to admit something else.

She didn't want to hurt him. Not in any way.

Lowering her gaze in indirect agreement and swallowing her barbed tongue, she helped him drag out backpacks then cut off the safety belts that still secured crates in the debris.

He dragged one between them, popped the lid open before looking at her with teasing back in his eyes, to her relief. "There's one thing I can't get over. How you don't take words lauding your beauty and effect as your due—my jasmine dew."

She followed his lead, loaded water bottles and packets of dry food into the backpacks. "Next you'll call me Mountain Dew."

A chuckle rumbled inside his massive chest. "Oh, no. You get your own brand names. But we do have canned relatives around."

She stuffed a compartment into one backpack, turned

to the other one, which she noticed was much smaller, as he pulled out another crate. "How nutritionally sloppy of you."

He opened the crate, produced guns, flares, flashlights, batteries, compasses and many other articles, which he distributed between the two backpacks. "I assure you, I never come within a mile of anything canned, except in emergencies. For easily stored quick fixes of hydration and calories, they work in a bind."

"Let's hope we don't have to resort to them. I'd rather drink detergent. But then we won't have to, since you have it all figured out, being the desert knight that you are."

He gave her a stoking glance. "That's right. And this desert knight says close your backpack and let's move on to packing our accommodations."

"You mean this tiny thing is mine?" She eyed his backpack. It was almost as big as her. "And this behemoth is yours?"

He nodded matter-of-factly. "I am twice as big as you are, and can carry four times as much or more."

"Listen, this is getting old. I won't stand by while you bust my sutures."

"I thought they were mine." Before the urge to smack him transferred from her brain to her arm, he added, "If I can't handle it, I'll tell you."

"Yeah, right. Right after you tell me you've sighted the first flying pig."

"But I'm the mulish ox here, therefore perfectly qualified for hefting and towing." Before she could plow into a counterargument, he cupped her face in both hands. The gentleness in his grasp made everything inside her crumple, pour into those palms. "Thank you for worrying about me, for braving exhaustion to spare me. But I've been through worse, have trained to weather the worst conditions for over a quarter of a century." His lips quirked. "Probably longer than you've been on the planet."

That shook her out of her hypnosis. "What? When I told you I've been practicing medicine for years? You think they grant babies medical licenses now?"

"They do, to prodigies."

"Well, I'm not one. I'll be thirty next August."

"No way." He looked genuinely stunned.

"Yes way."

"See? No end to your surprises."

"Stick around. They're bound to end sometime."

"Oh, I intend to. And I bet they never will."

"Didn't take you for a betting man."

"I'm not. But I'll bet on you anytime."

Only then did she notice he still held her face in his palms. And that she was shaking all over again. And that he knew that he turned her into a live wire, knew she was struggling not to succumb. He was also certain she would.

She glared back. *Never again.*

"Don't be so sure," he murmured, his tone a sweeping undertow, his exotic accent sliding over her, enveloping her.

She gasped. He'd heard her thoughts, was taking the challenge.

She shook her head, reclaimed her face from his possession.

With a last molten look of challenge, he resumed packing.

Afterward, he fashioned a sled from the helicopter's remains, using ropes for a harness. On it he loaded a folded tent, their quarters, as he called it, and piled on blankets, sleeping bags and mats.

She matched him move for move, followed his directions,

anticipating his needs as if they'd been working together for years in perfect harmony. And she felt that overwhelming in-sync feeling again, just as she'd felt when he'd assisted her in treating his wound, always reading her next move, ready for it with the most efficient action.

It wasn't only that. She felt her body gravitating toward him, demanding his closeness. She resisted the compulsion with an equal force until she felt she'd rip down the middle.

It's survival, she told herself. Seeking the one person around. Being out here would have been unsettling enough in controlled conditions. But she'd just learned that her predicament was far worse than she'd thought. And with him generating that field of reassurance and invincibility, who could blame her if all she wanted was to throw herself into his haven?

And since when did she indulge in self-deception?

This man had jolted things inside her, like electric cables forced life into a dead battery, from the second she'd turned to face him. Ever since, his nearness, everything he said or did, revved that life into something almost…painful. An edge that scraped everything aside. A knot of hunger that—

"You're hungry."

She jerked at the dark compulsion of his voice, and glared her resentment at him. Couldn't he have the decency to have one crack in his imperturbable facade? It might be self-defeating to wish that her one chance at survival be less than the absolute rock he needed to be to get them out of this, but she still wished it. No one could be *that* unflappable, could he?

He only looked at her with that boundless tranquility that she felt traversed his being. She answered her own question.

Yes, someone could be. And his name was Harres Aal Shalaan.

And he'd just read her mind. Again.

Before mortification choked her, he let her off the hook. "Like you, your stomach snaps its teeth." And she realized it was. She hadn't eaten in over twenty-four hours. "So here's the plan. We eat, prepare our gear then move out. It's 1:00 a.m. now. If we move out in an hour, we'll have around eight hours before things get too hot. When it does, we'll set up camp, hide out the worst of it, then set out again before sunset. The schedule throughout will be two hours on, one hour off. More off if you need it. At a rate of about five miles every three hours, we'll make it to our destination in about three days. If we ration ourselves, our supplies should last."

"If they don't, I'll use the IV fluid replacement. We have a few liters still."

"See? You *are* the best I could have hoped to be with in this mess."

"I'm sure you could have managed on your own," she mumbled, thrilled, annoyed, feeling things were about to get real at last, and struggling not to throw herself into his arms and cling.

"You're admitting I'm not a useless nuisance? I'm deeply honored."

She studied him for a moment, a suspicion coming over her.

Was he doing this on purpose? Every time she felt her will flagging, he teased her or provoked her and it brought her out of her funk and right back in his face.

Whatever it was, it was working. She grabbed at it with both hands. "It remains to be seen what exactly you are. You might still take us in the wrong direction and we'll end up lost. And fossilized."

He laughed. Rich, virile, mind-numbing laughter. Made all the more hard-hitting as it mixed with a guttural groan of pain. "I don't take wrong directions. It's a matter of principle."

Yeah. She'd bet. And she was willing to gamble her life on that. She was going to.

Then again, what choice did she have?

None.

But then again, why should she even worry?

He'd gotten her this far, through impossible odds.

If there was anyone in this world who could get them through this, it was him.

But what if there was no getting through it…?

He suddenly grabbed her hand and yanked her against him.

This time she met him more than halfway. As he'd told her she would.

And whether it was survival, magic, compulsion, or anything else, she needed it. He needed it. She let them have it.

She dissolved in the maddening taste of him deep inside her, with the thrust of his hot velvet tongue as he breached her with tenderness and carnality and desperation. She surrendered to his domination and supplication, all-consuming and life-giving.

Then he wrenched away, held her head, her eyes. "I said you were safe with me, Talia, in every way. I'll keep you safe, and I'll see you safe. This is a promise. Tell me you believe me."

She did. And she told him. "I believe you."

Seven

Talia wondered, for the thousandth time since she'd been snatched from her rented condo at gunpoint, if any of the things that had happened since could be real.

One thing was certain, though. Harres was.

And she was following him across an overwhelmingly vast barren landscape that made her feel like one of the sand particles shifting like solid fluid beneath her feet.

They'd set out over six hours ago. Before they had, during the hour Harres had specified for preparations, he'd studied the stars and his compass at length, explaining how he was combining their codes with his extensive knowledge of his land's terrain and secrets to calculate their course. He'd said he needed her to know all he did. She thought that impossible when she couldn't imagine how he fathomed different landmarks when sameness besieged them. Yet he'd insisted it was vital she visualize their path, too, and somehow managed to transmit it to her.

They'd just embarked on their third two-hour hike. He still walked ahead, seemingly effortlessly, carrying his mammoth backpack and towing the piled sled while she stumbled in his wake with her fraction of their load. Which was still surprisingly heavy. He'd been keeping them on paths of firm sand, so it wasn't too hard. At first. She'd soon had to admit anything heavier would have been a real struggle.

She still continuously offered to carry more. Each time he'd answered that silence would boost their aerobic efficiency and increased the steps he kept between them no matter how hard she tried to catch up with him. It wasn't only adamant chivalry, it felt as if he was making sure he would be the first to face whatever surprises the seemingly inanimate-since-creation desert brought, wouldn't let her take a step before he'd ascertained its safety, testing it with his own.

Acknowledging his protection and honoring it, she treaded the oceans of granulated gold in the imprints of his much larger feet, feeling as if she was forging a deeper connection with him with each step, gaining a more profound insight into what made this unprecedented—and no doubt unduplicable—man tick.

It had been hours since dawn had washed away the stars and their inky canvas, the gradual boost in illumination bringing with it an equally relentless rise in temperature. While that had made each step harder than the last, it had given her a new distraction to take her mind off counting them, off the weakness invading her limbs.

He'd shed one layer of clothing after another, was now down to the bandages she'd changed an hour ago and the second-skin black pants fitted into black leather boots. With his back to her, she was finally free to study him, to realize something.

He was perfect.

No, beyond that. Not only couldn't she find fault with him, but the more she scrutinized, the more details she found to marvel at.

He seemed to be encased in molten bronze spun into polished satin ingeniously accentuated by dark silk. His proportions were a masterpiece of balance and harmony, a study in strength and grandeur. She'd never thought a man of such height and muscular bulk and definition could display such grace, such finesse, such poise. How could such a staggeringly physical manifestation combine such power and poetry of motion? And that was when he was half-buried under the backpack and tethered with the sled's harness. *And* that was only his body.

His face was a testimony to divine taste, hewn beauty in planes and slashes of perfection. In the dimness, his eyes had dominated her focus, but now, as she saw his face from every possible angle, she found something new to appreciate with every self-possessed move of his head. Between the intelligence stamped on the width of a leonine forehead, the distinct cut of razor-sharp cheekbones, the command in the jut of a sculpted jaw and nose and the humor and passion molding sense-scrambling lips, she couldn't form an opinion on a favorite feature. Not when so many other things vied for her favor. The eyebrows, the lashes, the neck, even the ears.

And then there was the hair.

Since dawn's first silvery fingers had touched it, she'd become fascinated with it. But it had taken full exposure to the desert's merciless sun to highlight its wonders.

The color seemed to have been painted from a palette of every earth color in creation, forged from resilient gloss and blended with trapped solar energy. As he walked ahead, the undulating silk seemed an extension of his beauty and virility, transmitting the same power and purpose. Every few minutes, when he turned to check on her, the mass seemed to beckon to her numb fingers to come revel in its pleasures for themselves.

Just then he turned to her again, and that curtain of luxury swished around, catching the nine-o'clock sun, leaving her gulping down her heart. And that was before he gave her that look, that amalgam of encouragement, solicitude and challenge that injected willpower into her veins and pumped it to her limbs. And she realized something.

This was what the Prince of Darkness should look like. To seduce without trying, to enslave into eternity, to induce all sorts of unrepentant sins. To have a woman believe her soul was a trivial accessory.

And she must be starting to hallucinate from exhaustion.

Maybe she should call another time-out before she collapsed.

Problem was, she was exhausted, but nowhere near collapse. Which meant all those thoughts were originating from an unwarped mind.

She tore her eyes away from his hypnotic movements, tried to document the subtle yet rich changes every mile brought to the awesome desert terrain. This place might be a trekker's nightmare, but it was any geologist's, artist's, or nature-lover's dream.

There was so much to delight in as the landscape shifted from magnificent sand dunes to endless gravel-covered plains to sinuous dry lakebeds and stream channels and back again to dunes. The sky, too, transformed from a fathomless ink canopy studded with faraway infernos to a stratus-painted, multicolored canvas to a blazing azure void as the sun rose and incinerated all in its path.

As the heat and glare intensified, she felt so thankful

for the sunglasses he'd had on board—the one undamaged pair that he'd insisted she have—and the cool cotton cloth he'd fashioned into a head cover for her.

At 10:00 a.m. sharp, he stopped.

Though all she wanted was to sit down and never rise again, when he turned to her she rasped, "I can go on."

He shook his head and took off his harness and bag. "No use going farther only to exhaust you so you'll need longer to rest. Or worse, be unable to go on altogether."

"You're the one with the gunshot wound. And I'm used to being on my feet for days on end in my work."

He only took her bag, his smile adamant. "You've gone through the equivalent of four of your grueling days in the last twelve hours." Before she could protest again he overrode her. "But since it's against your principles to be catered to, you can help me set up the tent."

She nodded reluctantly. She was dying to rest, but she wanted to get this trek over with more.

He handed her the tent. Then she found out why he'd offered it to her. Because he knew there was nothing for her to really do. Once she unfolded the thing, it sprang into existence with very little adjustment.

After gathering supplies for the next hours, he led her inside and she was even more impressed. It was big enough to accommodate ten people, and he could stand erect inside it. The sand-colored fabric was tough and cool, the floor's insulation total, the openings sealed once zipped and the ventilation ingenious.

But it was still hot. Too hot. And most of the heat was being generated by her smoldering hunk of a companion.

She looked up from gulping water and found him staring down at her with eyes that flared and subsided like fanned coals.

"Take off your clothes."

She jerked at his dark murmur, a geyser of heat shooting from her recesses to flood her skin.

His eyes left hers, traveled down, as if looking for the origin of the flush that rose to take over her neck and face.

And that was before he added in a will-numbing whisper, "All of them."

She stared at him, at a loss for the first time since she'd seen him. This was the last thing she...she...

Then his lips twitched, one corner twisting up devilishly, belying the seriousness in his voice when he elaborated, "If you don't, you'll sweat liters we can't replace."

Oh. Of course. She bit her lower lip, nodded, dispersing the ridiculous alarm and temptation that had slammed into her.

Problem was, in a usual "all of them" clothes-removal scenario she would have kept her underwear on, which would have amounted to a conservative bikini. But with only a man's undershirt over her now undone corsets, she'd be down to her boxer shorts. And she didn't know what mortified her more. That he'd see her topless, or that he'd see how ridiculous she looked in them.

Oh, right. And that was grounds for risking dehydration?

She nodded, exhaled a tremulous breath. "Any hope you'll turn your back?"

He gave her a mock-innocent look. "Why?"

Then he began to take off what little clothes he had left. He started with yanking off his boots, then straightening to undo the fastening of his pants. Her eyes were glued to his every move, her tongue darting to moisten suddenly desiccated lips. It was only when she realized her eyes were sliding lower with her mouth open as she anticipated the big revelation that she felt fury spurt to douse her mortification and abort her daze.

She met the master-tormentor's gaze defiantly, then started to undress herself. If he thought she'd swoon at the sight of his endowments, that she'd turn around for modesty or try to shield her nudity with virginly arms, he could think again!

As she prepared to yank off the short-sleeved undershirt, Harres stretched and manipulated something at the ceiling. A heavy cloth partition snapped down between them.

She froze, staring at the opaque surface inches from her eyes, until his amused drawl from the other side roused her.

"I did say 'quarters,' plural."

And she cried, "You…you…weasel!"

"Now we move from the farm to the animal kingdom at-large."

The mixture of relief and chagrin choked her as she threw off the rest of her clothes to the sound of his teasing chuckles and tackled her thin matttress as if it were him.

But if she'd thought she'd toss and turn with him inches from her with only flimsy fabric between them, she was mistaken. She felt nothing from the moment she became horizontal, to the moment she came to. To his caresses.

She blinked up in confusion. He was kneeling beside her, running his hands gently over her hair and face and arms.

For a long moment she could only think what a wonderful way this was to wake up.

Then the wonder factor rose exponentially when he smiled down at her. "I called. And called. I even poked you through the partition, to no avail."

She blinked again, looked down, found herself covered in a light cotton blanket. But since he was the one who'd covered her, he must have seen everything. Still, he had covered her so that he wouldn't infringe on her. She struggled with the urge to throw her arms around him and bring him down to her, thank him for being so thoughtful. And more.

Instead, she croaked, "What time is it?"

"Sunset."

She jackknifed up in alarm. "But we were supposed to move out two hours ago!"

"You needed to rest. Now we'll move faster." Before she could reprimand him for not sticking to their schedule on account of her alleged delicacy, he ruffled her hair and winked. "Hop to it, my dewy doc."

She huffed as her heart fired against her ribs. He was suddenly treating her like his kid sister. And it *still* turned her insides into a mushy mess.

As she began to reach for her clothes, he turned back to her.

He took her undershirt away from a hand gone lax. He pulled it over her head, guided her flaccid arms through it, managing not to drop the blanket from where it covered her breasts. He drew it away only once the undershirt was securely in place.

Just when she thought she might suffer a coronary, his intent and serious expression turned incandescent with a surge of something dark and driven. Then he leaned down, opened his lips over the junction of her neck and shoulder.

The feel of his tongue and teeth there was like being prodded by lightning. She lurched under the force of sensations that thundered through her. Then he made it worse.

He glided to the tip of her shoulder, scraping her flesh

with his teeth, gathering the sweat beaded on it with his tongue.

He growled against her skin, sending a string of shock waves through her with every syllable.

She thought he said, "A reward…an incentive…"

Then he pulled back and disappeared into his compartment.

She flopped onto her back, gasping, before she forced herself up and into her clothes. Then she crawled to his side to check his wound before they resumed their grueling trek.

She'd have hours to contemplate the meaning of his words.

And the feelings he'd ripped from her depths.

By the end of the second day, their water supply had dwindled even though they drank only when absolutely necessary. They were losing gallons in this weather and with the exertion.

After midnight they stopped for their hour's rest.

As she drank, she noticed he didn't. She stopped, insisting he drink, that he was the one losing the most fluids handling ten times the weight she was. He only insisted on taking her up on her offer of IV fluids.

He hung the saline bag on his jacket so that she wouldn't have to stand and hold it for him. She protested the inefficiency of this maneuver, and he calmly unrolled a mat from the sled, propped it against the sloping edge of a dune, tossed a few blankets beside it, then caught her hand and pulled her down on it with him.

Before she knew what hit her, Harres was lounging with his back to the dune, his endless legs open with her between them, her hips in their V, her back to his chest, her head on his right shoulder. Then he cocooned them both in the blankets and crossed his arms over her midriff, plastering her to him.

After the first stunned moment, she tried to fidget away.

He tightened his hold, groaned in her ear, "Relax."

Relax? Was he insane?

And he wasn't only that, he was rubbing his lips against the top of her head, inhaling her and rumbling enjoyment as he talked. "Rest. Get warm. It's far colder than yesterday."

"W-we have enough blankets," she protested weakly. "We can roll in them separately."

"This *is* the best method of body temperature preservation."

"And to think I reminded you of that!"

His chuckle, reverberating beneath her ear, sent more waves of distress crashing through her. "Conserve your energy, my Talia. Sleep, and I'll wake you up in an hour, maybe two."

"I—I don't want to sleep."

"I don't either. I'd rather be awake, experiencing this with you."

And though she was far from cold, a tremor rattled through her.

He'd just put into words what she felt.

Though his arms were pressing beneath her suddenly aching breasts and her buttocks were pressed to what she suspected, if couldn't credit, was a massive erection, it wasn't sexual. Or not only so. She'd never felt this close to anyone. This intimate. Even during her now almost-forgotten sexual encounters, she hadn't been any closer to experiencing what she did with Harres than she was to one of the stars above.

She sighed, feeling as if her bones had turned to warm

liquid and the rest of her senses had melted in the sluggish heat of her blood. "Stars. They *are* still up there."

He nuzzled her cheek with his lips. "You don't see them much where you live, eh?"

She sighed in deeper contentment. "Make that don't see them at all. Not for years. But even when I did, I never saw so many. I didn't think there *were* so many. Scientifically speaking, I know there are endless numbers of them in our galaxy alone. But I never thought we could actually see them. There are millions of them."

Her voice sounded intoxicated to her ears. And she was. With the overpowering mixture of the virility enfolding her and the desert's magnificent menace.

His voice poured directly through to her brain, frying more synapses. "Actually, only about eight thousand are visible to us poor earthlings in any given hemisphere, no matter how clear the skies are. And you won't find any clearer anywhere in the world."

That piece of info she hadn't known. She turned in his arms languidly, looked up at him. "Don't tell me you counted them."

"I tried. Then had to borrow good scientists' findings."

"They seem so much more. But I'll take your word for it. I'm just glad they all showed up tonight."

"I ordered them to be present especially for you."

Coming from any other man, that would have sounded like an outrageous—and annoying as hell—line. But somehow, from Harres, this force of nature who seemed to be as one with the powers of this land, *his* land, it didn't seem far-fetched. She did feel as if he had an empathy, an understanding with their surroundings, as if they let him divine their secrets and share their strengths. And then, coming from the man who'd risked his life to save her, who'd lavished such care on her, showed her such admiration and restraint and solicitude, she could easily believe his wish to please her, to gift her. So even the sentiment behind the claim seemed right, sincere. Profound.

And if an inner voice told her it was his need to learn her secrets that fueled all of the above, she couldn't listen. No one could be that good at hiding ulterior motives. And she had experienced him through the worst that could be thrown at a person. He'd shone through with gallantry and resourcefulness, with kindness and control.

She at last sighed again. "I wouldn't put it past you. So they're your subjects, too?"

"Oh, no. They're just old friends. We have an understanding."

Just as she'd thought. "I sort of believe you."

"I could get used to hearing you say that."

The rolling *r*'s of the accent that caressed his perfect English thrummed that chord of ready desire that seemed to have come into existence in the core of her being. Instead of agitating her, it lulled her. She suddenly wanted to sleep. Like this. Ensconced in his power and protection.

She yawned. "You're comfy."

"*I* certainly am not comfy." His chuckle vibrated through her. But it was the powerful jerk against her buttocks, what she could no longer doubt was his hardness, seeming to be getting bigger, if that was possible, that lurched her out of her stupor.

He pulled her back against him. "Don't move."

"But you're...you're..."

"Aroused? Sure. I've been hard as steel since I laid eyes on you. And no, I'm not like that by default. But I don't mind."

"I thought men didn't mind anything more."

"I'm not 'men.' And even though it started out as uncomfortable, veered into painful and is now bordering on agonizing, I've never enjoyed anything more. I've never felt so alive."

She squirmed with his every word, only to be struck still when she realized it only made him harder. She'd never known mortification like this. Or arousal.

Her heart rattled her frame, until he pressed her closer to his body and whispered against her cheek, "I'll never do anything you don't invite me to, Talia. Beg me to."

She believed him. And she sagged back, savoring the way their bodies throbbed in unison. She'd probably be horrified later. But who cared about later when now was here? And like this?

She melted into him, felt her breathing and heartbeats match to his.

Endless minutes of shared tranquility and silent communion later, he kissed her forehead and sighed. "See that star? The one winking azure-blue? I'll call her Talia."

She nuzzled into his kiss, inviting a few more down her cheek, her core now so hot, so drenched and cramping she was breaths away from inviting more. Begging for it.

She pressed her thighs together, alleviating a measure of the pounding, and choked a thick murmur. "It must already have a name."

"I don't care. It reminds me of your eyes."

She giggled. "Maybe you should call it Talia's Eyes."

"Since it's only one, better yet Talia's Eye. So which will it be, *ya nadda jannati?* Talia's Left or Right Eye? I can foresee the myths that would one day be woven around such a name."

"Hmm, if I were a Cyclops, we wouldn't have this dilemma."

"If you were a Cyclops, they'd be the sexiest creatures to ever dominate men's fantasies."

She snorted. "And among all your skills, you acquired a black belt in far-fetched flirting?"

"You're right. I should have stuck with the truth. That it would dominate *this* man's fantasies. The two-eyed, sexy bundle of cuteness I'm wrapped around right now already does."

"I bet you wouldn't say that if you saw me in bloodstained scrubs with my hair spiked like a porcupine. Yeah, that 'atrocious' haircut wasn't for my disguise's sake. That's how I keep my hair out of my way and off my mind."

"You're talking to the man who found you overwhelmingly arousing when you were sporting a beard. I'd find you sexy if you were covered in mud. Oh, wait…now *there's* an idea."

"Mud-wrestling fantasies, huh? How mundanely male of you."

"I don't have those, no. But if it involves you and me, I'll definitely add them to my inventory of fantasies." She twisted around to glare up at him and he only whistled. "Whoa. Maybe I'll call it Talia's Glare."

"Since it's harsh and cold, huh?"

"Far from being either, this star, like your glare, is compelling, hypnotic, resolute, indomitable."

She almost did something stupid. Like kiss the aftertaste of those delicious words off his lips, or swirl her tongue in that solitary dimple that winked in his left cheek when he grinned.

She gave him a pseudo-self-important glance instead. "I'll have you know this glare has my interns and junior residents in the E.R. jumping and remaining in the air until I say down."

"I believe it." Suddenly he gathered her tighter. "Would you consider doing that here?"

Her heart veered in her chest. She struggled to spin

around further in his arms, came to lie sideways over him so she could more easily look into his eyes. "You mean work in an E.R. in Zohayd?"

"Actually, I'd love for you to consider training my men and women in field and emergency medicine."

"Oh…" The idea of remaining in Zohayd after they got through this, the fact that he esteemed her enough to offer her a responsibility like that, and elation at the thought of being where she could see him regularly erupted inside her.

Without thinking of the feasibility of such a scenario, she grinned up at him. "That sounds incredible!" It was only when his eyes blazed in return that she faltered. "I mean, we'll have to, y'know, talk this through when this is over…see if it's even plausible given why I'm here and all and—wait…women? You have *women* in your special forces?"

Impatience spurted in his eyes, probably since she'd changed the subject without giving him an answer. Then they softened again, perhaps in acknowledgment of the difficulties of their situation beyond the real and present danger. "Not many, since it doesn't seem to be one of the career options Zohaydan women prefer."

"I'm staggered that it *is* an option in Zohayd. That you have any."

His smile turned whimsical. "There *is* a difference between being a pigheaded, mulish ox and being a male chauvinist pig."

She rolled her eyes. "I'll never hear the end of that, will I?"

"Do you want to hear it?" he teased.

She thought for a moment. Then grinned impishly. "Nah."

With that, they both fell silent and snuggled deeper into each other as if by agreement.

After an hour of being melded together in deepening companionship, during which she'd simultaneously managed to remain molten and he to remain hard, they set off again.

The third day came. And passed.

At the end of the fourth day, their supplies had been all but exhausted. And there was no sign of the oasis.

On the fifth day, after sunset, as they'd set out on their cycle of hikes and rests, Harres had done something that had dread and desperation taking hold of her.

He'd dumped all their gear.

When she'd protested, he'd fallen silent for a long moment. Then he'd looked at her solemnly.

He'd said that she had no reason to believe he knew what he was doing anymore. But he could no longer afford to go at that pace. Would she trust him to know what they needed to survive, to reach the oasis?

And she'd trusted him.

But they hadn't reached the oasis.

Ten hours later, she'd been unable to go on.

She'd collapsed. Harres had managed to catch her before she hit the ground. He'd laid her down with utmost gentleness, held her in his solid embrace, raining on her soothing kisses and pleas for forgiveness.

She'd succumbed to unconsciousness thinking those would be the last things she felt and heard in her life.

But she woke up to find herself wrapped in the two blankets left with them. And Harres's jacket. She was parched and frying alive in the blistering heat of midday. Emphasis on *alive*.

And she realized another thing.

She was alone.

She struggled out of the tight cocoon, sat up. Harres was nowhere in sight.

He'd left her?

No. She knew he never would.

But what if something had happened to him? What if their enemies had found them? Would the prince of Zohayd be a bigger hand to gamble with in their quest for the throne? How would they use him? What would they do to him?

She sobbed. No tears came from her dehydrated eyes. She drifted in and out of consciousness. And even in waking moments, nightmares preyed on her. Showed her Harres, abused and worse, and all because he'd come for her....

Oh, God, Harres...please...

Then, as if in answer to her plea, he was there. She knew he wasn't *really* there. She was hallucinating with dehydration.

For this Harres was not the sand-car-and-helicopter-riding modern desert knight, but one on a white horse. Galloping her way as if he rode the wind, as one with the magnificent animal, made of the same energy, the same nobleness and fierceness and determination. Her knight coming to save her.

But there was no saving her. This was the end.

Not that it was too bad. She had only two regrets. That she hadn't saved Todd, and that she had let everything stand in the way between her and Harres.

If she had her time with him to live again, if she had more time with him, she would disregard it all and just be with him, experience all she could of him, while she could.

Now it was too late, and she would never know his passion for real.

What a waste.

Her dream Harres leaped off his horse before it came to a halt, spraying sand in a wide arc with the sudden abortion of its manic momentum. Harres descended on her, the wings of his white shroud spread like a great eagle's, enveloping her in peace and contentment. She was so thankful her intense desire had given her such a tangible last manifestation of the man she loved...yes, *loved*....

She could barely whisper her bliss to the apparition. "Harres...you feel so good..."

"Talia, *nadda jannati,* forgive me for leaving you."

"S'okay...I just wish...you didn't have...to leave, too."

His regal head, covered in a sun-reflecting white *ghotrah,* descended to protect her from the glare, his magical eyes emitting rays of pure-gold anxiety.

She sighed again. "You make...an incredible...angel, Harres. My guardian angel. Too bad you're here now...as that other angel guy...the death guy..."

"What?"

Talia winced. She'd been floating in the layers of Harres's voice, so deliciously deep and emotional. Now it boomed with sharpness and alarm.

"You're alive and you'll be well. Just drink, *ya talyeti.*" She found nectar on her lips, gulped it without will or question, felt life surging into her as she sank in the delight of his crooning praise and encouragement to her, pouring hoarse explanations. "If I'd carried you, I wouldn't have been able to reach the oasis. So I left you, ran there. It took me six more hours, and two to ride back. I died of dread each second away from you. But I'm back, and you're alive, Talia."

"Y-you're sure?"

His face convulsed in her wavering focus. "Sure I'm sure. Now please drink, my precious dew droplet. Soon you'll be as good as ever."

"Don't you mean a-as bad?"

She felt herself gathered into arms that trembled, pressed against a chest that heaved, her depletion probably shaking up her perceptions. "There you are. My snarky gift from *Ullah*."

"You say…the most wonderful things. You are the most w-wonderful thing…that ever happened…to me…"

Then she surrendered to oblivion in the safety of his arms.

In the dreamscape that claimed her at once, she thought she heard him say, "It's you who are the most wonderful thing that ever happened to me, *ya habibati*."

Eight

Harres ignored pain, smothered exhaustion.

He had to last until he got Talia back to the oasis.

Those who'd ridden with him offered again to take care of her, of both of them.

He couldn't let them. Wouldn't. He had to be the one to carry her to safety. As he'd promised.

He asked a few of them to go back in his and Talia's tracks before they were wiped away by the incoming sandstorm, to retrieve what he'd ditched. The medical supplies most of all. He let those who stayed with him help secure Talia astride the horse, ensconced in his arms like he'd had her during their rests between the punishing hikes.

The ride back to the oasis took longer. Too long. Each moment seemed to expand, to refuse to let the next replace it, bound on prolonging his ordeal, on giving him more time to relive the hell of being forced to leave her behind.

He'd gone further out of his mind with each bounding

step away from her. He'd struggled to force himself to focus so he could see his path to the oasis, their ticket to survival. But the sight of her bundled up in blankets and ensconced in the barricade of a steep dune had been branded on his brain. He'd lost chunks of sanity with each hour, knowing the blankets' protection would turn to suffocation once the desert turned from an arctic wasteland to a blazing inferno. He'd prayed the message he'd left her in the sand wouldn't be wiped away by the ruthless winds, that she'd heard his plea before he'd left, to please, please wake up soon, read it, unwrap herself and use the blankets as shelter with the tent prop he'd kept.

But the message had been obliterated. And she'd unwrapped herself but hadn't taken refuge from the baking sun. After more than five days of ordeals almost beyond human tolerance, it had been a miracle she'd lasted that long. The only reason he had was because he was bound on saving her.

He gathered her tighter to his body, his heart draining of blood all over again as he imagined her waking up alone and finding no explanation for his disappearance.

It had been his miscalculations that had led to this situation. The terrain had changed beyond recognition from the last time he'd been there, and fearing the lethality of the quicksand areas that were the major factor behind the segregation of the oasis, he'd taken a much wider safety margin around their now obscured boundaries. He'd ditched their supplies too late, when doing so no longer meant quickening their progress, with irreversible exhaustion setting in.

He'd stumbled into the oasis's outer limits a few stages beyond depleted. He'd seen how he'd looked in the horrified expressions of those who'd run to him with water and efforts to spare him another step. Their horror had only risen when they'd realized he was bleeding. In his mad dash, he'd torn Talia's meticulous sutures.

He'd let the oasis people bandage and clothe him in weather-appropriate clothes, gulped down reviving drinks only because he knew he'd be no good to Talia if he didn't get repaired and refueled. He'd still given it all only minutes before he'd jumped on their most powerful endurance horse and exploded out of the oasis with their best riders struggling to keep up with him.

It had been another eternity until he'd gotten back to her.

He groaned. Even in the face of death, his Talia had been the essence of composure and grace. And wit. A chuckle sliced through him as her words echoed inside him again. Until he replayed her last ones before she'd surrendered to oblivion in his arms.

You are the most wonderful thing that ever happened to me….

He shuddered, pressed her closer as if to absorb her into him, where he'd always protect her with his very life.

She might have meant those words for her savior. But he'd reciprocated them, had meant them, for her.

After one more interminable hour, he brought his horse to a stumbling stop at the door of the cottage that had been prepared for them.

He only let others support Talia's weight for the moment it took him to sway off the horse. Then he reclaimed her, folded her into him as if he feared she'd evaporate if he loosened his hold.

Once inside the dwelling that he couldn't register beyond it being a roof over their head and a door cutting them off from the rest of the oasis, he coaxed the mostly unconscious Talia to drink again, glassfuls of both water and a high-calorie, vitamin and mineral drink the locals had concocted for conditions of extreme dehydration and sunstroke.

With utmost care, crooning encouragement and praise, he undressed her down to those ridiculous men's underwear, bathed her in cool water, fanned her dry and then sponged her down again, cooling her raging heat. When he finally judged her temperature within normal, he dressed her in one of the crisply clean, vibrantly colorful nightdresses the oasis women had provided.

Throughout, though her consciousness rose and fell like waves in a tranquil sea, she surrendered to his ministrations, unquestioning, unresisting.

He finally laid her down on the soft *kettan* linen sheets freshly spread on a firm mattress on top of a wide, low platform bed. As he withdrew, a distressed sound spilled from her suddenly working lips, her brow knotting as if in pain.

She couldn't bear separation from him. As he couldn't from her.

He came down beside her, cocooned her with his body. She burrowed deeper into him with each ragged breath until he felt she'd slid between the layers of his being, making him realize again that he'd had so many vacant places inside of him, ones she'd exposed. Ones only she could fill.

He stilled, savoring the imprint of each inch of her, vibrating to her every tremor, his rumbles harmonizing with her unintelligible purrs of fatigue and pure contentment.

Then she went limp and silent, her breath steadying, indicating her descent into replenishing sleep.

But he couldn't take that for granted.

At the tattered periphery of his awareness he thought he should seek the oasis elder and ask if there was still time before the sandstorm to have envoys sent to his brothers. Maybe if they moved fast enough, they'd get ahead of it.

But he couldn't bring himself to leave Talia. His only concern was to see to her health and comfort. Until she opened her eyes and her beloved personality shone at him through her heavenly gaze, he could think of nothing but her. Even the fate of Zohayd came second.

He'd do nothing but watch over her until she woke up....

Talia woke up.

For long moments after her eyelids scraped back over grit, she couldn't credit the images falling on her retinas.

She was ensconced in gossamer off-whiteness, drenched nerve-tingling spiciness and sourceless light.

Her surroundings came into sharper focus. She was actually surrounded by a fine mosquito net, lying in a gigantic bed on the smoothest linens she'd ever touched. She'd smelled the scents more than once since she'd come to Zohayd, seemingly a lifetime ago, incense of musk and amber and *ood*. The light was seeping from openings below a low ceiling blocked by arabesque work so delicate it must be almost as effective as the net.

She hadn't turned her head yet. She couldn't. But she saw enough to fascinate her on the side she could see. A wall of whitewashed mud-brick, a palm-wood door and window with shutters, cobblestone floors, two reed couches spread with wool cushions handwoven in a conflagration of color and pattern, with the same distinct Bedouin design gracing a rug and wall hangings. Oil lamps and incense burners hung on the wall, made of hand-worked bronze, simple, exquisite and polished to a dazzling sheen.

Was this another world? Another era?

She should know where she was. The knowledge just evaded her. She also knew she'd woken up many times before. If she could call the hazy episodes waking up. Now fragments of recollection clinked and bounced around like a rain of beads on the ground of her awareness.

Then as moments of wakefulness accumulated, the jittery particles settled, coalesced, stringing together to form a timeline. And she realized what had happened.

Harres had come back for her. Her desert knight had ridden back on a white horse, leading the cavalry. But not before she'd compounded dehydration and heat prostration with sunstroke.

No wonder distortions and abridgments stuffed her head. Yet one thing possessed hyperreality in the jigsaw of the haziness. Harres. Caring for and healing her. Looking so worn-out, so anxious, she would have wept had she been able to.

"Are you awake for real this time, *ya habibati?*"

His voice was as dark and haggard as she remembered from her delirium.

She twisted around, homing in on it. She found him two feet away on her other side, sitting on the floor with one knee bent, primed, slightly above her level with being so tall and her bed so low. He was wearing a white *abaya*.

So she hadn't imagined it.

She closed her eyes to savor the sight of him in his land's traditional garb. He looked regal in anything, but in this, he looked…*whoa*.

Yeah. *Whoa* should become a sanctioned adjective to describe the indescribable. Him. The ultimate in mind-blowing virility. Especially adorned in what he was born to wear.

He stood in one of those fluid moves that never ceased to amaze her, considering his size and bulk. Before her eyes could travel up to his, he swept the net surrounding her away and his *abaya* fell open.

Her gaze snagged on his chest. But for his bandages it was bare, a bronzed expanse of perfection and potency.

This was where she'd sought refuge from jeopardy and exhaustion, the haven that had turned their nightmare into a dream she'd cherish for the rest of her life.

His bandages were now narrower than she'd made them, exposing more of the ebony silk that accentuated each slope and bulge of sheer maleness. If that wasn't bad enough—or good enough—the tantalizing layer arrowed down over an abdomen hewn from living granite, guiding her eyes to where it began to flare…before it disappeared beneath string-tied white pants straight out of *Arabian Nights*. Those hung low, dangerously so, on those muscled hips, their looseness doing nothing to hide the power, the shape and size of his formidable thighs and manhood.

She couldn't breathe. Her insides contracted with a blow of longing so hard, she moaned with it.

Which was good news. If she could go from zero to one thousand in seconds at the mere sight of him, all her systems were functioning at optimum.

"Don't, *ya talyeti*. I beg you, don't close your eyes again."

She hadn't realized she'd squeezed them shut. His ragged plea and the dipping of the mattress jerked them open and up to his. And she moaned again.

The urgency in his eyes, in his pose, doused the heat spiraling through her. Even though his expression made him look more imposing, intimidating even, and even more arousing….

Enough. Say something!

She tried. Her throat was sore and as dry as the desert from disuse and the aftereffects of dehydration and exhaustion.

Her voice finally worked in a thready whisper. "I'm a-awake. For r-real."

He loomed over her, his eyes singeing her with the intensity of his examination and skepticism. "You said that before. Too many times. My sanity can't take much more false hope." He looked heavenward, stabbed his fingers through his hair. "What am I saying? If you're still sleep-talking, this won't make you snap out of it."

She struggled to sit up, managing only to turn fully toward him. "I a-am awake this time. I sort o-of remember the false starts. But I'm not only awake, I feel as good as new." His eyes darkened. "No, really. I've self-diagnosed since coming around, and I'm back to normal. I'm just woozy, which is to be expected, and sore from the exercise of my life and lying in bed too long…."

Her words petered out as she tried to sit up again and took her first look down her body.

She was in a low-cut, sleeveless satin nightdress in dazzling blues and greens and oranges, echoing the exuberance of the room's furnishings.

Heat rose as she imagined him taking her out of her clothes and dressing her in it. Her imaginings scorched her as they veered into vivid, languorous enactment of him taking her out of it again….

To make it worse, he was coming nearer, his anxiousness to ascertain her claim trapping her breath into suddenly full lungs, making the nightdress feel as if it had come alive, sliding over her nipples, slithering between her legs with knowing, tormenting skims, intensifying the heavy throb within.

She wriggled, trying to relieve her stinging breasts, squeezed her legs together to contain the ache building between them. She looked up at him with eyes barely open with the weight of desire. "Say...h-how long have I been out?"

He snapped a look at his watch, before looking back at her, his eyes losing their bleak look. "Fifty hours, forty-two minutes."

"Whoa!" she exclaimed, her voice regaining power and clarity with each syllable. "But that's a very acceptable time frame to get over a combo of dehydration and sunstroke. Good thing I'm a tough nut, eh?"

Elation dawned in his eyes, intensifying their vividness and beauty. "That you are, along with being an in-evaporable dew droplet. And *shokrun lel'lah*—thank God into infinity for that."

Her lips managed a tremulous smile. "So what have you been doing while I was sleep-talking?"

His lips quirked, the old devilry she knew and adored reigniting his eyes. "I took care of you, sent envoys out to my brothers, took more care of you. Then, oh, I took care of you."

She slapped his forearm playfully in response to his teasing then patted it in thanks for his effort to paint his grim vigil in lightness. "Did you take care of *you* at all? Did you get any sleep?"

He gave her a delicious look of mock contrition. "Not intentionally, I assure you."

She now saw the strain and exhaustion traversing his face in lines that hadn't been there even during their worst times. Her heart compressed even as it poured out a surplus of gratitude and admiration. "Oh, Harres, you're such an intractable protector." She caressed his forearm, basking in mixing their smiles. Then she gasped. "What about your wound? Did you get someone to look at it? How is it?"

He gave a perfect impression of a boy mollifying his

teacher before he revealed something that would send her screaming. "Uh—I have good news and bad news."

Her eyes flew over him, feverishly assessing his condition. No. Whatever his news was, it couldn't be terrible. Apart from the evident fatigue, he looked fine.

Her heart still quivered in her chest as she said, "Hit me with the bad."

He gave a pseudograve look. "Your sutures were very good."

"Past tense?" she squeaked. "You busted them!"

He nodded, holding his hands up. "Good news is, there's no sign of infection. See?" He moved his left arm up with minimal effort and no apparent discomfort. "What's more, the oasis people retrieved our medical kit, so you can sew me up again."

"You bet I will!" She subsided in relief at the proof that he was okay. Her eyes darted away from him for the first time and took in the whole room. She could see the rest of the place through the open door behind him. "This place is incredible."

"It is a very special place," he agreed. "It was the previous oasis-elder's dwelling. He died two years ago. Elders' houses remain uninhabited, as a tribute to their lives and leadership. It is an honor to be given this place during our stay."

Her smile trembled again. "Only the best for Zohayd's Guardian Prince."

He shook his head, his eyes bathing her in warmth. "It's not that. Any refugees they claimed back from the desert would have been given the same treatment. I also have a relationship with the people here that has nothing to do with me being their prince. I'm not sure they consider the Aal Shalaans their ruling family, or if they do, that they give the fact much significance."

"Why not?"

"The oasis and its people are considered off-limits to the outside world they live independent of. They are...revered by the rest of Zohayd and all the region, almost feared as a mystic nation who will always exist outside others' time and dominion."

She digested this, the feeling of being in another world and time intensifying, validated. "A nation? How many are they?"

"Around thirty thousand. Yet their refusal to join the modern world in any way makes them unique. Uniqueness is power beyond any secured by numbers."

"Not if they lack the modern methods of defending themselves against intruders, it isn't."

His face closed. "There will never be intruders. Not on the Aal Shalaans' watch. Not on mine."

She believed him. Harres the knight whose honor dictated he protect the helpless against the bullies of the world.

Suddenly, she felt she'd suffocate if she didn't feel him against her.

She held out trembling arms. "So, do I get a welcome back to the land of the awake?"

His face clenched with what looked like pain. For a heart-bursting moment, she feared he'd been placating her about his wound. Then his eyes filled with such turmoil, she thought she'd imposed on him.

Just before mortification caused her arms to slump to her sides, he groaned and sank into them.

The enormity of the reprieve, after thinking she'd lost her chance of having him like that, of everything, had her hands quaking as they slid over the breadth of his back, the leashed power of his arms. Her fingers caressed his vitality, his reality, committed every detail of him to tactile memory, felt him being integrated into her perceptions and senses.

Then she reached his face and translated into awareness what she'd been looking at and not fully registering.

"You shaved."

He smiled into her nuzzling, letting her singe her lips with the pleasure of coasting them over his perfect smoothness. "It was the first thing I did the moment a blade and disposable water were available."

She rubbed her lips over the underside of his jaw. "You know…I've never seen you clean shaven. When I first saw your face in that bathroom, you were already sporting a mighty ten-o'clock shadow."

He rubbed his chin over her cheek, giving her further demonstration of his silkiness. "So you approve?"

"I far, far more than approve."

Her lips traveled up until they glided hesitantly over his, her tongue tentatively laving them in tiny licks, still disbelieving the reality of experiencing this, of their texture and taste.

A rumble poured into her mouth, lancing into her heart just as it spiked her arousal to pain with its unadulterated passion.

Then he broke away from her quaking arms.

She had no power to drag him back into them. And no right, if this wasn't where he wanted to be.

He sat up, severing their connection. Then he rose off the bed altogether.

He stood above her, his heavy-lidded eyes obscuring his expression for the first time since…ever.

Then he drew both hands through his hair and exhaled. "You might be awake, but you're not really all there yet. And you are—fragile, in every way." His shoulders rose and fell on another exhalation. "So now we get you back to fighting form."

Was that why he'd pulled back? He wanted her back to

full health, physically and mentally, before he'd consider changing their status quo?

It made sense. And made her even more grateful to him, if that was possible.

She was a cauldron of seething emotions and needs right now, had no control over any of them. And she needed to know if what she felt melting all resistance was the ordeal talking, the days of inseparable proximity and total dependence, or if the feelings originated from her.

Now that stress and danger were over, would the physical and emotional pull remain this overwhelming? Would he remain the same man who'd done everything to keep their spirits up? It had niggled that he might have exaggerated his attraction to her for many worthwhile ends. Survival, smoothing over a bumpy beginning. And maybe not so worthwhile ones. Gaining his objective—the secret to secure his family and their throne.

So many things hung like a sun-obliterating cloud over the whole situation. Todd's ordeal, the Aal Shalaans' role in it and their current danger, the info she'd stumbled on, Harres's duty as guardian of his family and people.

So he'd done the right thing by drawing away. She'd follow his lead, recover her health and clarity. Until she figured out what was real. Inside her, around her, about him, between them. Or until this mess, this assortment of *messes*, was sorted out.

If they possibly could be.

Nine

A string of eruptions reverberated in Talia's bones.

She would have taken instinctive cover if Harres's arm hadn't been around her shoulder.

He gave her a reassuring squeeze, chuckled in her ear. "No, that's not a firing squad."

Gulping down her heart, she let him resume leading her through the hurrying crowd, still not sure where their destination was, where the feast was being held. "A gun salute for the Guardian Prince of Zohayd, then?"

His grin widened. "That's just how they announce the beginning of their entertainment."

"With an aerial blitz?"

He threw his magnificent head back and laughed before looking his pleasure and merriment down on her. "The extra zeal is in honor of your recovery and your gracing of their feast tonight."

She raised him a wider grin, her heart zooming again

with elation, with anticipation. But mostly, with his nearness.

She'd been up and about for three days now, had recovered fully. But what relieved her was the condition of his wound. Her sutures had been very good. And had remained mostly intact, with only a few needing reapplication. The healing had been spectacular. She'd never known humans could heal that fast. She kept teasing that he must have mutants or local gods in his ancestry. Which wouldn't surprise her.

And during the idyll of recuperation and recreation, they'd remained in the cottage or its garden, with the oasis people coming periodically to check their needs and replenish their supplies. She hadn't wanted to go out, to see more.

She'd had Harres with her.

She now knew that the bonds of harmony and sufficiency they'd forged during their desert trek hadn't just been crisis induced. It hadn't been the isolation or the desperation. It all originated from their unpressured choices, their innate inclinations, their essential selves, and flowed between them in a closed circuit of synergy and affinity.

Being with him *was* enough. Felt like everything.

Tonight was the first night they would join the oasis people. She felt so grateful to them, so humbled by their hospitality. But earlier she'd felt embarrassed, too.

The oasis-elder's wife and daughters had come, bringing her an exceptionally intricate and stunningly vivacious outfit to wear to the feast. As Harres had stood beside her translating their felicity at her recovery and her thrill over their magnificent gift, the ladies had eaten him up with their eyes. She'd wanted to jump to their side and indulge in the pleasure of *oohing* and *aahing* over the wonders of him with those born equipped to appreciate them. Which was every female with a pulse.

But it had been when their eyes had turned to her with knowing tinged with envy that she'd realized. With her and Harres's living arrangement, they must think they were... intimate. And if she was truthful, and she was, they hadn't been only because of his consideration and restraint.

Not one to let misgivings go unvoiced, she'd asked. Was their situation compromising him, a prince in an ultra-conservative kingdom? Now that her staying with him was no longer necessary, couldn't she move elsewhere until his brothers came for them?

He'd said that the oasis people didn't follow any rules but their own. Being one with nature, living outside the reach of politics or material interests, they didn't police others' morality and conduct, lived and let live. But even if they hadn't, he cared nothing for what the world thought. He cared only about what she wanted. Did *she* want to move out?

Her heart thudded all over again at the memory. He'd been so intense, yet indulgent, not taking it for granted that she didn't want to. And she didn't. She couldn't even think how fast the day was approaching when she would move out of his orbit, return to a life that didn't have him in it.

She couldn't think, so she didn't. Plenty of time later to. Her lifetime's worth.

Now with her heart thudding, she investigated the external source of pounding.

In the dual illumination of a waxing moon and raging fires, she saw it was coming from the direction of the biggest construction she'd seen so far in the oasis.

Silvered by moonbeams and gilded by flickering flames, a one-story circular building rose among a huge clearing within the congregation of dwellings. It was made of the same materials but could accommodate probably a few thousand. It had more windows than walls, and flanking its single door, older women in long-sleeved flowing dresses with tattoos covering their temples and chins were squatting on the ground, each with a large wooden urn held between bent legs, pounding it with a two-foot pestle.

He smiled into her eyes. "When it's not used as a percussion instrument, the *mihbaj* doubles as a seed grinder, mainly coffee, and…" A storm of new drumming drowned out his voice, coming from inside the building, making him put his lips to her ears. "The whole rhythm section has joined in. Let's go in."

As they did, she felt as if she'd stepped centuries back into the ancient orient with its special brand of excesses.

The ambiance was overpowering in richness and depth and purity with an edge of mystic decadence to it. Heavy sweet-spicy *ood* incense blended with the distinctive smell of fruit-mixed tobacco that many smoked in their water-filled *sheeshas*. The fumes undulated like scented ghosts, twining through the warm, hypnotic light flickering from hundreds of polished, handcrafted copper lanterns.

The huge circle of the floor was covered in handwoven rugs, the whitewashed walls scattered in arabesque windows, most thrown open to let in the desert-night breeze and the rising moon rays.

All around, multitudes of exuberant cushions were laid on the floor and against the walls, with *tableyahs*—foot-high, unpolished wooden tables—set before them for the banquet.

On the unfurnished side, a three-foot-high platform hosted the dozens of drummers producing that blood-seething rhythm.

"The tambourine-like instrument is the *reg*. The *doff*, the large one with no jangles, acts as the bass drum." She followed Harres's pointing finger, eagerly imbibing the info. "But it's the *darabukkah*, the inverted vaselike drums, whose players keep up the hot rhythm. Usually they wow the crowd with some impossibly complex and long routines before the other instruments join in."

They sure wowed *her*. She felt the rhythm boiling her blood, seeping into her nervous pathways, taking hold of her impulses.

She let Harres guide her to the seating arrangement. But with every step she swayed more to the rhythm, her every cell feeling like popcorn, ricocheting inside her with the need to expend the surplus energy gathering in them in unbridled motion.

Suddenly Harres took her hand and spooled her away then back into his arms, all while moving as one with the beat. "Dance, *ya nadda jannati*. Celebrate being alive and being in paradise."

And being with you, she wanted to shout.

She didn't, let her eyes shout it for her. Then she danced, as if she'd been released from shackles that had kept her immobile all her life, riding the compelling rhythm, moving with him to the primal beat, her heart keeping the same fiery tempo.

Somehow, they wound up in the middle of a dancing circle that he'd either led her to or had formed around them.

The young tribe members swirled around them in intricate routines, the males swooping like birds of prey, bounding and stomping in energetic courtship and persistent demand, the females twirling around like huge flowers, gesturing and tapping in practiced coquetry and eager acceptance.

Harres led her in emulating them, then in improvising their own dance of intimacy and delight in each other.

And for an indeterminate stretch, she felt she'd been transported to another realm where nothing existed but him. She felt him, and only him, as his eyes and touch lured her, inflamed her, shared with her, joined with her, as he moved with her as if they were connected on all levels, as if the same impulses coursed in their nerves, the same drive powered their wills and limbs.

She surfaced from the magical realm to everyone singing. In moments she found herself repeating the distinctive, catchy melody and lyrics, without understanding a word.

Suddenly Harres pulled her to him, turning the energy of their dance into a slow burn of seduction, his lips at her ear shooting more bolts of stimulation through her. And that was before she heard what he whispered.

"Everything before you passed and went to waste."

Her whole frame jerked with the shock, the emotions that surged too fast, too vast to comprehend, to contain.

He pressed her nearer, his voice deeper, darker, the only thing she heard anymore. *"Koll shai gablek addaw daa."*

That was what she was singing along.

Harres was just translating.

But no. He wasn't. He meant it. Even if the magic of those moments, of their situation and surroundings was amplifying his emotions...

The music came to an abrupt end. The silence that exploded in the next moment felt like a freezing splash, dousing her fire.

No. She wanted this time out of time to continue, to last.

But she knew it wouldn't. None of it would.

She could only cherish every second, waste none on despondency.

She looked up at Harres, found him looking back at her with eyes still storming with stimulation. She teetered from his intensity, from the drain of energy. He bent and lifted her into his arms.

People ran ahead, indicating the place of honor they should occupy. She tried to regain her footing, but he only tightened his hold on her. She struggled not to bury her face in his shoulder in embarrassment, to be carried like that, and after the whole tribe saw her dancing like a demon, too.

At their place, he set her on the cushions, sat down beside her and fetched her water and *maward*—rose essence. Then he began peeling ripened dates and feeding them to her.

She fought the urge to do something to be really embarrassed about. Grabbing his hand and suckling the sticky sweetness off his fingers. Then traveling downward...

Going lightheaded with the fantasies, with holding back, she mumbled around the last mouthful, "You do know I'm fully recharged and in no need of coddling, right?"

He shook his head. "You used up your battery with that marathon jig."

She waved her hand. "I'm just saving up for the next one."

He smiled down at her, poured her some mouthwatering cardamom coffee in a tiny, handblown, greenish glass and brought it to her lips. "A sip with each bite of dates is the recommended dose."

She did as instructed, her eyes snapping wider at the incredible blend of aromas and flavors, of bitterness and sweetness, at the graininess of the dates dissolving in the rich heat and smoothness of the coffee.

She sighed, gulped the rest. Sinking deeper in contentment, she turned to adjust her cushions. He jumped to do it himself.

She leaned back on them, quirking her lips at him. "When will you believe you don't have to keep doing stuff for me, that I've never been in better shape? No emergency doctor could have done a better job on me."

"I know, my invincible dew droplet, but would you be so cruel as to deprive me of the pleasure of pampering you?"

Now what could a woman say to *that?*

Nothing but unintelligible sighs, evidently. That was all that issued from her as the oasis elder rose to deliver a word of welcome before waiters with huge trays holding dozens of plates streamed out to serve dinner.

More sighs accompanied the fantastic meal. The food at the oasis was the best she'd ever had. Tonight it rose to ambrosia level.

Harres fed her, cut the assortment of grilled meats, told her the names and recipes of the baked and grilled breads and the vegetable stews. He introduced her to date wine, which she proclaimed should replace nectar as the drink of the gods. But it was *logmet al gadee* that was truly out of this world. The golden spheres of fried dough, crunchy on the outside, soft on the inside and dipped in thick syrup were so good there should be—and probably there was—a penalty for it.

After dinner they danced again, then she shook hands with hundreds of people, thanked them all for the best night of her life. On their stroll back to the cottage, she decided something.

Everything in this place was pure magic.

But she knew that wasn't an accurate assessment. Had she been with anyone else, she wouldn't have enjoyed it a fraction as much. She'd been to idyllic places for vacations before, but had never enjoyed one after her parents died, had stopped trying to years ago....

"What are you thinking, *ya talyeti?*"

She shook off the surge of melancholy, smiled up at him. "This means my Talia, right?"

He nodded, sweeping a soothing hand over her hair, now

supple and sparkling from a miraculous blend of local oils. "Your Arabic is getting better every day."

"I find it fascinating, so rich and expressive in ways so different from English. I'd love to learn more."

"Then you shall."

It was always like that. She wished for something, and he insisted she'd have it. She knew he *would* give her anything, if at all possible.

Feeling her skin getting tighter with emotion, she answered his previous question. "I was thinking of my parents."

His eyes grew softer. "You told me they died. I didn't want to probe. Not a good idea bringing up death and that of loved ones in our situation back then."

"But you want to know now."

"Only if it doesn't pain you to talk about them."

"No, no. I love to talk about them. I hate it that people avoid bringing them up, as if it will remind me of their loss. As if I need to be reminded. It's actually not mentioning them that makes me feel their absence even more acutely."

His eyebrows knotted. "People can be misguided in their good intentions." His brow cleared, his lips quirking. "What I find amazing is that you didn't set them straight."

"Oh, I did."

He chuckled before gentle seriousness descended over his face. "Were their deaths recent?"

"It *feels* like yesterday. And like a few lifetimes ago."

"I know what you mean."

Her heart kicked. "You've lost loved ones, too?"

He shook his head, his gaze heating. "I meant knowing you. It's so vivid it feels perpetually new, yet so powerful it feels as if you have been there all my life, a part of my being." Now what could she say to something so—indescribable?

And worse, that sounded so spontaneous and sincere? Good thing he didn't let her struggle for a comment, but went on. "But I don't have a comparable experience when it comes to losing someone that dear. My mother died when I was five, so I hardly remember her. So tell me, *ya talyeti,* talk to me about your loved ones."

"I feel I lost them simultaneously, even though they died seven years apart. Okay, let me start at the beginning." She let out a shuddering exhalation, let him draw her closer into him, then began. "I never knew my biological father. I knew *of* him, but he didn't want a wife and a kid, let alone two. We had our mother's family name until she married the man I consider my father when Todd and I were two. As I grew up and learned the whole story, I thought my mother the luckiest woman on earth and my father—the man whose name I carry now—the best man in existence. I never saw anyone more in love or right for each other than they were.

"The only problem was, my father was almost thirty years older than my mom. He'd never been married before, always said he'd been waiting for her. For all of us. When I was in my second year in med school, right before his eightieth birthday, he passed away in his sleep, beside my mom. She never recovered. Seven years later, she overdosed on a concoction of the prescription meds I'd been begging her for years not to take. I could have saved her if I was there, but only Todd was home. By the time the ambulance arrived, it was too late."

For long moments after she fell silent, Harres said nothing. Then they entered their cottage, and he pulled her into his embrace, pressed her head against his endless chest.

They stood like that, sharing, savoring, her body throbbing to the tempo of the powerful heart beating below her ear.

Then he kissed the top of her head. *"Ana aassef, ya nadda jannati*. I'm sorry."

He said nothing more. Then they went about their bedtime routine. Once in bed, hearing him moving in the other room, she had a sudden realization. Why she'd always given up on any attempt at a relationship so early, so easily.

With her parents' example, she'd set her own bar high. Every connection she'd attempted had fallen miles below it. She'd soon given up on trying, had been resigned that she'd never have anything like they'd had, and that if she couldn't, she'd rather be alone. She'd become content with a life full of activity and purpose.

Now there was Harres.

"It's…huge."

At Talia's exclamation, Harres pressed his hard body to her back, murmured in her ear, "Yes, it is."

She nestled back against him, cast her gaze over the depression of *el waha*—the oasis that sprawled below them.

It had taken the past four days to cover the place on horseback. Now, on top of Reeh—or Wind, the white horse Harres had ridden on his charge back to save her—she had the best vantage point yet to appreciate it all from.

It seemed the explosion of life among the barrenness of the desert fed the conditions that fueled its proliferation in an endless cycle of balance and symbiosis. Date palms and olive trees numbered in the hundreds of thousands. Wildflowers and cacti were impossible in beauty and abundance. Farmed fruits and vegetables, especially figs, apricots, berries and corn, were astounding in size and taste. And besides horses, camels, sheep, goats, cats and dogs, there were innumerable representatives of the animal kingdom, all like the residents, unstressed and unthreatened.

Deer and foxes let her walk up to them, a few let her pet them. Even reptiles and birds humored her when she cooed to them and presumed to offer them food and seek their acquaintance.

She sighed her pleasure again. "Scratch huge. It's endless. It goes on forever."

Harres chuckled as he unwrapped her from his arms, jumped off the horse and reached up to carry her down. His effortless strength and the cherishing in his glance and touch as she slid down his body sent a current through her heart.

"We can see about three miles to the horizon if we're on the ground, farther the higher up we go. Since we're three hundred feet up, we can see for about twenty miles. And since the oasis measures more than that on its narrowest side, you can't see its end from any point, making it look endless."

She whooped, loving his explanations. "You should consider a career as a tour guide, if ever princes are no longer in demand…." She bit her tongue. Not something to joke about with a dethroning conspiracy going on in his kingdom. He only grinned at her, showing her he knew she'd meant nothing, enjoyed her joke. Grinning back in relief, she said, "I can now see how this place earned its mystical reputation."

"So it's worth the ordeal I put you through coming here, eh?"

"I would have welcomed a trash dump if it had water and shelter. But it isn't because this place meant life to us that I find it amazing. It is a paradise, like you said. Mostly because of its inhabitants. Everyone is so kind and bright and wise."

She left out the main reason why she found this place enchanting. The present company.

For minutes, as sunset expanded its dominion over the oasis, boosting the beauty to its most mind-boggling, he guided her to a spring of crystalline water enclosed within a canopy of palms. The air was laden with sweet plant scents and heady earth aromas, its temperature seeming to be calibrated for perfect comfort, all year round as he'd told her.

As they stopped by the spring, she said, "It would be so easy to live here forever."

If Todd was with her, she amended inwardly, or at least out of prison.

Harres spread a rug at her feet, looked up. "Wouldn't you go out of your mind without modern conveniences?"

She sank down on the rug, reached for their food basket. "Sure, I'd miss a few things. Hot showers for one. And the internet. Uh...I'm sure there's more I'd miss, but I'm drawing a blank right now."

He got out glasses. "How about medicine?"

"Oh, I'd practice it here like I have been so far. I'd probably do far more good in the long run than I do patching up people who go out and drive recklessly or OD again."

He raised a slice of apricot to her lips. "But you're a very complex being, *ya nadda jannati,* a product of dozens of centuries of human evolution. I am best qualified to judge how sturdy and tenacious you are, but beyond the comforts you'd substitute with the pleasures of healthy living and labor, you'd itch for what the people here can't conceive, need challenges they can't provide."

He knew her too well. And she could say the exact same of him. She nodded. "Probably. It's just the simplicity, the contentment and tranquility that breathes in this place is enchanting. If I had my way, this would be normal life and the bustle of the twenty-first century would be the vacation."

"Then you will have your way."

It felt like a pledge. As if he never meant this to end.

Yet she had no illusions, no hopes. Oceans of harsh realities, mountains of obstacles existed between them.

She was a commoner from another country and culture and he was a prince with a binding duty to his people. Then there was Todd's ordeal. She had no idea what securing his freedom would mean, to Harres, to his family. Even if there could be a solution that didn't end up harming them and making her Harres's enemy, he was probably—like that woman her brother had fallen in love with—intended to marry for king and kingdom.

Not that she'd ever put Harres and marriage together in a linear thought where *she* was concerned.

She now watched as he braided palm leaves into an ingenious basket for her fruits. Then she said, "You know, I came here thinking all of you Aal Shalaans were pampered perverts, mired in excess, useless at best, and helpless without your guards and gadgets, that all there was to you was unearned wealth and inherited status."

His nimble hands had stopped midway through weaving his own basket, his eyes becoming somber, contemplative. Then he inhaled. "So what did you think of me specifically?"

She owed him the truth, no matter how ugly it was. Feeling shame surge into her cheeks, she said, "When I first heard the tales of your valor and victories? I thought you were the most obnoxious of the lot, playing at being a hero, taking credit for the achievements of the true but faceless heroes, or at best relying on the safety net of your men's lives and your endless resources to play the role of Zohayd's Guardian Prince. I thought you'd show your true colors when you were stripped of your force field of assets."

He put a palm over his heart. "Ouch. And now you

think all that plus a few more choice put-downs and denigrations?"

She cast him a reproachful glance. "You know what I think now."

"Tell me."

The way he'd said that. The way he looked at her. As if he couldn't live without this vital knowledge.

Breath left her. "You know what you are. You have a whole kingdom who revere the dirt beneath your feet."

He sat up slowly. "Reverence doesn't matter to me. I never do anything in anticipation of anyone's thanks or admiration. I surely don't expect either, or care if I get them."

Her lips twitched. "Too bad. You'll just have to keep your chin up and take shiploads of both like the worshipped prince you are. Judging by the way the oasis inhabitants treat you, you're far more than that to them. And it *is* only you, not the whole royal family. You personally have done so much for them."

"I only do what I am in a position to do. I don't deserve credit or gratitude for doing my duty, but I would have earned disrespect and disrepute if I didn't."

"As you say around here, 'squeeze a lemon on it,'" she teased.

"So I can stomach the queasiness of adulation? Do you at least believe I never expect, let alone crave, any of it?"

"Oh, yes. I saw you squirming when they told tales of your glories last night. You sure don't crave anyone's adulation."

"I didn't say *that*."

Her heart punched her ribs. "You...crave mine?"

His nod was solemn. "I crave your acceptance, your approval."

"Uh…you have been around the past two weeks, right?"

He rose until he was on his knees, towering over her. "I need to hear it, *ya nadda jannati,* in your inimitable words. What you think of me is the only validation I have ever craved."

She struggled with an attack of arrhythmia. But he'd demanded. And the truth was his due, the least she could give him when she owed him her very life.

She gave it to him. "From the first moment, you forced me to reassess you. With every action and word, you showed me you are all that's advertised and far more. Stripped from all the trappings of your power, you proved to be the total opposite of what I thought, with stamina and resourcefulness and bravery that constantly awe me. You showed me you take your duty to protect anyone weaker than you, at whatever cost to you, more seriously than I thought possible in this day and age. I believe you're one of a kind, Prince Harres Aal Shalaan."

His gaze lengthened, heated, until she felt she'd burst into flames. Just when she was about to whimper, *please, enough,* he took her hand, buried his face in its palm for a long moment.

Then raggedly, still against her flesh, he whispered, "You honor me with your opinion. I will always strive to deserve it."

From then on, the atmosphere seemed charged with emotion, intensifying each sensation into near distress.

As if by agreement, they barely spoke as they had their meal. She was thankful for the silence. It gave her the chance to deal with her upheaval and face herself with more truths.

There were Aal Shalaans who hadn't hesitated to destroy Todd's life to gain their ends, but she could no longer dip the whole family in the bile of her anger and prejudice. And just as she didn't know who exactly among the Aal Shalaans and Ghada's family were culpable, there could be sides to the story that would change her perspective. Whatever *that* became, she now believed, from Harres's example, that the Aal Shalaans weren't an evil regime that deserved to be deposed.

Which led her to more realizations. And a decision.

Soon it got chilly and they rode through the now sleeping oasis back to the cottage under the blaze of a full moon.

Inside, they took turns bathing.

The moment he came out into the sitting area, she began. "I decided something when I thought I was dying."

His smile froze, his face slamming shut. "Don't say that again. Don't even think it."

"I need to tell you this." She waited until he gave a difficult nod, then went on. "When I thought it was over, I thought that if I had a chance to do things over, or a second chance to put things right, I'd do what I really wanted to do, with no thought to obstacles or misgivings or consequences. Then you saved me. And I got cold feet."

He didn't ask her to elaborate. He just stared at her, seriousness seizing his face fully for the first time.

She knew this would lead nowhere. And it made no difference.

She loved him. A love that permeated her soul and traversed her being. A love forged in shared danger, fortified by the certainty of mutual reliance. And she was no longer letting anything stop her from expressing that love, from taking what she could with him, of him.

She rose from the low couch, her steps impeded by the ferocity of her emotions. She stopped before him, looked up into the eyes that meant everything to her. Then she made the leap.

"You told me you'd never do anything I didn't want you to, didn't beg you to do. So here I am, begging you. I want you, Harres. I want nothing but you."

Ten

So this was temptation.

Unstoppable, irresistible. To die for.

This golden virago who'd invaded his being, occupied his mind and heart, conquered his reason and priorities.

She stood before him, open, offering everything. He could feel, in every nuance of his essence, the totality of her offer. It wasn't only of her body and pleasures. She was bestowing all she had, all she was, on him.

And if he closed the gap between them now, he'd take all of her, consume her.

But how could he when he couldn't give his all in return?

She *did* have all of him, Harres, the man, the human being. She had since that first night in the desert, when they'd been stripped to their essentials, when their souls had mingled in the most profound ways possible. If he'd had any concerns that the ordeal had augmented his feelings, influenced their depth and direction, the past ten days had erased them, had replaced them with certainty and wonder.

Added to how she'd awed him with the way she'd handled their trials, stood up to and beside him. She'd delighted him with every second of their stay in the oasis. After only a week, even with the language obstacle, she was already the more favorite among the inhabitants.

The day after the feast, she'd set up a clinic, offered her services. He'd thought those who'd relied on healing practices passed down through generations would shy away from her and her modern medical practices and instruments. But she'd anticipated that, offered only her medical skills and whatever the oasis provided of supplies and medicines. After a slow day, she'd been called to an obstructed labor, where she'd saved both mother and twin babies.

Then she'd become a legend. People had flooded in. They'd stood in queues from morning till sunset, when he, who acted as her assistant, insisted the doctor needed rest. She kept proving how she, too, needed nothing beyond her diverse skills to survive and excel anywhere, under any conditions. He told her she was the epitome of the Arabic proverb "A skilled woman weaves with a donkey's leg" and teased her about being Dr. MacGyver.

She wasn't just a healer, but a warrior and a protector like him. She shared his soul in all its breadth and peculiarities. He wanted, *needed* to share the rest of himself with her, for the rest of his life. There was no doubt in him anymore. Harres, the man, was hers. Forever.

And though Harres the prince had divided loyalties, that wasn't what stopped him from proclaiming his love, his devotion. Only one thing did. Her grievance against his family. If everything she'd told him was the truth, she had legitimate reason to want to bring his family—which she perceived as a unit that worked to the same end of retaining power—to her brand of justice. What if he couldn't secure her brother's release and redemption? How could he take her, when he couldn't promise that in return?

Turmoil ripped the bindings of his heart. And that was before she closed her eyes, her chin trembling as two crystalline tears escaped her luxurious lashes.

Then she raised glistening azure eyes and he nearly had a heart attack. "I thought you wanted me, too...."

He couldn't bear it. *Elal jaheem* with the obstacles between them. He *would* obliterate them.

With a sob, she began to turn away. He grabbed her hand, placed it on his chest, felt as if his heart would ram through it to feel the touch of that hand that healed so many, that had saved him.

Her hand shook under his, each tremor an electric shock. Her words' effect was more brutal.

"Just forget I said anything. I've put you in an awkward position, what with all the things that remain unresolved. And then you've probably been flirting with me with no intention of taking it any further, and I understand your motivation, totally—"

"Oh, shut *up*."

Her mouth fell open at his growl, her eyes snapping wide, those eyes that glowed an unearthly blue in the vividness of the honey tan the desert sun had poured over her.

He looked down at her in that satiny dress that hung from her shoulders in relaxed pleats to the floor, another that the oasis women had given her in a shade that attempted to emulate the eyes that so fascinated them. The dress was by no stretch sexy. Not on anyone else. On her, it was the ultimate in eroticism.

She fidgeted, tried to escape his gaze. He wouldn't let her, his other hand capturing her delectable chin.

"Do I have your attention, *ya nadda jannati?*" He waited until she raised moist eyes to him and gave a hesitant nod. "First, yes, ultimately major issues are unresolved." She gasped, tried to wriggle out of his hold. He clung tighter, his hold growing gentler until she subsided in it, gave him her wounded gaze. He groaned. "But not where I'm concerned. My father once told me a man is granted one certainty in his life, one perfection. And it's up to him to recognize it, to seize it, to let it bless his life. He wasted his, for reasons that seemed imperative at the time. My younger brother Shaheen just found his certainty, and learning from our father's mistake, didn't let anything stop him from seizing it. I thought *my* certainty was that I'd never have such perfection. I lived at total peace with that. At least, I did until I found it. Found *you*. So no, Talia, I don't *want* you."

The eyes that had been misting with an escalation of emotion jerked with stricken confusion. Eyes to bring a man, willingly, eagerly, to his knees.

They brought him to his before her.

She gasped, swayed, then a hot sound of protest broke from her as she tried to pull him back up.

He only brought her hand to his lips and pledged it all to her. "*Ana ahebbek, aashagek ya talyeti, ya noor donyeti*—I love you, worship you, and more, my Talia, light of my world."

She went totally still. Her tremors stopped. Her breathing. Her stare emptied of all but shock.

Then she shook her head. "I—I don't—you don't have to say that…I just want to be with you while I can…so don't… don't…"

He rose, gliding his aching body against hers, catching her around her hips and raising her up until she was blinking her surprise down at him. His heart quivered at the incredible sight and feel of the treasure filling his arms, his lips spreading with the pleasure. "I am getting good at getting you to shut up and listen. And yes, *ya talyeti,* I do have to say this, because it's what I feel, *all* that I feel."

She wriggled in his arms until she made him put her down. He smiled all his love down at her, willing her to read into his heart. But when the flabbergasted look in her eyes, the distress didn't waver, uncertainty crept up on him.

Had he seen and felt more from her than there actually was? She wanted to act on the desire that had raged between them from the first moment, but that was all?

The unbearable doubt with all its ramifications hit him like a barrage of bullets in his gut. He swayed back under its brunt.

At last, he rasped the most difficult words he'd ever uttered in his life, "If you don't reciprocate, just walk away, and we'll forget *I* ever said anything."

With his certainty shattered, the expressions that wove in her eyes tangled in his mind. He stopped trying to analyze them, too afraid to hope, too scared she'd end hope.

"You won't take me up on my offer?" she said, slow and husky.

His heart contracted. "Not if you don't feel the same."

Suddenly, something he'd never thought to see in her eyes almost had him flat on his back. A look of unadulterated seduction, so hungry and demanding and erotic, he could swear he heard hormones roar in his arteries.

His arousal jerked painfully. And that was before she gave him a reason-numbing body rub with her hot firmness.

"Sure I can't change your mind about that?" she purred against his neck before sinking her teeth in his jaw.

"Talia…" He growled his agonized stimulation, his

whole body turning to rock with the need to crush her to him.

Before he could push away, her hands tangled in his hair and dragged his head down.

He knew if she kissed him, he wouldn't be able to stop. And he'd rather not have her at all than have her in every way but the one that mattered.

He turned his face away, felt her scorching lips latch on to his cheek, open, moist, devouring. "Don't…"

"Oh, shut *up*."

Her aggressive growl ended with a sharp tug on his hair. Then before his overcharged nerves could fire one more impulse, her lips sank onto his, paralyzing him with their hunger, with their softness and fragrance and taste.

Before the pain of it all could travel to his core, shatter it, she moaned inside him, "I thought it was impossible, but I can love you more. You just made me."

He jerked back, she clung. His whole system was going haywire from the mixed signals. He groaned. "You love me?"

She spread nips and nibbles over his jaw, detonating depth mines of pleasure and ferocity in his blood. "Down to your last pore. I'm sure I'd find even your cellular structure pant-worthy."

The image her words painted, their import, struck him. And just like that, everything inside him surged with jubilation.

He squeezed her off the ground, held her up high, guffawed. "Only you. Only you would say this, my unique dew droplet. I did have to go fall in love with a doctor."

She braced her hands on his shoulders, her eyes burning with desire dueling with challenge dipped in insecurity. "Of all the women you wade in, huh? I did hear the Guardian Prince was also the sultan of a worldwide harem."

He put her down, caught her face in an adamant grip. "Only one woman for me. Ever. You. And I would say everything before you went to waste, but it didn't. It did serve a great purpose. To make me recognize the certainty of your perfection for me faster, appreciate it with everything in me."

She only nodded, her eyes now inundating him with everything in her. She believed him. With just his word. And she was making him believe, too. That he had all of her.

He now truly had the whole world.

He bent, breathed her in, angled his lips against hers. Then he sank. He felt life rush through him, passion cresting in dark, overwhelming waves, crashing inside him. Magic. And love. More. Adoration and beyond. His Talia.

"Talyeti, enti elli, wana elek," he growled in her mouth, between tongue thrusts that breached the sweetness she surrendered with such mind-destroying eagerness. "You're mine. And I'm yours."

"Yes, yes…" She snatched at his lips, hers rising in heat. "How do I say 'my Harres'?"

"Harresi," he groaned.

"Harresi. My guardian knight."

And he did feel hers. Owned. And delirious to be so.

He sank to his knees before her again, bunched her dress in his fists, raised it up in inches, replacing it with his lips, tongue, teeth, coating her velvet firmness in suckles and bites, skimming and tantalizing her, lingering and tormenting himself. Her moans echoed his groans, became keens, then pants.

When he could no longer bear it either, he exploded up and took her dress with him. She flung up her supple arms in a sweep of eagerness and surrender, helping him, urging him. He snatched the garment away as if it was his worst enemy. But before he could step back and look on the treasure he'd uncovered, her hands were attacking his clothes with the same vehemence.

She tore the *abaya* off his shoulders and down his arms. Then with him still entangled in its tethers, she devoured him, her tongue painting him in ravenous greed, her teeth sinking into his flesh in delicate bites, each nip a new lash of arousal. He lurched under the power of each one. Then she moaned, "You taste and feel as magnificent as you look. I want more of you, all of you."

He roared. The pressure in his loins was becoming unbearable. He had to stop her, pull back from the precipice or this wouldn't be the languorous seduction he'd planned it to be. Any more and it would be like a dam breaking the moment he thrust inside her.

No. He wouldn't let her first intimacy with him be less than perfect bliss. He would show her he craved her pleasure far more than he craved his, that his pleasure would always stem from hers.

He tore away from her, snatched his fetters away then stopped. Stood transfixed. Stared at her.

He'd struggled to respect her helplessness when he'd covered her nakedness in the tent. And when he'd tended her in her sickness, his male hormones had been buried under gallons of stress. *Now* he looked.

She'd wrenched an unprecedented response from him when she'd been disguised as a man. He'd thought her the most beautiful creature in creation when he'd seen only her exquisite head and hands. She'd had him balancing on an edge both distressing and intoxicating with glimpses at her assets. But now...

Now he could see himself truly devouring her.

Encased in golden, glowing skin, taut and tight everywhere, her breasts were turgid and peaked, her thighs and hips full and firm, her waist impossible amidst her voluptuousness.

And he could no longer just look, he needed to experience all that, claim it, wallow in it.

"Rao'ah, jenan..." He growled, filling his hands with sunlight and gold and honey made woman. *His* woman. "A marvel, madness—beauty like this shouldn't have been sanctioned by the heavens."

"Look who's talking," she moaned as he took the mounds of her breasts into kneading hands, yearning for their weight and feel.

He felt he'd blow an artery without a taste. He bent to have it, laved their peaks, answered their demand for the pull of his suckles, the grazing of his nips.

"Elahati, my goddess." He swept her up into his arms, didn't register the journey to the platform bed. He laid her on it, arranged her limbs as if they were flowers, tracing every line demarcating her tawny tan from her still-creamy areas with his tongue. "We'll sunbathe naked from now on. I want to see your inner lioness fully manifested. We'll do anything and everything."

A peach flush evened out her color and her eyes turned almost black as she writhed. "Yes...please, anything... everything..."

The totality of her hunger and trust shot to his heart, tampering with its rhythm. He anchored her as she began to buck beneath him, his fingers lost in the mindless pleasure of spanning her sharp concavity, digging into her taut flesh.

She whimpered a white-hot tremolo that attested to a pleasure she couldn't breathe for its power. "Harres, take me...*daheenah.*"

Hearing her say *now* in his mother tongue felt like a giant hammer shattering the last pillar of his control. He would later swear he'd heard the shrieking snap of his mind giving way, the howling implosion of restraint's end.

A rumble rolled inside him like distant thunder as he snapped her turquoise panties down her silken legs. She was golden down to her last secret. Rising on his knees, he barely pushed his drawstring pants down enough to release an arousal that was beyond rock now.

The look of feverish hunger, of shocked intimidation on her face made him want to hold back, take it infinitely slow and gentle. And they made him want to ram into her, ride her, grind his flesh into hers until she wept with the closeness, broke with the pleasure, dissolved in the fusion.

Feeling the world receding in a white noise of incoherence he grabbed her thighs, would have pressed them apart if they hadn't fallen wide-open.

She arched, writhed, tried to drag him to her, inside her.

He pulled back, tried to regain control. She was tampering with his sanity, at the verge of destroying it. He could hurt her. Even if he knew he'd pleasure her, too, he had to hold back.

He opened her folds, forged a path between their molten heat, but denying her the full entry she craved. She came off the bed at the first touch of their most intimate flesh. He laved his hardness in her nectar, rubbing her in escalating rhythm, until she was sobbing. He alternated between shallow nudges and circular strokes, over and over and over, teasing without fully taking.

She rose on her elbows, lips open with distressed gasps, her eyes spewing azure wildness and invitation of anything at all he would do to her.

Then he moved in a tighter rhythm until she fell back

on the bed, legs shaking wide, her back bowed deep as she convulsed into wave after wave of a screeching orgasm.

Seeing her lost to pleasure, pleasure he'd brought her, made his heart thunder with pride, with relief, with uncontrollable lust for more. He was already addicted to the sight, to the experience. He wanted it again. And he set about having it.

He stroked her swollen flesh, soothing it, desensitizing it. Drenched in tears and satiation, yet darkening with a deeper hunger, a wilder need, her eyes seethed as she watched him perform those ultimate intimacies on her, owning her flesh, manipulating her responses, extracting her ecstasy.

Soon, her pleas were a litany. "No, no more…more, you…you…take me, take me, *daheenah,* now, *now…*"

"*Aih*, now. I will take you now, finish you, claim you, brand you. I will plunder you and pleasure you until you weep with the satisfaction, *ya talyeti.*"

He rose onto his knees, kicked off his pants, cupped her buttocks in his hands, tilted her, opened her petals. He started to invade her…and it hit him like a sledgehammer.

He *couldn't* take her.

He almost keeled over her with the realization.

He did slump over her, his head to her breasts, his whole frame shuddering.

She cried out, tried to drag him up, but he resisted her, raised his head, the words cutting him on their way out. "When we get back to the capital. I can only take you fully then." He smoothed the look of distress off her brow, rasped, "But I'll pleasure you now, in so many other ways."

Understanding dawned in the pieces of heaven she had trapped in her eyes. Then a slow, sensuous smile spread her lips. She clamped her legs around his back, pulled him up. He acquiesced, slid over her slippery ripeness, mingling their moans and shudders and sweat.

Once he reached her lips, she gave a throaty moan of scorching seduction. "You *can* take me now. It's safe. For at least a week. You can trust me. I'm a doctor."

So it was a safe time for her. He almost wished it wasn't, and he'd take her knowing that.

If it was up to him, he was sure. He wanted it all with her, now, no waiting. He needed her to know, everything.

"I trust you, *ya habibati,* with my life. And more. And I only cared, for you." She nodded, her eyes adoring him into oblivion, the perfection of her belief pouring fuel on his conflagration. He filled his hands with her, unconditional love made flesh of his flesh. "And I'm safe, too."

She nipped his chin, as if chastising him for needing to voice this. She believed he would never endanger her in any way, didn't need to be told.

And she was opening her arms for him to fill, her beloved body quivering, her every cherished feature emanating her need in bludgeoning waves.

It was too much. He wanted too much. All of her. At once.

His growl sounded frightening in his ears as he sank his teeth anywhere in her flesh on a blind swoop. They dug in where her neck flowed into her soft, strong shoulder like that time during their ordeal when her nearness had meant life. She jerked and threw her head back, giving him a better bite. He took it.

He was a hairbreadth from going berserk. He tried to rein in the frenzy.

Then she made rationing his passion impossible.

"Show me how much you want me." Her voice reverberated in his brain, dark and deep. Wild. "Give me everything, take everything, ride me, finish me. I can't bear the emptiness...*fill* me."

With a growl of surrender he stabbed his fingers into

her short locks, pulled her head back for his devouring. She bombarded him with a cry of capitulation and command. He drove her into the thin mattress with a bellow of conquering lust. And on one staggering thrust, he embedded himself all the way to her womb.

They arched back. Backs taut, steep curves. Mouths opened on soundless screams at the potency of the moment. On pleasure too much to bear. Invasion and captivation. Completion. At last.

His roar broke through his muteness as he withdrew. She clutched at him with the tightness of her hot, fluid femininity, her delirious whimpers and her nails in his buttocks demanding his return. He met her eyes, saw everything he needed to live for.

He rammed back against her clinging resistance, his home inside her. The pleasure detonated again. Her cry pierced his being. He thrust, hard, harder, until her cries stifled on tortured squeals. Then she bucked. Ground herself against him. Convulsed around him in furious, helpless rhythms, choking out his name, her eyes streaming with the force of her pleasure.

He rode her to quivering enervation. Then showed her the extent of his need, her absolute hold over him.

He bellowed her name and his surrender to her as he found his life's first true and profound release, ecstasy frightening in magnitude, convulsing in waves of pure culmination, jetting his seed into her depths until he felt he'd dissolved inside her.

But even as he sank into her quivering arms, instead of being satiated, he was harder, hungrier than before.

Which didn't matter. He had to give her time to recover.

He tried to withdraw. She only wound herself tighter around him, cried out, clung to him.

"There will be more, and more, soon, and always." He breathed the fire of his erotic promise into her mouth. "Rest now."

She breathed her pleasure inside him, thrust her hips to take him deeper inside her. "I can only if you stay inside me. I can't get enough of you, *ya harresi*."

"Neither will I of you…ever." She was driving him deeper into bondage. He loved it. He drove back into her and she pulsed her sheath around him until he groaned. "Tormentress. But just wait. I, too, will drive you to insanity and beyond."

In response to his erotic menace, she tossed her arms over her head, arched her vision of a body, thrust her tormenting breasts against his chest and purred low with aggressive surrender.

Still jerking with the electrocuting release, he turned her around, brought her over him, her shudders resonating with his.

"Give me your lips, *ya talyeti*…" he gasped, needing the emotional surrender to complete the carnal abandon.

She groped for his lips, fed him her life and passion. Then her lips stilled, still fused to his, as sleep claimed her.

Only then did he let go. And he slept. Truly slept for the first time since he'd gone to rescue her.

She wanted to lie on him forever.

For the past four days she'd gone to sleep like that, after nights of escalating pleasure and abandon.

She propped herself up to wallow in his splendor.

Unbelievable. That just about summed him up.

Just looking at him, her heart tried to burst free of its attachments and her breath wouldn't come until she bent closer to draw it mingled with his beloved scent.

He smiled in his sleep, rumbled, *"Ahebbek."*

I love you. She caught his precious pledge in an open-mouthed kiss. He instantly stirred, dauntingly aroused, returned the kiss then took it over, took her over.

"Ahebbak," she gasped her acute pleasure and total love, as he swept her around, bore her down and thrust into her, knowing he'd find her ready and unable to wait. Their hunger was always too urgent at first, it took only a few greedy tastes of each other, a few unbridled thrusts, to have them convulsing in each other's arms, their pleasure complete.

After the ecstasy he drove her to demolished and re-formed her around him, he twisted again to bring her over him.

He sighed in contentment. *"Aashagek."*

He'd explained what that meant. *Eshg* was a concept that had no equivalent in English. More comprehensive than love, too carnal for adoration and as reverent as worship. It fit perfectly.

"Wana aashagak." She rose over him, took a deep breath. "And I can't believe I thought of this only minutes ago, but I wasn't in any condition to think of anything beyond you." She knew this would intrude on the perfection. But she had to say it. "I want you to know everything."

Harres stiffened beneath her. She frowned in alarm as he disentangled himself from their fusion, sat up. It was one of the few times she'd seen him totally serious.

"This time is ours, *ya nadda jannati.* We will not bring anything or anyone into it. Plenty of time for that when we rejoin the world. Now only you and I matter, *ya malekat galbi.*"

Talia shivered at the intensity of passion that permeated his voice. He'd just called her the owner of his heart. By now, she was certain she was.

She was also certain it wouldn't matter.

When they rejoined the world, it would tear them apart.

There was only one thing to do now. Cling as hard as she could to her remaining time with him. And tell him what he needed to know. "I need to tell you."

His golden eyes were explicit with his aversion to letting the world intrude on them now instead of later. But he finally squeezed them shut, giving his reluctant consent.

And she started. "A month ago, I got a letter. It was addressed to Todd. He'd been living with me since he came back from Azmahar, before his conviction. All his mail comes to my house, and I take it to him when I visit. But something made me open this one. Two things. That all mail so far carried only more bad news, and I decided that this time, I'd try to do something about it and tell him only if I failed. The other reason was that it had Zohaydan stamps."

His eyes went dark. He just nodded for her to go on.

"I didn't know what to expect, but it certainly wasn't what I found." She shuddered again with the memory of the explosive emotions the letter had elicited. "The writer said he knew who was involved in framing Todd, that he could expose them, exonerate him. He asked that Todd come to Zohayd, where he'd supply him with the information. He had a huge stake in exposing them, too, but he needed it to be at a stranger's hand. And who better than someone they'd so deeply wronged?

"I realized only after I'd read the letter a dozen times that the writer didn't know Todd was in no position to fulfill his demand. There was an email included, so they could drum out details of the 'mission,' as he called it. I wrote an email explaining the situation, but accepting their mission in Todd's place. Then, right before I hit Send, I reconsidered.

If the writer knew Todd was already convicted, he might give up on the whole thing. And from Todd's reports on the region, I thought he would balk at doing business with a woman. Not to mention that a female foreigner on her own would draw too much attention, all of the unwanted variety. And my plan formed.

"If this person didn't know Todd was in prison, then I could go as him. I had his passport, and I could pass for him with some disguise. I created a new email with Todd's name, emailed him with my acceptance. I got a response within an hour. All I had to do was buy a plane ticket to anywhere in the world to get into the airport's departure gates. Someone would meet me with a pass to a private-jet flight, so I could slip into the region without record of my entry. That worried me, about my departure, but I rationalized they would want me to leave, to carry out their exposé for them. I thought I could also run to the American Embassy if I got into trouble.

"They brought me here. I demanded the info I came for, and my contact told me it was bigger than I thought, that 'my' problems were a part of something that could not only exonerate 'me' but that would destroy the Aal Shalaans, as they deserved to be. Then he called on the cell phone they'd given me. He used one of those electronic voice distorters, said he couldn't afford to ever be linked to what he was about to reveal, wouldn't leave anything to be tracked back to him. And he told me about the stolen and counterfeited Pride of Zohayd jewels, and the consequences that would have for the Aal Shalaans and their regime. I asked how that would help 'me' and he only said I was a bright lad, would work out how to use that info to my benefit. When I started to protest, he said he was in a very sensitive position, had to go now or risk exposure, but that he'd call me later with more info.

"I emailed Mark Gibson, Todd's lawyer and our child-hood friend, to ask his opinion. I didn't specify what my contact had told me, just that I possessed info that could bring the royal house of Zohayd down. Two hours later, I was snatched from my rented condo. The next thing I remember was waking up in that hole in the desert. The rest you know."

Then she felt silent. And realized that tears were streaming down her face. Reliving those past events and anticipating even more anguish and hopelessness, not only for Todd but for her and Harres in the future, broke her heart.

Harres's bleak eyes were eloquent with his acknowl-edgment of the validity of her trepidation. He said nothing, just pulled her back into his arms. Soon, he was kissing her, inflaming her, taking her with a new edge of recklessness, of desperation.

The dread that their time together was counting down to a crushing end made their hunger explosive, their mating almost violent, their ecstasy almost damaging.

Afterward, she lay curved into his body, quivering with the enormity of it all. He pretended to be asleep. She knew he wasn't.

She couldn't sleep, either.

She wondered, once she lost him, if she'd ever sleep again.

As night deepened, the oasis's unique environment somehow warded off the bitter cold of the desert. Even if it had been as bone-chilling as it had been during their trek, Harres wouldn't have felt a thing. He was burning up, from the inside out.

She'd finally fallen asleep. He'd left her side, gone out to try to find air to breathe.

He couldn't find any in the vastness around him.

He stumbled to a stop at the far edge of the cottage's garden, stared up at the preternaturally clear and steady stars. They blurred, swam. The heat seething inside him was filling his eyes with the moisture of frustration and despondence. Just as he'd seen in hers. It had hurt, still did, like a knife in his gut.

What hurt more was that he couldn't wipe those feelings away. He couldn't promise her what he wasn't certain he could deliver. Promises now would torment her with hope. That was even more agonizing than resignation, and if for any reason he failed to keep them, the crash to despair would be far more devastating.

He *would* do whatever it took to secure her happiness. But until he did, he had to keep silent, had to suffer her suffering. And love her with all of his being.

He only prayed it wouldn't come down to a choice between him and her brother.

He couldn't afford to lose her. He wouldn't survive it.

Eleven

Talia lurched awake, the ferocity and satisfaction of Harres's last possession humming in her blood, in her bones.

She stretched, moaning at the delicious frisson of soreness zigzagging through her. He *had* kept his promise of driving her to insanity and beyond. She now thought sanity, like the soul she felt he'd claimed, was a highly overrated and mostly inconsequential trimming.

He wasn't there. But he would be any second.

She rose, freshened up. Just as she finished, she heard the steady clatter of Reeh's hooves at the back of the cottage.

She rushed to the door. The moment she stepped out, gazing up into the twilight of the skies she'd come to depend on seeing, a meteor flashed bright then faded, as if it had never been.

It felt like their time together.

But they didn't behave as if it would ever fade. They both pretended this was forever.

He rode around the cottage, approached her with the smile that was everything worth living for. She rushed to him and he pulled her up on Reeh's back, molded her back to his front, enveloped her within his hot, hard body.

After a while of trotting leisurely in their daily excursion to *al ain,* Talia sighed, snuggled back into the cherishing heat and protection.

"I've come to a conclusion," she announced. He kissed the top of her head, held her more securely, waiting for her revelation. "Getting kidnapped was the best thing that ever happened to me."

He chuckled, hugged her exuberantly. "What a coincidence, since it turned out to be the best thing that ever happened to *me.*"

She sighed, knowing he meant it, nuzzled back into his embrace, soaking up his feel, assimilating it into her being along with his scent, mingled with those of the pristine nature.

Then she teased, "Do you think it's possible I'll get to ride my own horse one day?"

"I have issues with seeing you in danger."

"What danger? Horses here, like the rest of the inhabitants, human or otherwise, are wonderfully understanding of inept foreigners."

"Then I have issues about keeping you in my arms for as long as possible...." He stopped, groaned, amended. "Having you in my arms at every opportunity."

She knew he must be kicking himself for phrasing it that way, for even hinting that their time together would come to an end.

She swerved from the subject, turned lips tingling with the numbness of fear into his neck. "A noble cause."

She felt a ragged breath empty his lungs as he gave her a tighter squeeze, as if to thank her for circumventing the emotional landmine. "None higher. I got addicted to holding you like this, ever since I rode back to the oasis with you."

"Buttuli." She tilted her head back to smile up into his eyes and caught the bleakness there.

Tenderness replaced it, making her wonder if she'd even seen it. But she had. And she wouldn't bring it up.

What was the point of worrying about the future but to taint the purity of happiness they shared in the present?

She rubbed the hair he'd told her he adored, called spun gold milled from sunshine, against his bare chest. Now that he no longer wore a bandage but a local dressing over his fast-healing wound, she'd been wallowing in the sensory nirvana of touching his sculptured perfection at every opportunity. Which was almost always.

"Harres…"

"Yes, Talia, say my name like that, like you can't draw another breath if you don't have me inside you. As I will be, here and now."

The blow of arousal at the thought of him carrying out his intention, here, was paralyzing. And not just because it was a fantasy she'd thought would forever go unfulfilled. They were out in the open, with the oasis people in the distance.

She thought he was only stimulating her, that he'd wait until they were by the *ain,* where they'd shared more than one explosive if hurried mating, but then he lifted her, dragged her voluminous dress from beneath her, let it flow over his lap.

Then, as one hand held the bridle, the other slid around to dip below the folds of the neckline, seeking her breasts. Fire forked to her core as his fingers manipulated her nipples. It burst into flames when he sank his teeth in her nape, like a lion securing his mate.

She swooned back, her already open thighs falling apart wider, moisture dampening her panties.

"Do you know what scenting your arousal does to me?" He growled in her ear as his hand slid inside her panties, his palm gently squeezing her for a moment, winding the rhythm of the throbbing there into a frantic pounding. "I want to taste you again, but I'll have to settle for feeling your heat and your satiny flesh as it softens and melts for me. Show me how much you crave my touch, *ya talyeti*."

Beyond caring that they might be seen, she bucked back against him, widening her thighs, giving him full access. "I'm out of my mind craving anything you do to me, all the time. Touch me, feel for yourself, do everything to me."

With a groan of male possession, he dipped a finger along the molten lips of her sex, sliding its thickness and power on a mind-numbing path to and fro, each pass tightening the coil of agonizing pleasure inside her. She writhed, whimpered, turned her face up to his. He thrust his tongue inside her mouth as he replaced his finger with his thumb and plunged his middle finger inside her. The coil snapped, and she unraveled around him, in his arms on bucking keens. He stroked her inner trigger, stoked it until the climax drained her of the frenzy he'd built inside her.

"Having you lost to pleasure is the most magnificent thing I've ever experienced," he rumbled against her mouth as his fingers still stroked her, avoiding her sensitive bud, until he soothed her, then he changed direction and rhythm, had her climbing to mindlessness again.

Once she was begging, she felt him release himself, his hard length slamming against her buttocks. He whispered in her ear, "Rise up with your thigh muscles like I taught you in the trot."

He was really going to take her here. Like this. The idea almost drove her over another edge.

She rose up and he positioned himself at her opening.

He was saying, "Settle down on me," when her muscles jellified. She crashed down on him.

He forged through her inner folds like a hot lance. She thought she'd gotten used to his length and girth, but it seemed that every time felt like the first time, felt as if he filled her more.

Now the pressure reached an edge of pain, of domination that redefined all her concepts of physical intimacy and pleasure. She was addicted to the impossible fullness, the feeling of total occupation, of trapping such a vital part of him so inescapably inside her and drawing both their pleasure from depths she—and he insisted he, too—hadn't known existed.

By the fourth or fifth buck and fall of the trot she was a mass of tremors, fully at his power, breached to her core, invaded, occupied, pleasured, taken, maddened.

"Ride me...ride me..." was all she could say anymore, all that was left in her mind. She was enervated with an overload of sensation, the pressure becoming beyond her endurance. She needed him to thrust her to release. Before anyone passed.

He only lay back into the trot, let its rhythm layer even more sensation. All the time, he said things that drove her deeper into bondage. "Filling you this way, invading you, being captured by you is all I can think of, I want to be home, inside you, pleasuring you, always...."

And she found another word. *"Please."*

She felt him jerk inside her, grow bigger. She keened, writhed, and he growled, nudged Reeh, pounded into her with all the fury of the gallop. Just when she thought her heart would stop and she would dissolve around him and be no more, his fingers massaged her bud in escalating circles, his teeth sinking into her neck again, his growls a carnal current knotting her heart and core. And she detonated.

A scream welled from her depths, too frenzied to form. The next one would have but he caught it in his palm, gave her his flesh to vent her agonized pleasure on.

She bit into the side of his palm, over and over as breaker after breaker of release crashed through her, receded, built only to smash into her again, scattering and reforming her for the next incursion. The convulsions radiated from the deepest point within her body, which he caressed, spread in expanding shock waves, each building where the last began to diminish. Then he plumbed a new depth in her, seeming to impale her to her heart, releasing his ecstasy there. Feeling him fill her to overflowing sent her thrashing once more. She wished…she wished…

She regained lucidity with a jerk. They'd reached *al ain*. He was still inside her. The pleasure was a continuous flow now, a plateau of contentment. Her head rolled limply over his heart.

"You should have told me you won't just drive me insane, you'll regularly knock me out, too."

He chuckled, a sound of profound male smugness. "I live to please."

She shuddered as he separated their fusion. "And how."

He adjusted his clothes and jumped off the horse, holding out his arms for her. "And no one saw us."

She closed her eyes in mortification. She couldn't believe she'd risked that. He did drive her insane.

His smile became pure bedevilment. "Let's hope for better luck next time."

* * *

There was no next time.

It was almost sunset the next day when she felt a bass drone reverberate in her bones.

In moments the distant yet approaching thunder became unmistakable. A helicopter.

Harres's people had come for them.

Their idyll had come to an end.

Harres turned to her, his eyes eloquent with the same sentiments. But he attempted a smile. "They'll be here in minutes. Do you want to leave immediately?"

She didn't want to leave at all.

She only said, "Yes."

He nodded. "Let's gather the stuff the oasis people gave us."

"I only wish I had something to give them, too."

"You gave them far more than souvenirs, made a lasting difference in so many lives. Many told me they were blessed the day the desert 'yielded you to them.' And you can bring them whatever you want later." She gasped. Then he articulated her wildest hope. "We'll be back here, *ya nadda jannati*. I promise."

In fifteen minutes, she was standing with Harres a hundred feet from the clearing where the helicopter had just landed.

Four men jumped down, walked toward them with movements made of power and purpose, not even acknowledging the brutal wind buffeting them from the still-storming rotors.

As they strode closer, Talia was left in no doubt they were Harres's blood.

Apparently Aal Shalaan men all descended from a

line that had originated the oriental fables of supernatural beings.

The men were close enough to be classed in the same level, yet different enough as to be totally distinct from one another.

But it was the man who'd been in the pilot's seat who captured and kept her focus. And not because she recognized him as Zohayd's crown prince.

Amjad Aal Shalaan had an aura about him that lashed out across space and punched air from an onlooker's body. He reminded her of a majestic black panther, perpetually coiled for attack, complete with startling, searing, soulless emerald eyes. And he had those eyes trained on hers. She could swear she felt her eyeballs about to combust before he turned his attention to his brother.

But that brief eye-lock had been enough for her to have no doubt. He was nothing like Harres. That perfect body housed a dangerous, merciless entity. No one got a second chance with Crown Prince Amjad Aal Shalaan. She doubted anyone got a first one.

For the next few minutes she watched as those male manifestations of the forces of nature descended on Harres with relief and affection. All but Amjad. He held back, his gaze on her.

She felt him slicing through the layers of her character like a mental CAT scan, cutting to her essence like a psychic laser.

Harres introduced the others, Munsoor, Yazeed and Mohab—the latter Ghada's reluctant fiancé—as the cousins who'd been with him for her retrieval operation. They shook hands with her, expressed their pleasure to see her well, if not exactly who they'd signed on to save. They exchanged with Harres dozens of questions and reports about what had happened since they got separated twenty days ago.

Suddenly Amjad spoke. "Enough with the reunion. You can all debrief each other, or whatever you do in this secret-service game you play, later." He focused on Harres. "After Shaheen spent the last three weeks tearing the kingdom apart with me looking for you, he couldn't waste one more moment away from his bride coming to fetch you and has jumped back into her embrace. He sends his 'love' from its depths."

Harres's lips twisted at him. "You tore apart the kingdom looking for me? I'm so touched. I hope we can now glue it back together."

Amjad shot him a look of demolishing sarcasm. She was sure a lesser man than Harres would have shriveled up. "The trials and tribulations of the oldest brother and all that. And then I couldn't let you get lost in the desert with my vital info, now could I? You can glue things back together yourself. Cleanup detail is why a man puts up with younger siblings."

Talia's mouth fell open. Harres only hugged her to his side and guffawed. "*Aih*, I love you, too, Amjad."

Amjad's gaze clamped the unit she and Harres formed.

Then he grimaced, rolled his eyes before leveling them on Harres disgustedly. "Not you, too."

Harres only laughed. "Oh, definitely me, too. And I hereby echo Shaheen's words. I can't wait until you make it three."

Amjad dismissed him like one would an insignificant annoyance, turned to her. Then, as he looked directly into her eyes, he talked about her in third person. "So what does she have over the rest of the women in the northern hemisphere? Since you went through them all, I'd be very interested to know what extra features she has installed that made you shed your sanity."

Harres nudged Amjad's shoulder, pointing to his own eyes with two fingers. "Eyes here, Amjad."

Amjad ignored him, kept looking at her, yet talking about her, not to her. "The way she's glaring back at me. Fascinating. Fearless, is she? Or is she just so perceptive that she read you right, knew she could pretend fearlessness knowing she has nothing to fear, and that would be what gets to you?"

This time Harres sort of punched him. "Quit your snide mother-in-law routine, Amjad, or prepare to eat some sand."

Amjad's sculpted lips twisted, the provocation in his gaze only rising as he looked down at her. "First you let Shaheen sink into Johara's thrall without throwing so much as a cursory rope and now you're eagerly rushing to join the collective of beached men. Is she pregnant, too? At least, was she any good..." Amjad allowed a beat for her to start to seethe, for Harres to take offense for real before he continued smoothly. "...for any info we can use?"

Okay. All right. The verdict was in.

They hired this guy to teach goading in hell.

The other three men had slipped away midconfrontation, went back to the helicopter to prepare it for the return flight. And, no doubt, to give the brothers a chance to have at it.

Though Amjad was formidable, Harres was clearly the more physical one and there was no doubt who would win in a fight. That was, if Amjad didn't fight dirty. Which she was sure he would, and did.

Keeping her hand clasped in his, Harres said with Amjad's same lethal tranquility, "I'll say this once, Amjad. Talia is my woman, my princess." Talia almost collapsed. Harres was saying what he wished for, wasn't taking into account the implausibility of it all. It felt like heaven. And like hell. And he was going on. "I owe her my life, and I have no life without her from now on. Deal with it. Nicely. Or else."

Suddenly Amjad addressed her. "See this? Your man, your prince, hits a snag, and he threatens, and may I add, employs, physical violence. Tut, tut. A bleak prognosis for a future with him, don't you think, doctor?" Then he swung his eyes to Harres. "And I had such high hopes for you. Have fun in your new life of mind-numbing sameness and soul-destroying emotional servitude."

Before she could finally set him straight, on so many accounts, before Harres could elaborate on his gag order, Amjad turned away, gave the oasis people who'd come to say goodbye a whimsical wave and headed back to the helicopter.

Then, as Talia hugged everyone who came to see her off, crying rivers with Harres beside her promising their return, the aggravating man had the nerve to honk.

Talia's return to the capital was the total reverse of her departure from it.

Going back in a royal helicopter surrounded by princes was certainly something she couldn't have even dreamed of when she'd been kidnapped twenty days ago. But being next to Harres as the real world approached made her realize the depth and breadth of the lifetime they'd lived together during that time.

After they landed in the princes' private airport, Talia changed into the clothes Harres had had delivered there, while he changed, too, before they drove to the palace in separate limos.

He told her they couldn't afford to have her tied to him. Apart from those who knew the truth, everyone thought he'd dropped off the radar on a mission as usual. But the traitors in the palace would know what this mission involved. If she were seen with him, they'd work out her true identity. So she'd arrive at the palace as a friend of Laylah, his cousin. Once that was established, he'd pretend to hook up with her, and it would seem natural to everyone that he'd be interested in the blonde beauty.

She told him she'd reconnect with her informant, get the rest of the promised info. And he forbade her to. He wouldn't risk her in any way, not even if the kingdom hung in the balance. He would find another way to discover the truth.

Then, reluctant to leave her but having matters to attend to, he gave her a cell phone so they could call each other until he could start seeing her again. Which he intended to be as soon as possible.

It took arriving at the palace—which was right up there with the Taj Mahal, just far more extensive—to take her mind off the turmoil of their situation, off feeling bereft at being away from him.

When she'd researched Zohayd before coming there, she'd read that the mid-seventeenth-century palace had taken more than three decades to build, and thousands of artisans and craftsmen to build it. But it was one thing looking at detailed photos, no matter how stunning they'd been, and something totally different treading this place with her own feet, feeling the history and grandeur saturating the walls and halls surround her, permeating her senses.

Just being there explained so much about Harres, how such a powerhouse had come into existence. The nobility and power and distinction, the ancient bloodline that had forged this place coursed through him. From what she'd seen of his relatives, it also did in them.

And no matter what he said, she had to do all she could to protect this legacy. Even if she hadn't fallen in love with him and would therefore do anything to protect him and his loved ones, Harres had been right. The whole kingdom was steeped in peace and prosperity. She'd been prejudiced when she'd thought that it would be better off without the royal family that had clearly done so much to produce and maintain that.

But if she played her cards right, she might help bring the danger to Harres and his family, to the kingdom and the whole region, to an end.

Just as she began to call her informant, reinitiating contact, her alibi for her long absence rehearsed, the phone came alive in her hand.

Knowing it was Harres, she pounced on the answer button.

His beloved voice poured into her ear. "I have news, *ya habibati*. The investigations and negotiations I had my family do while we were in the oasis bore fruit. Your brother will be released from prison. There won't be a retrial, just the charges dropped and he will be given a public apology in every international newspaper and anything he demands in compensation."

To say she was overcome would be to say her love for him was a passing fancy. She began to babble her shocked elation and thanks when he said, "I beg your forgiveness, *ya nadda jannati*. There is another pressing thing I have to attend. I'll call again the second I can. Until then, congratulations, *ya mashoogati*."

She stared at the phone, reeled. Todd. Released. It was over. Really over. She'd have her brother back. He'd have his life back. It was too much to take in. Harres hadn't told her that he'd been working to exonerate Todd already. But he had been, and he'd succeeded. And she knew it had all been for her.

She fell on the bed and curled into a tight ball. She

felt she might explode from too much love and relief and gratitude otherwise.

Then she burst up in a frenzy of purpose, dialed the number of her informant. She was told the number was no longer in service. She tried again, just to make sure she hadn't dialed it wrong. She hadn't. It must have been a temporary number so it couldn't be tracked. On the same thought, she went online, shot him an email, listing her phone number.

Moments after she hit Send, the phone's distinctive three-tone ring shot through her again. Harres. He must have more info.

Her flailing hand dropped it twice before she could answer. Then she almost dropped it again.

It wasn't Harres. It was a distorted voice that scraped her every nerve raw. Her informant's.

She hadn't dreamed he'd get back to her that fast. But it wasn't that that shocked her mute. It was what he'd said.

"Hello, Dr. Talia Jasmine Burke."

She squeezed her eyes. So their precautions hadn't worked. She didn't know how, but her cover was blown.

"Don't worry, doctor. I still want to do business with you. You're now in an even better situation to do the most damage. Harres is doing all he can to stay on your good side, to exploit you, so I hope you aren't falling for his charm and forgetting your original goal to redeem your brother." At her gasp, the distorted voice gave a macabre chuckle. "Yes, I know everything. That's why I went after you in the first place. Because I wanted someone with a cause, and because you are a woman. It suits me to have the Aal Shalaan's downfall be at the hands of someone who has a vendetta against them, and who better than a woman to bring all those mighty men to ruin.

"And now, I'll tell you who the mastermind behind the

conspiracy is. Yusuf Aal Waaked, prince of the neighboring emirate of Ossaylan."

Talia at last found her voice. "But why expose him and risk having the Aal Shalaans stop the conspiracy in its tracks once they learn who they have to fight and where they need to look for their missing jewels?"

"Oh, there's nothing the Aal Shalaans can do with his identity. My exposure will actually guard against him changing his mind. It will guarantee he'll see this through to the end."

Suddenly there was a long silence then the voice became uglier, scarier. "You idiot! You'll use the info to help Harres, won't you? He *has* gotten to you. I should have known, with a woman in the legendary playboy prince's clutches for so long. He must have you willing to sell your soul for him by now. But I'll prove to you that he and his family don't deserve your help, but your vengeance."

The line went dead.

She didn't know how long she'd stayed there, staring into space, shaking with agitation.

At last she roused herself. She had to call Harres, give him the new info. No matter what her informant said, she was sure Harres *would* do something with it, maybe solve this whole mess.

As she began to dial his number, two masked men burst into the room from the French doors that opened to a patio leading to the gardens. The gun in the first's hand made sure she didn't attempt a scream or a struggle.

"We won't harm you," the armed man said, "if you don't try to expose us. We just want you to come with us. There's something our master wants to show you."

They took her from the French doors, swept her around the palace through the extensive grounds.

They entered through another open French door into

a room. It was empty. Before she could say anything, she heard Harres's voice.

Her heart fired with hope, then dread crashed right on its heels. What if he walked in here, and they panicked, shot him?

But then she realized he wasn't moving. He was in an adjoining room, talking to someone. On the phone.

"…and how many women have you seen me take and discard? You think this American means more than any of them? The others at least were pleasant pastimes I remember with some goodwill. She, on the other hand, almost cost me my life. Can you even imagine the distaste I suffered as I catered to her for so long, struggled to save her miserable life, to get her to trust me and spill her secrets, and to change her mind about exposing them? Do you realize how enraged I was when I found out she knew practically nothing? But I had to continue to play along. I knew she could still renew her mission and secure the rest of the promised info."

He was silent for a moment, then he drawled, his voice pitiless, "Why do you think I gave her the trivial incentive of setting her brother free? She trusts me with her life now, will do anything to get me my coveted intel. I went so far as to proclaim my love, would have even offered to marry her if necessary."

He was silent for a moment more as the person on the other line interrupted him. Then Harres gave an ugly laugh, a sound she'd never thought could issue from him. "I might have afforded a measure of chivalry and human compassion in other circumstances. But anyone is expendable in my quest to fulfill my duty to protect this kingdom. So if she's useless to me on that front, do you really think I care if she lives or dies?"

Twelve

"**D**id you hear enough, *ya ghabeyah?*"

Ghabeyah. Stupid.

She'd been far beyond that.

She was beyond devastated.

The nightmarish voice continued. "That's what your prince says when he's having a private conversation with his crown prince, who's taking him to task over you. That's the ugly truth of his feelings. Still want to run to him with the information? Or will you now finally take the revenge you're owed?"

Talia stared at the phone on the bed. Who'd turned it on? How had she made it back to this room?

Her eyes panned around, unseeing. She was alone.

Her escorts must have led her back, turned on the phone's speaker. Their master, her informant, was pulling at the hook embedded inside her, shredding her insides.

Then at some point, the mutilation stopped. And silence decimated what was left intact of her.

She found herself on her side on the bed, a discarded body paralyzed with pain too huge to register yet. Her eyes were open and bone-dry. Harres's words revolved like a serrated wheel inside her skull, mashing her brain to tinier fragments.

He didn't mean it. Whimpers of denial spun in a countering direction. *There's an explanation. He was placating Amjad, his odious brother, to get him off his back, off my case. Or something. It must have killed him to say those things. He'll explain why he did. He loves me. I won't believe otherwise…*

"Talia."

Harres. Here? Or in her feverish hopes?

She jerked up. He *was* here. Looking down at her.

Please, my love, take it back, explain it away. Just look at me with love in your eyes and it will all go away.

But for the first time since she'd laid eyes on him, his were empty.

No. Give me something.

He gave her nothing, his face as expressionless as his voice. "Sorry to interrupt your rest, but my private jet is ready."

"Ready for what?" She heard her bleeding whisper, wondered how she could still talk.

"To take you home."

She stared up at him, the void emanating from him engulfing her. Then she found herself rising, as if a closer look would make her see inside him, decipher the truth.

She saw nothing. Only the abyss of uncaring he'd professed to feel for her.

And it all crashed down on her, the full weight of his betrayal, of his heartless exploitation. It crushed her.

But she realized one thing. Even hurt beyond expression or endurance, injured beyond healing, she couldn't retaliate in kind. She wouldn't. This was the one thing her informant hadn't taken into consideration in his quest to destroy the Aal Shalaans.

Harres had systematically destroyed her, for his duty, his family. But even had she wanted to exact revenge on him, she wouldn't destroy the royal family and the whole kingdom along with him. And she *didn't* want to avenge herself. She just wanted to curl up and die, far away from this land where she'd lost her heart and her faith in anything forever.

One thing was left in her wreckage. "What about Todd?"

"The procedures of his release are ongoing as we speak."

She saw the truth of this at least in his eyes. Or maybe she imagined it as she'd imagined everything between them so far.

And she gave him what he'd ruined her for. "The conspiracy's mastermind is Yusuf Aal Waaked, prince of Ossaylan."

His eyes flared. But she'd lost the ability to read them. She'd never had it. And she no longer cared. She just wanted out of his orbit. Wanted to go somewhere far to perish in peace.

"I know," he finally said in the same expressionless voice.

He did? How?

One thing explained everything. He'd monitored her phone call and got his coveted information the moment she had.

So the master secret-service man had adjusted his plan on the fly every second since they'd met, according to her reactions and based on an unerring reading of her character. She'd fallen in step with his every undetectable nudge. His masterstroke had been that last bit of reverse psychology. While indirectly stressing the danger Zohayd was in, he'd forbidden her to reinstate contact with her informant, knowing the first thing she'd do was just that. As the coup de grâce, he'd secured Todd's release. It clearly had required no effort or sacrifice on his part, had been insurance to make sure she would do anything for him.

Now her purpose to him was over. He couldn't wait to get rid of her.

It made sense. Far more sense than this all-powerful prince falling in love with her, so totally.

With this last shard of rationalization tearing into her heart, it was like a dampener dissolved and every memory of the past twenty days bombarded her, rewritten in the macabre new perspective.

Agony mushroomed to unmanageable levels, humiliation inundating her. She felt she'd suffocate, shatter.

She lashed out with all her disillusion and devastation. "So you know. But you can't say I didn't give you something in return for my brother's freedom and redemption. Now that I have them, I can't wait to leave this godforsaken land."

There was no mistaking what slammed into his eyes now. Shock.

Of course. He must have thought she'd simper and fawn and beg for him to keep her on any degrading terms he wished to impose. As he'd reassured his brother, he was an old hand at using and discarding women. He must have fully expected the dumping to be one-sided.

Before he could say anything, Amjad stuck his head around the door. "What's taking you so long?"

Harres tore his stunned eyes from hers, turned them to his brother. He still said nothing.

Then he shook his head, as if trying to credit what she'd said. She could only imagine how she'd sounded, looked as she'd said it. If a fraction of what was stampeding inside her had been apparent, he must be flabbergasted at the seemingly out-of-the-blue change that had seized her.

He stood aside, staring at her with eyes crowded with so many things it made her sick trying to fathom them. She gave up, on everything, preceded him out of the room.

Amjad was leaning on the wall outside the door in an immaculate sports jacket, his arms folded over his chest.

As she passed him, his eyes gleamed ruthlessly. "Give my…regards to your brother. He's to be congratulated for having a sister like you."

She stared at him, felt the urge to ask for an explanation. It fizzled out as it formed.

Feeling ice spreading from her center outward, she turned away, let Harres steer her outside the palace.

He sat beside her in his limo, the eerie silence that had replaced their animated conversations, his feigned interest and indulgence, deepening her freeze.

They arrived at the private airport they'd landed in only hours ago. What a difference that time had made.

He rushed out of the limo before it came to a full stop. He materialized on her side in seconds, handed her out of the limo, led her to the sleek silver Boeing 737 purring like a giant alien bird on the pristine tarmac.

His movements were measured, his hold the epitome of composure. The vibes emanating from him were the opposite.

At the stairs he turned to her. But though the move was controlled, his eyes were anything but, storming with emotions barely held in check. His voice sounded even more agitated. "What was that back at the palace?"

It couldn't be just his displeasure at her rewriting his expected dumping scene, could it?

Stop it. She *must* stop casting anything she felt from him through the prism of nobility and sincerity. She'd heard the truth with her own ears. What was she waiting for? To have it said to her face?

She wouldn't survive that. *End this.* Now.

She shrugged, started to turn away, to run away.

His hand snagged hers. But it was the confusion and hurt she thought she saw eclipsing the twin suns of his eyes that stopped her, captured her. "You're saying it was all for your brother? To manipulate me into setting him free?"

How could he still sound so genuine? How could she still be so pathetic that she wanted to believe him, melt into his arms, to answer her walking orders with proclamations of undying love?

Ghabeyah. Stupid. That was what her informant had called her.

No. She wouldn't give him the satisfaction of seeing her weep for him. She was so far beneath him, so disadvantaged, in every way, but especially in the depth of her involvement. She could only try to leave him on equal ground in at least that.

She heard the acid that now filled her arteries drip from her voice. "That wasn't too far to go to make you help an innocent man prove his innocence, don't you think?"

She'd seen him get shot. He hadn't reacted this spectacularly then. After his recoil, he stilled, seeming to loom larger, his vibe darkening until it was deeper than the night enveloping them.

Then he finally snarled, "It is *I* who has gone *far* farther to help a guilty man get away with his crimes."

For a moment she didn't get his meaning. Just as it dawned on her, he gritted out, "I guess committing fraud runs in your family, after all."

She staggered out of his hold. "I didn't think even you would go that far."

"*Even* me? What is that supposed to mean?"

"Nothing. None of it meant anything." She'd crumble at his feet any moment now. *Get away from him.*

She groped for the rails. He caught her back, twisted her around to face him. His face was a conflagration of every distraught emotion humanly achievable.

You're seeing what you want to see.

Pain skewered her, tearing the last tatters of her sanity.

"What is it?" she rasped. "Is your ego smarting? You want me to go but still want me to beg to stay? Or maybe you want another payment for Todd's freedom? On board your jet? I can give you one last go if you want to cross another fantasy off your list, with a reluctant woman this time."

For an eternity, it seemed, horror froze his features. Then his phone rang. He lurched, looked down as if not understanding where the sound was coming from, or its significance.

She broke away from his now loose hold, ran up the stairs. She wanted to keep running, out of her very skin.

Then she had to stop, heaped on the farthest seat in the jet. She begged the first person who came offering her services to please, leave her alone. She wanted nothing.

She only wanted to let the pain eat her up.

And for the duration of the flight toward a home she'd forgotten, a home no longer for now she'd remain forever homeless, she let it.

"Talia! You did it!"

Talia slumped against the door she'd just closed.

Todd.

She swung around, and there he was zooming toward her, his eyes filled with tears as he pounced on her and snatched her into a crushing embrace.

She shook, her battered mind unable to grasp the reality of his presence, here, so soon. How…?

She must have voiced her shock. He pulled back, held her at arm's length, his eyes, so much like hers, unsteady and avid over her face. "How did you do it? Mark told me you were trying to get me out, but I didn't dare hope that you would actually do it."

She almost told him, *I sold my soul to the devil for your freedom.* But that wouldn't be accurate. She'd given her soul of her own free will to said devil. And she'd asked for nothing in return. Todd's freedom hadn't been the price of her soul, just another strand in a convoluted, undetectable web of manipulation.

Yet to see him, free, here, was worth anything.

Not that she could bear more turmoil now, or contact, with even the brother who'd always felt like a physical part of her. Every nerve in her body felt exposed.

She pushed away, shrugged. "It doesn't matter what I did. What's important is that you're free and exonerated."

"How can you say that? I need to know if you got yourself in trouble for me."

"What's important is you're out and can resume your life."

"Oh, God, you did do something terrible, didn't you?" He caught her by the shoulders, his agitation mounting, shaking his whole slight frame. "Whatever you did, undo it. I'll go back to prison, serve the rest of my sentence."

"Don't worry, Todd. I'll deal."

But the lie must have been blatant on her face. Todd's

tears flowed down his shuddering, flushed face. "Please, Talia, take it back. I'm not worth it."

"Of course you are. You're my brother, my twin. And the most important thing is that you're innocent."

"But I'm *not.*"

She'd thought she'd depleted her reserves for shock, that all that was left in her was oceans of grief and agony.

She stared at Todd, denial still fighting to ward off comprehension. His next words ended its struggle.

"I—I committed all the crimes I was convicted for. I hacked into accounts I found out about when Ghada once let me fix her computer. She was just a good friend, and I made up the whole thing about us to give you a story you'd believe and sympathize with. I embezzled millions, sold dozens of vital secrets. I did far more than what they found out. But I couldn't admit it to you. It was part shame, part needing you to stand by me, to help me get out of this nightmare. I feared that if you knew I deserved what I got and worse, even with loving me, your sense of honor would stop you from trying. But I no longer care. I'll go back so you can stop paying the price for the freedom I don't deserve. I only hope you can one day forgive me."

She stared at him. This was too much.

It was all a lie.

The two men she loved more than life had both used her and exploited her unconditional love for them.

She tore herself away from Todd's pleading hands.

He sobbed as she staggered away. Before she stumbled into her room, to hide from the world and never exit again, she turned numbly. "Just don't get yourself in trouble again. I don't have any more in me to pay. And what I paid is forever gone."

The heart, the soul, the faith, the will to live.

All gone.

* * *

Seemed she was more resilient than she thought.

At the crack of dawn she was up, crackling with an unstoppable need. To confront Harres.

She'd thought she'd die rather than do it. But when she'd slept, her dreams had crowded with faithful replays of their time together. The contradiction between what she'd lived firsthand and the words she'd heard him say was so staggering, she knew something didn't add up. She hadn't been in any condition to realize that yesterday, too worn-out in every way, too shocked, too ready for bad news, too insecure, too you-name-it, that her mind hadn't functioned properly.

Now she was back to her scientific, logical, gotta-have-answers-that-fit self. More or less. And she would settle this, would ask the question she'd been too raw to ask before.

Why had he said those things?

She'd take any chance that he'd have a perfect explanation and remain the man she loved with all her soul, the memory of whom would enrich her life even if she could never see him again. Far better than believing he had no reason but the obvious one, and was the monster she couldn't bear living believing he was.

So she called him. For six hours straight. His phone was turned off.

Going crazy with frustration, she went back to work. Might as well do something with all this energy that others would benefit from.

She headed to the doctors' room, running on auto. But as she approached, she felt…something.

She shook her head. *Stop daydreaming, T.J.* What would that "something" be doing here?

She squared her shoulders, readying herself for the

storm of interrogation over her sudden month-long leave of
absence when she'd never missed a day of work.

The…premonition expanded with every step. The pull
became irresistible. She knew she'd feel like the stupidest
person in the galaxy in seconds when it turned out to be
all in her mind, but she didn't care. She ran.

She burst into the room.

And there he was.

Harres.

She hadn't been imagining it. She had *felt* him.

Which meant she had an infallible sense where he was
concerned.

Which meant she might have the man she loved back
after all.

He'd been leaning against the table that acted as
the doctors' meeting/dining/sleeping surface, pushing his
tailored jacket out of the way to dip his hands deep into
the pockets of molded-on-him pants, his feet crossed in
deceptive relaxation at the ankles.

He'd always looked incredible. But here, among mundane
surroundings and everyday people, he looked unequivocally
godly. The potency of the ancient pride and the birthright
of power emanating from him swept over her.

He waited until she entered and got a load of him dom-
inating the place, being gaped at by all present, before he
pushed to his feet, oh, so slowly, his eyes lashing out solar
flares.

She imagined herself breaking into a sprint, charging
him, pushing him flat on that table and losing her mind all
over him. A mind that flooded with images and sensations,
of tearing his clothes off as his magical hands rid her of
hers, before raising her as she straddled him, then lowering
her on his…

She swayed with the power of the fantasy. She felt as if

he was transmitting it directly into her brain, generating it, sharing it.

But it was his eyes that snared her in a chokehold. A tiger's. Crackling with scorching…rage? Pain? Both?

One thing was unmistakable. Searing challenge.

He straightened fully, cocked his head at her. "You called?"

"Saw my missed calls, huh?" She turned to her colleagues, who were watching her and Harres like they would their favorite soap. She wouldn't be surprised if someone ran out for popcorn. She twisted her lips at their audacious interest, poked sarcasm at all present, starting with herself. "I accumulated over two hundred. Must be why Prince Harres found a transatlantic visit to be the only suitable way to see what the hell was so pressing."

Taking her cue, showing her that he was embarrassment-proof, he walked up to her with seeming indolence. When he was within arm's length, he lashed out like a cobra, caught her to him, his gaze snaring hers in a fiercer grip.

"So, Dr. T. J. Burke…are you congratulating yourself how I, who could always smell the slightest trace of fraud, ate up your lies and am still back for more?"

She stood in his grip, her heart quivering with unfurling hope. "I never lied. In fact, like you once said, I can't lie. Just ask those guys." Grunts of corroboration issued from everyone around who'd been singed by her inability to hide the truth of her feelings. Suddenly, the pain she'd experienced yesterday welled up inside her. And she pinched him, in the sensitive underside of both arms. Hard. "But *you* lie like a bird can fly."

His frown cracked on a twitch of surprise at her unexpected action, at its sting, on a jerk of humor at her rhyme, before resuming full force. "I never, *ever* lied to you. And if you never did to me, as I would have staked my life on till yesterday, why did you say what you said? Or did you really think you needed to seduce me to get me to help Todd? If you did, didn't you know I would have helped the very devil to make you happy? That you didn't need to say you felt anything for me, because it's enough for me that *I* feel everything for you?"

His words washed over her in healing waves, wiping away all the pain and doubt in swell after swell.

Then she remembered Todd's staggering confession, and her heart compressed. Harres had probably done a host of illegal things to get him off the hook. All for her.

She soothed the flesh she'd abused, her heart brimming with sorrow and remorse. "I was just lashing out in shock and misery."

"Why?" He had the look of a man who was watching his sanity ebbing before his eyes.

She pinched him again, harder this time, dragging a growl from his depths, a mixture of pain and aggravation and arousal. "Because I *heard* you. Saying you don't care if I live or die. So you *were* lying, to someone. That's why I called you. To ask you who you were lying to, and why." She pushed out of his arms, stuck her fists in her waist. "So?"

Harres felt the mountain that had been crushing him since yesterday lifting. This explained everything.

She'd heard him.

"*Ya Ullah.* It's a wonder you didn't kill me and ask questions later." He laughed, with all the discharge of his confusion and agony. "So, the reason I said those things—which, by the way, made me so sick that I haven't been able to put a thing in my mouth since—is I got a phone call, someone telling me they know who you are, what you mean to me, and if I don't back off, they'll harm you. I had to say you meant nothing to me, to make you invalid as a target.

"After I said what I did to my extortionist, I had to keep playing it cool with you since I knew we had traitors in the palace, and your room was probably bugged. I would have explained things to you the moment we were outside monitoring range, but you hit me with that delightful surprise about never feeling anything for me. I couldn't believe it, but you seemed so distant, so different, until I began to lose my mind thinking it might be true. I wouldn't have let you go if Amjad hadn't called at that moment. As it was I sent a dozen men as your security detail just in case."

"So that explains all those *GQ* specimens suddenly hanging around outside my house. Way to go picking guys only I in my condition couldn't see for the elite secret-service agents they are." A smile, sheepish and adoring, trembled on her lips, still echoing pain. He wanted to devour them, soothe away the remainder of her agitation. She bit them, making him feel her teeth had sunk into his own flesh. "I can't tell you how sorry I am for…Todd. I should have suspected something, but I guess I am too stupid when it comes to him."

"I'm not sorry. In fact, I owe your misbehaving brother a debt I can never repay. Your misplaced belief in his innocence drove you to Zohayd and into my life. Amjad and Shaheen pulled some major strings, but I personally paid back with interest everyone he defrauded, and it feels like such a tiny price for having you."

Then she was in his arms, burrowing deep into his chest and deeper into his being and bawling her eyes out.

He filled his aching arms with his every reason for life, every source of happiness. When he'd thought he'd lost her, had never had her… He shuddered. He couldn't even think of those soul-gnawing hours. And he had to tell her something else.

"I'm not here because you called, *ya talyeti*. I was on my way here. That's why you amassed those missed calls. But I am ecstatic that you didn't give up on me, even after hearing the horrors I was forced to utter about you, that you still called, still gave me the benefit of the doubt."

She looked up from the depths of his embrace, her heavenly eyes brimming with love. "How could I not, when I sobered up and remembered what we shared?" She told him about her own phone call, and they both realized at the same moment. She articulated the realization. "My informant masterminded everything. Threatening my safety to you, forcing you to say what you did and forcing me to hear it."

"But that's where he went wrong." He gathered her to him more securely, feeling his heart stagger with the blessing of having her belief, so deep it had withstood that brutal test. And he had no doubt, would stand a lifetime of tests, come what may. As would his. "He didn't count on you being too ethical to lash out by doing his dirty work for him, and loving me so much that you'd give me a chance to exonerate myself."

The adoration in her eyes enveloped him, made him feel invincible. "And he didn't count on you being unable to believe I could use you that way, that you'd come after me, and that we'd talk, get past the doubts and hurt and find each other again."

He suddenly swung her in the air around and around. Her unfettered laughter echoed his overwhelming relief and elation, fell all over him like pearls tinkling off crystal.

He finally put her down, cupped her beloved face in his hands. "And now we have. And with your brother free and no doubt planning to atone, and with us being on the final leg of aborting the conspiracy now that all the pieces are in place, and now that I'm certain the threat against you was just a ploy to get you to hear me and lash out, all our obstacles have been removed." He kneeled in front of her. "I have nothing to give you while I make this offer but everything I am. So will you now take me, *ya talyeti, ya ghalyeti, ya noor donyeti,* all of me? Will you marry me and make me whole?"

Talia would have fallen if Harres hadn't caught her by the hips.

She stared down at him as he kneeled before her, shock and overwhelming joy twisting her tongue as she choked out, "Y-you're not—not promised to some m-marriage of state?

He smiled up at her, that annihilating smile that vaporized her mental functions at a hundred paces. "I'm not. I am free to marry the wife my heart chooses. And my heart, and everything in me, chooses you."

And she threw herself all over him, sobbing her love and relief. "Considering I'm yours forever, too, it's wise of you to make use of the fact."

From somewhere far away, she heard clapping and hooting.

Her infernal colleagues. They were still here?

Well, doctors in the E.R. didn't have much of a private life. She'd seen most of their revealing and embarrassing moments. They'd witnessed many of hers, too. Let them now share her most incredible one.

As she lost herself in Harres's fate-sealing kiss, one of her male colleagues said, "There's a very nice-size supply cabinet just around the corner, dude."

They both turned on him with a simultaneous, "Oh, shut *up*."

Then, exchanging a conspiratorial look with Harres, she grabbed his hand and they rushed out of the room.

On their way out, a female colleague asked, "What if the Chief sees you signed in but nowhere around?"

"Tell him I have a gunshot victim to tend to," she said.

"Yes," Harres added. "Someone who's so impressed by her uncanny medical skills, he's going to donate any number of millions she sees fit to your department in gratitude."

They left the room to an explosion of excitement.

Once they reached that supply cabinet, he dragged her inside, pushed her against the wall. "And to this golden virago who owns my heart by awakening it, my life by saving it, my faith by inspiring it, what would you see fit I donate?"

She dragged him down to her, begged in his mouth. "Just your love. Just you."

And he pledged to her as he made her whole, "You have it, and me, always. Forever."

* * * * *

Read on for a sneak preview of Carol Marinelli's
PUTTING ALICE BACK TOGETHER!

Hugh hired bikes!

You know that saying: 'It's like riding a bike, you never forget'?

I'd never learnt in the first place.

I never got past training wheels.

'You've got limited upper-body strength?' He stopped and looked at me.

I had been explaining to him as I wobbled along and tried to stay up that I really had no centre of balance. I mean *really* had no centre of balance. And when we decided, fairly quickly, that a bike ride along the Yarra perhaps, after all, wasn't the best activity (he'd kept insisting I'd be fine once I was on, that you never forget), I threw in too my other disability. I told him about my limited upper-body strength, just in case he took me to an indoor rock-climbing centre next. I'd honestly forgotten he was a doctor, and he seemed worried, like I'd had a mini-stroke in the past or had mild cerebral palsy or something.

'God, Alice, I'm sorry—you should have said. What happened?'

And then I had had to tell him that it was a self-diagnosis. 'Well, I could never get up the ropes at the gym at school.' We were pushing our bikes back. 'I can't blow-dry the back of my hair...' He started laughing.

Not like Lisa who was laughing at me—he was just laughing and so was I. We got a full refund because we'd only been on our bikes ten minutes, but I hadn't failed. If anything, we were getting on better.

And better.

We went to St Kilda to the lovely bitty shops and I found these miniature Russian dolls. They were tiny, made of tin or something, the biggest no bigger than my thumbnail. Every time we opened them, there was another tiny one, and then another, all reds and yellows and greens.

They were divine.

We were facing each other, looking down at the palm of my hand, and our heads touched.

If I put my hand up now, I can feel where our heads touched.

I remember that moment.

I remember it a lot.

Our heads connected for a second and it was alchemic; it was as if our minds kissed hello.

I just have to touch my head, just there at the very spot and I can, whenever I want to, relive that moment.

So many times I do.

'Get them.' Hugh said, and I would have, except that little bit of tin cost more than a hundred dollars and, though that usually wouldn't have stopped me, I wasn't about to have my card declined in front of him.

I put them back.

'Nope.' I gave him a smile. 'Gotta stop the impulse

spending.'

We had lunch.

Out on the pavement and I can't remember what we ate, I just remember being happy. Actually, I can remember: I had Caesar salad because it was the lowest carb thing I could find. We drank water and I *do* remember not giving it a thought.

I was just thirsty.

And happy.

He went to the loo and I chatted to a girl at the next table, just chatted away. Hugh was gone for ages and I was glad I hadn't demanded Dan from the universe, because I would have been worried about how long he was taking.

Do I go on about the universe too much? I don't know, but what I do know is that something *was* looking out for me, helping me to be my best, not to **** this up as I usually do. You see, we walked on the beach, we went for another coffee and by that time it was evening and we went home and he gave me a present.

Those Russian dolls.

I held them in my palm, and it was the nicest thing he could have done for me.

They are absolutely my favourite thing and I've just stopped to look at them now. I've just stopped to take them apart and then put them all back together again and I can still feel the wonder I felt on that day.

He was the only man who had bought something for me, I mean something truly special. Something beautiful, something thoughtful, something just for me.

A sneaky peek at next month...

Desire™

PASSIONATE AND DRAMATIC LOVE STORIES

2 stories in each book - only £5.30!

My wish list for next month's titles...

In stores from 17th February 2012:

❏ *Marriage at the Cowboy's Command* – Ann Major

& *How to Seduce a Billionaire* – Kate Carlisle

❏ *Dante's Honour-Bound Husband* – Day Leclaire

& *A Clandestine Corporate Affair* – Michelle Celmer

❏ *One Night, Two Heirs* – Maureen Child

& *The Rebel Tycoon Returns* – Katherine Garbera

❏ *Wild Western Nights* – Sara Orwig

& *Her Tycoon to Tame* – Emilie Rose

Available at WHSmith, Tesco, Asda, Eason, Amazon and Apple

Just can't wait?

0212/51

MILLS & BOON® Book Club

2 Free Stories!

Get your free stories now at
www.millsandboon.co.uk/freebookoffer

Or fill in the form below and post it back to us

THE MILLS & BOON® BOOK CLUB™—HERE'S HOW IT WORKS: Accepting your free stories places you under no obligation to buy anything. You may keep the stories and return the despatch note marked 'Cancel'. If we do not hear from you, about a month later we'll send you 2 Desire™ 2-in-1 books priced at £5.30* each. There is no extra charge for post and packaging. You may cancel at any time, otherwise we will send you 4 stories a month which you may purchase or return to us—the choice is yours. *Terms and prices subject to change without notice. Offer valid in UK only. Applicants must be 18 or over. Offer expires 31st July 2012. **For full terms and conditions, please go to www.millsandboon.co.uk**

Mrs/Miss/Ms/Mr (please circle)

First Name

Surname

Address

Postcode

E-mail

Send this completed page to: Mills & Boon Book Club, Free Book Offer, FREEPOST NAT 10298, Richmond, Surrey, TW9 1BR

Find out more at
www.millsandboon.co.uk/freebookoffer

Visit us Online

0112/D2XEA

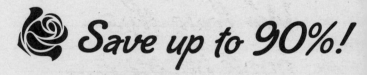

Have Your Say

You've just finished your book.
So what did you think?

We'd love to hear your thoughts on our
'Have your say' online panel
www.millsandboon.co.uk/haveyoursay

- Easy to use
- Short questionnaire
- Chance to win Mills & Boon® goodies

   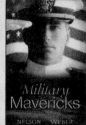